TIME FOR MILKING

On the planet of Sparta, Blis, a popular office holder, was revealed to be a member of the black market "shadow council." Pol Tyrees, Cadre One, was sent to interrogate him. Pol had a reputation for being able to "milk" unwilling prisoners.

Pol began by asking innocuous questions. He noticed that when Blis felt threatened, he clasped a medallion around his neck with his thumb and forefinger.

"After the epidemic on Bastion, vaccine was sold at exorbitant prices. Do you know anything about this?"

"No."

The medallion gave its verdict. "You are lying," Pol said.

"The accusation is absurd," Blis protested.

"You are lying," Pol repeated. Inside, Blis panicked.

The next day, Blis agreed to divulge everything he knew about the "shadow council". . . .

**ROBERT
O'RIORDAN**

CADRE
ONE

ACE SCIENCE FICTION BOOKS
NEW YORK

CADRE ONE

An Ace Science Fiction Book/published by arrangement with
the author

PRINTING HISTORY
Ace Science Fiction edition/January 1986

ISBN: 0-441-09022-2

Ace Science Fiction Books are published by The Berkley Publishing Group,
200 Madison Avenue, New York, New York 10016.
PRINTED IN THE UNITED STATES OF AMERICA

To the anchors in my life:
J. A. and the Guild

SY 3012

The building was tall and functional, towering over its neighbors, so that people laughed when told it was a nursery. It cared for children who had been orphaned or just tucked away for safekeeping; in either case, wealth and influence hovered in the background.

On a high balcony a middle-aged man and a young boy played an intricate game, shifting pieces on a triple-decked board. Far below traffic shunted silently. The sun was bright, the air keen. All was tranquil and orderly except for a saucy dark bird who banked into the balcony to strafe the players with taunts. The boy, waiting for the man to make a move, looked up.

"I think he wants to play the winner, Grandfather." The man frowned, undoing the collar clasp of his long black cape and letting it fall over the back of his chair. He did not take his eyes off the board. When he spoke, the boy listened as if his words were delicate flowers to be gathered with care and cherished.

"Don't let him distract, Pol. When something is worthy of your attention, give it *all* of your attention. Technically you're playing a fine game today, but your moves are out of a textbook, as if you have no flesh-and-blood opponent. Remember, your

1

enemy's *character* is revealed in his play, and that can be exploited. Now concentrate." The boy sobered instantly, dropping his eyes to the board.

"Yes, Grandfather."

"Perhaps we've been playing too long. Relax a moment. . . . You look a little pale, Pol. Are you feeling well?" A pair of startlingly blue eyes rose from the board again, tentatively.

"Yes, Grandfather."

"You had a good lunch today?"

"I didn't eat lunch, Grandfather."

"You didn't! Why not?"

"Well, when I started to eat breakfast yesterday, it . . . sort of felt bad. So I didn't eat any more." When the tall man in black frowned, his bushy eyebrows dipped together over his nose.

"You're telling me you haven't eaten since *breakfast yesterday?*"

"Just that tiny bit at first—oh, and other tiny bits when they fed us. Something was always bad, Grandfather, and I couldn't eat." The stark blue eyes were wary. The man reached across the board to push a forelock from the smooth white forehead.

"But that's more than a day and a half now. . . . Did the food make you ill?"

"Just at first. Not now." Small shoulders shrugged stoically.

"Not now?"

"Nope. Then I . . . shut the hungry feeling off. I won't let it come again until the food is better," he said proudly. "I told them about it." Another shrug dismissed the problem. "It's still your move, Grandfather."

The silver-haired man in black was already rising, but he pushed a piece forward.

"No, it's your move. Concentrate now. I'll be gone a few minutes to talk to one of the doctors."

He swept the long cape from the chair back and onto his shoulders with a practiced motion, but there was anger in it. He hesitated with his hands on the collar clasp to look down at his grandson. The boy's eyes were swallowing the board. He reached out as if to brush the hair again but arrested the gesture and let his fingers curl into a fist. He looked like a jeweler possessively examining the rarest of jewels.

"Pol?"

The eyes snapped back up to the lean face.

"Yes, Grandfather?"

"Pol . . . do you remember your father?"

The small forehead crinkled. "Not . . . not too good—too well, Grandfather. Just . . . he looked like you."

"No matter, no matter. Don't trouble yourself by thinking of the past. Think of the future. Think of you and me . . . and the Cadre. One day you will be my Cadre brother as well as my grandson." He parted one side of the cape to point down at the still creased forehead. "You carry special gifts, Pol. We must begin preparing you for this uniform so that those gifts will not be wasted. You will make me feel proud."

The very young, very blue eyes misted over at the words. They swam with worship and a determination that verged on pain.

"Y-yes, Grandfather . . . b-but . . ."

"Speak clearly, Pol. Remember: Intellect is power—*control* is power. You possess both in quantities that begin to astonish me. Dedicate them to the proper goals and nothing, *nothing* will stop you. Understand?"

In an effort to leash overflowing emotion, the pipe-high voice rose another pitch.

"Yes, Grandfather."

"Now. What were you about to say?"

"I . . . think I can do . . . anything when you're helping me, Grandfather, but . . . I don't want to be alone anymore."

The steel angles of the man's narrow jaw softened somewhat into a thin smile.

"Yes. We will be together more often now. It is time for more formal training. Remember, though: Solitude is not a curse—it is an opportunity to sharpen the disciplines of the mind and body. Remember also that you are a Tyrees. My blood flows through you. I will always be with you. Always. Understand?"

"Yes, Grandfather." The boy's smile was not a thin line—it was radiant.

"Now. Concentrate."

Petr Tyrees, Security Cadre One, swept along a busy corridor toward the nursery's administrative section. Youngsters who caught a glimpse of the tall, caped figure in black wore expressions of surprise and awe. Adults watched as peasants watch a king, his remoteness inspiring a respect that was speckled with fear. He descended on a white-clad aide who guarded the sanctum of the nursery administrators. She rose from her desk, mouth forming familiar words with difficulty.

"Oh, ah, good morning, sir. May I help you?"

"Yes. I want to see the director—Dr. Thoom, is it?"

"Uh, well, I don't know if . . . I don't think he's expecting . . ."

"Just tell him I'm here."

"Yessir." Her heels beat a quick tattoo around a corner. Seconds later she returned with a portly man of impeccable and expensive dress in tow. He dodged around her with outstretched hand and an ingratiating smile.

"Officer Tyrees! How good of you to drop in. All is well with your grandson, I trust? Remarkable boy—remarkable."

"I agree, Doctor. However, I am concerned about a medical matter. I've come to discuss it." The doctor's smile vanished.

"Of course. This way, please." He nervously led the way to a luxurious and spacious office. Cushioned seating, bright colors, soft, rich curves. Tyrees took it in with an expression of mild disapproval—not of its size, but of its comfortable self-indulgence. He declined the offer of a chair.

"I'll be direct, if I may. Has there been a problem with the food here?"

The doctor frowned. "Not a real problem, no. Just a minor thing today that was cleared up immediately . . . or is that what you're referring to? Perhaps . . ."

"Probably. Explain, please."

"Very well. One or two children complained of queasy stomachs after lunch. Before we even had a chance to check it out, the monitoring program ordered a part replaced in one of the food processing automatics. Apparently, oxidation was causing a very mild toxic—harmless in such quantities—to go into the meat. Now rectified." He darted a glance at the Cadre One.

"How was the connection made to the food?"

"We might not have made it at all, except for the monitor. Upset stomachs with children this young are pretty common, even with the best of food—and ours *is* the best, I assure you."

· "None of the children feel seriously ill?"

"None. Only two had any symptoms at all."

"Hmmmm. Hundreds here—how could Pol's stomach be that sensitive?"

"Sorry? . . ."

"This toxic chemical would also have been present earlier, then."

"Well, probably. To an even lesser degree."

"No, Doctor, not probably. *Certainly.* I'm Cadre, but also a scientist. That kind of oxidation would begin at an imperceptible level and gradually increase. You should have listened to Pol."

"I beg your pardon?"

"He told your people yesterday morning that something was wrong."

"I was told about that," said the doctor, his fawning replaced by a hint of testiness. "There can't be a connection. I can't see how he knew."

"He knew. That's what puzzles me. . . . There's something curious here. Doctor, what is your area of specialty?"

"Why, I'm a nursery director, of course. I—"

"Your *medical* specialty, Doctor."

"Oh. What you would expect—child psychology." The doctor was beginning to chafe. This man was too direct, oblivious to personal or social amenities.

"Good. Question: Should a child of five have the capacity to deliberately repress hunger pangs?"

"Well, it would vary, but not for any length of time in *any* case. Even most adults have little control over their instinctual need for food."

SY 3012

(Excerpt from) *The Personal Diary of Petr Tyrees, Cadre One*

I find this an indulgence I must allow myself—increasingly, of late. The Cadre, as it must be, is a hard mistress, demanding an unswaying strength and loyalty, but I think this small escape is harmless enough. I can muse and dabble on occasion, when I feel the need to break away. Sometimes it helps to calm me, and my visit to Pol's nursery yesterday has my mind spinning. At first I was only concerned about his health—he hadn't eaten for almost two days! I was worried enough to speak with one of the doctors myself, because Pol is not one of the whining, milking sort of brat that society keeps turning out these days.

But that is incidental. As a scientist, I can think of a dozen explanations for Pol's uncanny stomach; I can think of none that can account for the ability of a five-year-old to deliberately dampen out the pangs of hunger. Most Cadre Ones, after long training, cannot do that.

I will persuade the Vice-Proctor to keep my assignment directives local. My record will help. From now on, I will keep a closer watch on my grandson and take a personal hand in his training. He is unique . . . and it is imperative that such unique-

6

ness not be dissipated by an undisciplined mind.

Pol's father had potential, too, but his talents were squandered. I allowed his formative years to be shaped by a gentle but sentimental woman who had no fiber, no steel in her makeup. She had the sort of maudlin, romantic streak that cheap drama is made of—the kind that would encourage a woman to conceive a child, my son, without telling the father. She had nothing but emotional self-indulgence (and an embarrassing desire to please) to guide *herself*. How, then, was she to guide my son?

I saw him rarely then; those were the years when I was working on the Holtz Effect as my Cadre Five project, and by the time I took enough interest to see what was happening, it was too late. Mother and son were "soulfully joined" (her phrase); so he never saw me as anything but an interfering stranger. He died with that attitude. I don't know whether his mother lives or . . . No. That is self-indulgence. Nevertheless, she was a beautiful, glowing woman.

I will see that my grandson's life is not diminished by false causes or sloppy thinking. Waste is the greatest tragedy, and I will not be a part of another. Pol is my blood. It flows into his future.

I lost the game of snoff—to a five-year-old. And I never lose deliberately.

Encyclopedia Galactica
Computer Entry: SEC-HIS-SC-HE 107
"Holtz Effect"

The Holtz Effect is a quasi-scientific term first used in the Standard Year 701. A little-known physicist, Sydney J. Holtz, was conducting solar wind experiments while in orbit around ancient Terra. He was testing measuring instruments of his own invention. One of these was a complex device combining electrical, chemical, and biological components. It produced a "reading" that Holtz was unable to connect to any particular solar effect. Already the possessor of a dubious reputation, Holtz thereafter became noteworthy among his colleagues as an eccentric whose work was unreliable.

After Holtz's death the instrument itself found its way into a museum of scientific curiosities on Manplace, Sector II. In sy 1114 it was resurrected by a wealthy hobbyist for further study. He was able to determine only that the device was replicable, its readings consistent, and that it produced these readings only while in orbit around inhabited planets. "Holtz Effect" became a term used by scientists for "garbage output," or data without discernible significance.

Early in this century the instrument was resurrected once again by a young Security Cadre officer, Petr Tyrees, while working on his Cadre Five research project. (See entry, SC-AD-TYR 1001.) He was updating multivariable regression analysis programs designed to discover the relationship between seemingly disparate variables. Though he was primarily concerned with the programs themselves, one such relationship emerged that quickly caught public interest: it appeared that Holtz Effect readings were generated only by worlds whose mythology and cultural lore were strongly suggestive of alien species contact. Using the new programming techniques (that have subsequently gained him prestige even outside the Cadre), Tyrees produced a high statistical correlation between the two variables.

Tyrees's work led to the controversial "Alien Contact Theory," and concern about the probability of an advanced alien intelligence secretly observing our galaxy has gained credence because of it.

OPEN FILE >>> OPEN FILE >>> OPEN FILE

SY 3016

Petr Tyrees was in his study, one of a suite of rooms he now shared permanently with Pol and his grandson's tutor. There were few personal effects in evidence—and there would not have been any more even if the duty-ridden security officer had not spent so much time off-planet. He sat, hand over a thick sheaf of hard copy. Behind him were the dead fisheyes of a bank of small screens. Most of the other walls were covered with rows of cases for recording crystals, program modules, and printout carriers. His concentration was intense, palpable. The room, the universe, existed to enclose his thoughts—until a hum brought his head up. A sliding panel opened upon the small, somber figure of his grandson.

"You're ready, Pol?"

"Yes, Grandfather." The boy's face was almost pathetically set in a cast of adult determination. Only a slight quiver of the lips betrayed other emotions.

"I want you to be sure. You weren't sufficiently prepared last time."

"I know, Grandfather, but . . ."

"But?"

"You are right, Grandfather. I wasn't prepared." The small

chin rose a notch. This brought forth the man's tight smile.

"Fine. Let's begin." He hit a timer button on his desk terminal. "Your estimate of elapsed time?"

"I estimate one hour forty-three minutes—plus about ten seconds since I left my room." The man's eyebrows rose in surprise. He fought down a surge in his chest.

"Excellent. Excellent, Pol! You are only seconds off."

"Shall I itemize my observations, Grandfather?"

"No. Questions this time. What was its color?"

"Red."

"Red is a weak descriptor. A lazy word. Come. Concentrate. Did it shade toward orange or violet?"

"Uh, I think neither."

"You *think?*"

"No. I know. Scarlet. It was scarlet."

"A strong, deep, sharp red?"

"Yes, Grandfather."

"Good. You see the difference now. Concentrate. Was the ball round?"

"Uh, no. It was . . . a bit like an egg."

"You mean the ends were smaller than the middle?"

"No, Grandfather. The middle was a bit bulged out."

"Then it was not like an egg, my boy." A slender hand lifted to rest briefly on his head. "Concentrate. Be exact."

"It was not like an egg. It was fatter in the middle, like . . . like the shape of Regnum."

"Good. Was it smooth?"

"Yes, Grandfather."

"Very smooth?"

"Yes, very smooth."

"How do you know that when you were not to touch it, Pol?"

"Oh, I didn't touch it, Grandfather! I know it was smooth because . . . because no matter how close I got to it, with my nose almost touching, I couldn't see any, uh, different parts on it, uh, or bumps."

"You mean it had no discernible texture."

"Yes, Grandfather."

"Was it hard or soft?"

"Soft."

"How do you know?"

"Because I could see a tiny bulge around where it touched the table."

"Then how much did it weigh? An estimate. Concentrate. How much did it weigh?"

"Well, I would guess . . . about half a kilogram."

"On what do you *base* your estimate?"

"I . . . don't . . . it just seemed . . ."

"Pol! Stop that. If you don't know, just say so. Observation requires self-discipline and total objectivity. Intuition is a last resort and never to be trusted. Do you have observable data upon which to base an estimate of weight?"

The parody of adult determination on the boy's face had been dissolving into the more natural lines of childish despair. His eyes fell to the floor.

"I didn't think . . . I . . ."

"No. Look at me, Pol. Up. Yes. Look at me directly, please. . . . Thank you. Listen and remember. Failure is the reward for lack of effort. Failure is wrong if the tools you possess go unused. Or if you give up. Never surrender to circumstance, Pol, never. That is a denial of the powers of the mind and an abdication of its free will. Chaos is the enemy, Pol. The power of the mind and the body it controls are your weapons against it. Understand? . . . Understand?"

The young mouth still quivered involuntarily, but the head bobbed up and down, and stark, blue worship shone from the eyes. Petr Tyrees stood. His long fingers reached out again to touch Pol's shoulder.

"We will stop for a while now. You are tired, I think. You have not eaten or slept for—twenty hours. Sit. No, over here in my chair. Relax now. Relax and breathe as you have practiced. Good. Tell me how you feel. Be objective."

"Well, I *am* tired, Grandfather. But I never feel hungry unless I want to."

"Yes, I know. You are better at it than I already. But the fatigue—you must learn to know when it begins to affect your judgment—but that will come. That and other things will come to you sooner and in larger measure than for others. You will have much to offer."

"Grandfather?"

"Yes, Pol."

"What if . . . what if the Cadre won't take me? What if—"

"It will, Pol. It will. It needs men like you."

"But why should it need *me,* Grandfather?"

The man leaned back in his chair, stared at the ceiling. His voice took on the subtly evangelical tones of one who believes wholly in something gained at great cost.

"Because there are two challenges that are sacred, Pol—the struggle for order and the struggle for knowledge. The Regnum is the highest social and political order man has ever achieved. The Cadre is its guardian. By the time the Cadre examines you for inception, you will have won much of the struggle for *personal* order. You have already. The Cadre will one day honor the name Tyrees."

"Could I ever be a Cadre One like you, Grandfather?"

Petr Tyrees brought his eyes down from above, though his head was still tilted back. He looked down his fine, long nose and saw no incongruity in the little boy's form huddled in the high-backed chair. His voice was intense, powerful, certain.

"You will be *more,* Pol, more—regardless of rank. And I will help you."

Eyes and blood and belief leaped fifty years to lock in voiceless communion. After a time, the smaller pair of shoulders sagged beneath its weight. Pol's arms had been resting on the chair's, putting his elbows almost at ear level. Now he brought them down to hug his chest. He spoke from deep in his grandfather's chair.

"You said that the enemy is . . . chaos, Grandfather?"

"Yes."

"But how do you know it . . . uh, find it . . . or . . ."

"Another word for chaos is confusion, Pol. Another yet is fragmentation. Unity, symmetry, control, are its opposites. The Regnum is under constant attack from the forces of chaos. So is the human personality in the form of uncontrolled impulse, unharnessed emotion."

"Does that mean like . . . not crying?"

Tyrees hesitated. He fought down something old and dying inside.

"Yes." He was surprised by Pol's smile.

"I can do that."

"I know you can."

"Can we talk about the Holtz Effect again, Grandfather?"

It took a moment for Tyrees to adjust to the boy's sudden change of topic. He was a man of precise deliberateness and had to remind himself constantly that his grandson was a boy of nine. With an uncharacteristic flourish, he dismissed the subject.

"Oh, I'm still working on it, when I can spare the time. No progress of late." Quickly, he resumed the aspect of a commanding officer. Just as quickly, Pol took on that of dedicated obedience.

"It's time for you to report to your tutor now, Pol. He has a civics program ready for you. After that, you will return here to inform me of your physical status, particularly the effects of your fatigue. If you are still confident of your powers of judgment, we will continue with the observation exercises."

"Yes, Grandfather."

Ten hours later, Pol Tyrees confessed to his grandfather that he could no longer function properly without sleep. He was immediately ushered to his room.

He did sleep—deeply and fitfully. He dreamed that he sat in a doorless cage. His grandfather sat also, but outside the bars, holding a tray of food in his lap. Pol was wild with hunger, but the bars were impassable. He cried and cried, but his grandfather just sat there with the tray, sternly, kindly looking on, as he always did. But instead of strong, graceful fingers, holding the tray was a pair of hooked and ugly claws.

(Excerpt from) *Our Galaxy, Past and Present, Regnum History* Primer, Ministry of Information

Children all over the galaxy already know that a very important date in history is SY 474. It was this year that delegates from every colonized planet met on ancient Terra. They drew up a charter or plan of organization that later formed the basis of Regnum law. That charter also began the "Pax Regnum," an era of peace and prosperity that has lasted for over two thousand years.

In SY 474, there were only 103 colonized planets. Their delegates made up the first Regnum Council. However, this Council was growing so rapidly with new colonization that changes were necessary. "Sectors," areas containing many star systems, were formed, each with a sector council that now sends a representative to sit on the Council of the Regnum. The modern Council of the Regnum, then, has eleven sector delegates (ten-year terms), a Chairman (elected for life), and the Cadre Proctor (appointed for life), who is in charge of Regnum security. Policy decisions are made by majority vote. Each Council member has a "ministry," or area of responsibility.*

The main government offices are on the planet Regnum in Sector I. Almost the whole of that world, directly or indirectly, serves the vast and complicated machinery of galactic government.

Generally, local planet and system governments have autonomy (control or powers of decision) over internal affairs. The Regnum is responsible for interplanetary matters and keeps an ambassador on each member planet.

The Regnum Charter is accessible under program RCH–1000 through any legal or educational computer system. The following is a list of the basic principles of the Charter:

The Regnum

- owes allegiance to no single planet, system, or sector
- has the exclusive right to maintain interstellar military vessels
- has the exclusive right to monitor and regulate trade between its members
- acts as the final arbiter in cases of dispute between members
- may legislate and enforce regulations deemed necessary for the benefit of its members in totem
- has the sole responsibility of defense in the case of threats from nonmembers or aliens**

Unit Assignment:
Use your desk consoles to study the various responsibilities of the thirteen ministries. Note the areas that might overlap and be prepared to discuss them with your instructor.

* See Appendix D for the responsibilities of each ministry.

**The phrase "or aliens" was added by the Regnum Council in SY 2675.

SY 3018

(Excerpt from) *The Personal Diary of Petr Tyrees, Cadre One*

The Vice-Proctor died last night in his sleep. . . .

My reactions are strong and mixed. I feel anger—because this galaxy holds so many parasitical lumps who are allowed to breathe when he, who had and gave so much, stopped. I feel gratitude still—because he gave me the time and opportunity for my grandson and my work on the Holtz Effect. I feel elation and guilt—because I am to be his successor!

I know I can live up to the title, but I will miss the fieldwork even though I know I am getting too old for it.

The disturbing turn taken by my research two years ago continues. The new simulations on the Holtz Effect are almost conclusive. At first I was happy simply because of the progress made, but talks with Hans Bolla have thrown cold water on my naïve assumptions. He has strong opinions about the political and psychological effects of the notion of alien contact on the public consciousness. He may be right. I vacillate between fear and fascination. If my experiments lead to the conclusions I anticipate, the implications may be profound and pervasive. Hans has gone to some lengths to rob me of the illusion that the discovery of truth—or its revelation—is automatically justified. He is an academic to the bone, so I don't always trust those sweeping theories of his. He's also too inclined to take on the sins of those countless masses who are less talented and responsible than he; but that remarkable mind can't be ignored. Of one thing he has convinced me: I must take great care with my findings on the Holtz Effect. Hans's hypotheses are as impressive as they are shocking. I will talk with him again. Soon I will have to send my work to the Proctor, but not yet. If I am to be a worm in the apple, then I intend to eat the whole thing before I can be exorcised. Then I, at least, will know the whole truth.

It's a pity that Pol was always so fascinated with the HE and alien contact. I suppose he was simply infected by my own. Besides, we should be talking of things of more importance to a boy of eleven. My direction of his training has probably made him more serious and single-minded than he should be, but he seems content, and he's demonstrating some remarkable abilities. He reminds me of his father, whose death I suspect pierced deeper than either of us knows. But Pol has the Tyrees tenacity of mind without his father's unstable temperament. In fact, his self-discipline is a little frightening, and I sometimes wonder if I have gone too far. . . .

SY 3019

Petr Tyrees sat again in his study. In spite of the heavy burdens of his new office, there was little on his face to betray their presence or the passage of time. If anything, the power of the aura created by his concentration had increased. Silence seemed more a product of his will than an absence of sound. He broke it by moving to brush touch pads with deft fingers. Reading screen—off; intercom—on.

"Pol?"

"Yes, Grandfather."

"I'm expecting Dr. Bolla any minute now. Bring him right in when he comes."

"Yes, sir."

Tyrees folded his hands on the desk and closed his eyes. Silence returned. Visibly, his neck muscles relaxed and his shoulders fell. Breathing slowed, deepened. In seconds he appeared to be asleep, in minutes he was a manikin dressed in black, rendered by a craftsman with an obsession for realism. But when the door panel hummed, there was no sense of transition as his eyes flicked open and he began to rise.

In the doorway was a taller, more defined version of the boy who stood there two years earlier. He stepped aside and gestured in a short, dour-faced man. With the exception of a few tufts of hair over his ears, his pate gleamed whitely. Small, sturdy feet danced under a paunchy body. The two men were near the pinnacles of their careers, and galactic reputations attested to their achievements; yet visually, they were a classic comedy team: one tall and straight and sternly cut—the other saggy and slouched, as if the burdens of the spirit were too much for the body. They were near in age, but Tyrees gathered vitality with his years, while Bolla—at least physically—seemed to have sloughed off youth negligently. Tyrees had to pick up Bolla's hand to shake it.

"Hans. Good to see you again."

"Petr. You look fine. As always. So does your grandson." Pol smiled, ducked his head once, and left quickly.

"Pol is doing some programming for me," said Tyrees. "I think he's a bit preoccupied."

"He's very mature for his age, Petr."

"He's mature for *any* age. I'm very proud of him."

Bolla looked at his friend keenly for a moment. Then a yellow-toothed smile captured his face.

"I almost forgot! Belated congratulations! I haven't seen you since before your promotion."

"Yes, it's been over a year. But thank you."

"A Vice-Proctor. In charge of the most important sector, too. There's only one more step, Petr."

A subdued chuckle came from Tyrees. "There are eleven Vice-Proctors, Hans, and only *one* Cadre Proctor. No doubt this will be as far as I get. Even at that, I'll always feel like a Cadre One."

"Why?"

"Ones are the heart of the Cadre. Its men are at the peak of their powers, mentally and physically. They *do*. They *produce*." A rueful smile. "Vice-Proctors only administer."

"'Administer,' indeed. Your responsibilities must be incredible *now*. In the years to come, Petr, they will be awesome."

"Your book."

"Yes."

Tyrees sighed. "Why did you send the stuff to me, Hans?"

"A sympathetic ear—I hoped. And I had to get my preliminary findings to someone near the top without going public."

"I had you come here instead of sector headquarters because we need an uninterrupted talk. You don't seem to accept the possibility that I'll disagree with your conclusions."

"Disagree! It's not a question of agreeing or disagreeing, but of facing the facts. Face them! Even though the work is unfinished, the trends are undeniable." Bolla's jowls quivered with conviction.

"Facts. Statistical probabilities, you mean. Postulates for the future. And very frightening ones. Dangerous ones."

"Yes. Another reason I'm trying the Cadre before the political types. And I must be allowed access to the Cadre's resources—hardware and information. I've gone as far as I can go on the university's facilities. It's possible, Petr—just possible—that I will discover variables that will *reduce* the probabilities." Bolla was now sweating in rivulets. He looked around the Spartan room for a tissue to wipe his forehead, finally settling for the backs of his stubby fingers. For the first time, he could hear emotion in Tyrees's words—doubt, anger, fear.

"But you speak about the *Regnum,* Hans! You theorize about the imminent collapse of a galactic civilization that has kept man in an ordered growth pattern for two thousand years. You have it falling apart like a child's plaything!"

"Petr, Petr. Listen. You are a scientist—and the most ruthlessly objective man I know. You, of all people, should be able to listen with your head instead of your heart. The *size* of an idea doesn't render it unbelievable. You know how probability works—the Regnum's size itself makes the probabilities more reliable. You also know that social psychology is no longer crystal-ball gazing. Even if you believe me wrong, it's too important a possibility to ignore . . . and I'll go public if I must." The sacklike face and soft body belied the strength that rang in Bolla's voice, leaped from his eyes.

"How much time do you predict for—what do you call it?—*trend fulmination?*"

"Anywhere from twenty to seventy years. That's one of the figures I want narrowed. Anavex will do it."

"Anavex?"

"My new program. Unfinished. A few years should do it—but even now the university's best computer is choking on it. It will be the most sophisticated probability program devised, even without its capacity to assimilate psychological data. But it needs Cadre facilities—especially in the form of economic data."

"You call them the Trade Wars."

A nod.

"And they will begin in the Hub, the core of our galaxy."

"They have *already* begun, Petr."

Because of his incredulity, Tyrees's patience with his dogged round friend was flagging. Anger was back in his voice.

"There is no hard evidence of that!"

"There *is*. This is not a Hub sector, and you don't see the big picture anyway. The Cadre wouldn't be analyzing the data properly, but I'd wager that the Chairman and the Cadre Proctor can smell something by now—without realizing its significance."

"But you make it all sound so inevitable, like a . . . a tidal wave that can't be stopped."

"It can't. Not if the brew has reached . . . call it a critical mass. Even if it has, it *can* be influenced—deflected or dampened. And there is still the short end of the probability, the few percentage points that allow it not to happen at all. But I think critical mass *has* already been reached."

Tyrees had been pacing slowly as he talked and listened. Now he picked up the hard copy of Bolla's material and riffled its edges.

"All right, Hans. All right. I'll forward this to the Cadre Proctor. I'll also support your recommendations—on the simple grounds that they shouldn't be ignored. Your record is just too impressive."

Bolla heaved a long sigh of relief. "Thank you, Petr. You won't regret it. But you remain unconvinced?"

"Unconvinced, but . . . afraid. The Regnum . . . Hans, this is just *part* of your book isn't it?"

"Yes—*The Evil Star*. I know you won't like the melodramatic title. It's a study of the psychological effects of the Great Diaspora—man's explosive spread among the stars. I was plodding along quite innocently until a probability run sidetracked me into this. I'll finish it someday."

"You know you won't be able to release any of the 'Trade Wars' hypothesis."

"I took that for granted." Bolla smiled. "Assuming I got what I asked for. Not to the public. Council Eyes Only."

"A little blackmail, Hans?"

"Precisely." Tyrees shook his head glumly but did not object. "By the way, Petr. It was the part of my book about the public preoccupation with aliens that had you concerned about a year ago. Any progress on the Holtz Effect?"

"Sorry. All that is CEO now. Classified."

"And did you take my advice? Psychologically, perhaps more than ever in the years to come, we *need* aliens."

"Classified. It's in the hands of the Chairman himself."

Bolla shrugged, knowing Tyrees would say no more. "Well, who knows? If they set me up with a special commission, I'll have the clearance to see whatever I like."

"Quite possible."

"Well, I can only hope. I'm sure you won't agree, but the Cadre can be pretty narrow-minded sometimes."

"No, I don't agree, Hans. The Cadre has a specific function, a valuable one. What you see as narrow-mindedness is our dedication to that function. We have no time for philosophy."

Bolla's face fell sadly (his face could form no other aspect with such ease), and he raised a placating hand. "You don't understand, Petr." He summoned a clownish smile. "But no matter. You are just like the rest of the Cadre. Brass and buckle and ego. But I thank the Maker you are there. We need you. . . . By the way, your grandson. You told me some rather startling things about him last time. Still progressing?"

The granite set of Tyrees's jaw softened somewhat and he nodded. "Yes. He never ceases to amaze me."

"And you're still hardening him up for the Cadre, of course."

"Your choice of words tells me you still don't approve—though I don't know why."

"If you understood that, Petr, you'd understand what I said about the Cadre."

COUNCIL EYES ONLY

(Excerpt from) *The Evil Star: A Sociological Study of the Psychological Effects of Interstellar Culture* **by Hans Bolla**

Chapter X

The Maker Himself may have erred in letting slip the gentle tether that held man to Terra and to a less grandiose image of Himself. Perhaps even He is capable of losing control of His own creations. Fledgling man was allowed to go wandering before he came to grips with problems in his own house.

Though our civilization is spread across the immensity of an entire galaxy, ripples of cause and effect constantly alter its aspect, as would thrown pebbles a small pond. Sometimes a large boulder is dropped; ripples become waves, effects are dramatic and long-lasting. One such boulder was the Security Cadre. This iron-ribbed official body was responsible for virtually eradicating armed conflict on an interplanetary level; its presence was—and is—the single most effective ploy in keeping the beast of large-scare war at bay.

On the face of it, the elimination of war between planets, a rampant horror during the early years of the Regnum, seems an unqualified boon. But it is *not* unqualified. The weapons and tactics of military conflict have been torn from the hands of those foolish enough to use them; but they have been replaced by the weapons and tactics of *economic* warfare. These are more subtle, of course, especially when used inside the law, but their effects (as we saw in the last chapter) are ultimately just as destructive.

I have hypothesized that man's competitive nature demands a mode of expression regardless of his circumstances. Unconsciously, as a species, he remembers when he fought for his family, his tribe, his country. Reduced to its simplest elements, this innate and violent competitiveness over a patch of ground is a manifestation of his need for self-definition and belonging. It is stamped on his genes; he will fight to maintain the identity rendered by a particular group or territory, more conscious motives notwithstanding. The point is this: Take away his club and he will find another way to fight for precisely the same reasons. Now, he fights in the marketplace. This commercial mode of conflict has always been with us because it, too, defends or acquires definition and territory for a distinctive group; but for the past few generations it has been on the increase, thanks to the success of the Cadre in limiting the war mode. In my opinion we will soon live on an economic battlefield measuring a hundred light-years across. Inevitably, the "war" will become more and more overt, more and more vicious, perhaps to the point of resurrecting the club again.

The solution? Amazingly simple: Supply our compulsive competitor with a new patch of ground on which to stand and fight—the galaxy itself. But can a whole galaxy, which contains more nothingness than anything else, provide the identity or sense of belonging instilled by a plot of ground? I think that, having reached this stage of rapid communication and travel, it can indeed. But then what will he fight *against*? Aside from himself, most of man's traditional enemies—disease, starvation, the natural elements—have already been vanquished.

I do see one alternative, though I cite it with reluctance. Many pieces of evidence, including the now famous Holtz Effect, postulate the existence of an advanced civilization of aliens. Strictly from the point of view of one who studies man's collective behavior, I hope that "they" not only exist, but also *confront* man on his little patch of ground, his dirt-speck of a galaxy. It need not be a hostile confrontation—only a concrete statement of otherness and other-where. This would help to redefine and reunite us, if only in terms of what we are not, where we are not.

Let us return to the humdrum facts. They are dull and zest-less if one insists upon regarding them as rows of marching statistics. Remember that they are actually a paradigm of human behavior. For example . . .

SY 3020

"Be very careful, Pol. It is dangerous."

"Yes, Grandfather."

"That red door straight across from us is your objective."

They stood on a catwalk halfway up a sixty-foot wall. The nearest adjacent wall was smooth and featureless. The other walls and the ceiling were cluttered by a curious jumble of paraphernalia: spikes, netting, ladders, bars, ropes, wheels, drums. Some of the solid gear pulsed with a reddish light; parts were in constant motion, parts intermittent. It was as if a crazed engineer had gathered together odds and ends—perhaps spare parts from a circus and a plumbing warehouse—and stuck them together in an effort to construct the fabled perpetual motion machine. But it was not a maze of innocent junk. It was a CTH, a Commando Training Hazard built by the Regnum military. It was also a secret facility, because the kind of small, specialized, hit-and-run strike force it was used to train was not supposed to be needed in the Regnum. A Cadre Vice-Proctor, however, would have no difficulty gaining access from the sister service. Petr Tyrees looked at his timer. Pol looked at him. The boy stood quietly, but his eyes flashed with suppressed energy.

"I'll give you the same instructions they give to their commandos, Pol—though they'd be closer to thirty than thirteen."

"I'd still like to try it, Grandfather."

"I knew you would. But don't think of it as a game. A fall could be serious—even fatal. However, if I didn't think you were ready, I wouldn't have brought you here. The body as well as the mind needs discipline. It needs challenge in order to develop control. The CTH provides the first and demands the second."

Pol looked up and around at the maze of protuberances and then down at the slate-gray floor. His voice carried the barest hint of pleading in it.

"Will you stay here, Grandfather?"

"No. I don't want to distract you."

"I'm not afraid."

"Fear is not shameful, Pol—unless you can't harness it, *use* it, like a fist. Are you ready?"

"Yes, Grandfather."

"Very well. The unit has been set at its most difficult level. You have fifteen minutes to get to that red door. After that time, it will not open. There is a pressure plate on its threshold that will activate the fifteen-minute timing again, during which *this* door will open. The system keeps reversing itself. Neither door will open once the floor is touched."

"What happens if a man never gets to a door in time, Grandfather?"

"He must try until he succeeds—or until he injures himself. However, there is an intercom near each door." He tapped a grate on the wall. "If he asks to be let out, he is denied the right to join the special command unit. You, of course, would suffer no such penalty." Pol looked at the unseamed, ageless face and felt a pang in his stomach. He knew his penalty for such a failure: the unvoiced disappointment of this man who was everything to him, who burdened him with so much rigid affection and steely pride. His grandfather's eyes were light blue and far away; they lingered on Pol with a distant touch.

"Any lighted portion of the apparatus has an electric current passing through it. Not enough to kill, but enough to debilitate, or cause a fall. There is no single correct route. Some of the light and movement you see is random, some regular. When I close this door, the time begins. There will be no signal when time has expired and the far door locks.

"Those are the instructions received by the commandos,

Pol. Here are my instructions to you: Stay within yourself. Keep control. You possess the ability to pass this test." With a nod of encouragement the Cadre officer opened the door, then closed it quickly and firmly behind him.

Pol resisted the drag of his eyes to the indifferent gray floor and concentrated, using the attention-focusing techniques his grandfather had taught him. He studied the moving, flashing jumble quickly, looking for predictable patterns of light and possible routes. The best appeared to be a path diagonally upward to about three-quarters of wall height to the first corner, then an irregular path downward.

He would try to avoid the higher reaches of the ceiling—the wall could be an ally.

The first step allowed no choice. Revolving slowly two meters above him and with the same diameter was a runged wheel. He climbed up on the catwalk's guardrail, one hand on the wall. The jump was relatively short but would have to be timed perfectly in order to grab a rung and ride it up.

His mind told him it would be easy, but as he looked down an icy tide swept through him. He was four years old again, looking down to the street from a forbidden balcony. His fear angered and dismayed him. He shouted silently, No! No! Control. Control. Concentrate. Watch the rung, the rung. . . . Now . . . jump!

He almost overleaped but was able to grab the bar and swing gently from the rising wheel. Relief flowed through him, melting the ice. His first challenge had been more a battle within than one against externals. Well, his grandfather was always right about those things.

Knowing it would be draining and time-consuming to ride the wheel a full turn, he prepared to disengage as he rose to the vertical and could stand on the following rung. He had already rejected a flashing bar within easy reach, though its period seemed long and regular. Instead, he stood upright on the rung, balancing free for a moment at the wheel's high point, in order to grab a net at its anchor—a strut that jutted from the wall. He had more confidence in his balance than anything else because it came unflawed, without conscious bidding. Traversing the net would require strength as well. It was hammock-shaped, about ten meters long and sloped upward. Large, loose squares of cord would twist and tilt with the smallest shift in weight if a climber took the more obvious and inviting

course along its top. A strength-sapper. A muscle-jangler. Pol
swung to the underside, where he had to hang, taking his weight
in his hands; but this way his weight was concentrated, pulling
the net taut and steady above him. He pulled himself upward,
hand over hand. At the top, he wrapped his legs around the
supporting strut and hung upside down. He felt no fatigue and
was beginning to actively enjoy the challenge of the hazard.

At first glance the next choice appeared obvious. A simple
bar angled past him from the ceiling and sloped to the adjacent
wall at the corner. It would only require a ten-meter downward
slide. He had almost committed himself, hands on the bar and
legs about to release the net support, when the "bar" began to
give like a stick of licorice. With a spasm he let go and relocked
his legs. The thing was made of a spongy, elastic material that
would stretch with his weight, probably to a point far below
its anchorage at the wall. Even if he had reacted in time to
take the impact against the wall with his feet, he would still
have a climb back up—and the substance was greasy slick.
He wondered how many would-be commandos had dangled in
frustration at the bottom of that loop—or had fallen the twenty
feet to the floor after hitting the wall.

The only alternative was a horizontal ladder that led to a
small platform on the wall. But the ladder's side rails were
permanently lit up, and its rungs flashed on and off. He hung
there and watched the rungs for a precious moment. The clock
in his head told him he had already taken four minutes—that
left eleven.

The rungs flashed in a double pattern—one at a time in a
rapid, consecutive sequence, then again in a slower, but reversed sequence. Concentration and timing. Go with the slower
sequence, the flashes coming from behind. A rhythm. Hanging
below, hand over hand. Impossible to gain the top to walk it
because of the illuminated side rails. He would have to swing
up to the first rung.

Breathe deeply. Push the air out. Swing. Swing. Up. Higher.
Wait . . . Wait . . . another swing. . . . Now! Now! . . . Now . . .
Again . . . again . . . again. . . . Once . . . more! One hand fisted
the last unlit rung, just long enough to swing to the platform.

Pol smiled. He stood there panting lightly, savoring the
charge of a new drug, a brew of blood and adrenaline and
triumph, a potion spiced by the sense of danger faced, danger
snubbed.

At least nine minutes left. The rest looks no more difficult than what I've already passed, he thought.

He was right—until the last leg. He had reached the next corner quickly, with the only cost a bruised shin. Sweating now, and tired, he decided to take a few seconds' rest on another small platform. Then he saw something that unnerved him. His intention had been to pull himself up a vertical pole to another net—the last obstacle. The net angled down to a point near the catwalk at the door. He stared at the pole in disbelief.

"Hey!" he cried aloud. It was now an uninterrupted pillar of light. It had passed through his field of vision many times during his ratlike scramble through the hazard and it had never been lit. Why would they do this? Why would they have an impossibly long active period for a single obstacle near the end unless it was meant to *stop* rather than impede? It wasn't fair. It made judgment, decision making, a joke. It didn't seem *right*. What if he'd been on that thing when the current shot through it for the first time in ten minutes? He would wait a few more seconds. . . .

He was thirty-five feet above the floor. The only other route would take him right to the ceiling, and he'd managed to avoid it so far. It would take . . . hard to tell. He might not make the time limit.

The pole was still alight. He reached out and flicked a finger at it. Snap! He shuddered with the jolt. No choice.

He leaped for a wall ladder to the ceiling and climbed rapidly, angrily. The hazard should be difficult, not unpredictably dangerous. . . . Still, he had a slim chance. By the time he hung from a net at the ceiling, he was gleaming with sweat and acutely aware of the seconds rolling by in that special part of his brain that was never wrong. The net led to a long, almost vertical cylinder several feet in diameter, with its nether end gaping near the catwalk. There were other possibilities, but all would take more time than he had left. As it was, his traverse was muscle-tearing, because he was moving at a more careless pace now, though the net's capricious passivity was no longer threatening. His angry speed had brought him near exhaustion.

He made the suspended tube, breath rasping, and peered down its long barrel to a target of floor thirty meters below. His mind buzzed. He thought now only in fragments as he put all his energy into beating the clock.

Outside too large and smooth. Got to be inside. So. Shoulders and feet rammed opposite each other against the tunnel wall. Walk the shoulders down. Strength. Stamina. Speed. Rungs at the bottom for a swing to the catwalk. Enough energy left? Enough time? No matter. Have to try. Grandfather.

Up top. Now. Set shoulders and feet *hard*. Careful. Shuffle down. Okay. Not—so—bad. Keep a rhythm. Don't stop. Just maybe...

As he rotated his shoulders from side to side Pol stole a glance downward and nearly lost his hold in shock. Traveling up the inside of the cylinder was a meter-wide band of light.

No! No! This is insane! he thought. This...this is for stupid animals!

"Grandfather!" he cried aloud. "Stop this. I want to quit."

But the ring of light continued blithely upward as if it were coming to greet him. Panic stirred somewhere inside and began to spread. He bit his tongue. Again—no choice. He would have to release on both sides simultaneously and at exactly the right moment to fall past the light—then jam himself back almost immediately. If he fell too far or too fast, he would never be able to gain purchase again. But the panic threatened to erupt and he was still trembling. He caught his breath and watched the light rise from beneath.

Wait! Wait 'til it almost touches. Let...go! Jam back!

"Hummph!"

Pol had rammed himself so violently back against the plas-teel sides that his head rang and muscles vibrated—but he held. Blood screamed. Sweat stung his eyes. Breathing was a string of sobs. No challenge now. No eager excitement. Only pain and misery and the still exploding panic. He recovered only enough to wonder vaguely if he could begin moving down again. He no longer cared about the time.

He looked and saw that he was about halfway down; he looked and saw that another band of light was coming toward him. He threw his head back against the cylinder wall and screamed for his grandfather again. His knees increased their pressure against the rounded wall and began to bounce absurdly. They refused to release again—even when the ribbon of light began to pass under him.

But it brought no shock. It was just an innocent circle of light that continued up the cylinder. Then knees and hands and shoulders suddenly abandoned him and collapsed off the wall.

Semiconscious, fear only a fine gauze, a distant backdrop

in his mind, he fell down the tunnel like a sack of laundry and was spat at the floor. Dispassionately, he saw first the blur of the wall shooting upward; then a round eye receding in the distance; then a gray sheet rushing to meet him. It took a long time.

Pol hit the floor with the sound of a fist striking a pillow. The floor billowed underneath him, heaving like a soft stomach under an unexpected blow. It pulled away until the pressure was little more than the weight of his body. Then it belched him back upward and settled with a soft wave.

He was on his hands and knees, face sick white and tear-riven, arms quivering, by the time his grandfather stood over him.

"You did well, Pol."

"You . . . it . . . tricked me."

"What? . . . Nonsense."

"You . . . shouldn't have done that."

Pol staggered to his feet. Words came in spasms. "You didn't . . . tell me . . . you kept changing things . . . the floor . . ."

There was nothing observable in the expression of the man in black, but there might have been a hint of uncertainty in the voice.

"Experience is the only teacher, Pol. Crisis . . . you must learn to deal with it. And fear. It was necessary. Later on . . ."

"No!" Pol whirled and staggered for the door.

SY 3021

When Pol Tyrees answered the door, he was surprised to see Hans Bolla. The man's face was more baleful and houndlike than ever. His mouth was a trenched, downward-turning horse-shoe formed by sagging jowls. His customary air of assurance was gone.

"Oh . . . Dr. Bolla. I'm sorry, but Grandfather's not here. I haven't seen him for almost a week this time."

Bolla's eyes fell away. One hand reached out toward Pol and, as if its weight had suddenly become too much, fell away, too.

"May I come in, Pol? It's you I want to see."

"Uh . . . yes, please. Please sit down." Bolla walked stiffly past him into the living room and eased himself into the only comfortable armchair. Heaving a long sigh, he looked about the room, wondering again why the Tyreeses' apartment was so impersonal. Everything was of the best quality and well appointed, but also strictly functional and somehow institutionalized. Nothing was warm or frivolous. He forced his eyes back to Pol, who was watching him quizzically.

"You sit, too, Pol. I have bad news." Pol didn't move, but his face went pale.

"It's about Grandfather."

"Yes. . . . Pol, you know I'm chairing a Regnum commission now. Your grandfather helped put me there. . . ."

"Yes."

"Well, much of the work brings me into contact with the Cadre. . . . They know of our friendship—Petr's and mine—so they asked me to . . ." Pol's stare bored into him, pushed him into the chair. Bolla found it hard to breathe.

"They asked you to see me." The voice was totally without inflection, but the face was bloodless now.

"To see you . . . yes. Pol, I'm so, so sorry. Your grandfather is dead. I know what he meant to . . ." His voice faltered and died. The eyes that imprisoned his were so nakedly blue, so frighteningly deep, and in their depths he saw the unholy birth of despair.

The boy stood motionless and there were no tears. His voice was steady.

"What happened?"

"I don't know, Pol. They won't tell me. I'm only cleared for things I have a need to know. . . ."

"Why should it be classified?"

"I don't know that, either. I supposed there could be many reasons—but it won't help us to speculate. . . . Pol, I want you to come with me. My wife and I—"

"No."

"Pol."

"No."

"You're only fourteen. . . ."

"Thank you, Dr. Bolla. I want to stay here."

"Well, perhaps we can make some arrangements. . . . We'll go into it later. And we'll have to talk about the future, too."

"I know about my future, sir."

"Yes, yes. The Cadre," said Bolla with profound sadness. "Perhaps this will help: You have an appointment. In a few days. With the Chairman of the Regnum. The Chairman himself, Pol."

Pol nodded, turned, and walked from the room.

SY 3021

The highest officeholder in the galaxy, the Chairman of the Regnum, smiled as he watched the screen. One of his personal bodyguards led a very young man toward an outer office that was next to his own. The boy looked alert and self-assured— not to be expected.

He doesn't *look* unusual, thought the Chairman. Tall, like his grandfather. Slender. The resemblance is strong. Moves well, though. Graceful for an adolescent. Fluid. Interesting. I wonder if we've got something here....

The image on the screen vanished along with his smile as the door hummed open. He spun into his face lines and folds of concern. The Chairman was barrel-bodied, bullet-headed, but he moved with quick precision from behind his desk to greet his visitor, taking one hand in two of his own.

"Pol Tyrees. Please accept my condolences. Your grandfather was a great man—great. His contributions to the Regnum are inestimable—inestimable." He sadly shook his head.

"Thank you, Mr. Chairman."

"Sit. Sit down." Like a solicitous, hunkering bear, the Chairman hulked over Pol as he guided him to an informal grouping of deep chairs. "We must talk, you and I."

Pol was still dulled by his sense of loss and isolation, but he was being cooed at by the Chairman of the Regnum and so felt honored. For the past few days he had lived in a shell of his own making. His life had never had meaning beyond what had been inspired by his grandfather, and now that had been ripped away. What was left? There was the Cadre, but . . . the Cadre had really been his grandfather.

The Chairman had gorilla's arms—long, powerful, low—the wrists covered with a jungle of wiry black hair. One of these he draped heavily over Pol's shoulders.

"Son, your grandfather and I met many years ago when he was making some startling discoveries about the Holtz Effect and the Alien Contact Theory. A wonderful contribution. Wonderful. Over these past few months, we became very close. Very close. Did you know that he and I and Dr. Bolla were working together?" His tone was patronizing and Pol recognized that chant; but adults had always treated him as younger than he felt, so he did not resent it.

"No, sir. Just Dr. Bolla."

"Oh—well, fine. The work was—is—extremely important. But we found time to talk about you. He was very proud of you. Proud."

"Thank you, Mr. Chairman."

"He considered you a uniquely talented young man. Did you know he wanted you to follow in his footsteps? The Cadre, I mean?"

"Yes, sir."

"Excellent. Good. I thought it was the least I could do, to have a chat with you and help in any way I can." The Chairman's arm was still around Pol and he leaned closer as he talked, voice oozing sincerity. "Your grandfather and I were a *team*, son. We fought together in a . . . a vicious struggle, a fight to keep the Regnum whole and secure. Now you have to take up that fight with me."

He shook Pol gently for emphasis. Pol was unnerved by these words because they so resembled his grandfather's. However, the Chairman's little speech was delivered with a politician's sense of audience; his grandfather's words were those of simple, hard conviction.

"Yes, sir. But I don't know what I—"

"By doing what you were meant to do. By not permitting his passing to shake your resolve. Become the best Cadre officer in the Regnum.

"Now. Is there anything I can do for you? Just tell me."

"No, sir. Dr. Bolla is looking after me."

The Chairman beamed an impossibly warm smile at him. "Your grandfather was right."

"Sir?"

"Any other lad would have asked for help to get into the Cadre."

"I know you can't do that, Mr. Chairman."

"You're right. The Cadre Proctor sits on the Council with me and *he* controls the Cadre, not I. But I can do one thing— if you wish."

"Sir?"

"Ordinarily, you would be eligible for the initial screening process in about eight months. Correct?"

"Yessir. I'm fifteen in six months."

"Right. That's a flexible rule. I can have you started on the screening now. Then you should be cleared for the recruitment year right after your birthday. Would you like that?" The Chairman removed his arm after one last squeeze and sat back expectantly.

"That . . . that would be good, Mr. Chairman." Pol didn't feel good, though. Suddenly, the beginning for which he had been yearning all his young life was there in front of him, and he was alone and unsure.

"Fine. Fine. Consider it done." The Chairman reached for a pamphlet on a side table. "Here, son, take this. The Cadre Proctor himself handed it to me this morning."

Pol turned it over to read its title: REGNUM SECURITY CADRE—RECRUITMENT BROCHURE.

Regnum Security Cadre

RECRUITMENT BROCHURE

Citizens of the Regnum: The Security Cadre is charged with a single responsibility—to ferret out and eliminate any threat to the security of the Regnum.

The resources of "The Cadre" are available to member planets in the galaxy. LIke most other offices of galactic government, the Cadre's central headquarters is located on Regnum, and it oversees the activities of the eleven sector headquarters spanning the populated universe.

The Security Cadre is legendary for its dedication and integrity; its men and women are committed for life to the principle of the Pax Regnum. They are uniquely talented and trained to be the servitors of the most lasting and enlightened political order in history.

The Cadre was chartered over seven hundred years ago by an order in Council officially citing two concerns. First, the rapid colonization during the Great Diaspora was causing problems that were difficult to control, and a number of nonmember planets was disrupting Regnum unity. Second, reports of alien intelligence were on the increase. This potential threat has gained credence as evidence of a widespread, though discreet, incursion continues to accumulate.

Citizens, if you are parents with a son or daughter under the age of sixteen, you may wish to embrace a truly noble commitment. Contact your local sector headquarters (free of charge) for detailed information.

The Security Cadre is structured according to the outline following. A Cadre officer must manifest distinguished service in each sub-Cadre in order to be admitted to that of the next lowest number. Vice-Proctors, the Commanders of the sector headquarters, are selected from among the officers of Cadre One; the Cadre Proctor, Commander in Chief, has a seat on the Regnum Council.

Security Cadre Structure

Recruit Orientation (one year)

- Testing
- Policies and Procedures
- Physical Training
- Basic Mathematics
- Language
- Inception (optional to both parties)

Cadre Seven—Basic Training (Red—five years minimum)

- Mathematics, Physics, Chemistry
- Regnum Law
- Cybernetics
- Population Dynamics
- Political Economy
- Psychology
- Physical Training
- Operations Training (on assignment at a sector headquarters—six months minimum)

Cadre Six—Advanced Training (Yellow—four years minimum)

- Optional Academic Specialty
- Weapons and Combat
- Interrogation/Surveillance
- Covert Operations/Security Techniques
- Xenology
- Astrogation/Astrophysics
- Sociological Psychology
- Research Training (on assignment with a Cadre Three officer—six months minimum)

Cadre Five—Research (Brown—indefinite duration)
A Cadre Five officer chooses a project under the guidance of his Vice-Proctor. The project must add significantly to the knowledge, techniques, or intelligence data of the Cadre. A Cadre Five officer has access to the resources and data (with the exception of Council documents) of the entire Security Cadre.

Cadre Four—Operations (Green—indefinite duration)
A Cadre Four officer is assigned to a headquarters or a field support office to assist in operations or to support officers on field assignments. A Cadre Four officer may request permanent assignment where he may rise within the sub-Cadre.

Cadre Three—Investigations (Blue—indefinite duration)
A Cadre Three officer works in the field to gather information according to the terms of specific "assignment directives." He

commands the support of a local field support office and reports to a sector headquarters.

Cadre Two—Apprehensions (Violet—indefinite duration)
A Cadre Two officer works in the field according to specific orders contained in assignment directives, but he has powers of detention and arrest on any member world. He may also work covertly.

Cadre One—Sanctions (Black—indefinite duration)
A Cadre One officer holds the highest rank among field agents. Only a Cadre One may bear arms.
Only a Cadre One possesses diplomatic immunity on any member world.
Only a Cadre One has discretionary powers that may go beyond the mandate of an assignment directive.
Only a Cadre One may exercise judiciary prerogatives normally vested in local courts. (These special powers are entrusted confidently to a small number of the most superbly trained and talented men in the galaxy.)

A Cadre One officer reports to the offices of a Vice-Proctor or those of the Cadre Proctor himself.
The Cadre insignia is a simple circle that symbolizes the solidarity of the Cadre brotherhood within and a commitment to the unity of the Regnum without. The Cadre owes allegiance to no single planet, system, or sector of the Regnum.
The Cadre Charter revokes the citizenship of its officers and grants them universal diplomatic status. A Cadre officer is subject to local law, but not to local jurisprudence; the Cadre judges its own. The Cadre itself is subject only to the Council of the Regnum.
Officers of the Cadre do not draw salaries; they requisition funds they require for personal expenses, even in retirement. Off-duty travel is free and unlimited. A Cadre officer may not resign. For further information, contact your local sector headquarters.

SY 3022

Pol looked at the impressive structure and felt heat rise from his belly. He carried memories, not of a childhood now past, but as others carried locks of hair, of his grandfather's stories of Cadre training.

He was not prepared for the sense of power and permanence radiated by the complex. It had the off-white, dull gleam of an expensive nickel alloy, and it made the shabbier government buildings around it look like supplicants, poor relatives clustering for a handout. It soared and swept, lines curving in orderly intricacy.

Far overhead, a single dark bird flew a precise course, its size and color in chance contrast to the complex. Its flight tugged Pol's eyes into the distance and fear into his heart. The Cadre training complex symbolized a new and very romantic beginning for him—all the excitement and challenge of a calling in the Security Cadre of the Regnum. He had never wanted anything else.

But his grandfather, his hard yet benevolent god, was gone. The year of trial and probing ahead had seemed only a test of patience when he could draw strength from Petr Tyrees. Now he had to struggle to dampen the vibrations running down the lines of chest and stomach and loin. Grasping the recruitment brochure in one hand (though it had long been committed like a prayer to memory), he mounted the wide steps in reverence. He passed under the main archway, itself a huge replica of the Cadre insignia, and entered the reception area.

I'm finally here, he thought, forcing himself to relax by pushing his lungs empty with his diaphragm, holding, and refilling slowly. A year of orientation and he would be a Cadre officer, albeit a lowly one, without function except to study.

Then, as if suddenly animated from the picture on his brochure, an officer came striding toward him. He wore the soft boots and subtly shimmering black uniform of all Cadre; rank was indicated by the color of the thin cording around the top of the collar. This was red—Cadre Seven, Basic Training. To Pol, the long, flowing cape had an irresistible appeal, and his eyes were drawn to the red flashes along its trailing edge as the young officer walked past. There were those who saw the cape as an affectation, but his grandfather had told him that it had been designed deliberately hundreds of years ago to set the Cadre apart—and that it was also a fighting tool. It was illegal for a civilian to wear a similar uniform. It irked him that he would wear gray coveralls during orientation.

Pol joined a line at an information console, still tamping back the hum of his nervousness. When it was his turn he swiped at the hair on his forehead and pushed a key labeled DIRECTIONS. Immediately the screen flashed PROVIDE IDENTIFICATION. He fished in a pocket for his ID plate and dropped it on the transparent tray. The screen then commanded PROCEED TO RECRUIT RECEPTION and displayed a map. He disdained its offer of a printout, slapping the "N" key, but more words jumped up, this time flashing on and off: REMAIN IN WHITE-MARKED AREAS. He looked around him and saw that the reception area and some of the spoking corridors bore white slash marks along their walls. He headed down the passage matching the one in his head until he found a small lecture theatre containing a few dozen boys and girls of his age. They had that classic deadpan look that teachers recognize as nervous wariness in teenagers who await the prerogatives of unfamiliar authority. They wore rigid masks for faces and remained quiet. Pol walked down the center aisle. Some noticed a strangeness in his walk: it was lithe, cat-like and silent, inhumanly loose and liquid. He sat down between the two boys in first-row seats. Both looked up and saw the smooth, easy movements and placid expression of someone whose mask was more perfect than theirs.

"Greetings. I'm Dace Sestus," said one with mock formality. A shock of impossibly red hair bobbed above a quick smile. Pol liked him immediately.

"Pol Tyrees," he said, offering a hand.

"Ttig Hal," piped a stocky boy from the other seat, obviously grateful that someone was talking.

"Call me Ses," announced the redhead. "This is the big day, huh? I wish they'd get this ship in orbit, though. The Cadre has been too long staggering by without me."

The other boys laughed. The tension broke with the sound; others from nearby seats joined them, looking for an excuse to crack their forced reserve.

"Going by what I hear," said Ttig, growling nervously, "we'll be lucky to last first month." He pushed a cracking adolescent voice back down a full octave in midsentence.

"Yeah, I know," said Ses, grin fading somewhat, then rebounding. "But they really *need* me. I'm a natural symbol of justice. The public must be constantly reminded, you know, of the Cadre's glorious traditions. They use people like me to keep up the image—trot us out for the holovision cameras and such." Ses was a precocious boy even among an elite group of youngsters for whom precocity was the norm. His irrepressibility strengthened Pol's inclination to like him. Pol was more introverted, usually choosing to listen rather than speak. With people like Ses around it was easy to exercise that preference.

Ttig was still pursuing his point: doggedness was a fact of his character that the others would come to recognize as his trademark. He stuck a heavy round face forward.

"How many of us do you think will make it?"

"All I know is, a lot of us will get the chop sooner or later," said a voice from behind them.

"Well, all you guys have to do is follow my example," crowed Ses, "and you'll all be flying around in that cape a year from now. Keep your head on with the hair topside and it'll be nulgrav, right, Pol?"

It was a fill-the-silence quip, but Pol answered as he knew his grandfather would expect him to.

"Yes, I expect to make it all right. That's what I'm here for. I want the Cadre and I'll make it want me. The only thing that really bothers me is all the time it will take. But I know that's irrational. I'll wait my turn."

Again, the group took stock of the young man sitting so calmly among them. He looked more than just assured; he looked as if he were casually choosing his destiny. These teenagers were accustomed to bravado, even nurtured it, so they usually recognized it as a convenient, surface thing. Looking at Pol, they saw something more substantial and were surprised. They saw an unremarkable face except for eyes that were ruthlessly, magnetically blue; they started back disconcertingly, in uncompromising appraisal—the kind felt from behind.

The voice, too, was odd; it carried conviction without changing in volume or pitch, and it was controlled, deliberate. There was silence after his words. Those who were particularly sensitive felt as if they had suddenly discovered an adult in their midst. It was not a feeling they liked.

"I require your attention, recruits."

He was suddenly there, as if a spotlight had abruptly revealed a figure on a dark stage. The recruits did not know that even his entrance was carefully orchestrated.

It was the uniform they saw first, glinting softly in the artificial light, though its black was deep. The piping of the collar was green—a Cadre Four, Operations ranking. He waited until the silence was total, then stepped around the lectern and stared at a spot on the back wall above their heads. His face was elderly, cool.

"You are about to begin a year of orientation which will determine the level of your compatibility with the Security Cadre of the Regnum."

There was a short pause as the officer's expression became softer, almost kindly. His eyes dropped to take in their faces.

"There are forty-nine of you. You have proved your worth after a number of screenings or you would not be here now. The Cadre has already expressed its confidence in your potential; however, probability also says that some of you will leave in the next few hours. . . . Join me here, please."

The forty-nine were in semishock as they pushed awkwardly to their feet and shuffled down the aisles.

The Cadre Four officer waited patiently at what appeared to be the bare wall behind the lectern. When they had formed ragged lines in front of him, he turned and a section of the wall slid noiselessly aside. It revealed a wide, empty area at the head of a long corridor with an implausible number of old-fashioned doors ranked on either side. He led them inside and stood impassively as they gathered into a dense pack.

"These doors open onto small rooms—two meters square, to be precise. Each contains an automated food dispenser. I trust you all know how to use one." He was answered by a few stunned nods. He was tall, a head taller than the biggest recruit. A lined face and severely cut gray hair gave him a look of stern paternalism. Only Pol noticed that some of the ridges must have been formed by laugh lines.

"Each of you will enter a room. Its door is to remain closed unless you choose to open it." He moved down the corridor to the first door.

The recruits looked at each other apprehensively as he opened it and gestured inside.

"One of you—please." Ttig moved from the front of the group, hesitantly.

"Uh, sir?"

"Yes?"

"Is this a test or—uh, is it some kind of test?"

"Of sorts."

"We're going to be locked in?"

"No. The doors have no locks."

"How long are we to stay in?"

"As long as you choose. You are asked only to enter."

Now the recruits were as much puzzled as apprehensive. There were a few angry scowls on the young faces. A blond girl waved a determined hand from the back.

"Sir?"

"Yes."

"I'm sorry, sir, but I don't understand the reason for this. There's no time limit and we can leave whenever we want? it doesn't make—much sense."

"That is correct. As for sensible reasons, you may come to your own conclusions. No more questions, please. Next?"

The doors closed one by one on the forty-nine recruits. After admitting the last of his charges, the officer gave a small sigh and looked at his timer. He took a last look at the double row of doors before keying a tiny communicator unit built discreetly into the stiff fabric of his collar.

"Chicks are all tucked in. Normal reactions," he said quietly. "Your show, Supervisor." He walked briskly to the head of the corridor, turned, and folded his arms across his chest. His stance was spread-legged and his eyes unfocused. His pose suggested that he was a man at ease when standing motionless. A few seconds passed in silence; then his eyes jumped back into focus at the sound of an opening door. Down the corridor a mop of red hair emerged tentatively, the face in the other direction.

"You wish to leave?"

The head whipped around. "Uh, no, sir."

The slam of the door preempted any response. The officer smiled slightly, looked at his timer again, and resumed his stance.

Ses closed the door in a small panic. Had he already failed the test? But what *was* the test? Endurance? How long was long enough? Shit.

The room held a chair—not a particularly comfortable one— a food dispenser in the wall, and as far as he could tell, nothing else.

What the hell, he thought, I might as well eat. And since Dad kept me awake most of the night, I'll take a nap.

He fiddled with the dispenser until a stick of ersatz chocolate popped out. As he munched, he had second thoughts about a nap: maybe it was against the rules. Then again, he wasn't given any rules. With a shrug, he rolled up his jacket and put it against the wall for a pillow. He had just enough room to stretch out on the hard floor.

Sleep did not come easily.

The hardest part for me, he thought, is going to be not having anyone to talk to. Everyone knows I even talk to people I can't stand. How long is long enough? No timer to keep track. Come to think of it, the others don't have one, either. They told us not to bring anything but identity plates.

Wonder what the year will be like—it's off to a beautiful start! I'll never get to sleep on this floor. . . . The rest of them are probably abusing themselves . . . that one blonde . . . or they're snoring in real beds, having passed the test by realizing how stupid it is to sit in a barrel doing nothing.

That Tyrees is strange. I like him anyway. Dad is probably right—I should hook up with the sort that'll keep my feet on the ground. Where have I heard that name before?

Can't hear a thing. Rooms must be soundproofed. Shit, this is no place for the Cadre's symbol of justice!

Pol took in his room with a glance. The first filter trial. Uncertainty. His grandfather had avoided details of the orientation but had told him of the many unexpected "tests"—"like rats going from one maze to the next," he had said. Well, here was the first less than an hour into the complex. His purpose was simple: to survive whatever they threw at him. That's what he was here for, wasn't it? He had long ago accepted the Cadre; he had to convince the Cadre to accept him. He fought down another surge in his stomach. If he should fail the very first filter trial . . . Then he heard his grandfather's sacred words: "Control, Pol. Concentrate. Control. . . ."

He took a vicious grip on himself and thought about the nature of this particular trial. He decided that the lack of information was itself a clue; having none had to be a part of the test. It seemed reasonable that when forced into a position with no data upon which to base decisions, it was pointless to make any. He would simply wait until something happened.

In a nearby room, psychotechnics manned sensor monitors, two or three to each. Overseeing was a Cadre Four Operations officer with the rank of supervisor; he was also a psychologist and classroom instructor. His assistant was a Cadre Five working on the filter trial as his research project.

"Instrumentation check." The supervisor was addressing the technics at large. They punched affirmatives into their consoles, and green lights winked on at the master station.

"Begin standard observation procedure." The two officers huddled at the master station, flicking through the forty-nine monitor inputs.

"Look at fourteen, Murt," said the supervisor. "He's headed out already." The indicator light for console fourteen changed from green to yellow as its technic's voice emerged from the speaker.

"Number fourteen exiting, sir."

"We've already got him. Give us volume." The officers chuckled as the redhead made his hasty retreat back into the room. Yellow returned to green.

"Log this one. Good or bad, he's going to be interesting."

In the rooms the recruits went through various postures of confusion and frustration—all except number twenty-one.

"Twenty-one, sir. Outside normal behavior parameters." Twenty-one was keyed into the master station. The screen produced an image of the composed features of Pol Tyrees.

"One minute fifty. So far he's just been standing there. Noticed him earlier," muttered the number five.

"Close-up, facial," ordered the supervisor.

The camera, concealed in the food dispenser, brought a sharp picture of Pol's face to the observers. It was bland with tranquillity, a slight smile on the lips. From this close, closer than a friend could look without invading innate boundaries of privacy, the sculpted face looked as if it might be under the influence of a mild but pleasant intoxicant. The two officers felt vaguely uncomfortable under the penetrating blue eyes.

"Two-thirty. No obvious reaction," said the assisting officer. "Looks as if he knows he's being monitored."

"Don't jump to conclusions, Murt. *I* can't detect the instrumentation, and I know it's there. Besides, he doesn't show concern."

"But that's just it, sir. He's too passive . . . drugs?" The supervisor gave his subordinate a mildly ironic glance before leaning to the mike.

"Psycho-signs, please."

"Micromotor movement normal—no—subnormal, sir. Eye scan also subnormal. GSR negative. Macromotor is nonexistent. We've just gone to yellow."

The technic monitoring twenty-one had turned from his console and was staring across the room at the supervisor as if his superior were personally responsible for the unusual readings. The sensors picked up microscopic visual data simply by being focused on a human body. The raw data was fed into a computer programmed to correlate it with psychological and physiological behavior patterns. The supervisor scowled at the readouts.

"Huh. Log him. And get me his file."

An electronic call was made to Records. The officers watched Pol finally break his pose and move toward the chair.

"Three minutes, fifty-nine seconds. Back to green."

Pol lifted the chair, placed it with deliberation a few centimeters from the wall, and sat. After a moment he pushed the front legs of the chair off the floor until its back rested against the wall. The balance should have been precarious, but he remained there in perfect ease. Subtly, perceptible because of the unreal clarity of the camera lens, his facial muscles melted into total slackness. A curtain of glass fell gradually over the chilly eyes until the observers felt unaccountably cut off.

"Psycho-signs! And get those eyes!" Like a cheap horror holofilm, the screen was completely filled with the disturbing blue eyes. The pupils were dilating visibly.

"Psycho-signs all moving down," said the technic.

"Vital signs?" The supervisor's voice was crisp. During the last few minutes the status indicator light had automatically flashed from green to yellow and back to green when Pol had moved to the chair. Now it had progressed up to red, which was the computer's way of saying that the subject's behavior patterns were approaching some kind of extreme.

"Respiration, heartbeat, body temperature, all decreasing, sir."

"Watch your monitors!" said the supervisor in a burst of irritation at some of the technics who had removed earplugs and were turned toward console twenty-one.

"Vital signs still going down."

Murt was becoming alarmed. He read the data being pumped into the master station and looked at his superior with wide eyes.

"He's either dying or going into some sort of trance!"

"It's the latter," said the supervisor. "But alert Mother Hen. He'll have to go in if the vital signs don't level off."

As Murt relayed the instructions through his collar unit to the officer in the corridor, a call number appeared on an ancillary screen. The number was punched in and Pol's file began to roll slowly over the screen. With a grunt, the supervisor leaned toward it.

" 'Tyrees.' Is he related? . . . I'll be warped! This kid is the ex–Vice-Proctor's grandson!"

"Uh-oh," said Murt unhappily. "Any psychology postings in Sector Ten?"

"Vital signs leveling off," said the voice of the technic, "but I don't see how he could be conscious."

"Let me know immediately of any change," said the supervisor, voice growing hard. He returned his attention to the screen.

"I can't believe that this is anything but deliberate—self-induced. Lots of people are capable of it. As a matter of fact,

I've heard some scuttlebutt about Cadre Ones. . . ."

"Yes, I know. You don't have to be careful. I have access. Special training the Ones don't talk about—but nothing like this. Breathing, resistance to pain, reflexes—stuff like that. There are some religious types who spend their lives . . . you know, the Medi-templists on Foxfire . . . but this goes beyond all that. It's absurd! Control of parts of the autonomic system can only be acquired after years of practice. This . . . this *child* makes them all look like crib-ridden infants! There's a self-discipline here that's—"

"Self discipline is what the Cadre's all about. That and the ability to cope with a dearth of information are what this first filter trial is all about. I think this boy's been groomed for us, Murt."

"You mean by his grandfather?"

"Likely, but he's been dead for at least a year now."

For a long time they watched in silence as numbers flicked by on the timer readout. Then the technic's voice cracked through again.

"Twenty-one. Another parameter broken. All readings abnormally stable. *No measurable fluctuations.*"

Murt started to say something, hesitated, then resumed in a whisper.

"What about Cadre ethics? Family or no family, that boy was—and still is—an outsider." The supervisor gave the younger man a long, blank look.

"That is not my purview—nor yours. However, it *is* our job to investigate these anomalies and to make certain they don't indicate behavior inimical to the Cadre. Grandfather or not, that is exactly what we are going to do." He turned briskly back to the mike. "Lower the temperature in twenty-one five degrees. Keep a close watch on psycho- and vital signs."

Pol's image on the screen was a surrealistic still life: a young man in repose so utter as to appear deathly, balanced on the hind legs of a chair, eyes deep and ice blue and lifeless. The supervisor finished reading Pol's file.

"Aside from his heritage, I can't see anything unusual here." He glanced with professional speed at the status indicators. All but the number twenty-one remained green; it had returned to yellow when the vital signs had stabilized at their present low level. Murt chafed.

"I'd like to get a medic in there for a work-up, sir."

"Not a bad idea, but that would warp the first filter trial. For the time being we'll keep—"

"Respiration rate increasing, vital signs all increasing. Psycho-signs remain stable."

"His body is compensating for the decrease in temperature!" cried Murt. "I don't believe it!"

The supervisor was less surprised. He shook his head in mild rebuke.

"That's not so amazing in itself. It's the *sensitivity* that's remarkable. That is a pretty fine adjustment to a small change in temperature. Is he conscious or—hell, what's consciousness, anyway? I want another look at his file. I can't believe somebody didn't spot *something* before this." He punched it back in.

"Vital signs stabilized, sir. Still subnormal."

Another yellow light flashed among the rows of green and another technic's voice came from the speaker.

"Eleven, sir. Break from psycho parameters." To allow the supervisor to concentrate his attention on twenty-one, Murt moved over to the console monitoring eleven. When he returned, his superior was rubbing a furrowed brow.

"Back to green, sir. Little temper tantrum. Put a dent in the dispenser with his fist, but that seemed to make him feel better. Logged him anyway. Find anything?"

"That's the problem. I found *absolutely nothing,* nothing at all. I should have noticed it the first time. The medics really put these kids through the test tubes before they get to us; we're supposed to filter out the ones they miss. But *every* youngster who gets here has *something* wrong with him, usually minor things: stomach acids slightly off, atypical EEGs, hormone imbalances, and so on. This one has *nothing* wrong with him. If it had been one medic who did all the work-ups, he would have reacted. As it was . . . bending light, what is this boy made of?"

They stared at each other until the supervisor turned abruptly back to the master station. By nature, officers of the Cadre were angered by mysteries.

"Twenty-one!"

"Yessir?"

"Cut the oxygen in that room by twenty percent."

"Sir . . ."

"Do it. Watch the signs carefully." He glared at the image

on the screen; it remained unchanged. "Murt, give nineteen and twenty to two others. This one alone is enough for a technic to handle. And alert Mother Hen again."

While Murt was carrying out the instructions, Pol's technic was already reporting new readings.

"Oxygen down two percent—vital signs stable—psycho-signs stable. Minus six percent—signs . . . signs all increasing—cancel that—signs all increasing except respiration—it's going down."

"I just don't believe this," hissed Murt.

"Minus eight percent—respiration still decreasing—heart-beat and eye scan now increasing rapidly. Res . . . He's stopped breathing!"

"Steady, twenty-one. Other vital signs all right?"

"Sorry, sir." The technic resumed in his usual monotone. "Other vital signs stable. Oxygen now minus ten percent—no respiration. Oxygen down thirteen percent."

Pol's chair came down, front legs hitting the floor with a sharp crack, startling the observers. Quickly, Pol's features became animated, alert, eyes intense and casting. He stood.

"I'll walk with bent light," said the supervisor softly. "Respiration?"

"Still negative, sir. Psycho-signs fluctuating."

"Pump the oxygen back in. Log everything. From now on, log everything on twenty-one."

As Pol Tyrees gradually regained his customary aspect of composure, the Cadre Four officer watched, fear nibbling at the edges of his thoughts.

Forty-two hours later there was a conference involving the supervisor, his assistant, and a psychiatrist permanently attached to the training complex. He was a civilian. The supervisor opened the session.

"I believe you have met Murt, Doctor? He's been assigned to me while he works on his research project."

"Yes, we met briefly."

"Fine. You've got the data we sent you on twenty-one?"

"I certainly do. I must admit my first reaction was to question its validity. You have my undivided attention."

"Well, if you have no objections, Doctor, we'll deal with the routine cases first. You'll agree that twenty-one is something of an enigma. He may require more of our time."

At the doctor's nod, Murt began a long summary.

"Between four and seven hours: five voluntary exits, all exhibiting symptoms outside behavior parameters prior to exit; two demanded immediate withdrawal from Cadre orientation—granted; one wished to remain, but had displayed a pronounced inability to function under the data deprivation conditions of the first filter trial and we advised withdrawal. He acceded; the other two were within acceptable limits and offered to return to their units when given the choice; they were sent to billets and logged for close future monitoring.

"Between seven and ten hours: twenty-eight voluntary exits, one involuntary; the latter exhibited psycho-signs of severe anxiety at eight point five hours and began eating continuously; Mother Hen brought her out at nine point five when vital signs had begun to deteriorate; she's in sick bay now and we'll recommend withdrawal; of the remaining twenty-seven, three demanded withdrawal; one granted, other two sent to billets to think it over; twenty—"

"Excuse me, Murt."

"Yes, Doctor?"

"Would you be more specific about those last three?"

"Sorry, of course. The withdrawal had borderline behavior patterns. The two sent to billets actually demonstrated very little stress while in their units. We come up with these occasionally. Our diagnosis was plain old boredom spiced with a pinch of anger. Probably still good Cadre material."

"Agreed, but they should still be logged for observation." The doctor smiled. "A tolerance for boredom can be an asset at times. Incidentally, chronic boredom is often an indicator of self-rejection—or worse, a simple lack of imagination. The psychocomputer is not programmed to pick up such anomalies."

"That makes sense to me, Doctor," said the supervisor. "Log them accordingly, Murt. The decision will be made for us if they opt to withdraw later. I should remind the doctor however, that the first filter trial is extremely reliable. Our decisions are based on established principles."

The doctor's forehead furrowed, but he kept his silence.

"Continue, Murt."

"Yes, sir. Where was I? . . . Oh yes. Between ten and twenty-four hours: the other twenty-seven were within our parameters and willing to return to their units when given the choice; none logged, all sent to billets." Murt continued the litany in a monotone until he finished with three recruits who had been logged "high Cadre potential."

"One of the three was the one you logged near the beginning, sir. The redhead. He ate, had a nice nap, and woke up about twelve point five. That's almost a record, I think. The kids are usually too hyper to sleep that long."

"A good sign, indeed," said the doctor. "One must have a high degree of trust to relax in such a situation. Right, Supervisor?"

"It's only a good sign if that trust is discriminating, Doctor. A Cadre officer can't afford gullibility. Later we'll see if he knows the difference."

The psychologist bridled slightly under the implied rebuke. He was sensitive to the fact that he could never be a true member of the Cadre brotherhood. They used his knowledge and usually accepted his opinions—but he had never made a close friend of an officer.

"Not everybody is destined to reach the superhuman status of Cadre One, Supervisor. I'm sure that Operations, for example, could use a little 'nondiscriminating' trust."

The doctor got a sharp look from the supervisor; along with most of the service, he, too, was a Four. The look gradually softened.

"Your point is taken, Doctor. You were saying, Murt?"

"Well, the redhead had us worried for a while after waking up. He had a marathon conversation with himself."

"What!" The doctor's professional calm was shaken temporarily. Murt could not resist a chuckle.

"Sorry, Doctor. We had the same reaction at first. But the psycho-signs were fine and it became obvious that he was role-playing. He took all the parts—himself, parents, friends, strangers. Enjoyed himself immensely. Pretty soon all those people got around to discussing his predicament. After a lot of hot debate they decided unanimously on a close approximation of the trial's rationale. They also decided that our format was quite effective, although they had some suggestions for improvement, including the addition of a bed in the units. Finally, they had a close vote to elect him a spokesman: he was to come out and tell us that they had deciphered the filtering process, so there could be no point in wasting further time on it. He did."

The doctor was now laughing heartily. "I'd recommend him for inception right now! The Cadre needs more like him. Nothing personal, Supervisor, but if I were to cite a negative in the profile of the Cadre as a whole, it would be its predilection for taking itself too seriously."

"Really?" The supervisor raised his eyebrows.

"Yes. I think it may someday build into a serious problem, especially in a time of crisis. Permit me: because of the selection process and the nature of the institution itself, its officers have powerful, well-defined egos. If these egos are not tempered with a sense of humor, which is also a sense of their own fallibility, they will place themselves above ordinary men. The fact that this is quite *true* in many ways only increases the danger. Your people are canonized, you know, given sainthood. They are told that they are special, that they have gifts we lesser mortals rely upon, but lack ourselves. I shudder to think of the consequences should the Cadre break its already tenuous community with the rest of humanity."

The doctor realized that his delivery had been somewhat pedantic and doomsdayish, but he didn't expect the supervisor's blasé dismissal of the whole proposition.

"An interesting theory. Finish the summary, Murt." The doctor had to struggle to focus his attention.

"It's now forty-two point... six hours since Mother Hen signaled the count. Two subjects are still in their units—twenty-one and forty-three. At thirty-nine hours, the latter's psycho-signs began to indicate an onset of depression. We'll probably have to remove her soon. With that time tolerance I don't think she should be asked to withdraw."

"Agreed. Excellent will dominance. That leaves twenty-one. You have the raw data, Doctor. A unique case. We need your professional advice." The word "professional" had been slightly stressed. Some rivalry existed between the Cadre psychologists and its civilian psychiatrists. The doctor nodded in his most formal manner. "Twenty-one, almost from the beginning, has been in a comatose state—in strict medical terms, that is. Vital signs are extremely low, but constant and still positive. Our manipulation of the unit's environment suggests an incredible control of the autonomic nervous system. During 'threatening' conditions this control appears to be partially conscious; this is also indicated by a total lack of aberration in his medical history. His body seems to have escaped trauma of any kind. We have discontinued experimentation because we are operating in the unknown." The supervisor looked up. "Doctor?"

The doctor felt as if he had been asked peremptorily to jump over a tall building. His irritation grew.

"Then there is no possibility of data error?"

"None."

"He has not eaten since entry?"

"Nothing."

"And all the signs are absolutely stable?"

"Absolutely."

"I'm sorry, Supervisor, but this just doesn't make sense. I've had some experience with subjects who had a natural ability and a great deal of training: they were able to gain *some* control over *some* functions of the autonomic system. But this goes beyond credibility! Aside from the obvious departures from precedent, the most proficient of subjects in prolonged, self-induced hypnosis show measurable atrophy of the muscles and, unless fed intravenously, other declines in general body status. And this one's so young. What about previous training?"

"We have reason to believe that such training was possible— even probable."

"Still, no amount of training could account for this."

In spite of his desire to find some answers, the supervisor allowed himself a small smile. He watched the doctor put his elbows on the table and hold his head in concentration. "You have no opinions or suggestions, Doctor?"

"An injection? There are drugs . . ."

The reply was laced with exasperation: "No. Are you not aware of Cadre ethics here, Doctor?"

"I am *well* aware of them," said the doctor testily. "I would not suggest anything harmful to the boy."

"That is precisely why I stopped further experimentation. We're dealing with the paranormal here; we do not know with certainty what would or would not prove harmful. I had hoped you could suggest a line of attack that would keep us on safe ground."

The doctor heaved a sigh born of mixed emotions, pushed himself to his feet, and began to pace as actively as he could in the small room. He paused occasionally to glare at a wall. Finally he stopped to face the watchers.

"Very well. We can assume several things. Whatever else

it is, that body is an extremely efficient machine consuming a minute amount of energy to maintain a precise subsistence level of vitality; it's like a fine, self-monitoring computer program. I simply cannot accept that anything of such sensitive complexity and control can be totally conscious. The questions therefore are these: Just what are the capabilities of this human machine we call twenty-one? To *what* degree are these capabilities under conscious control? Will that control increase with maturity? How do we find some answers without compromising his health? And finally—just what *is* twenty-one? A genetic freak? A new kind of *human?* What?"

Despite the readiness to do otherwise, the two listeners were impressed by the doctor's quick and incisive grasp of the case; he had not come to any real conclusions, but he had clearly articulated the essentials of a difficult problem. Now it seemed more a target than a mystery.

"Thank you, Doctor. Your comments will be helpful."

"One more thing, Supervisor. We need help on this one—a great deal of help."

"I agree. I will file a special report to sector HQ. Now, would you care to have a look at the last two subjects at first hand? We could also use your opinion on the removal of forty-three."

"Certainly."

Mother Hen entered unit forty-three at fifty-eight point seven hours. The girl was given an injection by the psychiatrist, but the prognosis was positive enough to send her to billets. The blond girl had incredible determination. Unit twenty-one was entered by Mother Hen at eighty-eight point eight hours. No change had been detected in the subject's status for three and a half days. The young man "awoke" and followed the tall black shape to billets.

A report with an "urgent action request" was sent to HQ. The reply was almost immediate. The supervisor was actually reading it and had hit his desk with a heavy-fisted thump when the doctor arrived at his office the next morning. The psychiatrist was jingling with excitement, a bright boy anticipating a game of challenge and intricacy.

"May I come in, Supervisor? I'm not interrupting?"

"Uh, of course, Doctor. Sit down."

"Well, let's have it. What are they sending us? *Who* are they sending us? I've got an idea or two. I'm really . . ." The doctor stopped when he saw the very "official" expression on the supervisor's face. He'd seen it before. "What's wrong?"

"Nothing. Just a directive. I suppose it's all right for you to see this." He flipped a few inches of printout across his desk. The doctor picked it up gingerly.

Procedural Directive—Joll Machus, Cadre Four, Training Supervisor, Sector I

- Cease all special psychological/physiological testing of recruit Pol Tyrees: Tyr-p-sI-A7190
- Report any abnormalities in subject's status that may arise as a result of *routine*, repeat, *routine* procedures
- Classify all data gathered on subject to date, as well as all subsequent data, as CEO
- Proceed with normal recruitment procedures

The doctor read, put the paper back on the desk, and nudged it away from him with his fingertips.

"That doesn't make sense."

The supervisor shrugged. "Twenty-one is out of bounds."

"But why?"

Another shrug.

"Well, well! This is ... this is ridiculous, Supervisor. Ridiculous!"

"That's the way it is, Doctor. I'm disappointed myself."

"But why? Why!" The supervisor folded his hands and looked hard at the civilian psychiatrist.

"I don't care to speculate."

"Well ... well ... You'll keep me informed?"

"Of what? 'Cease special testing,' it said. Besides, everything on him is classified from now on. Sorry, Doctor."

The doctor stared back, rose abruptly, and left without speaking.

SY 3022

After the first filter trials Pol Tyrees felt confident. He didn't like the attention among the recruits that his successes brought, but they helped to salve that soul-deep tumor of fear that had always been there. Nevertheless, it was still a potent dormancy, precisely because of his reluctance to recognize its existence. His grandfather's training, while sheathing it in iron, had also sealed it darkly from his own vision. So it was after comparing himself with his peers and their performances in trial after trial that he became quite smug about his progress. Until the last filter trial.

It seemed innocuous enough at first—just another simulation game. Seven recruits (including Ses and Ttig) were seated before a large monitor that was to present them with a series of command problems involving a host of "mission" decisions.

The supervisor was Joll Machus again. He had just finished installing the program and was delivering final instructions.

"I have to tell you that this simulation will take a few hours—longer, if you run into serious problems. There is only one overriding directive: that the mission goal be achieved. Understood?"

Ttig said: "Uh, sir? Who leads? Don't we need a leader?"

This stopped the supervisor halfway through the door. Emer-

gent leadership was one of the main qualities this filter trial
was meant to establish.

"That will change as you go along, Mr. Hal. Just follow
the prompts. Hit the start key now, please." He left without
pausing for further questions.

"Standard procedure." Ses chuckled. "More filter trial mumbo
jumbo. Don't ask questions, kid. Just put your little hand in
this black box here, please." Ses parodied an expression of
hysterical pain, covering his eyes with one hand and pushing
the other forward spasmodically.

Zara, one of the two young women in the group, frowned.
"Stop clowning for a change, Ses. This looks like a bad one."
Their table was in the shape of a crescent, large enough to seat
all of them along its outside curve. Each had a keyboard, and
Zara tapped the start key on hers.

The room's lights dimmed. A voice came from the central
monitor. It had the rich intensity of a commander sending his
men on a life-and-death mission into enemy territory.

"Listen carefully. This is a commando operation. Here is
the target—planet X." On the screen before them appeared a
hazy sphere floating in space. The recruits leaned forward.
"This world is not a member of the Regnum. The Cadre has
no authority here; however, planet X has become a haven for
black marketeers. These criminals come here in secret to deal
in contraband, arrange illegal shipments to Regnum worlds,
and so on. Some have permanent residences which are actually
fortresses, heavily guarded against intruders, electronic and
otherwise." The image of the planet was replaced by that of a
palatial country estate surrounded by an imposing plasteel-
webbed fence.

"This is target center. You are a covert investigative team
on a mission—code name Locksmith.

"Your assignment directive is to gather information produced from a meeting of several black marketeers at this locale.
It takes place in three hours. You have no legal status on this
world and no local support. The pulsing light marks your drop
point five hundred meters from the perimeter fence." A blip
flashed on and off at the edge of a stylized forest as the image
expanded to show a view of several square kilometers with the
estate in the center.

"Input your plan of action," said the voice. Then the screen
went blank.

The recruits looked at each other.

"What?"

"Plan of action?"

"How the hell . . . ?"

"Hold it . . . hold it now!" hollered Ses. "I have an absolutely brilliant plan!"

"Ses—"

"No, just listen, will you? Here's what we do: We zap the whole festering planet with a tranquilizer ray, see? Then we hop on our faster-than-light broomsticks and we—"

"Stop that, Ses! Be serious."

"Oh, sure, sure. I considered serious until I realized we didn't have enough information. What's *your* plan? Crawl in and listen at keyholes?"

"Well, we can't say much, but it may not be necessary. Suppose we input something general—you know—place the house under observation or something. Then maybe we'll be given more data."

"Bullshit, Zara. Computers never give you something for nothing. . . . Maybe the direct approach will work." Ses pulled his board to him. "I hate this old-fashioned junk. And why have we *all* got one? Here goes nothing." He typed in IN-FORMATION?, a standard request. The word appeared on the screen followed by an instant response: SE.

"You're wasting our time," said Zara, exasperated. "It's not going to respond to simple-minded requests." Ses was smiling his smile.

"Ah, but I have just been informed that you are wrong, my dear. SE is syntax error—old-fashioned machine lingo. All I need is the right command."

He tried DATA? and got the same response. The same with QUERY? He slapped the table. "Well, that exhausts the standard tripe. . . . Wait a minute! Everything's been a million years out of date—why not the commands? Here's a real golden oldie, folks." He typed RUN LOCKSMITH. A menu appeared immediately.

TEAM	TARGET
1. equipment	1. defenses—physical
2. personnel	2. defenses—electronic
3. off-planet support	3. terrain

"Atta boy, Ses!"

"Computers are my meat," said Ses smugly. "Zara would have had us running around in circles."

The girl pouted. "I don't think so," she said. "It probably would have given us the menu after we input a plan."

"Nuts. It would have asked a pile of questions. Ring around the rosy stuff."

"What do you mean?"

"Well, when you really get to know these guys"—he patted his board—"you get on to their way of thinking, you know? Suppose you input your plan to 'observe.' The machine would have gotten snarky and said something like 'With what, dumbbell?' Then you might respond with—oh, let's say 'a directional listening device,' or something like that. It would say, 'You do not possess this device.' Get it, Zara? Now if—"

"Quit the lessons in basic computer psychology, Ses," said a particularly intense young man named Rom. "Let's get on with it. See what equipment is available first."

"No." Pol's hard voice fell into the discussion like a rock through a glass window. "The target first. Get all the info we can. Get hard copies. Then we'll have something to base the planning decisions on."

"Right." Ses ignored Rom's protests and typed in TARGET 1. "Holy shit." A list of dozens of details—armament, manpower, physical barriers, and so on—appeared on the screen. "This is gonna be fun!"

The group spent a long session discussing the information about the target and selecting from the limited choices of personnel skills and equipment available so that they might penetrate the defenses and "eavesdrop" on the black marketeers' meeting. Each of the seven was then "tagged" by the computer according to function. Pol became an explosives expert, Ses an electronics specialist, Ttig a locksmith, and so on.

"So," said Zara, "we know our roles, we've chosen our equipment. What's the plan?"

"We have the gizmo that junks up their heat detection around the periphery," said Rom. "We can start with that."

"Okay. I'll put that number one. What about the fence?"

"Pol can blow it open."

"Don't be stupid. That would alert them that we were there before we got near the place. He'd be fried sausages in about ten seconds."

"The gate. Put Ttig on its lock."

"He'd be seen."

"Oh, yeah. I forgot. The lights and the cameras."

"Why not knock out their power supply?"

"Good idea!"

"Hold it—not so good. That would alert them, too."

"What if we made it look like a temporary malfunction? Just long enough so we can get inside the gate."

"Hey, yes! They're solar-powered! We can low-beam the accumulator on the roof. Just climb a tree!"

"Sounds good. Have to be fast, though. How much time will we need?"

"Who knows?"

"Put that as our first move anyway," said Ses. "This program can only get so cute. It may even be impressed."

"All right, we're inside the fence. What next?"

Given their restrictions, the group built their plan as carefully as they could. When they were ready, Ses began to key it in. After his first sentence, the screen flashed:

STEP ONE: ACCUMULATOR MALFUNCTION—SUCCESSFUL

The group cheered.

Ses continued, now pausing after each step for the computer to react. It accepted everything until six of the group were safely and secretly inside the building at various crucial posts before power had been restored. It had been decided that Pol, as their explosives man, would remain outside to set off a charge at the main gate—should that be necessary to create a diversion or cover their escape. Ses and Rom were on the roof and had just lowered a listening device to a position near the window of the meeting room on the top floor.

MICROPHONE PLACEMENT—SUCCESSFUL

"What's the next step? This is beginning to look easy."

"Uh, well, just 'Record conversation,' I guess."

"Go ahead, Ses."

"Right."

Ses keyed the words in, but this time the computer did not respond immediately. "Uh-oh. I smell a rat," he said. In a few seconds, the screen flashed a simple message.

NOTHING BEING RECORDED

"Shit. Is there something wrong with the mike?"

"Beats me."

"Have we got the right room?"

"Yep, here's our layout copy and—"

"Idiots!" shouted Zara. "Look at the timer!"

They all looked at the readout at the bottom of the screen. The numbers indicating seconds continued to bump each other on and off.

"Oh, great. It's more than thirty minutes 'til the meeting."

"Now what?"

"We just wait, I guess. No problem."

"No problem my ass," said Ses. "The timing isn't programmed into this beast for nothing. Now we have to remain undetected that much longer. Anything can happen. We should have timed the whole thing closer to the wire."

"Do we have any option now but to wait?" asked Pol.

No one had any workable suggestions, so they did just that.

"Hell, I might as well be on that friggin' roof for *real*," said Rom after a few minutes. "My palms are sweaty." Ses laughed.

"Mine, too. But stay cool. Ol' Sestus has been in tight spots like this before. Just tune in next week for the further adventures of..." A message appeared on the screen.

PATROL APPROACHING LOOKOUT POSITION—INPUT REACTION

The words faded into a schematic of the house and grounds. A flashing dot of light was moving slowly toward a stationary "X."

"Damn! I knew it. That's you, isn't it, Zara?"

"Yeah. I'm in the bushes over there where I can see your position on the roof, and Pol's post outside the gate at the same time. We've only got a few seconds. What do we do?!"

"Run for cover?"

"Wait. How many in the patrol?"

"Who knows?"

Ses held up his hand and began tapping at his board again. HOW MANY IN PATROL? It answered: ONE.

"Only one?" said Zara. "I kill him, then! I've got our only rifle. Put it in, Ses, and hurry!"

"Okay. Here goes."

LOOKOUT KILLS PATROL WITH RIF—

"Hey, what's going on?"

"Pol hit his override!" yelled Zara.

"We can't go around killing people," said Pol. His voice

was strangely pleading and he kept his finger on the override key.

"These are criminals, Pol! Don't be ridiculous!"

"They're not criminals on this world . . . *we* are, remember? We don't even have a right to be here. Now we're killing." The others were amazed by his reaction. He was sulky and pouting like a child scolded for attempting to feed a doll.

"C'mon, this is only a game!" said Ttig. "We're running out of time!" Zara reached over from her place beside Pol and lifted his finger from the board.

"Okay, Pol Tyrees. You're a real goody-goody. It's on record. Now leave that override alone. Put it back in, Ses."

"Now I know why everybody has a board," muttered Ses as he typed. The moving blip on the screen had almost reached the lookout's position. It disappeared.

ACTION SUCCESSFUL—PATROL KILLED

"It worked! That's that. How much time before the meeting?"

"About ten minutes. We sit tight again."

"Let's use it constructively then," said Zara, her eyes on Pol. He sat facing away from the group. "We almost blew that one because we didn't act together."

"Not necessarily," said Ses, defending his friend. "There would have been a way out. That's part of the game."

"*Maybe.* In any case we've got to let Ses do all the inputing—nobody uses any other board." There were nods from everyone but Pol. He was feeling rejected by the group and, in some vague way, betrayed. As always, he masked his confusion under cool silence; as always when circumstances placed him on the unfamiliar ground of intimacy with his peers, he took the deliberate mental step backward and away. Ttig, the practical realist, was not satisfied with the arrangement.

"What if we can't *agree* on strategy?"

"We'll vote, then. No ties—there are seven of us."

"What if we don't have time? Don't you see? We need a leader to make quick decisions."

No one spoke for a time. The recruits knew Ttig was right, but none had forgotten that this was another filter trial, and each was afraid of being, and not being, the leader.

"Let's draw lots," said Ses, reaching into a pocket without waiting for approval. He drew out a small pack of cards and riffled them with dexterous fingers. "Anyone wish to cut? . . .

No? Very well, ladies and gentlemen. Holder of the high card becomes our illustrious leader." He began to toss the cards nonchalantly, one at each recruit. "A jack! Looks good, Rom. A three—too bad, Zara. Just as well. You'd just use your power to have your way with me. A nine, Ttig. Good try. Six ... two—tough luck, gents. A queen, Pol! Now let's see a bullet for the ol' redhead!" With a grand flourish Ses slapped the last card in front of him. "Oh, lovely—a lousy two yet. Well, the glory goes to you, Pol ol' son. Too clumsy to get the ace off the bottom for myself." Ses laughed, hugely pleased because Pol's queen *had* come off the bottom.

The others voiced no objection. With the exception of Zara, they were satisfied that someone who had already demonstrated a high ability in the filter trials had been chosen. Pol was not happy at all with his "fortune" but could not bring himself to renounce it. Zara looked at him frostily.

"I assume we still discuss things?"

"Of course," he mumbled. "I—"

The screen beeped.

MICROPHONE ACTIVATED—RECORDING

"Hurray! About time."

"How long will it take?"

"Ask it, Ses," said Pol. Ses bent to his board.

REMAINDER OF MEETING IN FUTURE TIME—UN-KNOWN

"That figures," said Ses. "More waiting. . . . Say! Why don't we have a game of cards?" Before they could agree on the game, there was another beep.

PATROL UNIT REPORTED MISSING—SECURITY CHECK

"Another monkey wrench," snorted Ses. "You see, Zara? No matter what decision you make, this thing will use it to throw another problem into the works."

"Oh, Ses, you're just a pain in—"

"Do that later," said Pol, rising from his chair. He was the leader, he told himself. He had to take control. "A security check is bound to uncover at least some of us. Any suggestions?"

"How much time have we got?"

"We don't know, stupid." Ses sighed. "And the computer won't tell us."

"A diversion, maybe?"

"Hey, yeah! Blow the gate!"

"No," said Pol. "They'll stop the meeting—and most of us would be trapped inside."

"Is there any way we can divert them without raising an alarm?"

Pol nodded, his excitement rising. "That's the right track, I think. If only . . . Yes! Let's have that dead man steal something!"

"What?"

"We can have our diversion and explain the missing patrol at the same time! Ses, they have ground cars, don't they?"

"Yep. Four. And I see where you're heading, ol' buddy. It just so happens that Ttig is now on the garage roof to keep an eye on them."

"Input this, Ses: 'Garage lookout steals ground car. Escapes at high speed.' They'll think their man stole it, I hope."

Ses reached for the board, but Zara put a hand over the keys.

"Wait a minute!"

"Get lost, Zara," said Ses, pushing her hand away. "You heard the man. Time's awastin'."

"Just listen, will you? What if the garage is locked? And how does Ttig get into and start a car?"

"Ttig's our lock expert, sweetheart." Ses turned his most saccharine smile on her. "Have more confidence in our commanding officer, huh?"

Zara's mouth went grim, but she said nothing. Ses completed the input, and they waited. Pol stared at the screen with an intensity that hinted of pain. The wait lasted only a few seconds.

DIVERSION SUCCESSFUL—TWO GROUND CARS IN PURSUIT OF STOLEN VEHICLE—LEADERS ALERTED BUT MEETING CONTINUES

"Atta boy, Pol! That did it!"

After some backslapping the recruits settled down again to watch the screen, but Ses was particularly restless.

"You know, there's something funny about this program."

"What do you mean?"

"Don't know—exactly. Inconsistent, maybe. And very sophisticated at the same time. For instance, it knew precisely *why* we made that particular move, and I can't believe that anybody but ol' circuit-brain here"—he gestured at Pol—"would have thought of it. I wonder if—" The beep interrupted him.

MEETING TERMINATED—RECORDING SUCCESS-
FUL—INPUT WITHDRAWAL PLAN

Their escape strategy was basically a reversal of their entry,
with the added precaution of the explosives charge at the gate.
The recording crystal was secured quickly, having been dropped
from the roof by Ses to Zara, who threw it over the fence to
Pol outside. The computer reviewed the steps onscreen, pro-
claiming each "successful"—until it came to Ses's dash for the
gate. He was the last inside the compound.

PURSUIT CARS RETURNING—CONVERGE WITH
LAST WITHDRAWAL AT GATE

"Aw, c'mon!" said Ses. "Too much already!"

"Blow it, Pol! Blow the gate!" screamed Zara. "Hurry!"

"We'll kill Ses!" Pol was white. Ses shrugged.

"What's the diff? We got the goods." He reached for the
board. Pol leaped forward and pushed his chair over backward,
sending Ses to the floor with a crash.

"Hey!"

"You damn fool!" Zara lunged for another board. Pol caught
her by an elbow and spun her away. He was panting hard, arms
outspread between the others and the table. When Rom made
a move toward yet another board, he screamed, got there ahead
of the boy, and tore its cable viciously out of the terminal.
Then, one by one, in a fury whose passion totally immobilized
them all, he ripped out the other cables.

When he had done, he stood there for a moment with wild
eyes, killing blue eyes. No one moved.

The door hissed open. The supervisor, an uncharacteristic
look of surprise on his face, hurried in. What he saw in those
eyes gave even him pause. He stopped, deliberately assumed
an aspect of resigned cynicism, and shook his head.

"Wonderful. Wonderful. Recruits destroying Cadre property. Some trial." He waited until the killing look in Pol's eyes
faded. Finally the eyes fell, along with the last of the cables,
to the floor.

"All of you. Get back to billets."

"Uh, sir?" Ses was struggling to his feet. "Can we talk about
this? That program—"

"Back to billets! Now!"

They shuffled out. Tyrees, the last, walked as if hypnotized.
Machus looked at the wreckage and thought about the phony

program. He himself had put most of the responses on the screen. He thought about the directive from the Cadre Proctor after the first trial. He thought about reality.

He kicked at the tangled cables.

"Shit," he said.

SY 3023

The orientation year was over. Of the forty-nine recruits, twenty-six had survived for the simple inception ceremony involving the donning of the black uniform with the red piping around its collar. Parents were invited to the more elaborate affair the day after when they would legally sign away their influence over their children's lives. They were now the property of the Cadre.

Although every uniform fit perfectly, the young men and women wore them self-consciously. They struggled with the cape when moving or sitting: they fidgeted, as adolescents do when suddenly expected to be adults. Pride flushed their faces. At sixteen they had become members of a brotherhood elite that made up the most powerful institution in the galaxy. It would be many years before they were practicing professionals, but that never occurred to them; they had proved their mettle through a grueling year and considered themselves worthy.

They walked in a knot, stiffly upright, into the same lecture theater they had come to as raw recruits a year earlier, full of the meaning of this juncture in their lives. They did not march; their training had not been designed to encourage rigid conformity.

They sat and waited like expectant fathers. Pol, Ses, and

Ttig were again together, again in the front row. As usual, Ses was the first to break the silence.

"Well, gentlemen, the Cadre is finally committed to the wise course. With my brains, my natural skills, my resourcefulness—and, of course, the loyalty of two devoted followers—I—"

"Ses, do you ever quit?" muttered Ttig. "Your brains may set the Cadre back a millennium. Pol, are you really crazy enough to share quarters with this neuron? You'll forget how to talk in a month! You don't say much as it is."

Pol felt the pride and relief even more deeply than the others, but as usual it was caged in the iron of his control. He had to be the best Cadre officer ever. *Had* to be. His grandfather had expected it. There was a tightness between his shoulders that never left him. It was always welcome because he wanted it to be his grandfather watching him. Except for Ttig and Ses, the others had begun to shun him, mistaking his resolve for vanity, his remoteness for disdain. They didn't know he was afraid of failure more than death itself. He turned his slow smile and steady blue gaze on Ttig.

"Ttig, you lack foresight. Remember, there are no holovision sets in shared quarters—and Basic Training allows only three days' leave a month. With Ses right there on hand, I'll have light entertainment to take my mind off the drudgery."

"A holovision set you can turn off," said Ttig with mock scorn. "Now, if entertainment were your only concern, you'd use your vaunted influence around here to get Salaan as a roomie."

Salaan Napi, a bouncy blonde, was the fantasy queen among the male recruits, the object of a cloud of wishful locker room thinking. Many a boisterous but wistful conversation itemized her manifest charms. Male and female recruits were carefully watched during orientation free time because legally, if not in practice, the recruits were still the responsibility of their parents. In Basic Training, males and females were no longer kept apart, but were not allowed to share quarters.

"If I did that, I'd see even more of pimento-head here. He slavers after Salaan even more than the rest of you."

"Guilty," said Ses without hesitation. "But I deserve special consideration. I have conducted a careful survey which proves conclusively that I am the only male recruit—strike that, 'officer'—who has actually looked at her face! You may just have enough scientific curiosity to take interest in the fact that she's going to be my Cadre Five research project." He looked back a few rows and sighed audibly. "There she is. I knew this cape had to have a practical function."

Ttig looked back, as well.

"She doesn't give a sputtering ramjet about your virginity, Ses, so don't bother defiling your new cape. She's madly in love with the Cadre and that's all she cares about. I crossed her off a long list of potentials very early on." Ttig was usually quite taciturn, but loquaciousness on the subject of Salaan was a common phenomenon.

"Ses, if you looked with your eyes instead of your gonads, you'd see that she's indifferent—no, oblivious—to anything but training."

Ses was about to disagree when the panel behind the podium hummed and slid open. Striding to the podium was a Cadre One officer. No one had seen a One during orientation; most had never seen a One in the flesh. Silence was quick and complete.

Cadre One.

The man was physically unremarkable; however, his demeanor was quite the opposite. His movements were swift, decisive, assured, his bearing aristocratic. The silence expanded as he looked with open curiosity at the young faces. Arms akimbo, he studied them as if they were a new breed of pets recently acquired. The black piping was unobtrusive against the dark collar, but it drew every eye. Unlike their own, his cape was part of him, the folded wings of a hawk.

The silence became awkward. The new officers flicked sidelong glances at each other. At the corners of the Cadre One's mouth, a tiny smile threatened; otherwise, he remained impassive. Tension rose. Just as some were thinking that this was some arcane filter trial, an ultimate test reserved for the eleventh hour, Pol Tyrees rose from his seat. He stood at stiff attention and held his right forearm across his solar plexus; the back of his wrist and forearm were a rigid line ending in a clenched fist. It was the standard Cadre salute, and this was the first occasion demanding its use by the new Sevens. At first slowly, and then with frantic haste, the others stood to duplicate it.

When they were all standing, the Cadre One allowed his smile to break. He returned the salute formally and released it. The solemn group hesitated briefly, then sat.

"Good evening, fellow officers." The voice was relaxed, good-natured. "You are aware that I'm not an education officer; as a matter of fact, I have never been here before. I was a recruit quite a few years ago in Sector Four, but I remember very well how I felt.

"My function here is a simple one. The Cadre sends a One—on leave, as I am—to talk to new Sevens and answer questions. I mean that literally; I will answer, as candidly as I can, any question you care to put. There is only one classification for information forbidden to officers—excepting the CP, of course—Council Eyes Only. It means precisely that. Anything else, everything else, is available to you as members of the Security Cadre brotherhood. The kind of information to which you now have access could mean enormous wealth and power; it could topple governments or take lives in the millions. I do not exaggerate. Consider what that means, in terms of responsibility: it is heavy, and it is never absent.

"One last point. You are no longer citizens of Sector One planets; that allegiance has been severed. For the rest of your lives, you are Cadre. It is your family, your world. If you have not already accepted that, do so now."

The young audience had listened with rapt attention. Though the content of the Cadre One's remarks was serious, his tone had been mild and his delivery friendly—that of an indulgent father speaking of important things to his young and knowing he would not be fully understood. After his first words, there was another long, uneasy silence because the new officers were puzzling over the meaning of a change in his expression. The man in black had cast his eyes downward and his face had hardened into a frown. Abruptly, he seemed to come to a decision. His head snapped up and he burned out a dark stare that every one of the twenty-six felt like an electric shock. His tone was now brittle and uncompromising.

"Just one more thing. Chisel this into your minds. Because you are Cadre officers—my brothers . . . I would kill for you. I would die for you. I would expect no less in return. No one is ever going to say that to you officially, but I'm saying it to you now, as a brother who has reason to know it well. Remember—and believe."

The new officers swallowed with dry throats. Pol looked at Ses. He wanted to say something, something full of faith and binding. But he could not. Ses looked back with a rare cast to

his face, because it was devoid of humor. But the look said—
yes!

"Right. That's something to absorb slowly, but prepare your
resolve now. I lost a friend—a number Two—a few years ago,
because he hesitated to kill. Those things don't happen often,
but they happen.

"Enough. Now." Once again he was the friendly officer.
"This is probably one of the few times this year that an officer
spoke to you without giving orders. You'll get lots more, but
not tonight. Questions. Fire away—I'll stay as long as you
like."

Deftly the number One hooked a stool under him with one
foot. He raised his eyebrows expectantly. The first questions
were halting and tentative, but he was indulgent, even with the
pointless ones.

"Uh, sir?" A hand wavered at shoulder height. "Do you like
being a Cadre officer?"

There were a few "what a stupid question" scowls, but the
man in black pursed lips and answered deliberately.

"That's like asking if I like myself. Most of the time I do,
but 'like' isn't the proper word." He flipped his cape to one
side, put his hands on his knees, and paused in thought.

"I don't know what the last census produced, but there are
billions of people working at millions of jobs in the Regnum.
Most of them are probably content doing what they do and
live, I suppose, good lives. They at least make a living. But
I'm certain about this: Most lack a sense of commitment to
what they do. If you want to feel alive, feel as if the blood
pumping through you has a reason for pumping, you've got to
believe in something bigger than yourself and you've got to
become a part of it. A Cadre officer has that sense of belief
and belonging—whether he actually 'likes' it or not. The nature
of our work calls for some unpleasant duties, but I pity those
who hack off a chunk of their lives and call it 'work' because
it's what they must do to eat and keep warm. I'll be blunt:
were I forced to choose between the Cadre or the Regnum—
the Cadre's reason for being—well, don't ask."

To youngsters brought up in the shadow of the seat of galactic government, his last words bordered on heresy. Frowns
of confusion darkened some faces before a girl's voice shunted
their thoughts to another track.

"Are you married, sir?"

He smiled, somewhat ruefully, and shifted on the stool. He hadn't expected personal questions that rumbled over the barriers of rank. But he answered, and he seemed more fallibly human.

"No. To put it mildly, the higher ranks are not encouraged to marry. It's almost impossible to build a home base when you're jumping light-years every other month. Even when you're not, wives—or husbands—find it difficult because the Cadre has a heavier claim on you than they do. It's one of the prices you pay, I guess. Besides, if I were to marry, my wife would be a natural target, a way to get at me. The Cadre doesn't need that kind of vulnerability. And I'd feel guilty when I couldn't act like a family man should. Ah . . . perhaps when I'm not an active field agent . . ." He shrugged and left it at that.

The questions gathered momentum as the Sevens relaxed and responded to the man's candor. Curious and intelligent, their young minds probed eagerly.

"Sir, what are your duties?"

"Ones have no specific duties, really. We do tend to remain in one particular section, like the Alien Section, or Political, but duties vary with the assignments. Directives come down, we go in, do a job, and get out. I've never had an assignment that lasted more than a few months. Most of the legwork is usually done before I get there."

"Sir, do you—"

"One moment. I should elaborate on that. A higher rank in the Cadre usually means you work alone and in the field until you get too old. Historically, this is the reverse of intelligence or security services; they often paid dearly for the poor decisions of inexperienced men in the field where decisions counted most and where the most accurate information was available. But don't misunderstand. In my opinion, the best minds tend to remain in Four, Operations. They make the 'big picture' decisions and keep the Cadre running. Ones tend to be loners, and they like to be where the action is."

"How many Ones are there, sir?"

"Point zero three percent of total Cadre personnel."

The young officers cringed.

"Are Ones often undercover?"

"That depends on individual talents more than anything else. Personally, I'm almost always in uniform."

"You may be sent anywhere in the Regnum, sir?"

"Anywhere in the galaxy, including nonmember planets, but there are too many to carry that too far. Briefings take too much time. We usually operate in one sector."

"Sir, from who do you get your assignment directives?"

"From *whom*. From sector Chiefs of Staff, or a Vice-Proctor directly. Or from the Cadre Proctor himself."

Every age has its heroes, and the young make those figures into idols because that is their nature and their need. Especially when they begin to suspect that real human beings cannot contain the greatness they can conjure up, they invest that stature in men too remote to become tarnished with reality. So it was with the Cadre Proctor, because he was ideal for the purpose: inaccessible, mysterious, and with a function that begged for glory. The reference to him ignited the teenaged memories of times not long past when the Cadre Proctor was the embodiment of power and patriotism, righteousness and revelation in their games and stories. Even this uniquely mature group of adolescents had too much of the Cadre's "Black Ghost" haunting its backwaters of experience not to feel heartstir at the sound of the title.

"Is it true that no one knows the Cadre Proctor's real identity, sir?"

"No. The Regnum Council knows. No one else even sees him."

"Then how does anyone outside of the Council communicate with him?"

The Cadre One laughed. "I've wondered about that myself. I just don't know."

The twenty-six were thirsty for more on the subject, but their source was obviously not about to engage in professional gossip.

"Sir, what is the most dangerous threat to the security of the Regnum?"

"Well, that's not an easy question. On the whole, though, I'd say that illegal trading practices are the most destructive, and they're on the increase. The worst sort are those who— these are *member* planets, by the way—those who attempt to monopolize goods that are essential to others. As you know, the Regnum regulates all external trade, but it's a big galaxy, and a lot of people—and some governments—are greedy enough to profit at the cost of somebody else's survival."

"Sir, aren't the nonmembers a threat anymore?"

"At times they are, but personally I'd rather have an enemy that proclaims himself. At least he's recognizable; there are enemies in our house who are not. And some nonmembers are quite friendly. It's been years since the Regnum has engaged in a military action against even the unfriendly ones."

The man in black flipped the edge of his cape back and forth and frowned once more. Once more, he seemed to be debating with himself, ignoring the small forest of raised hands. They fell quickly when he spoke.

"Here's something the general public doesn't know. We are in trouble. The Regnum itself is in jeopardy."

A hum of surprise. Heads turned to one another, seeking confirmation of the evidence of their ears. The hum became a buzz. The Cadre One held up a hand.

"Hold on. Hold on! . . . Thank you. Nobody is about to tip us over today—or tomorrow. *However,* for the first time, the Regnum faces a lethal enemy. But he doesn't bring a gun to bear or get caught with his hands around a throat. It's a quiet, deadly struggle—two wrestlers in the dark.

"In the Hub especially, economic competition is becoming more destructive, more vicious, and Regnum unity is eroding. They're beginning to call it the Trade Wars. It's growing in intensity. It will be a long struggle—a test of our strength. It's an insidious thing that attacks subtly from within. There will be one winner and no compromises. No military solution is possible, so it'll be up to us. The Cadre."

The listeners were shocked. Appalled. A cruel baptism plunged their heads into alien waters. They didn't know how to react, what to ask. Finally, a small voice piped up.

"Sir, what . . . what are we doing about it?"

"We're doing what we've always done. Enforcing the law. Sniffing out those who break it. But . . . there's a new game here. New weapons. We see death and—horrible suffering, but no violence. We see inhuman deprivation, but no one with blood on his hands. It's a chess game, with power the prize. The Regnum's own enlightened law makes that deadly game harder to win."

"Are you directly involved in these Trade Wars, sir?"

"Yes."

"Uh, how?"

"My last few years probably makes me one of the galaxy's foremost experts in 'brain burglary,'" he said with a bitter smile. "Brain burglary is Cadre jargon for the kidnapping of specialists. It's theft of human commodities—skills and knowledge that are in high demand."

Sir, do you mean that a planet which is short of, say, metallurgists, will just kidnap one from another planet?"

"Well, no. That wouldn't be likely. It wouldn't make sense to mount an expedition to capture an expert or two. What does happen is that rogue traders will form a phony 'personnel procurement company' and find an unchartered boulder in space for a base. Their front is legitimate, but the real money is made by raiding vessels and small colonies to build up a bank of skilled human resources—like your metallurgists. Then they are—quite literally—sold to the highest bidders, usually to worlds having slave cultures."

The youngsters were alarmed. The stuff of popular drama, the pap served up to hungry holovision viewers for easy entertainment, was suddenly not altogether unrealistic. There actually *were* shadowy criminals on a grand scale—and a proportionate level of human suffering. Salaan Napi was so agitated she stood, instead of raising her hand.

"Uh, sir? You mean these people kidnapped, you mean they might spend the rest of their lives as slaves somewhere?"

"That's right. Especially if a nonmember has bought them. Once on-planet, we can't interfere. If a Regnum world is involved, though, we go after them with sharp claws." Salaan persisted.

"Sir, are entire governments involved in that sort of thing? I mean, Regnum governments?"

"It used to be never. Recently, there have been several cases in the Hub, perhaps because trading competition is so raw there. But it's still relatively rare: governments still hesitate to defy the Regnum unilaterally."

Being young, the listeners tended to see things in black and white; being what he was, Pol Tyrees possessed more than his share of that tendency. Then and there, he wanted to strike out against the evildoers, the enemies of the Regnum; then and there he wanted to rise, fly with the Cadre One to fight the good fight and leave the years of training to those less dedicated than he. Salaan remained standing.

"But sir. That's a terrible thing! Can't the Cadre go to an independent world to free—slaves like that? Those poor people!"

"I'm afraid not. They're not Regnum. To them, slavery is an accepted custom." He looked with some sympathy at her. "You'll have to accept that sort of thing, or you won't get far in the Cadre. I'm not a particularly philosophical man, but I believe that law is a thin, delicate bubble that separates us from chaos. Don't break the bubble. Change it, if you can, but don't break it." Salaan pouted and sat.

Sensing an impasse, someone threw a diverting question—one that had been saved like a favorite firecracker.

"What about aliens, sir?"

"What about them?"

"Do they really exist?"

"I haven't the foggiest idea. However, the probability of their existence was one of the reasons for the creation of the Cadre—and the Alien Section does a lot of work investigating reports. I know some people in Alien, and they seem to believe . . . but I still haven't the foggiest idea."

The hypothetical alien was another mystique that veined deeply into the memories of the twenty-six young people. Indeed, the topic was always current with the public; it had become woven into the popular cultures of the Regnum. Mothers used them to frighten children into obedience; comedians joked about them; singers put them into their lyrics; priests revered or reviled them; soothsayers had them in their prophecies. So the number One was not suprised by the barrage.

"Have you ever had any Alien Section assignments?"

"What about the Holtz Effect?"

"If they exist, why haven't they contacted us?"

The Cadre One held up both hands. "Hold it now. One at a time."

"Can you just tell us what you know about aliens, sir?"

The unhurried, unyouthful voice turned the number One's head. He found the strange blue eyes in the first row and felt slightly uneasy. His intention had been to pass off questions about aliens because his information was sketchy and his thoughts on the subject ill formed.

"You probably know as much as I do. The connection of aliens with the Holtz Effect is still, as far as I know, a theory. It remains under active investigation, though. I've told you that Ones tend to specialize, so I've had no involvement with that sort of thing. In any case, I suspect that anything startling would be classified CEO—Council Eyes Only." He looked for a mo-

ment longer into the hypnotic blue eyes before turning and
waiting.

The Cadre One was remembering how his own mind had
teemed with questions when he was in their place, many years
ago. They would probably not meet another of his rank for
many years; even then, they wouldn't be in a position to fire
salvos of eager questions. He sighed inwardly and resigned
himself to a lengthy session. His audience was trying to sort
questions now—those that *should* be asked from those it *wanted*
to ask. Finally, one of the more daring launched one, like a
frightened soldier throwing an incendiary.

"Have you ever killed anyone?"

The Cadre One looked at his inquisitor with the same black
intensity that had frightened them earlier. One hand slowly
opened, then closed the dark cape more securely around him.

"Address me with 'sir.' The answer is yes. One day you
may find out what that means. Next question?"

SY 3024

The nul-gravity chamber was a recreation and exercise room for the Sevens in Basic Training. The walls of the huge chamber were rounded and thickly padded, and the lack of gravity encouraged experimental games.

Pol's classmates had invented "floating buckets," a rough-and-tumble game that had become rapidly popular even as a spectator sport. Two teams of a dozen would don colored vests. Two buckets matching the colors were tossed in, along with a hard, fist-sized ball, to start a match. The object was to control the ball, eluding the opposition long enough to throw it into their bucket, which was in constant motion. Only a very accurate throw would pop the spring-loaded lid for a goal. If a bucket were touched, a penalty throw was awarded to the other team. Since the padding soaked up velocity as the buckets careened from wall to wall (floor and ceiling were only abstractions in the chamber), players often threw the ball at their own bucket (taking care to miss the lid) to increase its speed and rotation. This made it a more difficult target for scorers.

Aside from restrictions on dangerous play, there were few other rules. There were always bodies in motion. Players had to make quick judgments about carom angles, velocities, and the positions of buckets, ball, and players. They continually launched themselves off the spongy walls on intercepting vectors. Immediate goals depended on a player's situation at a given moment: he could send himself on a flight meant to block an opponent, throw or catch the ball, or help a teammate who had lost "flight control," a common condition because midair collisions were frequent. Once in a tumbling motion, a player was useless until he hit a wall; even then he had to be in a position to use hands or feet to stabilize before pushing off. Floating buckets produced comic situations that delighted the spectators. The flight control problem was helped along by players who were proficient at sending opponents into windmilling gyrations by catching a passing foot or knee; they would convert the reaction energy transferred to their own bodies by going into a deliberate roll that they could control at the next wall.

Unobtrusively, Pol had quickly become the most skilled floating buckets player in the complex. He found that the more he played, the more his perceptions seemed to slow down the chaotic action. It was as if some magician had condemned the others to play in a medium that made them more sluggish, less able to anticipate; he gave Pol more time to calculate the next move, to judge the angle and force needed to propel himself from the next wall. Soon, embarrassed at his advantage over the others, he began to concentrate more on the subtle creation of comic confusion than on scoring. He felt like the director of a holofilm production when the spectators laughed at a particularly ridiculous tangle of bodies created by his engineering. Games in which Pol played tended to end in his team's favor, but were low-scoring.

On this occasion, things were different. The group of Sevens one year ahead of Pol's classmates had issued a challenge, claiming supremacy in the game invented by their juniors. They were older, more confident, and more steeped in the pride nourished by the mystique of the Cadre.

Portholes at all levels were filling with heads of excited friends and amused instructors. Pol's team would have recognized the officer of the corridor—the "Mother Hen" of the first filter trial. He was there with the supervisor in charge of that and other trials, who had maintained a lasting but discreet interest in Pol.

"C'mon, Hen, I'll put a half day's leave on the junior class and not ask for odds."

"Supervisor, you're a good psychologist, but I've run into better gamblers. With due respect, sir, you assume your pigeons are gullible. You've obviously been watching Tyrees play."

"Yes, as a matter of fact. He's good, but nothing special. Not enough to make the difference," said the supervisor with a look of innocent candor.

Mother Hen sighed. "Nothing special, huh? He plays his own game out there, all by himself. I wouldn't have noticed what he does if there weren't this funny picture in my head of a kid walking into twenty-one, sitting in a chair for a few days, and strolling out exactly the same way."

The supervisor lost his smile. "Forget the picture in your head, Hen."

"Is that order still in force? I'll never figure that one."

"Don't try. Strictly out of bounds. Do we have a bet or not?"

"Very well, Supervisor, I will offer *you* a day's leave to a half that the youngsters win."

"No bet. You know I hate to pull rank, Hen, but . . . Hold it. Here comes my extra leave in a less cynical form. Play along."

Hen turned to see the second-year trainees' combat instructor strolling along the corridor, looking for a spot at a porthole. It would betray too much interest to órder a lowly Seven from a place.

"*Our* extra leave," muttered Hen.

"Over here, Cratt," called the supervisor. "Join us. Looks like this will be a good one."

"Yes, it should be interesting. I'm told the younger lot invented it."

"That's right. Hen and I are partial to this bunch—a high survival rate through the filter trials. Mind you, they're young, a long way to go yet. What do you think their chances are against your lot?"

Cratt gave the supervisor a long look. "I can recognize an overture when I hear one. How much leave did you have in mind?"

"Cratt! You shock me! A bet never entered my mind. However, I wouldn't be averse to a small wager—just to demonstrate my loyalty."

"Well, I'm partial to my chicks, too. I wouldn't mind risking a day or two."

"Now, Cratt. Your chicks are a year older, and you've taught them your dirty tricks, too. But I'd be willing to up the bet for some incentive."

"Incentive! Loyalty isn't enough, huh? Oh, never mind. I will lay you six days to four that your chicks discover just what chickens they are."

"Done!"

Hen was unable to control a wide grin as the three turned to the porthole. He held up two fingers behind Cratt's back and refused to lower them until the supervisor nodded with a mock scowl.

They watched the players warm up, tossing balls to each other while in flight and bouncing off the padded walls. A Cadre Six, solicited as a referee, blew a whistle. The teams gathered at the entrance, whites and blues densely packed and hanging on to each other to keep to the "floor." The referee threw white and blue buckets in diverging diagonals upward, then the ball on a path between. Two by two, he sent opposing players into the fray.

To less experienced spectators, the action appeared random, even pointless; but the practiced observers could appreciate the specialists at work. Some players, termed in the vernacular "busters," interfered with the other team's passers and ball handlers and broke up offensive patterns. Occasionally, spectacular collisions generated a cluster of spinning bodies and not a few bloody noses. The "bucket bugger" followed the flight path of his opponent's bucket to protect it from throws meant to set it spinning faster. The more skilled members of each team were involved in the intricacies of controlling the ball and attempting to score.

Early on a melee surrounded the ball, with players trying to use each other for flight stability. A cluster grew like a grotesque snowflake in the center of the chamber. Controlled mobility was essential, so a mass of bodies dampened productive action. The proficient were able to shove off an opponent, float to a wall, and regain controlled direction.

Suddenly a pure, clean motion pierced the confusion of bodies like a hawk through a panicking flock of sparrows. A hand plucked the ball from the fumbling grasp of a potential receiver at the edge of the cluster. Pol used a nearby foot to change direction and turned into a smooth somersault to hit a wall, the ball already poised to throw.

"Good maneuver—but lucky," muttered Cratt. "An opportunist." The supervisor kept his poker face intact, but Hen's was tight-lipped with the strain. He stretched his neck and rubbed his jaw to disguise his glee.

Pol threw the ball crisply at a far wall and catapulted himself on another vector, arrowing for open space. His speed and the fact that he no longer had the ball discouraged interference.

"Ahh, now that was stupid," said Cratt with more confidence. "He just dumped it to nowhere."

Now the cluster was beginning to disperse, players maneuvering toward the walls. With buckling knees, Pol hit the "ceiling" hard and pushed off with such force that he plummeted past the bettors' porthole like a captive shark headed for dinner at the bottom of a tank. Then the watchers realized that the opponents' bucket had bounced off the floor and was headed up toward Pol. Meanwhile, the ball had made two banks; as Pol neared the bucket, it made another carom off a side wall to form an intersecting vector. Body, ball, and bucket "fell" toward the same point as if the three were sliding into a hole. With a slight twist at the waist, Pol caught the ball neatly and merely had to hold it for the instant necessary to flick it into the passing bucket. "Click." One to nothing.

The applause from Pol's classmates could not be heard by the players, but it was as loud as it was gloating. Mother Hen didn't try to hold back a burst of laughter as he broke protocol to pound the supervisor's back. Cratt did not make noises of disappointment; he simply turned an intent look of inquiry on his two colleagues.

Pol scored another goal before the word went out to get him. The older team was frustrated and embarrassed, and there was something about him they didn't like, something besides his skill. A powerful boy named Jon Chaas—"King" Jon—was duly appointed. He stayed out of the action, making short wall-to-wall flights until he saw Pol in the midst of a long plunge, with no possibility of changing direction. Jon came at him diagonally, from above and to one side. Pol had just enough time to turn his head, so the elbow blow took him flush in the face. Blood exploded from his nose in a cloud of tiny globulets that were scattered by the spin of his own body. The whistle shrilled. The referee, who had not seen the incident because it was away from the ball, swooped over to dampen Pol's wild spin.

Pol assumed it was an accident, but he still felt shame through his pain. He wanted only to escape and held his hands over his bleeding face as he was towed to the exit.

SY 3025

It was a thing of growing certainty, though not as much to Pol as to his classmates, that he didn't fit. He was respected but not liked. With the exceptions of Ttig and Ses, they were obscurely afraid of him. Hard-pressed, they might express a feeling of nakedness in his presence, as if their hidden thoughts and feelings were exposed to him. They distrusted his impeccable neatness and the mildness of his response to their enthusiasms. He always seemed to know where he was going and what he wanted. His angers were gentle and short-lived, his irritations (if he had any) invisible. In short, he was not like them; being what they were, they had not been like their friends beyond the complex, so they would have sympathized had they not also sensed that he *preferred* his isolation.

Most grew accustomed to his quiet, assured manner, but they did not like the directness of the blue eyes that seemed to see things in them that they had difficulty admitting to themselves. When they lied, he looked away; when they considered reaching for something, he handed it to them.

Pol thought of his difference as the result of a singleness of purpose and a training in self-discipline that the others lacked. At first, he assumed that they, too, could sense when a person said things that did not match their thoughts; that they, too, could guess an instant before a thing was done that it was about to be done. As he became aware that this was not the case, he decided that it, too, must be generated by the sharpened awareness nurtured under the tutelage of his grandfather. He tried to hide these small talents; like an overly bright child in a classroom, he left things unvoiced lest the others resent him. He thought these to be minor quirks, something a bit freakish that occasionally provided an unfair advantage.

Pol was also aware that his worship of his grandfather had affected him in ways that others could not understand, so he avoided that topic. Memories of his mother and father were dim and ill-formed, drifting through his mind like ghosts. He had been brought up under the institutional kindness of strangers, those who had taught and fed him in nurseries. During those years, his grandfather was the only one who displayed affection for him—it was stately and stern, but it was there.

When news reached him of his grandfather's death just before entering the complex, he was surprised at his own lack of reaction. He had been cauterized. Emotional trauma was the unforgivable sin. He would simply carry on. It was as if his grandfather had never died. Perhaps, after all, he was still there, as always, watching over him. . . .

But Pol was an adolescent. One aspect of his emotional life had yet to be strained. He felt, like the others, the strong sexual urges that only the young and healthy can know; unlike the others, he distrusted these urges and was wary of their powers of distraction. He was confused and out of his confusion sought hard decisions: he reasoned that if other strong impulses were things to harness and channel, was not this as well?

"To lose control to emotion is to deny the efficacy of the mind and directions chosen by that mind," his grandfather had said. He had chosen only *one* direction—the long and rigid path that led to Cadre One. For him, that was enough. He was afraid of sex because it was a tempting mystery—and a threat to his control.

Pol may well have been celibate indefinitely had certain events not linked, forming a chain that led to a new and, for him, terrifying experience.

It was the second year of Basic Training, and the uncertainty of orientation had long since been replaced by brashness on the part of the young officers. But studies were hard and long, and the supervisors were practiced at trading off rambunctiousness with physical activity. Sexual liaison was made difficult, but, by design, not impossible. Again, experience enabled the staff to nudge their charges through the minefield of pulchritude, puppy love, and passion.

One afternoon, Pol, Ttig, and Ses bantered their way into a canteen. Typically, Ses was doing most of the talking.

"If we're expected to believe these sociology neurons, the Regnum's headed for the shit pile, Cadre or no Cadre. It's got to be a hoax, just so much theory spinning. The habit comes with their Ph.D.s; besides, the more complicated the theory, the longer the textbooks they get to write."

"A lot of that stuff isn't theoretical anymore," said Pol in a more serious tone.

"Are you kidding? Thousands of populated planets spread across a whole galaxy, and these 'experts' predict behavior as if they were talking about a bunch of people in a single room!"

"As usual," said Ttig, "you've got it backward. The larger the numbers, the better probability theory works."

Ses grabbed Ttig's arm. "I just lost interest in probabilities. *That*, though *not* probable, is beautiful reality."

Salaan came bouncing through the entrance swinging a sheaf of printout carriers. Ses never tired of pursuing her long after the younger age group had despaired. She was the lusting youth's image of a holovision queen, the kind they joked about publicly and dreamed about privately. In reality, she was a serious young woman dedicated, even more than most, to the Cadre. She recognized the ogling for what it was and, beyond taking mild advantage of it occasionally, like a worker in a chocolate factory, ignored it. In spite of having one or two interludes with older Cadre Sevens, she was not, to Ses's undying regret, promiscuous. Mind and body were her own.

"Salaan, you luscious wench! Come over here!" She responded to Ses with an indulgent but friendly smile and came to their table. The three watched her movements appreciatively. Ses produced a low growl. Salaan stuck her tongue out.

"Are you three characters ever apart?" She sat and eyed them with amused affection. "You're like three potentates, always presiding over—something—wherever you are."

"Yes, my dear." Ses beamed. "We accept our responsibility as the conscience of our lessers with reluctance, but it is a burden of some honor. We must endure."

"Well"—Salaan laughed—"it's nice to see you all bearing

up under it." She looked at each in turn. "Ses, the spokes-mancum-court jester; Ttig, the trusty knight-at-arms; and Pol . . ." As her eyes turned to Pol, they lost their humor, becoming sad and quizzical. She brushed silky blond hair abstractedly from her breast. "You don't really fit, Pol. You're the catalyst, or something. You don't say or do much; but . . ." She felt the bite of the now infamous blue eyes. "Well, I'll just have to call you 'the Holy Ghost.'"

"You have to use ancient religion to find a function for me?" said Pol mildly. Underneath, he was feeling hurt at being viewed so impersonally, an object of passing, though curious, interest.

"I'm surprised you could find one at all," put in Ses. "But 'ghost' isn't bad at that, Salaan. There's so little flesh to him that Ttig and I can't find him a date for the Breakaway Party."

Salaan laughed again. "Oh, you warper. I don't buy that one. I happen to know that Judi asked him. Actually, Pol, you have a problem there. She's a bit miffed at your refusal."

"What! What is this?" exploded Ttig indignantly. "We . . . he claimed that nobody was interested—though I'll admit it sounded like a good argument." He glared at his friend as Ses took up the lead.

"Marga asked you, too, didn't she, roomie? What's going on? Got a surrogate woman you threw together in the chemistry lab?"

Pol cast his eyes away from the others, something he rarely did. But his face showed no reaction except that when the eyes returned, they were flashing and there was a subtle warning in his voice.

"Look, you two, quit making a nova out of it. Like a good little Seven, I'll be using Breakaway Night and Hangover Day to get ready for the next session. Simple as that."

The Breakaway Party, held twice a year in the breaks between changes in syllabus, was a tradition of the complex. The usual rules were relaxed, including the one forbidding alcohol. Many of Pol's classmates had lost their virginity at the last Breakaway. Pol was not one of them. Realizing that his outburst was a surprise to his listeners, he continued in a softer and deliberately pedantic tone.

"There is a telling statistic that you may not be aware of: Ninety-six percent of Sevens have to repeat one or more of the sessional subjects. I intend to be on the short end of that stat. You two are already one behind, and I'm shaky in Regnum

Law. I won't be wasting time repeating it."

Ses started to argue about such a short time loss but thought better of it. He had never known Pol to waver after delivering such decisions. He spoke to Salaan instead.

"Salaan, my lady, I don't suppose you would consider enriching my shabby life by accompanying me to the Breakaway?"

"You neuron. We both know you're going with Fax."

"Merely insurance, love. Have pity."

"I'm going with Jon." She shrugged an apology.

"Salaan, you disappoint me. To reject my advances just to favor a last-year man. Shame!"

"If I didn't know you better, Ses, I'd pop you one. He was the first to ask—period. Wait a minute! He can pop you himself. Jon!" Salaan waved at a group getting up from a far table. Her Breakaway date led a train of older Sevens toward them.

Though Salaan didn't realize it, Jon coveted the trappings of the Cadre most, the paraphernalia of authority, not its responsibilities. In a place where egos and ambitions were strong, most of the Sevens were too young to recognize the difference. Since Salaan was regarded as one of the most attractive females in the complex, Jon saw her as a fitting companion.

"Hello, Salaan. I hope this junior triumvirate isn't boring you. How's everything, striplings?" Nods from around the table. "If you youngsters don't mind, we won't sit." He winked at Salaan and, with a bow and a hand flourish, invited her to leave.

Ttig was a practical soul, a doer. His stocky, efficient body was a reflection of his mind. Subtle social or verbal games went against his grain. To him, Jon was such a gamester. Ttig also rose rather quickly to proffered bait. It was a sign of Ses's acuity that his jibes were obviously in jest when aimed at Ttig— and Ttig was the only one for whom he took such care with his remarks. He relished taking verbal shots at people like Jon.

"Sit at attention, recruits!" said Ses in a loud whisper. "You may be in the presence of the next Cadre Proctor."

"You may be right, my boy. Salaan, let me rescue you from these adolescents. We have plans to make for the Breakaway. Besides, turkey-top is starting to drool on his bib." As the group around Jon laughed, Ses broke out his beaming grin and touched Salaan's arm to stop her from rising.

"Salaan, your sense of pity knows no bounds. Only someone

of your generosity would accept such a dolt as a gesture of charity." Some of the sheen left Jon's confident smile.

"Take care, Red, or I'll be tempted to take you seriously. Let's go, Salaan." Her flawless brow marred by a frown, Salaan gathered up her materials.

"Idiots! I'll come, but only to separate the egos around here."

"There's more mouth than ego at this table," sneered Jon, trying to deliver the parting shot. "Well, maybe the three of you could make up one ego." He looked at Pol. "But with Tyrees in the mix, it might turn out to be the wrong gender." Pol kept his composure but felt as if he had been slapped in the face by a passing stranger. Why should he be attacked when he took such pains to avoid trespassing on others' emotions? And since it was so absurd, why should he feel so insulted by Jon's remark?

All this time, Ttig had been simmering, but now he had come to a boil. His voice had none of the banter with which Jon and Ses had taken the edge off their insults.

"Look, *King*, are you trying to prove something, or are you just a stupid clot?"

Salaan was acutely aware of the rising heat, but she was afraid of taking sides. She looked to the nearest tables in search of a Six who had both the duty and authority to break up a potentially violent situation like this. A brawl meant isolation and a session or two with a psychiatrist. She saw only Sevens, the nearest showing a morbid interest in the deepening conflict. Ttig and Jon were flushed and tense. She noted that Pol, the brunt of Jon's most pointed insult, seemed relatively unaffected. He merely looked up at Jon with raking blue eyes and waited. In fact, Pol was ashamed of a very real desire to kill.

Salaan recalled some veiled comments about Pol's apparent lack of interest in girls—but never from girls; from them, she heard only sounds of mild frustration when their advances failed beyond a certain point. The thought that Pol might be a homosexual never occurred to them. She also sensed in him a willed control, a deliberate lock on things emotional. She didn't understand it, nor had she dwelt on it before; but she knew that he was somehow special, marked for the future. In the moment of this small crisis, the telltale minutiae of his uniqueness flooded into her; and suddenly she wanted to know more, and to help him. She was deeply chagrined by Jon's attack.

Jon had actually begun to turn away, satisfied with a draw, until he saw the faces of his cronies; he had been adopted as their leader, and in the ephemeral mix of adolescent loyalties, draws were unsatisfactory. He felt the psychological pressure of his group as a spider feels a tremor in his web. He drew his face into an expression of casual contempt and turned back to the table.

"Prove? No, I've nothing to prove," he spat as he jerked a thumb in Pol's direction. "But your friend here does. Come to think of it though, a 'candy bar' fits your bunch."

"Jon, you're an ass!" hissed Salaan. Ttig drove to his feet with murderous intent. Chairs scraped as others scrambled to join the audience. Pol spoke to his antagonist for the first time in a low, even, inordinately calm voice. Inside, he was afraid— but only inside.

"Jon, you're pushing more than you want to. If there's something worth fighting for, we'll use the combat room. Ttig, sit down. The rest of you, shove off. There'll be no fight here."

Salaan was amazed at the effect of Pol's words. The listeners acted as if triggered by a reflex of obedience. Ttig sat, glaring out of a purple face.

"Me or Pol," he growled. Jon looked at the burly, peasant shoulders and made his decision quickly.

"I want Tyrees. I don't like his sort having an influence on officers in training. I'll make arrangements for tonight."

He turned on his heel and strode imperiously from the canteen, his retinue in his wake.

Salaan sat again as the last of the onlookers were dispersing. The remarks of the last two were typical.

"You hear what he said about Tyrees?"

"Yeah, and he's full of shit."

"Probably, but that won't stop King Jon from carving him up. Tyrees is smaller and he hasn't had combat training yet."

"Yeah, I know. Did you see the King give that gorilla— what's his name, Ttig—the once-over first? He wasn't taking any chances. Built like a landing shuttle. Still, Tyrees didn't look worried, did he?"

"No, but he never does. There's something about him that's scary, you know what I mean? Maybe King Jon picked the wrong one after all. Do you think Tyrees really is queer?"

"Who knows? Who cares?"

"Whatever he is, he'll make a better officer than the King. What an asshole!"

"He'll make a better officer than most of us."

Back at the table, Ttig looked resentfully at Salaan, who was visibly distressed.

"You pick some great friends, Salaan."

"Let her alone," said Pol. "It's not her fault."

"As of now," she said in a low voice, "he's not a friend. I'm sorry, Pol."

"It's his problem, not mine. Forget it."

"His problem!" exclaimed Ttig. "Tonight it'll be *your* problem. I hate to see friends get mauled. If you'd kept your mouth shut, he would have challenged *me*. And I'd kill the bastard!"

"If he'd kept his mouth shut," said Ses, "both of you would be grounded by now for fighting in the canteen. It's really my fault, though. I should have kept *my* mouth shut."

"Maybe. At least Pol wouldn't get reamed by that posturing idiot."

"What difference does it make?" said Pol. "I won't get maimed. No flaming nova, okay? Let's go. It's time for cybernetics." Ttig's pug nose was still off-color and he was muttering invectives as they started out. Salaan trailed behind. Before they reached the exit, she suddenly grasped Pol by the arm and held him back, her face full of compassionate intensity. She backed him to a wall as if she were cornering a pickpocket. They stood nose to chin. Pol could feel her breath on his neck and the slight pressure of one thigh.

She let go of his arm and looked up straight into his eyes. Her voice trembled. "Pol, come to the Breakaway with me?"

He looked just as directly back, noticing the fleck of perspiration amid the fuzz of her upper lip, and smiled his slow smile.

"No, Salaan. Thanks, anyway. You don't owe me anything. I said it wasn't your fault."

"That's not why I asked!" she spat. "At least..."

She moved back then, swiping angrily at her hair. She was confused about her motives and hurt by his refusal. At the same time, she still marveled at his calm. Those eyes!

"Okay. Then at least see me tomorrow. There's something I want to talk to you about."

"Sure."

"Ses has Population Dynamics at ten hundred, doesn't he?"

"Yes, he's—"

"Then I'll come to your quarters. I want to see you alone." Head down, and knuckles shiny around her printout carrier, she hurried out. Pol blinked and watched her go. She was lovely. And he was more afraid of her than of Jon.

SY 3025

Most of the Sevens were entering the challenge combat room for the first time. It was a smaller facility than the main combat room where regular training was conducted, but size was the least of the differences. It had lavish and formal appointments. Deep black carpeting was ingrained with slashes of muted red. A vaulted ceiling thrust down in a sharp curve to strike a steeply inclined floor that poured ruddy plush seats to the brink of a round pit in the center. Sound was deadened. Lighting was subdued except for the slab of glare that stabbed upward from the pit itself, forcing eyes to focus there.

A stranger standing in the pit would feel himself at a nexus, would sense a clashing convergence of things—with himself as the target. He would know instinctively the room's function because it was a shrine to the pure and terrifying concept of one man pitted against another; it was a stage for violence, a place where primitive struggle was ritualized, exalted. It said what the Cadre said: be prepared; combat is a serious endeavor that puts you into the vortex; note the consequences; fight well, for much hangs in the balance.

A mass of Sevens and a scattering of Sixes filed into the room until the seats were filled; then the entrances were closed.

Hushed voices turned to silence when a supervisor marched to the lighted pit. He spoke with formality.

"Officers of the Cadre. A combat challenge has been issued by Jon Chaas, Cadre Seven, against Pol Tyrees, Cadre Seven. It has been accepted. Combat rules: No striking blows; no attempts to cause permanent injury. The victor will force immobility upon his opponent until he yields. Combat will cease when a yield is called, an injury occurs, or I, as judge, terminate it. On their honor as officers of the Cadre, this combat marks the end of all hostilities between them.

"Onlookers will remain silent during the combat. It has been staged because two officers could find no other redress for their differences. It is also staged for your edification, *not* for your entertainment."

He turned toward an aisle that spiked to the pit from under the rising seats.

"Officer Jon Chaas." He spun to face an aisle opposite. "Officer Pol Tyrees." The two young men, naked except for protecting belts at their loins, walked out of the darkness to face each other. Both gave the Cadre salute.

Jon looked magnificent. His muscles bunched and relaxed as he shifted from one foot to the other and glared across the pit. Pol stood loosely, almost negligently. His body was smaller, lighter, its muscles not in knotty bulges but in smooth, flat curves. The supervisor motioned them to the center of the pit. He grasped each by a wrist, raised their arms high, and pressed their palms together. In the piercing light, the three looked like votives engaged in a holy rite; one black-draped priest bracketed by two naked acolytes, hands aloft in supplication of the gods. The light probed from beneath, allowing shadows only in the sockets of their eyes.

The supervisor spoke first to Pol.

"Is the challenge just?" Aware of the moment's sanctity, Pol barely hesitated.

"It is."

"Do you wish it met?"

"I do."

He turned his head to Jon.

"Is the acceptance worthy?"

"It is."

"Do you wish it answered?"

"I do."

"Are you both prepared in mind and body?" he intoned. The answer was in unison.

"I am."

The supervisor lowered their arms and stepped from the pit. "Begin the combat."

Jon's fingers clenched and unclenched as the two began the ageless, crouching, circular motion wary fighters have always used when facing a single opponent without weapons. It was a dance of tight muscle and violence held in check, a double motion moving to rhythms felt in the blood. Jon began to vary the rhythm by moving quickly in and out as he circled, looking for an opening. It seemed a dance of lovers, one pressing his desire, the other reluctant; every so often a hand would slap flesh and pull away. Pol reacted defensively to his opponent's thrusts but tried none of his own. He was afraid of failure, not defeat—of humiliation, not pain.

Suddenly, Jon's hands went high and he lunged as if to secure a headlock. It was a good feint. In reaction, Pol snapped backward at the waist, forearms flying up. Jon converted his lunge into a low dive, driving a shoulder into Pol's midsection, grabbing one leg, and throwing him backward. Pol landed several feet away, on his backside, with a hard thump. He regained his feet before Jon could follow up, but Jon was in no hurry. He did not notice that the throw had failed to change the blandness of Pol's expression. His confidence grew as he saw in his mind's eye the spectacle friends would see of his prowess carved on the body of an enemy. He had drawn first blood—mandatory for psychological reasons, according to his combat instructor. He smirked and began to circle once more.

Pol was hurt and angry. Why am I here? he thought. I didn't choose this. What is it that I'm fighting for? I'm going to lose. What will it mean to the Cadre?

Then Jon was on him again. Pol grabbed for a wrist, which Jon let him have as he slipped around behind and threw Pol over the back of his hip. Pol landed with another loud thump on the same ignoble spot at the base of his spine. His vision of Jon's smile was bleared with pain, but he felt something else as well. Pain and anger had triggered a new alertness that was mushrooming inside, that sharpened with the pumping of his blood. His senses were pouring data into his mind with a cold precision he had never known before. His fear was leaking away. He sprang to his feet.

Jon made another feint, but this time Pol saw it for what it was—the muscles tensed to stop before following through, the movement too exaggerated to be authentic. The real attack was another lunge that was intended to lock his arms behind Pol's knees. Instead, just before Jon's chest hit the floor, arms embracing the air, his opponent's feet flew over his head. Pol's leap had cleared the length of Jon's body. A high-pitched giggle came from one of the seats. Jon's face burned. The supervisor interrupted his circling of the pit to glower at the sound.

Pol was now heady with his new sense of acuity, drugged with its promise of power. He watched Jon scramble to his feet and begin another stalk. Adrenaline surged as he took his defensive stance. He could hear the soft pad of the supervisor's circular vigil, the susurration of the air system, even the diffused breathing of the watchers. He began to key his movements to Jon's, perceiving the notion of an action before it happened. He was an infant again, discovering his own limbs and his control of them; he took a marveling joy in ducking, dodging, sideslipping Jon's attacks. He watched his man's uncertainty change to frustration, then desperation. It was a new dance, and Pol could smell the dew of fear on the forehead a meter away.

Jon's attacks became more frantic. He backed a step to leap feet first for a flying ankle lock. Pol sidestepped, plucked a shin from the air, and threw it sideways. Jon hit the floor on buttocks and hands and spun like a top. This time, there were only smiles from the spectators.

Jon was unhurt, but trembling with rage. When Pol approached, he threw a wild and vicious kick from the floor.

"Foul! Stop!" The supervisor leapt into the pit. "Officer Chaas, you have committed a foul." Jon's face went white.

"Yes, sir," he said from the floor. "Unintentional, sir. I apologize to my opponent." He got to his feet and saluted Pol. The supervisor glared sternly before continuing the formula.

"Officer Tyrees, do you wish to continue?" Pol could now walk from the pit without loss of face, but he was caught up in the new glory of his control; he wanted to sing to the fine thrum of the music he had found in his muscles and his nerves. He returned the salute.

"I wish to continue."

The supervisor addressed Jon once more. "You will not be

allowed a second foul. Continue the combat." He backed from
the pit.

Jon now began to fight with total earnestness and more than
a little courage, for he knew that he was overmatched, although
he did not understand it. He knew that he could fight well; yet
in this conflict, he felt clumsy and was sure he appeared so.

Pol studied his man again. His movements seemed to be
even slower; tiny ones became gross, gross ones ridiculous.
He was watching a comic actor parody a fighter in slow-motion
pantomime. To this point, he had remained on the defensive;
but his keening blood would no longer allow that passivity. He
remembered the ignominy of the first throw and imitated it.
The high feint he made obvious by matching his enemy's awkward speed. When Jon reacted to it, Pol drove downward in a
blur and threw his man as he had been thrown; but before Jon
could recover, Pol took the backs of his thighs in his armpits,
forcing knees to ears and pinning wrists to the pit floor. Jon
struggled like a trapped animal, but only his head was free to
move with impunity. Pol could feel the desperation subside as
Jon's breathing turned to shudders. After a final spasm, a spark
died in his eyes, quenched by a film of tears. For a moment,
there at the center of things, the two young men looked at each
other, faces close, and shared a new awareness.

"I yield," said Jon in a soft voice.

Pol released him immediately and stood. The vaulted am-
phitheater spun and blurred the watching faces into flashing
white spots. Like a collapsing dam broken by exploding waters,
his body let the tension flow out. It left him disoriented and
he felt strangely depressed.

Jon struggled slowly to his feet, eyes down. The supervisor
entered the pit wearing a look of puzzlement, but he completed
the ritual in the traditional manner by repeating the palms-
together stance.

"Is the conflict resolved?" he chanted.

"The conflict is resolved."

"Is it resolved forever?"

"It is resolved forever."

The supervisor lowered their arms.

The next morning, Pol was returning to his quarters after a
class, still struggling with glimpses of a darker self he had not

known was there and did not *want* to be there. The combat had opened deep crevasses into a disturbing substratum. It pulsed with primordial power—and threatened chaos. He had tapped that power to turn the fight his way, and he had been swept up by it. There had been some control, but it was the control of a beast, blood deep and lusty, sweet and horrible.

On a more superficial level, he felt like an honest man who suddenly realizes that he has won a huge sum with loaded dice. He no longer doubted that others simply did not possess some of the abilities he was more and more deliberately drawing upon. The realization had been there before, but lurking dimly, a weapon kept out of sight. It gave him a strange, mixed feeling of pride, guilt, and fear. Yes, he was different. The fear came from the suspicion that, whatever else, this difference would mean a destiny apart from others, a solitary path more isolated than even he wanted.

Preoccupied, he slipped his identity plate into a wall slot in the corridor, and his door slid open.

"Wha . . . !"

A tall man in the gray coveralls of a maintenance technic stared at him blankly. Absurdly, he was standing on Pol's bed.

"Oh—uh, hello . . . sir." The man pointed at a grate in the ceiling with some kind of metal tool. "Problem with the circulation system, sir. Okay now. Uh, sorry about the bed." He tucked the tool in his belt and, with a peculiar half gesture of his lowered hands, hopped to the floor. Though he was technically an officer, Pol was uncomfortable with the "sir" from a man twice his age. He also felt vaguely resentful of the invasion.

"How did you get in?"

"Oh, well. Some of us trusty types have a master card. Need it for emergencies, you know." He bent to snap shut the lid of an incongruously small case on the floor. Pol studied him closely. Something didn't fit. He was a lowly maintenance man, but the cut of face and body was fine and clean and hard. Movements were decisive, the voice oddly articulated. A smile revealed perfect teeth.

"Be going now. Won't be any more problems. Thanks." He left quickly.

There was a niggle in Pol's mind. Something . . . He hadn't noticed anything wrong with the air circulation. The man didn't *look* like a maintenance technic, but . . . Then it hit him. The funny gesture before he jumped off the bed! It was the beginning of the ingrained "clearing" motion made—before an action like jumping—by someone *accustomed to wearing a cape*. But why would a Cadre officer . . . ?

Before he had time to think further, there was a low hum from the entrance panel. He reached out to press a stud and the panel slid open to reveal Salaan. She stood with arms akimbo, saying nothing. Her height was average, but framed there in the doorway, she seemed oversized and powerful. In fact, every single feature of her could have been described as "average": it was their harmony that pulled and widened the eyes.

"Salaan! Come on in. Throw Ses's junk off that chair and sit down. I'm sorry, but I forgot you were coming." He smiled his apology. The territories of the two roommates could have been marked off with chalk: one side in chaos, the other neat, almost fastidious.

Pol was apprehensive as he watched the serious-faced young woman shift things from the chair. She wore brief exercise togs and her skin glowed. Before, he had appreciated her looks with dispassion. Now, filled with a new sense of loneliness, he wanted to hide in her. He dampened these feelings angrily and with elaborate formality removed the other chair from under its study console and placed it precisely opposite Salaan's. When he sat stiffly and looked a question at her, he had to force his heartbeat down. Blond hair slightly disheveled, face and throat still ruddy from a shower, expression still etched into some kind of determination, she let slip unbidden stirrings in him.

"I'm glad you kicked a hole in Jon's ego last night, Pol."

He shrugged. "So am I. But let's keep it in perspective. It wasn't a nova in the first place, and now it's over."

"No. It's not over. The things he said about you—they're not true." Again, she looked directly into his eyes, a thing few people did with him. He felt his own gaze falter and slide away, feeling strangely vulnerable.

"Well, as I said before, what others think is their problem, not mine."

"But it *is* your problem." She spoke with a soft intensity that shook him. "You're going to be somebody special in the Cadre, Pol, but not if you or the people around you think you have a sex problem."

"That's ridiculous, Salaan," he said, some of his anger leaking out.

"No, it's not! Her voice rose. "The Cadre is everything to me, but I'm not blind to its flaws, and one is that certain types walk around as if they were gods or supermen or something. Maybe it helps if the public accepts that image, but it's not right if our *own* see themselves that way. But that's not the point—the real point is that the Cadre hates certain kinds of 'weakness.' If they believe, or even suspect, that what Jon said is true, you'll end up shuffling paper in the lower echelons for the rest of your life!"

Salaan stopped her tirade, panting slightly. Pol sat hunched forward, hands clutching the edges of his chair seat. Beads of sweat popped out at his hairline.

"I . . . I never thought of it that way." He paused to think. Could she be right? Could something so—so stupid hold him back in the Cadre? The thought was appalling. "Look, Salaan, I'm not a homosexual, but I've never had sex with a girl. I know a lot of the guys haven't, either, in spite of what they say, but with me, it's . . . it's hard to explain. It scares me, I guess. I don't like feeling . . . well, I'll just have to sort it out myself. I'm not really worried about it, so you shouldn't be."

"We'll sort it out *now*, then, so others won't be, either." Salaan stood, walked over to Pol's bed, and turned to face him. His head snapped up, eyes flaring.

"Salaan, I don't need your pity. And sacrifices are . . . I'm used to solving my own problems." Hands on hips, legs spread aggressively, she leaned toward him and spoke as if at a child.

"This is one problem you're not going to solve by yourself, you stubborn neuron. You're letting your silly pride get in the way. Besides," she added in a softer tone, "this isn't much of a sacrifice."

Chin with a slight upward tilt, she unzipped her exercise top in a single motion. She hesitated a moment before shrugging it off and letting it fall to the floor. Pol discovered with a shock that he could not prevent his heart from racing faster. She truly was beautiful. Her breasts, in the smallest of motions, swung forward as she leaned to remove her footwear.

Without thinking, he rose from his chair, reached out, and gently touched one nipple. Salaan raised her eyes to his. A thrill, deeper and more irresistible than anything he had ever known, surged inside as he felt, saw, the nipple stiffen and grow. His trembling fingers moved, and the brownish areola erupted, fissured. He felt faint. Salaan shuddered slightly; the look of adolescent determination melted into the softer lines of a woman aroused. With slow deliberation, she took his other hand and placed it on her other breast. A second surge gushed through him. Pol's eyes swam with curves and softnesses and darknesses. After a few moments she said, "Take off your clothes, Pol."

He fumbled with his clothing, using fingers that belonged to someone else. When he finished, she moved against him and they fell clumsily on the bed. Pol was taken out of himself, released into a mindless frenzy. . . .

A short time later, Salaan quietly swung her legs over the edge of the bed and dressed. She said nothing, but her expression mingled tenderness with triumph. She turned to look at Pol as she touched the door panel stud. His eyes were blank, his mouth slack. She smiled and left quietly.

Pol looked at the empty doorway. He felt a deep melancholy because he knew that he could never again permit himself to stand helpless at that edge. He was afraid of the dark forces stirring within, waiting to claim him, waiting to tell him things he did not want to know. He wept.

The following day, a mournful Dace Sestus informed Pol that Salaan had been peremptorily transferred to the training complex in Sector II. No explanation was offered. By then, Pol had forgotten about the maintenance technic.

SY 3028

Pol came down the ramp of the Cadre vessel *Honor,* thinking that honor was poorly served by this particular piece of transport. It was old, cramped, and uncomfortable; its equipment had been jury-rigged, cannibalized, and improvised. He hoped it was due for mothballing because it seemed to perform every function grudgingly.

This had been his first interstellar flight, a journey of twenty light-years, lasting a bare three weeks. *Honor* was several generations old but, he mused ruefully, suited for milk runs like the delivery of a lowly Seven for his stint of training duty at a sector headquarters. If his first six-month assignment was satisfactory, he would return to the complex to become a Cadre Six officer and begin Advanced Training, with yellow piping on his collar. He wanted that badly—and soon.

A loud clang sounded behind him and he turned to see a crewman working at a cargo bay. He smiled at the man's casual use of a heavy sledge to jar the pitted door from its comfortable seating.

The journey itself was part of his training. He was expected to learn the rudiments of space travel, because at least a part of his career would involve light-year trips. The first successful interstellar voyage undertaken by man had lasted seven years;

most of Pol's three-week trip had been consumed by initial and terminal maneuvering. He knew the basic theory. Man's senses and most instruments perceived space as distance to be traversed in "straight" lines. But fine peculiarities of light had led scientists long ago to discoveries that resulted in the modern mode of space travel. Under certain conditions, some light particles seemed to disappear near their source light-years away and reappear near the observer with no apparent lapse of time. Research gradually revealed that space was immersed in a vast and intricate network of invisible pathways—another dimension woven into conventional space.

Pol had to think of himself looking down a long, tunnellike street with a tall building etched in the far distance. Then he imagined a giant hand that grasped the building and bent the whole street around in a great loop until the building was right beside him. But he could still see it in the distance, because he was looking in a 'bent' path around the loop. However, in terms of the shortest distance between it and him, he had only to step sideways to touch it. In space travel, this "sideways" distance was the one traveled if a pathway was there to use. Scientists had connected the pathways with galactic gravitational forces. Gravitons, theoretically postulated particles of infinitely small size, traveled in waves along the pathways, occasionally herding light waves along with them. The trick was to place a vessel at a point where a pathway interfaced with conventional space, alter the ship's gravitational field to conform with that of the gravaton waves, and the short cut was open. The ship could get off the pathway by reverting to its normal gravitational field and powering away. In terms of distance, all star systems—in effect—existed simultaneously at the end of the "street" and "sideways" right beside the observer.

Intergalactic patterns were another matter; their nature was different, and the waves fewer and weaker in the voids of outer space. (Even galactic graviton pathways had to be closely charted to be useful; for instance, it was often necessary to travel to a star system in one direction in order to pick up a pathway to a target star that lay in another.) It was dangerous to place a ship on an intergalactic pathway because it was almost impossible to predict where it would end up.

Pol left off his daydreaming with a whimsical question: Was man to be denied the privilege of exploring other galaxies when he had already gone so far and done so much? Or had that gift been granted to others more worthy? Then he saw a Cadre ground car on the apron of the spaceport. A Cadre Four got out as he approached. Pol saluted, stiff forearm across his body; it was returned and followed by an outstretched hand, which he shook.

"Pol Tyrees?"

"Yessir. Reporting for B. T. assignment."

"Welcome. I'm Section Head Georg Wal. You've been assigned to me at HQ. They'll send your kit over later. Jump in." He gestured at the car.

On the way to sector HQ, Pol studied the man who would be his immediate superior for the next six months. He was slightly less than middle age and had the easy manner and ready smile of one content with his lot in life. His size and obvious physical strength made him an imposing figure in the Cadre uniform, in spite of a rather craggy-ugly face. He did not set any automatics, choosing to drive himself.

"My little section is concerned with data analysis, Pol, but not the usual stuff. We look for patterns, trends, what have you, by matching up gross data not readily available to field men." Pol was already confused.

"Uh, a 'little' section, sir? My assignment says 'Economics Department'—and I assumed that it would be huge."

"Oh, it is, it is, my boy. But we're their *specialists*. We perform magic tricks the other computer boys only dream about." He laughed with a booming sound before turning to Pol. "They call us 'ferrets.' I rather like the name." Pol wondered how he could have been selected for such specialized duty. He was too inexperienced. Since the man was patently indifferent to formality, he didn't hesitate to ask questions.

"I'm sorry, sir, but I don't really follow. How is your work different from ordinary information analysis?"

Wal's first response was a naturally crooked smile. "You know, I haven't come up with a satisfactory definition of my job yet, and I've been at it for seven years. If I don't come up with one soon, I'm going to have an identity crisis. Let's see . . . I'll have to give you an example instead, okay? A few months ago the computers told us that Beatrix was importing eleven percent more quarzium than usual. No big nova, right? But since it was an unusual datum, I decided to check it out. By the way, you have to know that quarzium is one of the newer synthetic isotopes used to make superconductors—very expensive. We started by looking for other anomalies and found nothing unusual from Beatrix herself, so we expanded the search to include her trading partners.

"Remember now, at this point it's very low priority, having begun as a hunch on a slow afternoon. I've got one Six on it—on assignment, like yourself. You're our first Seven, by the way. One of the nice things about our section's work is that we go pretty much our own way without interference from the brass because they don't know what we're doing, either." Wal took time out from his "example" to boom out another laugh. "Anyhow, another strange fact turns up; Erewhon's industrial output is taking an unexplained dive. Ordinarily, we wouldn't take note of it because they themselves put it down to temporary energy supply problems. However, Erewhon is Beatrix's main competitor in the trade of manufactured goods. We up the priority and dig deeper. Erewhon's energy production is down six percent. On an industrial planet, that's a lot. Their main source of energy comes from solar collectors in deep space, things so huge they'd clutter up orbital traffic lanes—and they wanted to hide them as much as possible. Follow so far? Any comments?"

Pol thought for a moment. "Erewhon report any specific reason for the energy loss?"

"Nope. Just recorded current energy production in their annual report as required by Regnum law. We assumed that a reduction of that size had to be connected to the solar collectors."

"You said superconductors earlier?" said Pol tentatively.

Wal again laughed loudly and reached across the seat in a very un-Cadre-like gesture to swat Pol's shoulder.

"You've got it, son! It takes a crazy kind of mind for this work, and you may just have one of them. The brass sent a number Three to each planet, and they find industrial sabotage all over the place. Beatrix had been using superconductors to make energy bleeds off the Erewhon collectors and storing it in a ship that was really a spacefaring storage battery. Real hit-and-run operation: by the time Erewhon could get out to one collector, Beatrix would be bleeding another. Erewhon assumed a transmission malfunction at first, and it was a while before they could put two and two together and put permanent patrols on their collectors. They didn't report their suspicions because they had industrial saboteurs playing games on Beatrix themselves.

"To make a long story short, Ones and Twos went to both planets and hauled in half of both governments. A bad indicator of the escalating Trade Wars, but I like the case because it's a classic example of a good 'ferret' job. Fire-eyes actually used her smile muscles."

"Fire-eyes, sir?"

"You'll find out shortly, son. Here we are." Wal swerved recklessly into an underground tunnel beneath the sector HQ. Pol had seen only a maze of interconnected buildings. It held the wherewithal for coordinating the affairs of the Cadre in hundreds of member planets scattered through as many light-years in space. After parking the ground car, Wal led the way to an elevator.

"I'll take you to our warren and introduce you to the staff. Your quarters are ready, but I know they're unpleasant enough to encourage a lot of duty time."

They emerged into a corridor several floors up; it was full of officers talking excitedly in small groups. Wal held up a hand to stop Pol in the middle of a question.

"Something's up. Something big. Hey, Paccer! What's going on?" A young Four detached himself from the nearest group.

"Bad news, chief. We've lost a number One."

"What?"

"His monitor started buzzing a few minutes ago. All I know is that he was on assignment. All hell's breaking loose around here."

"It damned well should," said Wal over his shoulder as he started down the corridor. Pol chased after, feeling the electricity in the air. Invisible speakers blared.

"Attention, please! Section heads report immediately to the conference room. Section heads report immediately to the conference room."

Without missing a stride, Wal changed direction. Still at his heels, Pol knew the reason for the excitement. Every Cadre One officer had a permanent implant in the base of his neck. It was a nuclear-powered sender that had only one function: to send continuously the simple message that its carrier lived. The implants were tied into the Regnum network of galactic communications. The system utilized transmission stations parked on the graviton pathways so that even the farthest part of a sector was only seconds away. Pol assumed that this number One had been operating under cover, because a man would have to be out of his mind to murder a Cadre One deliberately—if he had a choice. On the rare occasion when it did happen, the Cadre went about its business with a special vengeance: aside from brotherhood sentiments, Ones were produced only after years of expensive training, and their value to the Regnum was inestimable. The Cadre was tightly knit, a single, many tentacled body. When one of its arms was lopped off, it writhed in anger.

There was a bottleneck at the entrance to the conference room and Pol fell in behind Wal. It may have been the excitement, or they might have assumed he had a right to be there, but there was no reaction to his youth or the red piping on his collar. In Operations there were many ranks, as there were in all sub-Cadres, except One. They were indicated by the number of gaps in the pattern of the piping.

Two section heads in front of Pol were muttering back and forth as the press of bodies thinned.

"I'd rather have ramjets for toilet paper than Fire-eyes on my back for this one."

"Me too. But if it's one of ours who goofed, he'd deserve what he gets."

"Naw. Not a chance. This place is so far from the action that I sometimes forget why we're here. Any goofs were made by Chiefs of Staffs or in the field."

"Listen, Lavvi. If you keep forgetting why we're here, you'll end up counting machine parts on Ceti Three."

Pol wished the same fate on the section head and then made a nervous decision. He shuffled into the conference room with the rest of the tense group. Inside, they filed down two sides of a long table that bristled with computer consoles, screens tilted toward immovable seats. The near end of the table was dominated by a massive chair festooned with instrumentation, the armrests dotted with keys and buttons. Just clearing its back was a collar with green piping in a two-gap pattern—supervisor rank.

He passed the chair, trying to look inconspicuous, and saw that the collar was worn by a striking woman with spiky flames for hair. Though it was close-cropped, it was even more dramatic than Ses's orange mop. It was brighter, redder, spearing the senses.

The face was in direct contrast. It was set in stone. The features were fine, beautifully chiseled, and of the creamiest hue. Pol could not guess her age, but the skin was clean of lines, so smooth it glowed like rubbed milkstone. Tiny, pointed ears peeked through the hair, pixielike, but they were the only suggestion of frivolity. The rest was hard, cold business, with a pair of flashing green eyes. Fire-eyes.

She looked up from her console and the last of the entrants made haste to find seats. Her sweeping glance scorched past Pol, stopped, and did a quick return. Like aiming a laser beam, thought Pol, controlling his apprehension.

"Who is he?" she demanded at large. Her voice had the edge of a scalpel. When he saw the reason for the question, Wal's face reddened.

"I'm sorry, Supervisor, I just brought him from the spaceport—our newie. I guess he just tagged along. Officer Tyrees..."

"Never mind now. Leave him." She looked again at Pol. "Sit down. You may learn something."

"Gentlemen, we have a crisis. A few minutes ago Communications informed me that the life implant of a Cadre One stopped sending. I have read his assignment file, and it originated from this department. I don't like that." She paused to let her words sink in.

The section heads cringed subtly. They were reacting both to the loss of a fellow officer and to the accusing eyes of the supervisor.

"If we sent a number One into a dangerous situation without one datum that might have saved his life, I'll have the balls of the section head responsible." No one smiled. "Here's what I have." She punched a code into the terminal. Words and figures appeared on the smaller models ringing the table. She summarized tersely.

"Member planet Shalom reported galloping inflation about six months ago. Claimed that two competitors were making concerted and illegal attacks on her currency. We recommended a Cadre Three research assignment. Chiefs of Staff concurred and sent a digger in. His report..." She tapped in another code. "His report confirmed the suspicion of a conspiracy and probable counterfeiting, but failed to identify methods or perpetrators. Chiefs of Staff sent in a number One under cover as an underworld expert in distributing phony money. He was to establish contact with counterfeiters and work as close to the top as he could—an infiltration assignment. He barely had time to get started." The supervisor stopped and looked up, pinning one section head with her green eyes. "Your section came up with the original recommendation, Bool. Any comments?"

An officer at the end of the table cleared his throat and stabbed furiously at his terminal.

"Pretty straightforward, as I recall, Supervisor. All I can add are the actual figures: in spite of a healthy production profile, Shalom's economy was in trouble because inflation made the import of raw materials excessively expensive. She claimed that Cosmos and Leaf were undermining her currency. That's about it. After our recommendation for a digger search, it was out of our hands."

"There was no information that may have pointed a finger?"

"No, nothing hard—only that, in general terms, Leaf and Cosmos have the most to gain from Shalom's problems. I understand that the digger's report confirmed counterfeiting, but we were not involved by then."

"Did you do a run on Leaf and Cosmos?"

"Yes, a very cursory one, I admit. But we saw nothing to indicate anything illegal."

"Did you ask Wal to put his ferrets on it?"

"Uh, no, Supervisor, it just didn't seem like that sort of thing. The annual reports were all routine, and it was my judgment that illegal currency dealing wouldn't surface there; hence our recommendation for an on-the-spot digger."

"Your judgment was probably correct, Bool. However, it's the ferret's job to see connections others can't—especially when we think something may be there in the first place. Remember that. Wal, put your people on this. Priority One until I tell you otherwise. If we couldn't help to avoid the death of a Cadre officer, maybe we can help to point a finger. Use the digger's report, for a starter."

"Digger" was jargon for a Cadre Three, data-gathering field agent. A hand went up.

"Yes, Valsi."

"Supervisor, any reaction from Chiefs of Staff?"

"Yes. *Fury.* Too soon for anything else. My guess is they'll send in One-Two teams to the three planets to scare up reaction, if nothing else. In the meantime, they better not see anybody in HQ smile. We have received no specific orders, and I doubt that we will. But *I* require, starting right now, a full review of the economic status of all three members. Those of you not directly involved, get involved. Dismissed."

The group dispersed quickly. On the way out, Pol offered a sheepish apology to Wal for following him into the meeting. He did not say that his act was deliberate.

"Forget it, son. My fault for ignoring you. Let's join the ferrets and start in on the bleary-eyed stuff. If I know Fire-eyes, and I do, she'll be riding our tails nonstop until we turn up something. And I'll be surprised if anybody but us stumbles onto anything significant here. The others are good at their jobs, mind you, but too accustomed to dealing with stuff that looks routine." He stopped long enough to stab a large, bony finger at Pol's chest. "A good ferret gets suspicious when the routine looks too routine."

Wal led the way to a large workroom. A table, like that in the conference room, was cluttered with consoles and personal effects. Five officers interrupted a heated conversation as they entered. Their attitude and the ambience of the room confirmed Pol's opinion that Wal ran an informal ship. No one rose from the table, but Pol could detect nothing suggestive of disrespect. Because of the growing acuity of his senses, he was adept at reading body language, though it had long become a habit to conceal it. He saw scorn under the masks of two of them. They felt insulted that someone actually thought that a Seven could contribute to their work. Pol's own, more perfect mask sealed itself.

Four of the men were permanent Operations. The fifth was a Six on assignment. Wal stopped the opening barrage of questions with a wave of his hands.

"I'll tell you all I know in a second. You're not going to like some of it; but first, meet Pol Tyrees from Sector One." After Pol was introduced, Wal gave an account of the meeting.

"The juicy part, gentlemen, is that the ferrets are going to be the ones who bring in the goodies, no matter how much we have to flatten our asses in the process. First,"—he rubbed his hands and grinned—"the digger's report." He strode to a nearby terminal and tapped some buttons. "I'll set for multiple display and divvy up the parts. Pol, you just float around for the time being and watch the geniuses at work." He looked at his timer.

"All right, assignments are in your consoles. I'll hear summary reports in two hours. Get at it, gents."

Two hours later, the group reconvened at the big table, oral scripts in front of them.

"Right, here we go," said Wal. "Sal, you first."

Sal was the Cadre Six. He had been with the ferrets only four months, but Pol had seen him work with incredible speed and confidence. No doubt that was why he was here. It took special skills to become a good computer man; they seemed to have a sixth sense when it came to knowing how and what to retrieve from the bowels of the machines. Like dog trainers, they were able to coax the beasts into doing things no one else believed they could do. Sal seemed already to be such a man.

"Okay, chief, but you won't be impressed." His oral script began to hum as his notes, dictated earlier, began to roll by on the drum of thin metal before him. "I was looking at the fine data the digger dredged up on Shalom's GNP. Everything appears normal until about four years ago. Gradual but steady decline since. Imports become more expensive as the value of their currency dropped. Parallel declines all over the place. In a nutshell, the digger's breakdowns reflect the general conditions shown in Shalom's routine reports. He supports their claim that inflation is the major problem. So do I, if that means anything."

"Anything strike you as unusual, aside from the inflationary situation itself? No bad vibrations?"

"No, the figures feel right, chief."

Pol was beginning to sense what Wal had meant about the ferrets' special talents; they developed intuitive powers that told them when apparently "normal" data didn't "feel" right or failed to fit a larger picture as snugly as it should. One of the old hands delivered next.

"I've been looking at the digger's stuff on currency flow. Did a fine job, incidentally. Took gross figures from industrial and banking sources and did a probability run on them. Indications were that there are billions of credits' worth of Shalom currency flowing in the system that was never minted. He drew the only possible conclusion: counterfeiting on one hell of a massive scale."

The pooling of information continued until Wal finished his own report. Nothing substantial had been unearthed: they suc-

ceeded only in doing a detailed review of a highly skilled Cadre
Three's report. Pol realized that this was one of the ways the
ferrets became adept at their own work; they followed the
footsteps of the most talented computermen in the galaxy when
they sifted through diggers' reports—and they had the added
advantages of hindsight and unlimited resources. An assignment he once feared might be dull was rapidly becoming fascinating.

At the moment, however, the others were not fascinated.
Pol noted the minutely increasing breathing rates and postures
that were becoming more tense as the meeting progressed.
He diagnosed frustration because the tiny telltales matched
behavior patterns that, in his experience, were the responses
of people thwarted, denied progress toward an important goal.
None sent the signals more clearly than Wal, and he infected
the others. To Pol, he was like a hunting bird tethered to his
perch, trembling with trapped energy as a squirrel paused below. The others saw only their genial leader urging them on.
Finally, when no one had anything constructive to offer, the
crack in Wal began to widen. The Cadre personality loathed
mystery; in many ways, Wal was not typical of his fellows,
but in this, he was classic.

"Damn it, there's got to be *something* here. The digger's
only human! The bastards who got our number One are only
human! I'm not asking for a pile of corpses, just a little smell!"

"We're only human, too, chief," muttered someone.

"No you're not! You're ferrets. And Fire-eyes isn't human,
either," he added, breaking the tension with his crooked smile.

"All right, all right, I know I'm pushing and we've only
been at it a half day, but there's a dead man a few light-years
away who left us a job to do. . . . It's funny, I can't get the
thought out of my mind of his going without the black on.
Doesn't seem right." The others nodded. "This is the second
number One this year. Before that, I can't recall *any*." The
expressions around the table said a great deal—the mouths,
nothing.

"Okay, gents, I'll send out for eats; we'll relax over the
Cadre's sumptuous fare, and get back at it."

During the lunch break, Wal could not resist shop talk, but
his manner was more relaxed.

"We know it's there, boys. Nothing that radical can happen

to a whole economy—a *healthy* economy—without the culprits leaving a diltz or two behind.

"Pol, say something."

"Sir?"

"Call me chief. This bunch uses it as a sign of their disrespect, but I'm the only man in the Cadre with that title, so I keep it. You've got a fresh mind. You didn't get here by being stupid; in fact, our conversation in the car led me to believe the opposite. So say something."

"Yes, sir—uh, chief. What's a diltz?" The others laughed, and one cried, "Oh, no, don't ask that!" but Wal launched into an explanation.

"A 'diltz' is spacecrew slang for an unexplained malfunction, a bug in a system. Let's say an elevator refuses to stop at a particular level. Everything's checked—nothing's wrong. When that happens to a mechanic, he just shrugs his shoulders when asked what the trouble is, and says fatalistically, 'I dunno. It's the diltz, I guess.' The diltz is the gizmo that's causing the problem when you can't find out what's causing the problem. Got it?"

"Chief," said one of the men, "you're getting worse. I don't think *I've* got it anymore."

"I think I understand," said Pol. "We look for something that might appear innocent, but doesn't belong, like a harmless flaw in the pattern, only it isn't harmless."

"Well, that's close enough. It doesn't really matter, though. If you have the right kind of weird circuitry for a mind, you spot them even if you don't know what you're looking for. Sal, here, is going to be one of the best, if I can talk him into going permanent Operations." Sal smiled noncommittally.

"Let's get back on track, shall we? You two youngsters have a look at the currency flow on the other two planets. Staas . . ." Wal rifled out new assignments that were spreading farther afield from Shalom. "All right, go. Two more hours."

This time, two hours wasn't enough for most of the men to complete thorough reviews, but Wal insisted on partial reports at definite time intervals. He felt that it added to the team effort, giving each a clearer idea of the general picture. They also took turns for naps on a makeshift cot. No one noticed that Pol never took a turn.

Pol became absorbed in the process. Sal summoned information from his terminal in a chain reaction series as one set of data led to another. Occasionally he paused to dictate notes into his oral script. Early on, he said, "If you see anything, Pol, just holler." Pol laughed, thinking of his lack of experience.

"Don't worry, I will, but I've never seen a diltz before." Sal laughed, too.

"Well, sometimes you see it like a spanner in your soup, and sometimes you never see it and swear it isn't there—until someone else spots it. If it's here this time, I hope somebody trips over it soon, because the chief'll run out of suggestions and we'll be starting over again. He doesn't like Fire-eyes on his back."

"He doesn't like the supervisor?"

"Oh, I wouldn't say that. I don't think he's afraid of her, either, but he makes sure things happen when she's involved. He's jumpier, pushes our asses harder, you know? But don't get me wrong. The chief is the best there is. They're a real team here. He knows how to run a section, and he does it without rank getting in the way."

Pol settled down to concentrate on the rhythms generated by the statistics. He stayed with Sal because the Six was inclined to explain things as he went along; in fact, his chatter was constant. When he came to a point where a summation or suggestion could be made, he would dictate a note into his oral script. His speed was incredible, fingers racing over the keys like a concert pianist. Pol complimented him on it.

"Yeah, well. The chief says I'm *too* fast, that I probably miss things I'd see at a slower pace. He doesn't understand that I feel comfortable like this. The chunks actually go together better this way, you know? I can concentrate on the whole rather than the parts. I like to see things grow."

Pol's experience in fiscal matters was limited to classroom Advanced theory, but with the help of Sal's running commentary, the figures became more organic and he was able to ingest something of the overall picture of currency flow. A very large but finite sum of money would branch into smaller streams, branch again and again, rejoining into myriad combinations. Under trained or intuitive eyes, patterns emerged and words that were once more appropriate to physics seemed to apply: inertia, momentum, fulcrum, vector, and so on. He began to sense the addiction that struck computermen, making them into ascetic slaves. With these machines, everything was imbued with order, so long as it was rendered into quantity, given a number. And the right buttons were tapped. He was almost mesmerized by it when Sal jolted him back.

"Well, I think that's as far as I can go. The digger was able to establish the entry times for large, unaccounted for influxes of money into the system on Shalom with a small margin of error. That would have to be phony stuff."

Sal leaned back in his chair and fiddled with the toggle switches on his oral script. Then he shrugged elaborately.

"Can you think of any way that those entry times would be reflected on Leaf or Cosmos if one of them was the bad guy?"

"Uh, you mean like certain people are suddenly richer when they're not supposed to be?"

"Yeah, like that . . . but we wouldn't have that kind of minute data. I doubt that it was available locally, either, or the digger would have been after it. Those worlds aren't highly computerized. If Shalom had been, she wouldn't be in this mess, because a credit system would be in use instead of old-fashioned currency."

"Well, if we're stuck, why don't we just do a broad spectrum correlation on whatever we *do* have, then—or can we?"

"Oh, we can *do* it all right. This baby"—he patted the terminal as if it were a pet—"can do handstands. But it'll take a while, and we'll get a hell of a lot of crap, you know? But who cares? I've done all I can think of, anyway. Okay, I'll program for a match between the times of influx on Shalom and everything we have on the other two worlds.

"Hey, Pol. How come I feel like shit and you look as fresh as mother's milk?" Sal peered at him with mock suspicion before resuming a smooth finger beat on the keys. "The chief has been after me to apply for his section after Basic Training—cook up a number Five project that would fit—but even though I love this stuff, the hours get to me. Hemorrhoids always in orbit, you know?"

He had just enough time to put in the program before the next bull session. Sal was as nervous as a hummingbird when he wasn't playing his music at a terminal. His fluttering became more accentuated as the session progressed, because he was unconsciously reacting to the frustration and fatigue of the others.

"It's just possible that there *is* no diltz," said a Four, after a negative report. Sal jumped when Wal's fist came down hard on the table.

"No! It is *not* possible! That much phony money cannot flow through a system without leaving tracks. We just haven't seen them yet. Change your mind-sets. Give!"

"All right, chief," said Sal. "You asked for it. I hope you're ready for this. We did a broad spectrum correlation between the currency entry times on Shalom and the whole economic picture on the other two. It's been cooking and should be ready by now." He began punching.

"I'll be warped," said Wal. "We *are* getting desperate."

"Do we have time for this?" asked another. "Just like rookies. Games that waste computer time." Sal began without waiting for permission.

"Only the double correlations for openers. That narrows the field, okay? Entry times on Shalom match the following fluctuations on *both* Leaf and Cosmos: ladies' jewelry sales, up; holovision sets, down; alcohol, down; income tax for male prostitutes, up (there were tense guffaws); dental supplies, down; tourism, up . . ."

On it went, a long litany. Soon there were only blank stares as information overload took effect. Pol began to feel ashamed that his suggestion was wasting time. But Sal continued quite happily until Wal interrupted.

"Enough! This may help later, when we have something to filter out some of the garbage. Right now"—he rolled tired eyes to the ceiling—"I'd rather wallow in space bilge."

Until this moment, Pol had said nothing at the bull sessions, but wanting to contribute had become almost painful. He leaned his arms on the table, making himself part of the group before speaking.

"Can I ask a few questions, er, chief?" Wal nodded. He welcomed an opportunity to shift to solid ground—answering the queries of a greenhorn—because he didn't know where to go from here.

"So far, we have no idea how the counterfeit money actually entered Shalom's economy?"

"Nope. The digger didn't unearth a single source. It looks like it came in all over the place, like a rainstorm on a pond. Apparently, the phony stuff is good and passes easily. The Shalom authorities have picked up literally hundreds of people who were using it since the digger's report was made available.

No connection to a source, though. Frankly, I can't see how such massive sums could be squeezed into the flow without collusion from the banking interests on Shalom."

"Neither did Chiefs of Staff," interjected a sharp female voice from the open doorway. "Remain as you are, gentlemen." Fire-eyes strode into the room, gesturing them back into their chairs. "But Shalom denies the possibility of an internal conspiracy. Considering the fact that their 'banking interests' run the place and are losing more than anybody, I'm inclined to believe them." She sat on the table's edge, a sleek cat claiming ownership of anything she touched. Her eyes flashed around the group.

"All right, what have you got so far?" Wal snorted out his disgust.

"Not much . . . nothing, actually. We've just been brainstorming, fishing for the diltz."

"I beg your pardon?"

"Sorry, Supervisor, shop jargon." The others made silent prayers that their chief would not dive into another explanation of his notorious diltz.

"We've been over the works. We need something new. I have a feeling about this one—too neat, too pat. There are usually hundreds of false trails in a case like this, and we track them down until something hits us in the nose. This one is as big a systems problem as we ever get—an ocean of data— but we haven't even found false trails." He held thumb and forefinger over the table as if holding an eyedropper.

"My gut says that if we squeeze a drop of the right stuff into this ocean, the whole damn thing will gel."

Wal spoke as bluntly and naturally to the supervisor as to anyone else. That was why, though he was unaware of it, Fire-eyes favored him. Pol, however, had become quickly aware. When her famous eyes rested on Wal, they lingered a half second longer than was necessary. He detected subtle shades of compromise in her tones when she spoke to him, and her body-set softened. As well (Pol surprised himself in this), he could detect an elusive scent of sexual fragrance that he had never recognized before, yet he knew instinctively what it was. It disturbed him simply because he was male, even though it was not meant for him. Like the pheromones of a bee, he thought. To the others, Fire-eyes was, as always, the supervisor with uncanny eyes, startling hair, and tough hide.

"Your 'gut' is no doubt a sensitive instrument, Wal. But it's not pointing anywhere, is it? However, continue your brainstorm. At the risk of getting wet, I'll sit in for a while."

"Our new lad was asking questions about how the large sums of counterfeit currency got into the works. You answered yourself—we don't know."

The piercing green eyes moved to meet the penetrating blue ones; they locked.

"Were you simply asking for information, or did you have an idea?" The green eyes flickered when the softly controlled, curiously compelling voice answered. She was accustomed to inspiring self-consciousness, especially in young officers. She didn't know Pol shook inside. He made his decision and jumped off a cliff.

"I have the germ of an idea, Supervisor. Do you have any new information about the Cadre One officer?"

"Yes. Murder confirmed. Poisoned in a nightclub favored by prosperous crooks."

"His cover involved being recruited by the people we're looking for as a big-time money passer?"

"That is correct. It was arranged so that an impressive reputation preceded him. He even had his own phony money to disperse as bait."

"Do you think he was murdered because his cover was broken or because it wasn't broken?"

"I don't follow," she answered in a clipped voice. Pol took note of the signs of impatience and plunged ahead.

"I mean, did they know he was Cadre?"

"Field investigation is not my department." The eyes locked again, momentarily. Then, reluctantly, she continued. "But I will say this: Cadre One covers are rarely broken, and rarer still is a One murdered. Most know better."

"So in all probability, he was killed as a money passer." Wal's interest suddenly flared higher.

"But if they fell for his cover, why should they kill him? He would have been useful to them!"

Pol nodded. "Or they might decide to get rid of a man whose activities would interfere with theirs, especially if they had what they considered to be a foolproof distribution system already."

The supervisor's figurine features remained lifeless, but her lashes dropped and her scrutiny of Pol became more intense. She spoke softly.

"I don't know if the thinking of Chiefs of Staff has led in this direction, but it smells right to me. Keep going."

"Your correlations, Sal. You said that tourism was up on both Leaf and Cosmos in a cycle matching the influxes of counterfeit on Shalom. Where were the tourists from?"

Sal stared curiously at Pol until he was prodded by a simple "Well?" from the supervisor. His fingers flew over the keys. He finished and looked up in amazement.

"The only significant increase is from one source—Shalom."

The heads around the table swiveled comically back to Pol like inspection globes on an assembly line. Before anyone could comment, he asked another question.

"Is that very unusual?" More rapid-fire tapping from Sal.

"Before the period of Shalom's inflation, tourism to both Leaf and Cosmos was lower by several degrees of magnitude—and it wasn't cyclical."

"And the cycles match those of the phony money."

"Yes, or it wouldn't have come out of this program."

Pol frowned and spoke cautiously, beating down his excitement. "Then this may be the diltz."

The supervisor brought the full force of her green glare on Wal. He was speaking before she could. "He's got something, Supervisor! Disgorge it, Pol."

"Do we have the names of those picked up by Shalom authorities for passing phony money?"

More tapping from Sal.

"Yes, we do."

"And the names of her tourists to Leaf or Cosmos?"

Sal's fingers were a blur. "Of those questioned by Shalom police, eighteen point nine percent made visits to Leaf or Cosmos in the last four years."

There was a long silence. One by one, each began a careful reappraisal of the young man with the plain features and extraordinary blue eyes.

"Is that significant?"

"Significant!" cried Wal. "It's the diltz! You're not bloody human!"

Later investigation found that highly placed officials on Leaf and Cosmos had conspired in the manufacture of vast sums of counterfeit Shalom currency. They set up front companies to offer inexpensive tourist packages to Shalom natives. In return for the savings, tourists had to make all currency exchanges through certain banking institutions during their visits. Thousands of loyal Shalom citizens eventually returned home as passers of counterfeit money. Large amounts of legal currency remained behind in the hands of Shalom's competitors. It was a double-pronged attack because they could use the good money to exacerbate Shalom's balance of payments problem.

The accolades that fell on the shoulders of the ferrets finally brought the chief and Fire-eyes together. In their more restful moments, Pol was a main topic of conversation. Both were surprised at how quickly he had become a good ferret. They found him intriguing also because they saw few of the symptoms of the young tadpole fresh out of Basic Training.

They decided to file a special report of commendation on him to central HQ. They were disappointed and a little angry when it was acknowledged without comment.

At the end of his stint, Pol returned to the complex, as did his classmates. They came in from all over the galaxy, full of stories about strange places. Now they were magnificent young men and women of twenty-one and twenty-two. They lusted after the yellow piping that marked the end of Basic Training.

Again, the ceremony was simple and solemn; again, it was in the little lecture theater that always seemed to house new beginnings for them. The commanding officer of the complex stood on a small dais. He was old, pushing upright a body bent under the weight of years and the cape of his shoulders. But he lent his office dignity, and it was considered appropriate for officers of all ranks to spend the last stage of their careers in the training of those following.

Pol watched with burning eyes as the C.O. finished a short speech about Cadre traditions and raised the ceremonial parchment with its list of names.

"Officer Tass Pel." A young woman rose from her seat, capeless, walked to the dais, and saluted.

"Congratulations, Cadre Six," murmured the C.O. She turned to face the audience, and with a grand flourish, the C.O. swept a cape onto her shoulders, its collar glowing gold. She saluted once more before marching, straight-backed, to her seat.

"Officer Dace Sestus."

Ses popped to his feet and strode down the aisle wearing a smile that bounced off the walls. As the cape settled, the C.O. added a sentence to the ritual.

"A special commendation for exemplary duty removes the gaps in this officer's collar piping. Congratulations, Cadre Six."

Pol was proud of his only real friend but winced inside when he found a hot layer of envy there. Feeling that his contribution to the ferrets' coup had its element of luck, he was not resentful, but he was chagrined that some seemed to be leaving him behind. Two more trainees received the special collar; he donned the yellow without fanfare.

With the ruthlessness of a fighting cock at an enemy's throat, he ripped out the shameful envy when he congratulated Ses afterward, but it was a long time before he could talk about it. They were walking back to their shared quarters after a class when Pol made a casual remark about the gaps in his collar. Even this little foible took Ses by surprise.

"Listen, ol' buddy. The collar doesn't fool anybody. You're the only one around here who doesn't concede that you're the best of our bunch." He looked hard at Pol. "You're too good for your *own* good, maybe. Bothers me sometimes." Pol sniffed loudly at that, but he was moved by his friend's rare seriousness.

"Thanks, Ses, but the collar does mean something. I had fooled myself into thinking I deserved it, too, that's all."

"Hey, that sounds interesting. Tell me about it."

"What?"

"Your B.T. assignment. You haven't said a word about it. Give."

So Pol told him about his part in the computer investigation with Wal and Fire-eyes. As he talked, Ses became more somber. He threw a hand in the air when Pol finished.

"I don't get it, Pol. I don't see the *luck* in that. You should have got that commendation. Shit." Pol only shrugged.

"Obviously not. Yours . . . Hey!"

"Yeah, I know, roomie. Never told you. Never told anyone. Not like me, right?"

"Your turn to give, Ses."

Ses pursed his lips, lowered his head—and blushed. The unruly orange mop that even the Cadre had failed to tame fell over his forehead.

"Okay, Pol. I'm telling you this because you think the Cadre's infallible. Because you think I'm a hotshot and you're not. I'll track you to the ends of the universe if you . . ." Then his cocky grin came back. "Sorry, I know you wouldn't. Besides, nobody would believe you."

"C'mon, Ses."

"It's embarrassing, but I'm getting there, okay? They put me on a surveillance assignment under a number Two."

"No kidding! Surveillance. A number Two!"

"Relax." Ses chuckled. "I *think* I saw a Two there once. From a distance. Mostly, I worked with Operations types. Turned out the glamorous assignment consisted of baby-sitting a wall full of listening equipment in a jail-size room. Real exciting."

"Then how . . . ?"

"Give me a chance, will you? I don't even know why we're looking for this guy, but we've got the ears on his piece of fluff on the off chance he'll try to contact her. Anyway, there's really nothing to do. Three days produce a couple of videophone conversations with her hairdresser, so I'm really getting bored. I'm yawning into my late shift while my aging partner sleeps right through his." Ses rubbed his chin and looked sideways at Pol as they walked. "So I decided to call her." Pol stopped in his tracks.

"You what!"

"Yep. I figured we were covering a long shot and it wouldn't make any difference. She was dumber than she was sexy, Pol— and she was sexy! The old stereotype. Crook's bimbo. If I make the call, I get to see her again on the video, right? One other time, she answered from the bathtub. Didn't care who was calling, either."

"But, Ses . . . you were taking an awful chance. You could have been . . . the Cadre . . ."

"Naw. Nobody would know." Pol was distressed, though he didn't know if it was because he was worried about Ses's welfare or his friend's cavalier view of duty.

"Anyway, I get her call number from the signal tone on the recording crystal by putting its sound through this little specialized computer. Nifty machine. Then I take the crystal out of our recorder and call. I'm not on video, but *she* sure is." Ses made smacking noises with his lips. "Luscious thing. Happy to have somebody to talk to. I tell her that a 'mutual friend' gave me the number, but can't say his name over the phone. She nods like a rocking horse, all excited about getting into the action, right? Big, bouncy boobs. Pretty soon we're old friends. She's even throwing hints about being lonely. 'Love to meet one of—uh—*his* friends,' she said. I put her off and tell her I have to see him right away. 'Is he still at the same place?' I ask. And she gives it to me! Dumb!" Ses laughed so hard he stopped to lean against a wall.

"You found out where the man was?"

"You got it, roomie. I sign off and put the crystal back in. But now I'm getting nervous because I can't *tell* them, right? A two-bit Seven playing games like that. But the ol' master sees a light go on." Ses grinned, winked, and tapped his head. "When I get back to HQ, I request computer time for 'study purposes.' I have enough info to pull the case file. I'm only after one thing—and sure enough, it's there: a full description of the guy they're after. Off duty, I get some civvies and check out the address the girl gave me. Turns out he's managing a cutthroat credit bureau under an assumed name. I go back to HQ, tell them—sheepishly—about this guy I run into in a bar who brags about slipping his hand into the till, and shouldn't they cue the local constabulary. I give them a *very* detailed description. Of course, they put it through their own mill first, and eureka—they find their man! And I'm a hero."

Pol shook his head, bemused. His image of the Cadre and of Ses vibrated, threatened to jar out of place.

"Ses, you're crazy. One of these days you're really going to get in trouble."

"Not me, ol' buddy. I was scared enough to learn my lesson. The point of all this, my friend, is that I stumbled into a commendation—and this no-gap collar—through the back door." Ses turned to Pol at their door. "The Cadre's not a religion, Pol; it's not God."

"Well . . . you did get *results*, Ses. What else matters?"

Ses just smiled and shook his head ruefully. He slapped his plate into its slot and was whipping his cape off and slinging it through the entrance before it was fully opened.

"You're incurable, ol' buddy. But what the hell. Number Five, here we come!"

SY 3028

COUNCIL EYES ONLY

Internal Security: Recording Transcript

(Ass't. Dir've ds 2a)

Recordees: Cadre Six Officers Pol Tyrees, Dace Sestus
Time: 06 23 3028
Place: Shared quarters, Advanced Training billet, Sector
           I
Occasion: CEO directive—ongoing, random

(RECORDING BEGINS—TRANSCRIPT BEGINS)

Sestus: ...what the hell. Number Five, here we come!
Tyrees: I should be hitting the math. It may be responsible for
         the first-known suicide of a number Six.
Sestus: You should worry. Either your name's on the complex
         letterhead, or it's on the top of all the evaluation lists
         around here.
Tyrees: Yeah, well, you already know that it came the hard
         way—sweat, not brains.
Sestus: Tell me the difference, roomie. I haven't exactly been

126

on vacation around here, either.

Tyrees: You don't know how to concentrate, Ses. If you'd do those exercises I showed you . . .

Sestus: Pol, ol' buddy, if I practiced your 'exercises,' I wouldn't have time to do anything else.

Tyrees: Forget it. You decide on your research project yet?

Sestus: Are you kidding? Mind if I finish Advanced Training first? They may decide to keep me a Six just so I can nurse mindless romantics like you. Doubtless *you* have the project nailed down five years early—or are you going to skip the brown entirely? I realize it would clash with your eyes.

Tyrees: I told you, Ses. I'm going to work on the Holtz Effect.

Sestus: I obliterated that little tidbit from my memory because it's such a nutty idea, ramjet. The best minds in the galaxy have been slugging away at that ever since your grandfather released his findings. And they've come up with damn little.

Tyrees: Not necessarily. There may be classified stuff that I'll get when my project is approved.

Sestus: Birdshit. There's nothing classified. They've been trying to solve that joke for so long that they'd be afraid of keeping information from anybody who might stumble onto something.

(Recording crystal verified—legitimate twenty-one seconds silence—minor background noise)

Sestus: The Holtz Effect. You're just trying to add glory to the ol' family name, aren't you, roomie?

Tyrees: No comment.

Sestus: I know you, nova-nose, you'd walk with bent light to follow Granddad—wouldn't you? Seriously, Pol, I'd hate to see a headlock put on that famous Tyrees determination, but this wild gooser may do it.

Tyrees: Listen, child, the Holtz Effect, for all its mystery, is just another problem to solve. Besides, I've got something the experts haven't.

Sestus: Oh, have you now? So give.

Tyrees: I've got Grandfather's personal notes. Just speculations and such, but if I know him as well as I think I do, there's something to work on there. He never quit on anything in his life.

Sestus: So?

Tyrees: The Cadre released his initial findings a long time ago. He was the first to tie the Holtz Effect to the Alien Contact Theory. He wouldn't just leave off there— unless something deathly serious got in the way.

Sestus: In other words, he was just like his grandson. What makes you think he found anything new?

Tyrees: Well, his best friend, Hans Bolla, hinted that he was on to something before he died. Wouldn't elaborate, though.

Sestus: That ancient reprobate? The one whose books have been squeezing my brain? What would a psychologist know about the Holtz Effect?

Tyrees: That "ancient reprobate" is doing classified work as a Regnum commissioner, so he doesn't just write text-books.

Sestus: The brass has probably already been through those papers, chum, and don't tell me it would be illegal to tamper with a bequest.

Tyrees: Even if they have, they don't know him the way I do.

Sestus: You are a stubborn bastard. Two in one family. It warps my mind.

Tyrees: Careful, or I'll be defending the family name in the combat room.

Sestus: Okay, tiger, I give up. What happened to the old boy anyway?

Tyrees: Don't know. I saw him last when he was Vice-Proctor, not long before our orientation. I was told he was dead—officially. Everything else was classified.

Sestus: Classified?

Tyrees: Yeah ... and I was told by the Chairman himself, too.

Sestus: What? No kidding! Sonofabitch!

Tyrees: Yeah. It still bothers me. Something...

Sestus: Something what? Your granddad must have been quite a guy for the Chairman to—

Tyrees: That's just what I mean, Ses. Why would he do that? The Chairman doesn't go around holding the hands of Cadre orphans, does he? Maybe, just maybe, Ses, Grandfather is still alive, so—

Sestus: Pol, don't say it! Now I know why you're so red-eyed obsessed about him. Shit.

Tyrees: Ses, don't start again. Please. I shouldn't have said anything.

Sestus: But it's fucking crazy! I'm beginning to see where you get that God-awful dedication from. Don't do that to yourself. You're better off thinking he's dead!

Tyrees: Don't say that. He's all I ever had . . . but I know you're right. I suppose I just *want* him alive—watching me do well in the Cadre.

Sestus: It's gonna do funny things to your head, Pol.

Tyrees: No, it won't. I just can't let anything get in the way. I . . . can't really explain, but I have to start with the Holtz Effect.

Sestus: Back to the HE shit.

Tyrees: I owe it to Grandfather, Ses. He believes . . . *believed* in me.

Sestus: Listen, Pol, I envy you. You've got . . . drive, and, well, you know where you're going and you've got what it takes to get there—more. And a famous grandfather to be proud of. I come from a long line of cutthroat merchants. But you scare me. . . . Don't let a dead man dictate your life, roomie. You're not used to me talking like this, but . . . blast it, you're special. The guys know it and I know it better. I mean it. Don't go nova because you feel you should finish somebody else's life. Pol, are you listening to me?

Tyrees: I appreciate your concern, Ses, but there's no need for it.

Sestus: Someday you'll be a big boy like Granddad, chum, only you don't have to do what he did, okay? Okay?

Tyrees: You can drop it now, turnip-top.

(Recording crystal verified—fifty-nine seconds silence)

Sestus: Pol?

Tyrees: What?

Sestus: Your granddad's not the only one you've got, so you don't have to keep him alive.

Tyrees: What?

Sestus: You've got *me*, you stubborn bastard. Kill that light.

(TRANSCRIPT ENDS—RECORDING ENDS)

SY 3032

CHAIRMAN'S EYES ONLY

(Excerpt from) *Recording Transcript*—**Chairman's Automatic Surveillance System**

Recordees: Chairman, Council of the Regnum; Proctor of the
              Security Cadre
Time: 18 49 3032
Place: Chairman's private offices
Occasion: Automatic surveillance

(RECORDING BEGINS—TRANSCRIPT BEGINS)

Chairman: Well, Proctor, how's our little chick doing?
Proctor: He's doing well, sir. But he's no longer a chick.
           He's about to don the Brown, you know. He did
           a splendid job in his two field assignments.
Chairman: I know, Proctor. You're not the only one keeping
           tabs on him, though it's a hobby I can ill afford
           the time for. This morning was the first occasion
           in about a year I punched for an update. And I
           saw something that would lead me to believe you've
           been trying to keep him under wraps.

Proctor: Chairman, you know perfectly well—

Chairman: All right, all right, simmer down. You know what's bothering me. He wants to work on the Holtz Effect. Should he be stopped?

(Recording crystal verified—legitimate sixteen seconds silence)

Chairman: Come on, Proctor. I know it's difficult for you to be objective in this.

Proctor: Yes, it is, Chairman. But that doesn't prevent me from making the right decisions. He's so absorbed with the Holtz Effect that we might destroy his usefulness to the Cadre by thwarting him. Besides, the Vice-Proctor is not supposed to refuse any "reasonable" project request.

Chairman: Cadre traditions have a low priority in this. Are you certain that allowing him his project won't backfire in the long run?

Proctor: Actually, I'm not certain; I'm worried about it. But I still feel a loose rein is the best course. We can accept his project as completed if he starts getting close. I've said before that I consider him to be an important potential resource for the Cadre.

Chairman: Yes, a resource that you insist we don't exploit!

Proctor: Chairman, I feel strongly about this. He's only now becoming aware of his own capabilities. If we make him into a guinea pig, he may never develop that potential. Besides, putting him under a microscope doesn't guarantee results, either, especially if it's against his will.

Chairman: Relax, Proctor. I'm still willing to go along with you for the time being. I gather that a medical study would be impossible anyway?

Proctor: Absolutely. We could do nothing that would directly affect his body functions without his knowledge. If he is allowed to develop naturally, in his own fashion, he will have a great deal to give to the Cadre when the time comes.

Chairman: But what if these things are not teachable? What if it's a question of straight genetics? And how long does he need?

Proctor: Well, he may need years, Chairman, but it's a good investment. As for his talents, we already know that some of them *are* teachable. Some of our Ones—I, for that matter—can do things he can do. After training, of course.

Chairman: Humph. He was doing most of those little tricks when he was a child.

Proctor: That doesn't change anything, Chairman. If we assume the worst—that few of his abilities are trainable—we still have *him*. I know his mind as well as I know my own, and if he ever comes to suspect that the Cadre would treat him as an experiment, he would . . . well, he wouldn't cooperate. And the psychological assessments back me up. In my humble opinion—

Chairman: You have yet to express a humble opinion, Proctor.

(Recording crystal verified—legitimate twenty seconds silence—minor background noise)

Chairman: Very well. Carry on. But you'd better pray those years you're asking for don't turn into hours, because that's what would happen if the Council decided to take an interest. You're fortunate that most of them don't know of his existence, but remember that they have access to the information, should they care to look. I suppose there's more than enough to distract them. The Trade Wars could swallow us all if we don't keep the plug in, and our little hobby wouldn't be worth a fart in a vacuum anyway. Which reminds me . . . he's got to be kept out of the action if he's, humph, "a valuable resource."

Proctor: "*Potential* resource." Yes, Chairman. That will be a simple matter. The Holtz Effect will keep him out of the present trouble.

Chairman: All right. Humph. I just wish he'd chosen a more useful project. His utility to the Cadre won't exactly be enhanced by work on the HE, will it?

Proctor: In one sense, it's better this way because I can control things more tightly.

Chairman: All right, all right. Just keep me informed, will you? I haven't the time to keep double-checking you.

Proctor: Chairman . . .

Chairman: Never mind. Let's get to more important matters, shall we? Have you worked on the manpower problem?

Proctor: I have. I've increased the personnel in the Hub by twenty percent, overt and covert, though it's getting harder to get them into the trouble spots. I've reduced the Political Section for that purpose. Alien Section was already cut to the bone, and I can't see making it any thinner—not without starting talk even outside the Cadre.

Chairman: Humph. That'll have to do for now, I suppose. I don't mind admitting I'm getting frightened. Things are starting to boil over. Can you push recruitment?

Proctor: Yes, but I can't guarantee discretion. The process has too many mechanisms that touch the public sector.

Chairman: Forget it for now, then. I may have to dip into the military—but, humph, that has its own problems. If I had only one enemy, in one place, I would blast him to oblivion. . . .

Proctor: I wouldn't recommend that sort of thing, Chairman. The Council—

Chairman: Damn the Council! . . . Ah, forgive me, Proctor. Tired, I guess.

Proctor: Of course, Chairman. Uh, are Bolla's people . . . ?

Chairman: Still working, still working. You know that crusty old hullbut won't pontificate until he's ready, and he's more likely to go to full Council than just to me.

Proctor: I urge you not to minimize his work, sir. Without him, we may not have begun at all.

Chairman: Yes, yes. I've been rereading his stuff lately, and I've decided that it's time to stir up a little more healthy xenophobia—all in the interest of public education, of course. A holovision documentary about the probability of hostile aliens . . .

SY 3034

Pol Tyrees's career progressed relatively smoothly for several years after leaving the training complex. He did feel the disappointment of a boy sent to bed in the middle of a favorite holovision show when he was pulled off his Cadre Five research project. He thought it premature because all he accomplished were some improvements on certain programming techniques. (Even they sprang out of suggestions from Hans Bolla.) The Holtz Effect itself, a brittle wall of mystery, had bounced back his puny charges. However, his Vice-Proctor expressed high satisfaction with the minor technical achievements and proclaimed his project terminated—an automatic promotion to Cadre Four. The fact that Operations was the *real* beginning for a Cadre officer softened his chagrin.

As a Four, he worked like a man pursued by devils—as indeed he was—and built an excellent record. Evaluation reports praised his drive. To him, problems were rats to a terrier, targets that enticed him and narrowed his vision, focused his energies. Like a dog bred for the purpose, once his teeth closed on flesh, they would not release. He developed a bloodhound's skill in research investigation. His background work pointed the way for field men so successfully that he was often requested by name for support by Ones and Twos.

Still, it wasn't long before he chafed to be unshackled from the display screens and swivel chairs, from the artifice of the electron. The Hub was seething to the point where Cadre personnel expressed their anxiety openly. He wanted to join the cause. But when the blue collar of the digger came, his first assignment sent him far from the Hub to a hideously misnamed world called Eden. She was a "degenerate"—a worthless chunk of wasteland feebly colonized during the Diaspora. She had regressed into semibarbarism because she possessed nothing worth trading or stealing. Internal squabbles had reduced her to a patchwork of tented fiefdoms—hundreds of them. This rendered Eden's appeal to the Regnum for economic aid ridiculous. It had come from a single brigand leader who claimed to speak for the whole planet. It was delivered by a laconic free-lance trader who had been forced to land there to barter for provisions. Pol allowed that the leader's name, "Crazy Max," was quite appropriate.

Nevertheless, the authorities had never had a legitimate opportunity to gather information about Eden, so it seemed prudent to send a Cadre Three to do just that. Accordingly, Pol's assignment directive was vague; he was ordered to observe and gather information that might be "germane to Regnum security." He had no negotiating powers and was ordered to impress this upon "those in authority." The job was strictly a passive one, suitable for a fledgling digger, but Pol soon had reason to regret that passivity.

Using the coordinates provided by the free-lance trader, Pol's transport made landfall where *he* had, near the encampment of the fiefdom chief, Crazy Max. The sight from the top of the ramp should have been enough. Into the middle distance stretched a shambling collection of makeshift tents and shacks propped up out of the thin mud. They were made of boards and scrap metal, cloth and hides, with low-lying smoke drifting over and between them. Odors from unimaginable sources obliterated Pol's nostrils, making them pinch closed convulsively. He could see no suggestion of order except for a few ditches meant—he hoped—to carry off excess water.

Gathering quickly under the small Cadre vessel was a ragtag mob of long-haired, skin-clad, vagabondish people staring up at him with blank eyes. Hope had never shone in them—but hunger had, and so had rapine. When the bearded mouths parted, he saw mostly black holes. Teeth in evidence were dark and wide-spaced. The young had distended stomachs. Few were old.

"Good luck," muttered the vessel's captain with as much pity as sarcasm. "Your kit's already below. Remember, I can take a signal in six days as I swing by. Two weeks again, after that." With a crinkle of his nose, he stamped back in, bellowing at his crew to ready for lift-off immediately. Pol knew that six days would be far more than enough. Those eyes sent a mixed message of apathy and violence. He shivered at their touch.

As he came down the ramp, several muscular types, well fed relative to the rest, shoved open with forearm swipes a ragged passageway through the mob. Through it shambled a tall figure in outlandish costume. It was skirted and belted and tied in a tailor's nightmare of leathers and hides and thongs. Poking in all directions were knife handles and hatchet hafts and chain loops. Like Pol, he wore a cape, except that this was some sort of matted fur in a confusion of dull hues. When he reached Pol, he stood there grinning, gap-toothed, a parody of a king with a parody of a smile.

"Welcome, Cadre! Welcome to Eden!" Pol took the hand that swung out from the long pile of hangings. Where skin showed, it was a dull slug white, speckled with discolorations.

"Pol Tyrees, Cadre Three. I—"

"You are young, no?"

"I—"

"No matter." The apparition laughed and scratched a large hair-tufted wart on his cheek. "I didn't think *anybody* would come. Not to *us*, eh? But you *did*, eh? You give us food, metal—guns, mebbe. Money? Money to buy from other worlds. Then Crazy Max delivers Eden to the Regnum like meat on a spit, eh?"

"I'm sorry—sir. I'm only here as an observer. I have no authority to make any decisions. But I will certainly carry back your requests." Crazy Max's bushy eyebrows pulled closer together. The beard lifted.

"Then why come? You are"—he waved disdainfully at his bodyguards—"a lackey!"

"Not exactly. My superiors will base their decisions on my report."

"Huh! Well . . . then you come. Come and—and 'observe' *all* you like, eh?" The horrible grin returned. "You will see that Crazy Max is obeyed. Look." He pointed at several of his bodyguards. On the forehead of each was branded a crude fist. Crazy Max raised his own and laughed. "I am not weak like the other fools on this world who try to lead like children. I am obeyed!" With a grand flourish, he opened his cape wide. The underside revealed shriveled, caplike discs, sewn edge to edge. It was only then that Pol realized that the cape was made from human scalps. His head swam. He could only nod dumbly. Crazy Max reached out a hand to touch Pol's cape, as if in instinctive recognition that it, too, was a totem dipped in blood. The soft, shimmering cloth of deepest black seemed to mesmerize him. Before his fingers actually made contact, his eyes sought Pol's and found there such frozen, implacable blue that his fingers curled back on themselves and the gesture was arrested. Instead, he spat on the ground.

"Come!"

That afternoon, Pol sat on a dirty cushion, waving at tiny but voracious insects, as Max explained how he was going to bring Eden into the Regnum as a unified world—under his leadership. He was going to do this anyway, but Regnum's help would speed up the process. Pol heard nothing, saw nothing that he liked and little that he understood. He felt unclean and absurdly embarrassed that he shared a common species with the Edenites. Slowly, Crazy Max's crude eloquence began to flag in the face of his visitor's noncommittal silence. Finally, he stopped and sat, pulling on his beard, fixing Pol with that blank, unlit gaze. Then he stood abruptly to bark an order. A shapeless woman appeared carrying a basket of flyblown, applelike fruit. Every eye within fifty meters turned to that basket. It was apparent that food was the legal tender on Eden— probably because so much valuable time was devoted to fighting instead of growing, thought Pol. Crazy Max raised his eyebrows in surprise at Pol's refusal of one of his delicacies. He shrugged and flopped back down to his pillow. Idly, negligently, he crossed his ankles, waggled his booted toes, and bit into the fruit. He chewed abstractedly. Pol took in the loose and sagging flesh under Crazy Max's chin, the fenced and yellowed horse teeth. The body is languid, but the eyes are cunning, moving like steel bearings captured in dull glass, rolling to the lolling of an indolent neck. He watches his people watching him. Between lazy bites he lifts the end of his beard to wipe his mouth. His people watch closer. He stops chewing and grins. The gaps between his teeth are as wide as highways.

Limp-wristed, he tosses the half-eaten fruit up and down. Once, twice, three times. He pauses. His people watch and, quite literally, lean forward. Again: once, twice, three times. His eyes roll back and forth, watching his people watch.

Then, with a careless motion, a gesture born to those convinced of their own divinity, he flips the fruit into the air. His people watch it arch and fall into the mud. He watches his people clamp shaky wills on bodies that would lunge at a piece of overripe fruit gathering a swarm of insects out of the mud. His heavy-lidded eyes watch theirs fall away. Now they watch the fruit only in their memories as it fell through space and landed a million miles away. He yawns elaborately, draws up splayed feet, and pushed himself upright with a grunt. He takes a last look, grins a last grin, and shambles, arms heavy and low, to his tent. Before he enters, he turns to wink at Pol.

The fruit was still there in the morning.

Pol spent several days with a permanent ball of acid in his gorge, waiting for the six days to come to an end. So many of the Regnum Charter's principles were violated on Eden that *any* kind of negotiation was impossible, let alone membership. On the fourth day, one of Crazy Max's far-casting patrols came back with several prisoners, and Pol couldn't believe his eyes. They were clean, handsome, unscarred. Even more surprising, they seemed relatively unafraid, though the patrol was delighted with its catch and the nod of approval from Crazy Max. Pol questioned one of the henchmen eagerly, thinking he had landed within the barbarian fringes of a world that had its civilized element after all. That hope was short-lived. The half dozen unblemished specimens were simply house pets. Over the past few months, Crazy Max's brigands had been mopping up after routing a rival horde in the next river valley. The vanquished mogul's fondest hobby had been to breed, raise, and cloister a covey of personal lapdogs in the form of people. They were taught nothing but basic speech and some amusing games. They were pampered, fed well, and kept in total isolation from all but the "royal" family, who were little more sophisticated than Crazy Max. Miserable and confused after fending for themselves the past few weeks, they were relieved to have been found by new masters. Pol was amazed by Crazy Max's friendliness when he questioned his childlike captives. He even clasped one—a fair, curly-haired young man—to his breast. The cherubic but strong-looking Adonis (who seemed to dote on an

equally young and beautiful woman beside him) smiled shyly.
Crazy Max pinched his cheek and muttered reassurances before
sending them all to a tent under heavy guard.

"We have found others like these before," he said to Pol,
and tapped a split-nailed finger on his forehead. "But I did not
understand. I let them die too soon. We will see them again
later, eh?"

Pol turned away.

The fourth night, he sat cross-legged in a ragged circle with
Max and his favorites around a sputtering fire. Its smoke stung
his eyes. The grease from their dinner—something lank that
was skinned, spitted, and roasted—still sizzled when flames
hit a drip spot. The atmosphere was morose: Max was angered
by the aloofness of the Cadre whelp he was forced to impress;
his henchmen simply reflected his mood; Pol stewed in the
funk of his revulsion, anxious for the return of his transport
and worried about the next travesty he would have to witness.
He had eaten almost nothing since his arrival and knew that
Crazy Max had taken this as an insult.

Finally, Max tossed a piece of fat at the fire and leaned over
to mutter into the nearest ear. The man rose hastily and scurried
off. In a few minutes, he returned with two of the house pets—
the handsome couple—in tow. Both ducked and smiled, quite
flattered when invited to join the group for a bowl of wine.

Max's eyes never left the two. They touched constantly and
whispered back and forth. She would giggle and tease softly,
controlling the young man with the velvet reins of instinct. She
darted back and forth to feed the fire or replenish Crazy Max's
bowl. A lithe young thing she was, with raven hair and a cupid's
pout. Pol soon realized that she was actually coy and a bit sly,
too; she knew that when she moved, every eye moved with
her. She had come into the encampment a few days earlier as
a nervous rabbit; now she had the self-assurance of a filly.
Fewer of her smiles were directed at the young man—more at
Crazy Max. Pol began to feel inklings of horror when Max put
a lank arm around the curly-haired lad, whose expression radiated a ridiculous desire to please. It didn't start to fade until
Max told the girl to dance and he saw the looks on the men's
faces around the fire. Even then the Adonis just hung his head
between elbows and knees.

Something turned in Pol's stomach. He wondered if he
should—or could—interfere. He looked at the young Adonis's

bowed head, saw his lips quiver in confusion. Innocence is supposed to be a virtue, he thought. If so, it's the one that costs the most. Tragedians reserve it for ghastly downfalls. At one time or another, we are all innocent; that is to say, we are at the mercy of those who have a better fix on reality. He wondered whether innocence equated best with purity or stupidity. Certainly it was sustained only if cloistered; otherwise, it begged for destruction. And he who marked the virgin tablet first, be it with slashes of blood or lines of harmony, became its maker. Innocence is a colossal excuse, he concluded, and for the first time felt he understood the significance of the original Eden's fig leaf. It is a horrible crime not to know.

A man with a homemade stringed instrument strummed it into a harsh, heavy rhythm. At first the girl was self-conscious because of the ring of male stares around the leaping fire, but Crazy Max's indolence seemed to reassure her. Her white teeth flashed, flashed, flashed as she began an awkward twirl. She couldn't really dance, but she could move, and as the pride she had in her body reasserted itself, her motion and the music gradually blended. The music pushed her into the classic paradigms of seduction. The fire drew her around it with an invisible cord. The eyes of the men, too, were drawn: around and around, pausing for the impact felt in the loins of a thrusting hip, a thrown-back breast curving into the line of a high-flung arm.

The player pounded his rhythm into a harder, faster throb. She, caught in its delirium, went with it. The eyes of the men, the silence of the men, were part of her music. Now her hair was flying and the firelight shimmered off her moistly glowing skin. Now the poses at the heaviest beats were aggressive, taunting, a single undulating line from the delicate curves at the bottom of her trailing foot, over calf and buttock and waist and shoulder and neck. The forward leg bent at the knee, thrust out of a rough shift. The hands and arms were no longer flung to the blackness above, but to the men, to the ring of staring eyes in the firelight.

Yes, Pol's eyes, too. And he *knew* that something ugly was coming. The Adonis didn't look up—not until Crazy Max threw a pot at the player to make him stop. The young man's face held the petulant, still quivering mouth and now pleading eyes. Max smiled at him benignly and told the girl to take off her clothes.

Pol could see that the music and the eyes were still with

her, because her breasts and the soft skin under her chin heaved
with the awareness of her magic. She nodded. Pol saw the
Adonis's head duck down again and his fingers curl tightly.
He saw, then, in shadowy dimness, *everything* that was to
happen, because it had the inevitability of all tragic dreams.

The music began again, and she danced again, in her nakedness even more fervently than before—and she was beautiful. But now Pol's attention was on Crazy Max and the young
man sitting beside him. The one was slouched semiprone with
a bowl of ersatz wine sloshing on his belly and the other was
dipping his head lower to the ground. He was learning, learning
about deceptive appearances and how deeply humiliation can
burrow. What a purging.

Max waited until her skin was agleam, sheening with her
sweat, with the fire from the light of the ring of the eyes, before
he kicked the player silent again.

He bid her to come to him. She stood there with her shining
smile, breathing heavily, proud and triumphant. The Adonis
looked up once again.

Pol felt an impulse to rise and stomp away, like a sensitive
theatergoer putting a vision of human nature behind him because it was hideously distorted and repulsive. The high ideals
of the Regnum and the Cadre—why should they require him
to tolerate this?

Crazy Max told the girl to lie down and the men to line up.
The Adonis shattered the air with a wild scream and dove into
the fire. He came up with smoking embers on his clothes and
a smoldering brand that was already arching toward Crazy
Max's head. He was a strong man, and the club was heavy.
With the kind of irony that is humorous to men who study
insect colonies, he tripped over the body of his lover and the
club landed between Max's splayed feet.

He died an instant later. Max's knife had been at the ready,
but he would have been too late, had fortune not favored him.

Pol boarded his transport on the sixth day. It was a long
time before he resumed his normal eating habits.

SY 3039

Pol Tyrees, a young Security Cadre Two, lived a lonely life. However, his work generally conspired to keep this solitude at bay. The Cadre was a monkish institution that could absorb the time and energies of its best and ask for more. A minority of family men was less isolated from the common run of life, but inevitably their professional lives stagnated. Pol's colleagues were quick to recognize him as a remarkable man. They accepted his abilities gratefully on the job as long as comparisons were avoided: they did not wish to compete with a "robot." Off duty, they tended to avoid him because they felt uncomfortable in his quiet company. He made them feel as if they were always being caught in a lie, as if they should be on guard lest he expose embarrassing flaws.

But Cadre officers were practical, no-nonsense men. The incidents that sometimes arose around Pol during his younger years had stopped. Adult males usually resisted the urge to challenge him. Women were intuitively more drawn to him, but they always reached a wall beyond which he would not allow them. They never saw the fear behind the barrier.

Pol noted the softer, deeper relationships of others and often regretted their absence in his own life, but he refused to dwell on it. Occasionally he was able to seek out his old friends. Ses or Ttig, now number Threes, and renew their old camaraderie. And there was always work.

The Political Section had a reputation as a pedestrian posting because it moved cautiously for reasons of diplomacy and the work was seldom dangerous. The adversaries of Political were not desperadoes; their lust was for personal power, and they worked cautiously, breaking the letter of the law only when stakes were high. Their taste was for intrigue rather than blood. Officers without patience were not happy there, and Pol's was strained. There was a gnaw in the back of his mind about his "rocking chair" assignments. In spite of his excellent record, he was afraid that he had been found wanting. He sensed that he was being more carefully scrutinized than others, perhaps because of his heritage. Very well. He would strive harder.

He had just finished an assignment in a far corner of Sector III and was reporting back for duty at his HQ. Technically, the Vice-Proctor was the only permanent officer in any sector HQ who outranked a Cadre Two. He had not returned to his quarters from his carrier but went directly to the VP's offices. The female administrative officer looked up and recognized Pol as he came in. His youth, given his rank, always startled her. Since she was sitting, a salute was not required, but she started to rise. He gestured her back with a wave.

"Hello, Lanni. Is the VP free?" She was surprised that he remembered her name. Blue eyes pinned her to the chair.

"Welcome back, sir. Yes, in a minute or two. Have a seat?" She smiled her "unofficial" smile but fidgeted nervously, suddenly at a loss for something to do. He seemed to notice her uneasiness and turned away to sit looking out a window. He stared without seeing. On someone else, the obvious turning inward would be self-conscious; on him, it was natural.

She found him intriguing—a layered fruit she would enjoy peeling, but she was angered by her loss of composure. She was a tough, capable officer. Functioning daily as the right arm of the VP, she had a great deal to do with the running of the sector. She was also confident of her personal charms and asked herself why this particular number Two should set her skin tingling when others she thought more physically attractive did not. In sexual relationships, *she* was accustomed to being the aggressor, regardless of rank. And why did she have the feeling that he *knew?* Characteristically, she decided to deal with it head on. She would reel him in for a closer look. She pretended to punch a code into the computer file.

"Uh . . . Officer Tyrees?" The blue eyes came back like an invisible tide, and her blood moved with it. She tried to make her manner as relaxed as his.

"Can you answer some questions, sir?"

"Call me Pol, Lanni. That can't be my report you pounded out because you hit one key too many. What questions?"

She flushed. "You know I can't use your first name—a number Two on duty. He'd warp me back to a Seven . . . Pol." He smiled easily and she felt better. He unfastened his collar clasp and let his cape slide to the back of the chair.

"It's nothing crucial. Just a few clarifications. The VP feels this case could be touchy on the diplomatic level, you know? Your man was a big fish, locally. Uh, it'll save time for him if I debrief while you wait." She let out a breath she didn't know she had been holding.

"Fine. Go ahead."

"The arrest of Talon's cabinet minister—it was done with the knowledge and consent of the government?"

"Their knowledge, not their consent. He had influence and a lot of favors to call in. His colleagues were afraid to condone his arrest, but they did keep quiet while I was stalking him."

"Could that mean trouble from indignant patriots?"

"Unlikely. After the arrest, the celebrants came out of the woodwork. Once they were sure I had him in the FSO lockup, they dumped more evidence than I needed. Which reminds me—I had to do a supplementary. Here." Pol took a recording crystal out of his cape and tossed it to her. She picked it neatly out of the air but was slightly miffed at the notion that his casual manner was designed to put her at ease. Well, she thought, it was working. But what *was* it with this man? . . .

"I'll file it later. You made the arrest personally—Pol?"

"I did."

"Uh, no complications?" She had to do this properly because she would have tracks to cover with the VP and she wanted to keep him talking. Pol had read the signs of her interest and, like a little boy, wanted to reach out for her. He was very much aware of his desire, but not of his need, and desires he excised with the long practiced skill of a surgeon.

"If you're asking whether he tried to use his political cronies—no. I didn't give him time to muster forces. He blustered a lot, called me a few names, offered bribes, delivered threats— just to observe the amenities—before I dragged him off." Pol smiled at her patiently as he waited for the next question. She looked away, tapping her stylus.

"Your rating of the field support office?"

"Excellent. Good legwork, better support."

"Fine. Well, I guess that's all. I don't see any problems. The VP is pleased with your work." She felt more herself now and smiled again. He remained unchanged. She had never known anyone who could maintain such stillness. Could she handle a rejection if she made an overture? He had been friendly but had said nothing that she could read as inviting; in fact, she could not read him at all. Besides, involvement with a Cadre Two was a bad bet, given their itineraries. She sighed and keyed the VP's channel.

"Yes, Lanni?" A clipped voice came out of the miniature speaker in her collar, so designed that only the wearer could hear—but Pol heard.

"If you're through, sir, Officer Tyrees is here. Uh—he's been debriefed."

"Debriefed? Since when do you debrief a number Two?"

"Sir, I—"

"Never mind. Just as well. But next time, wait for an order. You run the place, but let me go on pretending to be the C.O. around here."

"Sir—"

"Send him in."

"Yessir."

Pol, sheepish at overhearing the dressing down, neglected to allow her to pass on the order. He walked briskly past her darkening face. Her uneasiness returned as she watched his back.

The VP's office befitted his rank: rare hardwood decor, reds mingling with blacks in tasteful harmony. The stiff-backed man behind the desk became it, too. He had the look of a manikin, the central exhibit of a display.

"Tyrees, C-Two, reporting for assignment, sir."

"Welcome back, Tyrees," said the VP. "'For assignment'? You just made landfall. No request for leave?"

"I'd just as soon get back on the job, sir. I was a month in transit. Tired of doing nothing."

"I see," said the VP without inflection, not knowing that Pol registered his pleasure in any case. "Well, I can accommodate you. Sit."

The VP was a stereotyped Cadre officer: tireless, talented, concerned with results over all else. He drove himself and his subordinates hard. His body was a whipcord, making him seem younger than he was. Short black hair gleamed around his skull; white teeth gleamed inside it. His features were sharp and delicate, but muscles stood out on his neck over the solid black piping. Irreverent juniors claimed that he'd mastered the art of defecating without removing his uniform. He had the deft movements that men of physical confidence possess. He also embodied the negative qualities of the classic officer: his tolerance for weakness was as thin as his humor. He found the administration of his Political Section difficult because compromise was inimical to his nature.

The VP's youngest C-2 often left him mildly frustrated because he couldn't make him respond. With others, even Ones, he could evoke anger, exasperation, sometimes fear. He prodded them, not out of a sense of perverse amusement, but to judge them. They questioned orders because blind obedience was not the Cadre way, but Tyrees never went beyond that. The same blank, pleasant exterior presented itself in all contingencies. He found this irksome, but the young man's record was flawless, and for some reason central HQ had an interest in him that went so far as to alter certain of his assignment directives. Nevertheless, the VP never coddled him. He made Pol wait while he arranged objects on his desk in a symmetrical pattern and sculpted a look of absentmindedness into his face. Such tactics were usually puzzling to his people and they diagnosed eccentricity instead of cunning. As men in high positions will, when they lack the opportunity to see their charges on the job, he played small games to draw out reactions for assessment. Finally, during a fastidious nose blowing, the VP looked up; he had not expected to see impatience—and he saw none. With a small sigh, he took up business in his clipped fashion.

"I've had a case waiting for you. By the way—a good job on Talon."

"Thank you, sir."

"This is another touchy one. Too touchy. Are you familiar with Raven?" The VP knew the records of his Twos down to the finest detail, so the question was unnecessary, but he liked to catch them even in harmless lies.

"No, sir. Never heard of it."

"Well, you are about to," he snorted. "There's a situation unfolding there that may have serious repercussions. She's out toward the Hub. So far, the trade mess has been pretty well contained in the Hub sectors. But Raven's getting too pugnacious. There have been complaints. At first, I thought 'sour grapes' because they were coming from competitors. But the situation was showing signs of deteriorating though there wasn't enough hard data to move on it. Then, a few weeks ago, the Council released a new probability system to the Cadre. Called 'Anavex.' Been classified CEO for years. Brain child of some commissioner named Bolla." At this point, the VP registered his pique with bureaucracy by rolling his eyes to the ceiling. Pol's heart skipped a beat at the mention of his old friend's name.

"I gather it's been used by a Regnum commission for some special work until the Proctor got them to realize that it could serve a vital security function. Anyway, we ran the Raven stuff, and Anavex produced a rather shocking predictor: a probability of sixty-one point eight percent that information, available *only to the Cadre*, was being made accessible to Raven. This is the explanation the program postulates for Raven's new prosperity. Understand?"

Pol nodded slowly. "Shocking" was an understatement. The VP settled back in his red chair and looked at Pol with a smug tilt to his neck. A high-level Cadre leak was unheard-of, and this smacked of conspiracy. Pol knew that the VP, in spite of his implied confidence in the probability system, simply did not believe its conclusion. He also knew that those who worked on a daily basis with the awesome capacities of computer technology resisted the urge to deify it.

The VP studied his number Two from under half-lidded eyes, waiting. Such a leak meant a traitor. The Cadre was not supposed to foster traitors. For the first time, he saw something unguarded on the face across from him. It was as if a skin-thin mask had been peeled from the young, unmarred face to leave it predatory. Eyes narrowed and nostrils flared; the body tensed and leaned slowly forward in the chair. If I were looking at a cat, thought the VP, I would be expecting it to leap right now: for an instant, he actually felt fear. Then the moment passed. He was pleased that he had finally been able to draw this one out of his shell. The man was only human, after all.

The thought of a traitor had set blood burning in Pol, but it was more than that. For a long time he had felt caged and cushioned. "Action assignments" never came his way. He resented the feeling that the Cadre lacked full confidence in him and yearned like a hound to slip the leash and prove himself.

"So. Your job will be to find out if Anavex is right. And if it is—to nail the one responsible." Then the VP saw his man pull everything back inside. The mask was in place again and the blood-hungry look gone. Pol asked the question that begged to be asked.

"I'm sorry, sir, but I don't understand. This . . . shouldn't this be handled by Internal Security?"

"Ordinarily, yes. I almost assigned it to them, but several considerations made me change my mind. As you know, Internal Security usually deals with non-Cadre personnel—technics and such. Also, most of my Ones and Twos have been shifted to the Hub, and I don't want inexperienced field men blundering around in a situation this delicate. Besides, there *are* political elements to this case—your bailiwick—and finally, Cadre involvement is not a proven fact."

"Will this assignment be under cover then, sir? I have no experience there. For some reason I've never been even connected with covert investigation."

"Coincidence. This one will be under cover to the extent that no one in the FSO will know the exact nature of your assignment. They will be told only that you are investigating certain government officials on Raven. No one will assume otherwise. Informed support will come from here. Understand?" The VP hesitated before trading his brisk tone for one more confiding. "Yes, I'm skirting some regulations on this one. You'll get no assignment directive in print and no direct field support. Whether this Anavex is right or wrong, I won't have my personnel tainted by even the suggestion of a turncoat."

"I *am* looking for a traitor, then."

"Yes."

"My authority is . . . ?"

"Carte blanche."

"But . . ." Pol's eagerness was now salted with uncertainty. This was too big.

"I know you find this as distasteful as I do, but remember that we are not certain that there *is* a traitor. It's a possibility that must be checked out discreetly . . . discreetly. Understand?"

"Yes, sir."

"Good. Let's go into procedure. None of this will be going into Records or the communications net. . . ."

SY 3039

Pol made landfall on Raven. From orbit the world had a somber look because of the gray, brackish clouds that shrouded it. On the ground, its aspect was even more gloomy. As Pol was stretching his legs toward the spaceport perimeter, *Farstar*'s captain stood with his exec on the ramp. Both squinted into the nightfall mist.

"You'd think they'd provide better facilities here, wouldn't you, Captain? This is supposed to be a busy port."

"Yeah, it's a hole in other ways, too."

"That bad, huh? Unfriendly?"

"You could say that. They like to fleece visitors, anyway. Aggressive bunch. Quick to take offense. Goes with their climate, I guess. Everything here is cold and wet—including the people. They're dedicated to utility on Raven, never comfort."

"That should suit our passenger, then."

"Stow it. He's coming back.... Will you be heading in now, sir? Shall I have someone get your kit?" Pol peered up at them through the mist.

"Thank you, no. The FSO will send somebody for it." He came up the ramp and shook hands formally.

"Thank you for a smooth journey," he said, and turned, heading back down.

"Good luck, then, sir," the captain called after him.

The two watched the flowing cape swirl into the mist before the exec picked up where he had left off.

"Yep. This place matches his personality. He'll like it here."

Pol walked toward the distant terminal in a melancholy mood. The dank air was palpable, suspended between fog and rain. The foliage drooped and dripped, weary of its own weight, its color more black than green. In spite of the chill, everything gave off its own steam. Lights flickered through the murk and pushed out muzzy, tainted yellows into the heavy atmosphere. Things at a middle distance were obscure; things afar ghostly.

Raven was a place rich in material resources, but Pol wondered if it claimed in return a price scraped from the tender rind of the human spirit. He was mildly surprised by his own reaction to the place. He put it down to his concern about the assignment and the fact that he had heard the last words of the exec. He had the uneasy feeling usually reserved for a greasy, undigested meal.

The spaceport was busy, but the fibrous gloom turned it into a crazed mural, a staging area for souls freshly released from the bondage of flesh. Sourceless voices called out. Strange noises came from nowhere. Indistinct bodies would burst out of the steely fuzz, faceless because of the lights in their helmets, only to be swallowed up again. Pulsing beeps warned of port machinery plowing short tunnels into the fog. To Pol's acute and keening senses, it was demented. For the first time in years he found it a struggle to dampen and analyze a flood of incoming sensory data, and he remembered feeling the same stretched nerves as a boy under the strain of one of his grandfather's tests.

He followed a walkway, a thread of light stretching brokenly through the blear toward a terminal. Inside the entrance through which all arrivals had to pass, he saw two customs officials sitting behind a counterbarrier. They were throwing dice and muttering soft invective. Because of their game and the fact that brightly colored clothing was the norm on Raven, they failed to notice Pol until he was almost on top of them. They were startled by the disembodied white face looming out of the mist, the black cape becoming visible only when he stepped inside. The younger of the two was annoyed by the sudden jump in his chest and spoke abruptly.

"Huh! Sit over there. We'll get to you in a minute." Pol

stood where he was, waiting for recognition, in his present
mood reluctant to speak. The man rose, puffing out a garish
yellow tunic. He had already loaded his tongue with sarcasm
when his partner's hand clamped on his shoulder.

"Cadre," he whispered, and drew him back. He addressed
Pol with a voice oozing deference.

"Ah, good evening, sir. Worse than usual out tonight. Just
arrived in the Cadre ship? *Farstar?*"

"Yes."

"May I see your identification, please?"

"Tyrees, Cadre Two." Pol dropped his plate on the counter.

"Thank you, sir." The customs man shifted it with a practiced hand to a scanner. His partner self-consciously stuck hands
into pockets.

"And how long will you be a guest of Raven, sir?"

"I have no idea. May I pass now, please?" Pol put out a
hand for his ID plate.

"Of course. Certainly, sir. I didn't mean to keep you waiting.
May I find you transport? Our pool can spare a groundcar for
the Cadre."

"Thank you, but that won't be necessary. I'm sure the Cadre
keeps something here."

"Excellent. Just step through. And enjoy your stay, sir."

The footsteps of the man in black receded down the passageway. The customs official's lips curled in derision as he
turned to his partner.

"You idiot!"

Pol walked briskly through the public section of the terminal
and experienced a common phenomenon. The large concourse
was crowded and buzzed with anonymous human noises, but
as he moved, voices around him fell silent and heads turned.
A rough path formed ahead of him, wider than necessary;
behind, it closed in and the voices resumed in hushed tones.
Strangers turned to one another.

"Cadre."

"You see him? Cadre."

"Yeah, I know. I've seen them before. Lots here on Raven."

"Not Cadre Two. That's a Two, isn't it? Purple collar?"

"I dunno. Those guys give me the creeps, anyway."

"Why? They're on our side, aren't they? Look at that kid!
You can see his tonsils!"

"Dad? Is he here looking for crooks, Dad?"

"Who knows, son. Probably."

"Will he kill them, Dad? Will he kill them?"

Officer Tyrees had heard it all before. He pulled his cape closed around him as he stepped to an information terminal, seeking the location of a Cadre groundcar.

As he rode to the FSO he decided that he had to cast all doubts ruthlessly aside. He needed this one. He was on his own, and it was an opportunity to be seized and shaped. He would disregard the VP's words about discretion. Cadre One was still there ahead of him. He was fed up with waiting, going through the motions. It was time to squeeze events into *his* design, to pound them into the future his grandfather had envisioned for him.

The first thing he saw at the field support office when the door to the C.O.'s section opened was the beaming smile and saucy red hair of Dace Sestus.

"Ses!"

"Pol, you ol' ramjet, it's about time you got here." Ses checked an impulse to throw his arms around his old friend. Better than anyone else, he was accustomed to Pol's impregnable reserve, but he also knew of the man underneath. He settled for a hand on Pol's shoulder.

"It's been almost five years, roomie. Seems like more than that."

"I'm not sure, Ses, but I think that was my last leave," said Pol, feeling his spirits lift at the sight of the one person to whom he felt close.

"You look great, ol' buddy. Still look like a kid. It's funny, but when you were a kid, you looked like an old man. I heard about the violet a while back. You're leaving your old friends behind, as predicted." He fingered the dark purple piping on Pol's collar.

"Yours will come soon, Ses."

"Nope. I know better. I'll be a Three for the duration, and that's okay with me."

"How did you know I was coming?"

"Listen—uh, *sir*—I've been assigned to this backwater for three years now, and I know everything that happens here. Work is the only salvation on this ball of sludge."

"Really?"

"Well, I can take the planet, but not the people. They're all burning with patriotism and greed. But it's interesting work. The C.O. can't make a move without me because I'm the one who makes the machines sing around here."

All Threes were computermen. The very best tended to remain in the sub-Cadre for the natural reason that skill and contentment go hand in hand. The average ones were automatically denied access to Cadre Two and usually became administrators. Pol realized that Ses's case was different, because talented Threes were rarely given postings that lasted so long; usually they were on short field assignments. Knowing that Ses's brashness had irked his superiors in the past, he didn't ask questions.

"Come on, Ses, only the C.O. is supposed to know I was coming at all. I don't think even he knew exactly *when*."

Ses laughed uproariously. "Listen, ol' friend, I can suck *anything* out of those machines, whether they like it or not. Come on, I'll introduce you to the old man."

There was something in Ses's manner that Pol found discordant. Ses had always flown higher off the ground than most, but his altitude had increased. There was a pitched quality to his voice. Actions were more abrupt. Pol knew these were signs of tension, a tautness under the jovial gloss.

The session with the C.O. was brief and businesslike, partly because Pol found his subterfuge uncomfortable. They assumed he was there for a political investigation, and all he added was that his assignment involved the possible conspiracy of two government officials with factions in the Hub. It was taken at face value.

The C.O. was an elderly Four who was floating with the current toward retirement and desired nothing more than the captaincy of a ship that plied still waters. When decisions were involved, Pol saw eyes that had a tendency to shift, hands that became needlessly busy; he heard a voice that lost volume and precision near the ends of sentences. Ultimately, the C.O. would send an unconscious signal to Ses that said, "Look after this, will you?" The signal was always received (with a higher awareness), and the unspoken answer was always, "Sure, ol' man. Leave it to me." Then Ses would take over. The C.O. would then revert to an air of easeful command. Technically, Ses outranked him, so he found it easy to abdicate when de-

cisions were difficult. He was pleased to be able to help the
number Two by providing his invitation to a government function that would be attended by the men under investigation.

Ses bombarded Pol with chatter after the meeting as he
hauled him off to a quiet corner in the canteen. He peppered
his monologue with affectionate insults, trying to fill the gap
since they last met. When the avalanche abated, Pol asked a
question of his own.

"Ses, what's wrong?"

"Huh? What do you mean?"

"Well, for starters, why have you been here so long?"

The light went out of his old friend's eyes and he stared
blankly back across the table. Then he shrugged and a cynical
smirk broke out on his face. He was suddenly a stranger, because Pol had never seen its like on Ses before.

"We all get mothballed sooner or later, ol' buddy. My turn
came sooner."

"You're lying, Ses. Something's happened. Please tell me."

"Nothing to tell," mumbled Ses. "They just don't like my
nose-picking habit, I guess."

Pol said nothing. He waited until Ses brought his eyes back
up from the table; they, too, were a new and disturbing land-
mark on the familiar terrain of his friend's face. A flow of pain
and resentment had risen from somewhere beneath to find an
outlet there.

"I should have known better than to try to keep anything
hidden from *you*," he said softly, "but it doesn't matter. It's
over now, You know, I never understood how you could always—"

"We're not talking about me. Out with it, Ses. I've never
seen you like this."

Silence. Pol tried to lighten the mood and remind Ses of
their old bond.

"The Cadre can't function properly if its symbol of justice
is frayed at the edges."

"Shove the Cadre!" cried Ses in a hoarse voice. "I . . . Sorry,
Pol." He took a deep breath and began again, "Do you remember Salaan, from the training complex?"

A flood of sweet-hot-painful memories.

"Yes."

"She's dead."

Ses looked carefully at his friend's face and could detect no change in the bland expression. His ire rose.

"Did you hear me, Pol? I said she's dead!"

"Yes, I heard. I'm sorry," said Pol through barely moving lips. He wasn't given time to say more.

"She turned up here just after me, about three years ago. She was just as beautiful—*more* beautiful than I remembered. She . . ." Ses's voice grew huskier. He stopped to clear his throat and raked fingers through thick red hair. "But I wasn't a kid with his brains in his pants anymore, Pol. I really fell in love with her, you understand?"

Pol wasn't sure that he did. At the moment, he felt only an emptiness. Salaan. . . . He had a premonition, and he didn't want Ses to continue. Ses did, almost as if a switch had been thrown and he was a recording crystal turning precisely, irresistibly, tracing the fine, etched lines of what was unalterably there.

"She was still in Operations and she was busting apart trying to become a digger. *I* was busting apart trying to make her feel for me the way I did for her, so we made a fine pair. I loved her and she loved the Cadre. One-way orbits."

"She was a smart woman. What was keeping her back?"

"That one I thought about a lot; in fact, I made it a personal project." The cynical smirk reappeared like an evil face in a dark window. "It was a triumph of my digger's art, and it killed her."

"Make sense, Ses."

"Don't ask the impossible. I'll just tell you the story. Even you won't be able to make sense out of it, Pol, and I know you'll try. Incidentally, that's your weakness, ol' friend." No response.

"You don't know this, but I'm a good digger, better than even you were." Ses stopped his harried eyes long enough to stare defiantly at Pol. The look asked for nothing.

"The first thing I did was change my assignment so I could be here longer."

"You what?"

"That's right, ol' buddy. I—me and my machines—did it. They'll never find out *how,* assuming they *try* to find out. Anyway, several communications went through the net and I ended up with a long assignment for a digger." His hand went

forward over the table as if to grasp Pol's but stopped short.
"I would trust that with no one but you, Pol." Pol's impulse
was to disclaim that trust, but this was Ses. He didn't know
how to respond. There was no doubt in Ses's mind, for he went
on, absorbed in his story and taking Pol's loyalty for granted.

"Then I looked into Salaan's assessment files—"

"Wait now, Ses! You don't have access to those. Only Internal Security . . ." A laugh and waving fingers stopped him.

"I hate to disillusion you, roomie, but Cadre procedures are
full of loopholes if a digger wants to use them. Personnel files
are hidden under codes, but that's the extent of the security on
them."

"That's not telling me how . . ."

"Very simple. It's like an electron tunnel, see? I went down
the right one until I ran up against a wall—the code for Salaan's
file. Now, the machines were told to build that wall, so the
best practice is to ask *them* how to get through it. A good digger
knows that they're just like kids, right? So you coax them,
cajole them, and sooner or later they come around. Being naïve,
they don't know that there's more than one way to ask the
same question. They also love a challenge. So what I did was
ask them what they would do in my position. I asked them
what questions to ask."

Pol shook his head. "Ses, quit dancing and tell me."

"I *am* telling you. In effect, I said to them, 'If you wanted
information hidden by a code—by the way, my lovelies, here's
the *kind* of code—how would you get at it, huh? In the end,
they told me enough to get through." He sighed. "I suppose
even computers should be pushed into an awareness of sordid
reality. . . . Sorry, that's pretty profound for me, isn't it?"

"Ses . . . No, Ses. You've . . . I don't want to know any . . ."

"You don't want to know why Salaan is dead?"

Inside the still composed shell of what was Pol Tyrees, a
hard fist of fear grew. He knew, *knew* where this was headed—
Ses or the Cadre. In his mind, he cursed both. It was unjust.
The fist would smash him, either way.

"Go on," was all he could say.

"Salaan's performance reviews boiled down to one recurring
negative: she took outrageous liberties because she was soft.
She was compassionate and she was human and she always
took the time to try to help people and this was a dangerous

luxury. You probably never saw this in her, Pol, but—"

"Ses, this is ridiculous!" Pol winced inside. "I can't—"

"Let me finish. I'll tell you why they denied her the one thing she really wanted—their approval. She worked on a surveillance assignment and left her post to give medical aid to an accident victim. Saved his life. Another time, she covered for a relic who had a drinking problem. He wasn't even Cadre, just an old Technic close to retirement. Internal Security loved that one! The worst was when she refused to interrogate a petty crook about her black market activities because she was dying of syphilis in the hospital. She was a broken-down hag who fenced worthless junk from off-planet for eating money when she couldn't fuck for a living anymore. Shit!"

Pol could barely distinguish Ses's hair from the growing course of red on his forehead, which marked the flow of his rage.

"So you told her."

"Damn right I told her! I told her they were holding her back because they want us to be unfeeling bastards with snowballs for hearts. I told her to stop groveling for a lover who used her like one of my machines. I told her—"

"Take it easy, Ses," begged Pol. "Don't work yourself into a nova. You loved her, so it's got to have colored your judgment. Try to be fair. You know that the Cadre has a rotten job to do, and that often demands sacrifices." Pol had a painfully clear memory of the use of that word between him and Salaan years ago, but he went on. "I understand how you felt, but some of the things she did could have had serious consequences. She may have caused more suffering than she prevented."

"After her initial shock, that's more or less what she said. She called it a lack of judgment—maudlin sentimentality— and vowed to change her orbit. She even convinced me she was right."

Ses put down two taut, knuckled fists and stared at them as if they were obscene.

"Not long after that, they killed her."

"Please, Ses. You can't—"

"They killed her. It's true. You listen, Pol. You wanted to know, now you listen. I have to tell it to *somebody,* and you're the only one I can trust. You *should* listen, because maybe it'll do you some good, too, give you a more . . . realistic perspective maybe. Listen!"

"All right, I'm listening."

"I asked her to marry me, but she refused because she said she had enough on her record to overcome. Another black mark, she said, can you imagine? She did agree to live with me. I had a few months of the happiest... Never mind. It was good. Through my machines and the C.O., I kept our lives quiet for a while, but Salaan was impatient. She had to *prove* herself, she said. Without telling me, she put in for 'special assignments.' You know what that means—'hazardous duty'— jobs for glory-seekers and idiots. And officers desperately trying for recognition. I found out about it because nothing goes through this FSO without my knowing. Anyway, when I started to confront her with it, she cut me off like a ramjet blowout. I was angry, but in the end I had to accept it. I reasoned that that kind of duty was never dumped on a young Four because of their inexperience, right? I mean, the assignments are dangerous, one-shot things, but they still want them to *work*."

Pol could only nod.

"But I was wrong. Some asshole number Two in Sector Five wanted a whore, Pol. He wanted someone with Salaan's 'special qualifications' as a human sacrifice to nuzzle up to a Trade Wars baron in the middle of that mess in the Hub, and get information out. I caught it coming down the pipe, but I couldn't stop it in time. Too high a priority. But special assignments can be refused, right? It took me hours to find her because she was on the other side of this—this stinking bog they call a planet. I found her just after she'd got word of it."

Ses stopped and drew his two clenched fists together on the table's surface, then pulled them toward him. His skin made a squeaking noise on the plastic. In the quiet canteen, the only movement came from flickering shadows cast by the mobile of metal birds revolving overhead.

"She said she would take it. She said it would clear her record. She said she would turn me in if I tried to stop her. It was suicidal, but I couldn't stop her." Ses's voice was now a whine. "And she said she loved me. And she left. I never saw her again, Pol. She was dead a month later."

Pol looked at his old friend and saw pain, self-pity—and hatred. He wanted to reach out, pull Ses to him, and cry with him. He wanted also to stand and leave quietly—forever.

"That's a terrible story, Ses. I'm sorry. But I know what Salaan would think, and she'd be right. You've got to get a hold on things again. There's a long life ahead of you, and you can't bury yourself here forever just to nurse your misery."

"I've just decided that, unlike Salaan, I won't be doing any whoring for the Cadre, that's all."

"Ses—"

"I've given up on commitment and opted for a little pleasure niche here. The Cadre can provide for *my* comfort for a change. You get the promotions, Pol, and I'll be my own number One—okay?"

The ruts and twists of bitterness were back on Ses's face, and Pol knew they were now permanent landmarks. He vowed to himself that he would neither ask for, nor listen to, any more.

"Ses, let's find a spot, have a few drinks, and talk about old times. It's been too long."

A blank look came into the redhead's face. Then, as if the trite words were words of wisdom that he found wise indeed, he nodded and rose from the table.

Pol dealt with the buried fist in the only way allowed by his nature: he froze it—encased it by an act of will in the ice of his resolve. He used a mental discipline that had been developed into a fine and practical tool and wiped it from his surface consciousness as a mechanic wipes grease from his hands. When Ses was not present, this was possible. He knew instinctively that to dwell on the dilemma of conflicting loyalties was dangerous to his well-being in a way that nothing had ever been before. He prayed that circumstances allowed him to carry on as he was; if they did not, he knew that he would no longer *be* as he was.

That night, he covered his eyes with his arm so they would close and willed himself into oblivion. Because only dreams remember things that go back beyond the age of four, he met his father that night. The dream came with the bright reality of hysteria. He sat, a little boy, writing in a book. He didn't know what he wrote, but he stopped when he heard the footsteps. Though the tall figure wore the black cape, Pol knew it was his father. It nodded sadly and said, "Little Pol, stop that silly game. Go and play outside. Don't you want to be big and strong? The world doesn't like hermits, you know." Then he reached and gently removed Pol's marker. Slowly, deliberately, he drew a cage of thin bars around him. As his father bled the dark lines into the air, his arms and hands became ropier, like twisted tree roots emerging from the cape. The fingers formed into talons with long, hooked barbs. The cage finished, the talons spread and reached between the bars for Pol. He screamed with no sound.

SY 3039

The reception was in honor of Raven's acquisition of the mining rights of a large asteroid belt in a nearby system. The negotiations had ended in something of a coup. Their neighbor had been lacking certain commodities necessary for her industries—a fact she had been at pains to keep secret. Raven offered her trade incentives involving those very goods in return for the mining concessions. The neighbor regarded it as a fortunate coincidence that what she needed was available without exposing her weakness, and she agreed.

As a sign of the importance placed on a Cadre officer of Pol's rank, he was provided with an aide for the festivities. He hovered discreetly behind Pol's left shoulder and whispered details about the dignitaries. If Pol wished, he made introductions, though the highest officeholders had already been presented as a matter of course.

Pol's thorough briefing on Raven's leaders had already given him a good background, but he found that the aide was helpful in adding to it. He was a friendly, talkative sort, much impressed by the Cadre uniform and anxious to please. With a little coaxing, he threw in valuable tidbits and gossip that sketched in the finer features of Raven's power brokers.

Pol had decided on his line of attack long before landfall.

If information restricted to the Cadre was getting to Raven officials and providing an illegal advantage in the galactic marketplace, certain elements had to be involved: the officials had to have influence in interplanetary affairs, and they had to have some connection with the Cadre. Since his cover involved a political investigation, the best course would be to start with the government and trace links to the Cadre.

Although Pol's presence was considered special on the social scale, there were those who were less than delighted about it. The Cadre was not in the business of public relations, and number Twos did not visit planets solely to attend their functions. Those with skeletons in their closets were upset by the presence of the quiet man in black, but that reaction provided Pol with his first tenuous evidence. It would have left them incredulous had they known, because it consisted simply of Pol's reading the level of their anxiety in his presence.

He strolled past one man who was the center of a quiet conversation with several others whose body-sets told him that deference was being paid to power. As he moved across the man's arc of vision, Pol saw his eyes go blank, as if a glass curtain had been dropped. Unless he consciously wills it otherwise, a man's eyes will automatically track whatever passes through his field of vision.

"Who is that man, Emar? The one with the goblet in his hand—tallish, gray hair."

The aide responded quietly from behind. "Uh, Klist Rav, sir. Economic adviser to the secretary of trade."

"An important position?"

"Well, with advisers it's difficult to say, sir."

"Come now, Emar," said Pol with a confidential murmur. "You are a man with a sharp mind and keen eyes. Your knowledge of these people goes far beyond their titles, doesn't it?" Pol had turned to speak directly to Emar, and this, as much as the words, flattered him. Aides to special guests were trained to be discreet, as their charges didn't want others to think they were needed. Emar was accustomed to whispering over disdainful shoulders.

"They do say he has the secretary's ear, sir."

"A man of some influence, then? One who remains behind the scene, as it were?"

"Uh, I would say so, sir. I might also add that his stature has grown rapidly in the last year or so."

"What makes you say that?"

"Nothing tangible, sir, just the way others act around him."

"Ah, you are perceptive, Emar. The Cadre could use your talents. By the way, do officers from our FSO often attend functions such as these?"

"Very seldom, sir, though I have seen the commanding officer on a few occasions."

"And Regnum officials? Do you see them often?"

"Oh, yes, sir. Our government maintains very friendly relations with the ambassadorial staff."

There were interruptions for polite chats with overdressed and gushing socialites anxious to meet a Cadre Two. They were usually disappointed with his attempts at small talk. Pol circulated in a pattern that appeared random but was designed to bring him into close visual contact with the power brokers. With the help of Emar's comments, which were growing more candid, he was editing a list of targets.

"Ah, there's our Mr. Rav again, Emar. He must be a brilliant man, considering Raven's rising prosperity—if he's as close to the decision-makers as you think."

"Oh, I'm sure he is, sir. I've seen members of the Inner Cabinet seek his advice. *They* come to *him*."

Although Emar was unaware of it, Pol was close enough to eavesdrop on Rav. He could wash out the general babble of voices and listen to conversations at a distance impossible to ordinary ears. Rav was speaking to an undersecretary of trade.

"Jon, what is that creature doing here?"

"Uh, who, Rav?"

"The black crow, of course. The Cadre man behind you."

"Oh, right. Tyrees, I think his name is. The FSO's commanding officer was the one invited. I believe that this one had just made landfall and came in his stead. Youngish, isn't he? The secretary's wife was very pleased to have him. Not often you see a number Two. Standoffish chap."

"You don't get the point. What's he doing on Raven? Getting his cape laundered?"

"Oh, I see what you mean . . . Political Section, too. But that doesn't have to mean that he's sniffing at us, does it? Could be on leave or between stops. . . . You don't think he's looking into our mining rights deal?"

"Doubtful. I would think that would mean one of their

sleuths from Economics, not Politics. Besides, the deal is perfectly legal. Still, I'm curious."

"Why don't you just ask him, Rav? I'm sure the secretary would be interested, and he would sing your praises even louder."

"Ask him yourself. Those characters repel me almost as much as your sarcasm. Aloof bastards. Long capes to disguise the fact that they're ordinary men. Petty policemen, most of them, but they try to intimidate by posing as superhumans. The kids call them 'dark angels,' but they're just men in funny costumes—pah!"

"Rav! You surprise me! If the Regnum is to survive . . ."

"If the Regnum is to survive, my naïve friend, it will not depend upon the childish intrigue of overtrained zealots in melodramatic uniforms. It will depend upon the leadership of men of vision. You would do well to think on that."

As Rav's companion pondered this advice, Pol spoke again to Emar.

"Time for an introduction, Emar."

"Rav, sir?"

"Yes, he interests me."

"Of course, sir."

Pol led the way toward the twosome and watched Rav's body stiffen. His own adrenaline surged. With Ses in the back of his mind, he was anxious for speed and, ultimately, escape. Emar spoke smoothly from behind when they arrived. The two men had their eyes on Pol, ignoring the aide.

"Excuse us for interrupting, sirs. May I present Officer Pol Tyrees, Security Cadre Two? Klist Rav, adviser to the secretary of trade; Jon Laast, undersecretary of trade."

Pol saluted, Cadre fashion, drawing a slight smile from Rav and the barest of nods.

"Welcome to Raven, Officer Tyrees. Enjoying your visit?"

"'Enjoy' is a word I rarely apply to my work, sir. I deal with too many men I consider enemies." Rav was taken aback by Pol's bluntness and reverted to a natural aggressiveness without thinking. A long neck pushed his beaked nose closer to Pol. The undersecretary, a man of more caution, remained silent.

"Then your lack of courtesy suggests you are now in the presence of enemies. I'm sure that Raven's most honored citizens, most of whom are in this hall, would not be flattered."

Pol grabbed the trailing rope of Rav's anger and swung on it. "Those who believe in Regnum law would prefer justice to courtesy."

Rav tried to reconcile the challenging words with the emotionless tone of their delivery and failed; but he was a perceptive man and now suspected that he was being baited. The thought reassured him, because it was a kind of mental swordsmanship he knew well.

"I take your point, Officer Tyrees. I would make the same choice. I assume you have questions to ask, since you are obviously a man who works with directness?"

"Yes, I do. What is your function in the Raven government?"

"My function? Surely you already . . . ?"

"I mean precisely—your specific responsibilities."

"I'm afraid my title is about as precise as I can get. I advise the secretary of trade, and my responsibilities vary with his orders."

"You have no decision-making powers, then?"

Rav laughed softly before answering. The undersecretary was impressed by his calm. But that sound and other minute signs told Pol that he was about to lie.

"I can assure you on that point, at least. I make suggestions—if I am asked—and write reports, if I am so ordered, and the secretary makes the decisions. On the rare occasions when my suggestions become policy, I feel that my work is worthwhile."

Rav's short speech was beautifully delivered: the unctuous words and tone of the dedicated civil servant who is content to do his small part. But with most men, Pol could recognize the difference between a voice keyed to natural impulses and one that was deliberately shaped for a listener.

Then Pol made a mistake. As he chased Rav, he was running from Ses, and so his haste revealed his own designs.

"Do you have any dealings with the Cadre, as part of your responsibilities?" Rav's face darkened. The dedicated civil servant disappeared.

"None whatsoever."

To Pol, the terse response was also a lie, and therefore a hot lead; but Rav was now aware that he was searching for a link between the government and the Cadre. Pol took his leave with a curt nod, realizing that he had been phenomenally lucky in discovering a hard suspect so soon, but careless about forewarning an enemy. Nevertheless, like a child who considered his immortality undebatable, he felt secure in the cradle of Cadre invulnerability. He continued his casting tactics and dodged collectors of social trophies. Rav watched him from a distance, watched him like one of claw and feather watches a rodent moving through underbrush below.

A few hours later, Pol walked back toward the FSO, planning his next line of attack. Rav was an exciting lead. Even thoughts of Ses and the dank mist obscuring the lights on the walkways failed to dampen his spirits. Success could mean the black collar.

There was no warning. As he crossed one of the low bridges that spanned the capital's drainage canals, a tight, soundless beam of ultrasonic waves passed through his brain and wiped away his consciousness as cleanly as a cloth wipes glass. Puppet limp, his body dropped over a low railing into the dark water with a soft splash.

The assassin moved to the canal's edge warily. He set himself to wait for the body to resurface. He was a cautious man, but he was confident. The cause of death would be drowning. The Cadre would not assume that it was accidental, but neither could they proceed as if a murder had taken place on a planet demonstrably loyal to the Regnum. It was possible that the body would never be found.

The assassin felt something close to sexual ecstasy at having claimed a prize possessed by no one in his experience.

SY 3039

COUNCIL EYES ONLY

***Procedural Directive*—Vice-Proctor, Sector V**

- Recall immediately Officer Pol Tyrees, Cadre Two, Political Section, from present assignment on Raven

- Place yourself on censure report: failure to follow assignment directive procedures

- Report completion of procedural directive to Cadre Proctor

SY 3039

Pol's body sank to the bottom of the narrow canal. Like the life-support system of a space vessel, its automatic mechanisms took over to fulfill the function of their only reason for being— survival. Its windpipe sealed itself against the incursion of water; it braked its metabolism to conserve precious oxygen; it locked itself into motionlessness. The body waited for the mind to return.

As it began to do so, its first perception was that of suffocation, but its own systems allowed that only to trigger greater awareness. Flashes of fire shot along the channels of the brain as it reached for control of the body that gave it expression. The impulse to draw breath was short-circuited. Growing awareness also brought panic and a demand for hands to claw to the surface, where a surer death awaited. *There is enough!* screamed the center of reason. *There is enough time, enough oxygen. Enough strength. Hold to the bottom. Wait. Yes.*

Many minutes later, Pol Tyrees, a different Pol Tyrees from the one who had folded into the water, allowed himself to rise slowly to the surface. Before he emerged, he pulled his cape over his head to cover the whiteness of his face. When he broke softly into the air, he forced himself to inhale slowly, quietly, before resubmerging and stroking to the canal wall. Knowing he could see through the murk above better than his attacker, he took a careful survey. Silence. Cold, swirling mist. Bleary lights. Smells of decay from the canal. The sour taste of his own fear.

He heard the footsteps first, then sought their source over the lap of water. Above and a few meters away, he saw a shadow pass over the low mist light at the base of the bridge. His assassin was stooping over, hand on knee, to peer into the darkness under the bridge span. A light flashed on and traveled quickly over the scummy walls at the water line. It was three or four seconds, no more, before the thin beam vanished and Pol knew he was dealing with a professional. A man who works in darkness dislikes using a light because it draws attention and because the aftereffect inhibits nightsight.

Pol clung to the slippery wall, ready to submerge again. He heard the approaching footsteps, but could also hear the assassin's soft grunt as he rose from his stoop. Even through the gloom, Pol could see that the man's body-set was losing its tensed alertness. He had been there for a long time, longer than a less disciplined man would have been, but growing certainty brought carelessness. He flipped back a dark hood that had shrouded his features. Pol could make out a heavily boned forehead as he turned to mount the steps to the walkway—and froze for an instant; then the assassin moved quietly into the deeper shadows of the bridge wall. A man was walking toward them, preceded now by the sound of a tuneless whistle. The assassin and his secret sharer watched him walk through the mist. He created a strange effect as he moved in and out of the mist lights illuminating from below. The first spat out an image of a man preoccupied with destination rather than journey, the future, not the present. Then he was just a shadow until the next light conjured up his luminous image again, but from another perspective. Shadow once more. Then the bleared shape of his back, his stature diminishing with the sound of his comic whistle. He moved in and out of the dying lights, deeper into the obscuring folds, like a nonchalant ghost teaching himself a tune. Then he was gone. The man had occupied a space quite precisely at the time of an event of some significance. But he was not a true witness. His perspective was limited compared to that of the assassin whose hand had guided events, and watched as another moved obliviously through the small cataclysm. But the assassin was not a true witness, either, for he did not know that he, the watcher, was being watched in turn—by a man he had every right to believe had been ripped out of the flow of significant time.

The assassin moved out of his niche and marched up the steps, no longer taking care with the sound of his passage.

Seconds later, Pol stood facing the direction taken by the executioner. He did not know his identity, but he did know the motive, and he could guess the weapon. The face was that of a stranger, but the mind belonged to Rav—though of that, he must make certain.

With the wetness, his hair cleaved to his head, and his cape to his body; inside, a new, raw compulsion was being born. He began to follow the sound of the receding steps, and he moved eagerly, with the mind of a hunter. Fear was gone. He smiled thinly at the notion of stalking a man who thought him dead. Now—and the urge was so powerful there was no room for surprise—*he* wanted to kill.

The assassin was riding a high hum of excitement as he headed for a favorite watering hole. He was thinking that he had almost refused the ridiculously rushed contract on the Cadre Two—*would have*, if the man paying for it were not who and what he was. A Cadre Two! How could he keep this to himself? The prize of a lifetime, a testament to his craft, a guarantee of monstrous fees! He would find a way to whisper the tale into the proper ears. He had been told *never* to report back, successful or not. Perhaps he should take it upon himself to ignore that.

In the meantime, he would celebrate, buy the most expensive wine, the most exclusive women. He could see the garish lights of a marquee pushing through the gloom ahead, and he quickened his pace.

As he passed a narrow lane snaking between looming buildings into yet another darkness in this city of darknesses, a hand closed on the fabric of the cloak at the back of his neck. His feet were swept forward and upward and were suspended absurdly at eye level for a moment before his head was jerked down and the backs of his shoulders were driven ruthlessly into the rough pavement. Air exploded out of his chest and lights leaped from behind his eyes. Pain shot the lights with color, and before his lungs could suck back the lost air, a forearm crushed across his throat. His body was a grotesque rag doll in the hands of a cruel child. Why couldn't he move? He couldn't even call out. Silence drove out shock after a few seconds and replaced it with fear. He couldn't breathe. His eyes began to bulge and he had to open them to escape the painful lights. A white, innocent face was thrust centimeters from his, just a quiet face, with wet, plastered hair, but it belonged to a ghost.

Its voice seemed disinterested.

"Cadre," it said, and waited while he begged for air with his eyes; then, "Who hired you?"

The assassin moved his lips soundlessly, pathetically. The forearm was lifted long enough to allow a squeak of air to enter before it clamped down again. The assassin's vision swam with the pale face. It came even closer, out of the darkness, and cool breath from its mouth washed over his sweating cheeks. He fought to keep consciousness, but with it he kept his fear, and he had not yet thought about the answer to the question. He was afraid to close his eyes lest the face be there beneath, also. Slick hair, white, innocent face, soft voice.

"Who hired you?"

"I cannot answer!" screamed the voiceless mind behind the protruding eyes. "Let me answer!"

But the vise on his throat stayed tight and the lights were returning, even with his eyes open. Then the voice came again. Were voice and face and arm not connected?

"One answer. One name," said the ghost. "I will not wait."

The forearm lifted a second time, but only a little, and air had to scrape down a tortured throat. When the assassin's lungs pushed it back out to reach for more, his lips used its force to say:

"Rav."

Only minutes later, Pol was in the shadows near the reception hall. He saw the last of Raven's social elite enter a line of chauffeur-driven ground cars. He still felt the strange, atavistic thrill, strong, burning, and targeted. Soon, Rav emerged with the secretary of trade. Pol could see that the dialogue was between equals, not master and underling. Rav left the secretary with a gesture of reassurance and entered a car. Quickly, Pol approached the last car in line and opened its door. The chauffeur jerked back at the sight of the intense blue eyes and plastered hair.

"Get out."

"Wha?"

"Cadre. Get out."

The chauffeur hastened to open the other door.

By the time Pol saw Rav's dim figure enter the warehouse, his clothes were starting to dry, in spite of the damp air. He followed silently. Inside, the light was dim, but he could make out two figures standing near a loading machine. One of the shapes threatened to merge completely with the surrounding darness, but Pol knew it wore a Cadre uniform. Something inside him went cold when he saw the dull flash of red hair. He felt fear so obliterating, so utter, that it was he, he was it. It was not a frenzied thing that explodes into blind passion; it was too purposeless for that, too numbing.

Without a sound, he moved in a trance toward them. As he neared, their outlines became sharper, and the soft mutter of their voices began to form distinct words. When he could recognize their features, he had to stop and bank his cold fear, as a smithy banks a hot forge.

"You say these crystals contain the Cadre's data on the production and secret trade negotiations of two of our main competitors?"

"Yes, down to the finest detail. You'll know their moves before they make them."

"You're sure everything's here? Only two crystals..."

"What's not there, the Cadre doesn't have."

"Fine. I have no reason to doubt you, Sestus, considering your services to date. Your account will be credited with the fee agreed upon, though the secretary has never put such a sum in the hands of an individual before."

"We both know that the investment will bring a thousandfold in return. And my risk is...well, if the feel of this uniform on my skin didn't fill my guts with...no amount of bribery would tempt me. Which reminds me—no more deliveries until I see the plans for my 'disappearance' and relocation. It had better be good—in fact, it had better be infallible. You know how the Cadre reacts to this sort of thing. If I go down, you and your cronies go down with me."

"No need for threats, Sestus. The plan will be foolproof. We're working on it now, but we hate to lose you."

"Ultimately, you'd lose me anyway, because a diverted information flow of this nature reveals *itself* in time. Computer surveillance is too sophisticated to miss it for long, even if the culprit has machines for children."

"What?"

"Never mind. I computed a timeline before I started this, and that line turns red soon. Be ready for me within a month and I'll have some more goodies as a parting gift."

"How did you arrive at your timeline?"

"My machines—they told me when their brothers and sisters would probably begin to get suspicious."

"Well, I have some bad news for you. I'm afraid you placed too much faith—"

Pol's fear broke and pushed him once more toward them. The two heads swiveled in his direction with comic simultaneity, but there was nothing amusing in the pallid faces glowing sickly in the dark. Their eyes grew large and round; their bodies froze in surprise and fear, each with a different surprise, a different fear. Ses fought to recover his composure. He blinked away his shock and his eyes tried to focus on the implacable, frozen blue of those accusing him. Rav remained as he was, rendered impotent by his own terror, fed by the certain knowledge that he was a dead man. He was ignored.

The two men in black confronted each other in motionless silence: one seemed to be delivering, unvoiced, an absolute and terrible proclamation of justice; the other, a hopeless but defiant assertion of his right to be.

Somewhere outside, a bird shrilled. Dace Sestus sighed, and the tableau was broken. He shook his head. "No, Pol. No, please." Pol couldn't speak. He was damning the universe and his guts writhed in bile—and he couldn't speak. Ses could only see the cold blue eyes.

"Pol...Pol, ol' buddy. Just give me a few hours. A head start." There was a twisted imitation of the old warm smile. "Give it to me, roomie." His voice cracked. "You never gave anybody anything, you know."

Pol shook his head because he couldn't do anything else. He shook his head because he was denying the cackling, lunatic Maker who had put him there to see his only friend beg for life. Ses saw only a Damoclean sword. He sighed his resignation—and leaped.

Rav cried out, because he had never witnessed such sudden, potent human action before—not one born of such stillness. The attack was simple and direct. Ses lanced his body across the few feet of abyss between himself and his Cadre brother. The middle rows of knuckles on both hands were a spearhead.

The targets were cold, blue. it was a standard but deadly Cadre attack: the body was a projectile; if the knuckles should miss, the bowed head aimed its thick frontal bone for a lower blow; if that should miss, the knees would rise for one lower still.

Unfettered reflex drove Pol's head down and under the rigid arms, drove his right shoulder low and back up to power a whipping elbow, like a rock on the end of a rope. The elbow impacted with the bridge between Ses's eyes with a sickening crunch. Shattered bone exploded into his brain. Ses was dead before his body hit the floor.

The conflict had taken less than three seconds. For one man, they measured the time between fragile life and the black wall of death; for the other, they measured the time between the security of ignorance and the knowledge of despair.

Pol stood for a time unmoving, feeling only the headiness of nerves still accelerating. He knelt beside the body but could not touch it. As if arranged delicately by a devout altar server, his black cape was draped artfully on the damp floor. Head bowed, hands clasped, shoulders drooping, the figure over the body looked like a defrocked priest praying desperately to a God he suspected was not there.

Many long days later, *Farstar* broke out of the seamless black of warped space. Pol was returning to HQ on the same ship that brought him to Raven. He sat on the observation deck, staring out the glassteel bubble, watching the Void form and stride in. The transparent dome between him and it provided no comfort—a thin, brittle barrier hung there like a chunk of obsidian around a savage's neck, a bauble meant to ward off the inevitable.

The Void strode in, a violent interloper, confident not of welcome, but of its power to come. It required no indulgence, offered no apologies. *Farstar*'s motion made the stars icy white spikes, light pricks that slaked into him insidiously.

He stood and leaned his forehead on the cold glassteel. He raised two fists and pounded, pounded, pounded, filling the small chamber with a howl, like a wolf.

SY 3039

"Why did you kill him?"

The VP's face was drawn with fatigue, but his voice held its customary bite. He looked at his number Two and, for the dozenth time in the last hour, took note of the changes. Tyrees presented the same washed blandness for a face, but something was missing. The rapier-sharp eyes had lost their piercing quality and their immediacy, as if they didn't care where they lingered. They moved without haste, looking at this object or that with equal disinterest. Something vital was gone; before, the man had always seemed relaxed, but still exuded a reserve of energy, a ready stock of power that buzzed beneath the skin, waiting to be drawn upon. Why was he now a mined-out asteroid, shell hard but coreless?

The VP wondered if his imagination were overactive. He had been pulled through a sieve on this one; HQ on Regnum had taken an unholy interest in Tyrees and the Raven affair, and he had been caught blatantly ignoring procedure. Fortunately, things had turned out well—except for the traitor in the brotherhood: high-ranking, in *his* sector, and dead at the hands of a fellow officer.

"Tyrees, I asked you why you felt it necessary to kill him."

"Sorry, sir. I . . . he attacked. I reacted. I'm afraid it's as simple as that."

"Did you confront him? Challenge him, trap him? What?"

"Uh, I don't follow, sir." A shrug.

The VP was exasperated. Lassitude was another thing he didn't expect.

"Look. I have exchanged more priority one messages with HQ over this than I have in the last two years. That's in *spite* of a 'successful' assignment. A lot of it is my responsibility because of the way I had you go in. I didn't go by the book and I daresay you didn't, either. I'm paying for my decision and that's okay—but I don't want any more surprises!" To punctuate his last words, the VP bounced a stylus off his immaculate desk. His listener watched the rolling cylinder like a retarded child.

"So I'll try again. Was there any way that the digger's death could have been avoided?"

A long silence. For the first time Pol raised his eyes and looked directly at his questioner. He started to speak, then stopped. Finally, his eyes fell again, seeking out the stylus, and he spoke to it softly.

"Given the circumstances . . . given the circumstances, no. I followed Rav. Ses . . . the Cadre man was there. He attacked. If I could have predicted his reaction, maybe . . ."

"All right." The VP sighed and settled back in his chair. "Nobody asks you to be a mind reader. What about the Raven bunch?"

"I arrested Rav before my recall. That's all I had time for. Handed him over to the FSO to wait for your number One."

"Any others implicated?"

"The secretary of trade. Probably others . . . I don't know. . . . Sir? When will I be reassigned?"

"Relax, number Two. First things first. Get your evidence—you seem to have damn little, except for the actual culprits—suspicions, guesses, whatever, into a crystal, for transmission to our man on Raven. Have it to me by tomorrow."

"Yes, sir."

"Then get some rest."

"Yes, sir." The dismissal was obvious, but Pol remained in his chair, now staring at nothing.

"Tyrees."

"Yes, sir."

"You did a good job—an *amazing* job, considering the timeline. The digger was a traitor and the Cadre court would have executed him anyway. You've cut out a rotten pustule that was growing inside us." The VP's voice was easy and low, but it resonated with conviction. "You could not have done otherwise."

"But there may have been—extenuating circumstances. The court . . ."

"The court would have delayed the time of his dying. That is all."

There was still no defined response from Tyrees, but the VP was more certain than ever that something serious was wrong. The man was spiritless.

"I know you've never had to kill any man before, let alone a brother. Your assignments have taken you into little violence, but personal feelings are irrelevant here. It was your *duty,* nothing more, nothing less. The Cadre requires it, so don't waste time on regrets." His words stirred some animation from Tyrees, though only in his voice. There was an undertone of pleading in it.

"But I didn't *decide* to kill him."

"What?"

"I didn't *choose*. I just . . . reacted. There was no thinking, no reasoning, no decision. I . . ."

"Look, Tyrees! I gave you more credit than this. If you hadn't acted as you did, if you had stopped to consider pros and cons, *you* would be the corpse back there and the Cadre would still have a traitor in its ranks! Now get out of here and get some rest."

Pol stood silently, saluted, and moved to the doorway.

"And Tyrees." Pol looked back. "After that report is done, after you get some rest, go out and get drunk or something. Find a woman. I don't want to see you in here like this again."

"Uh . . . sir, why, why was HQ so interested?"

"Don't know. Because they caught me playing games, I guess. Now get out. Get out. Oh! One other thing. In three days, report in for your psychological assessment." Pol frowned.

"But the last was only a year ago. . . ."

"Orders. Do it. Three days."

"HQ again?"

"Yes."

Pol looked as if he were about to protest, then shrugged his shoulders and left, walking slowly like a drunk very aware of his condition.

The VP sat in thought. He was not a man who spent much time on imponderables, having long been in the habit of making hard decisions and living with them. Violently, he stabbed at a key.

"Lanni!"

"Yes, sir?"

"Get in here to take a priority one transmission to HQ. I'm going to save a career and do the Cadre a big favor at the same time."

"I beg your pardon, sir?"

"Get in here, dammit."

He flipped the key closed and went to retrieve his stylus from the floor, muttering as he went. When Lanni entered, he was dictating before she could sit down.

SY 3039

COUNCIL EYES ONLY

Procedural Report—Vice-Proctor, Sector Five

- Censure Report, justify procedures re Raven assignment
- Debrief Officer Tyrees, Raven assignment
  - record and transmit—CP
- Psychological Assessment, Pol Tyrees
  - record and transmit—CP

Report

Directives implemented. Details following.

Supplemental Recommendation

Assignment completion—Pol Tyrees, Cadre Two, Raven file: speed, discretion, effectiveness. Recommend promotion to Cadre One.

Transmissions re . . .

SY 3039

COUNCIL EYES ONLY

Psychological Assessment

Subject: Pol Tyrees, Cadre Two, Political Section
Examiner: Dr. Ammas Tiir,
             Chief Examiner

Synopsis
Raw data was generated from "The Standard Test Bank—Field
Agents" (see Appendices A,B,C). This was supplemented as
usual by a series of personal interviews. As directed, hyp-
notherapy was *not* part of the assignment procedure.

Intelligence/aptitude
- The intelligence rating is slightly above average for a Cadre
  Two officer
- Ratings in all aspects of sensual acuity are off the top end
  of test scales—extremely unusual, perhaps unprecedented
- High aptitude ratings in extrapolation facility, assimilation,
  and thought sequence control
- Slightly below average ratings in mathematical abstraction
- All other ratings average for category

Emotional Matrix

Responses complex, often contradictory. Rigid superego control of natural volatility, especially libidinal impulses. Potential adrenaline production extremely high (0.93). High empathetic responses in conflict with task-oriented will. Overall responses suggest strength of purpose, perhaps a too rigid self-control.

Subjective Assessment

A "subjective assessment" is the prerogative of the chief examiner. I feel strongly enough about aspects of this personality to exercise that option, especially since they do not surface obviously from the measured data.

It is my professional opinion that from the Cadre viewpoint, this subject has extraordinary potential for *both* productive and counterproductive endeavor, depending upon circumstances. I recommend that he not be exposed to situations in which he would be forced to doubt his present value system.

My personal contact with the subject created a clear impression of drive, power of will, and a natural magnetism that is quite palpable. It is akin to what was once called "charisma." These strong personal qualities must have, as a fundamental source, strong passions. Yet, as the data does indicate, he keeps them under total control. He forms powerful loyalties and is very goal-oriented; but if his repressed passions ever become incompatible with those goals, or if he comes to perceive those goals as unworthy, I fear the outcome. He is a believer; he must have something to believe in. Others will believe in *him*.

I do not apologize for the apparent contradictions in my prognosis, for my profession embraces such things—as does the human personality itself. I *do* apologize for the subjectivity of my report, but my convictions are born of experience.

Addendum

For the first time since I began to work at the Cadre Two level, I have been denied access to the hereditary history and physiological reports on a subject. I request such access, in the interest of carrying out my duties fully.

SY 3043

The Cadre's highest ranks—Ones, Twos, even Threes—were made up of loners. They could be nothing else, because they were field men cast like stones into the vast and indifferent desert of spotted space, first here, then there. Roots could not take—friends were rare. They were set apart even from their own brotherhood.

Pol Tyrees, Cadre One, was a loner among loners, untouchable, remote even from those of the sparsest rank called number One. Those in contact with Tyrees never knew him to take leave, never knew him to express interest in anything but his present assignment. And they never liked him. Perhaps it was that he was too much the reality of what they were expected to be.

Pol didn't permit himself to care what others thought. He welded the memory of Raven in a steel coffin and buried it deep. He clung to the Cadre as a shipwrecked sailor clings to a spar. Even his grandfather had been relegated to the nether reaches of his mind, a statue of a saint tarnished by time.

His latest assignment directive put him on a tightly managed planet called Sparta. All the legwork had been done, the evidence gathered with meticulous care by the Cadre team before him. The arrest had been made and a conviction was expected.

Pol had been sent to conduct the final interrogation. He had established a reputation for "the milk—" the process of extracting information from unwilling prisoners.

It was a quirk of Regnum law that the Cadre's powers of arrest and detention were almost unlimited, but the use of interrogation drugs or implements *before* conviction was prohibited. After a guilty verdict, such devices were allowed, if information were still required. This law had been upheld for decades, but with the Trade Wars still escalating, factions in the Council had been moving to have it repealed; for the time being, it was even more scrupulously observed because of the controversy.

The fact that a Cadre One was sent for the interrogation attested to the importance of the case. The prisoner was Vääs Blis, a popular officeholder on Sparta until his arrest. He was reputed to be the wealthiest man in the sector and controlled a number of quite legitimate industrial conglomerates. Until his exposure, it was assumed by Spartans that the visible style was the actual man—a wealthy philanthropist who dabbled in politics and social reform causes out of a spirit of civic duty. In fact, he was one of a small group of ruthless men who secretly controlled the black market activities of the entire sector. It was thought that they had affiliations with similar groups in other sectors, forming a perverted version of the Regnum Council. It was also believed that these men had more than profit as a motivation; that they were in active partnership with the overt rebels in the Hub; that they had as their ultimate goal the carving up of the galaxy into personal baronies measured in light-years. This was abhorrent to those who espoused the ideals of the Regnum: only megalomaniacs would nurture such an insane dream.

In reality, these men were voicing a bold proclamation of their right to individual grandeur in an age of faceless, bureaucratic technology. Their defiance was directed at a galactic technocracy that denied the efficacy of individual aggrandizement. The single human being was too insignificant to cast a shadow over the vastness of space, over the diversity of planetary cultures; he could not absorb or encompass them. Even the Chairman of the Regnum could claim only a power of influence rather than edict, because he voted, like the rest of the Council, on policy limited to interplanetary affairs. The rebels in the Hub—and a few others under deep camouflage—

were making a daring statement of their right to be set above other men, above the dehumanizing machinery of classless order. The validity of that statement, they felt, would be demonstrated quite simply by succeeding in their efforts to destroy that order.

The Regnum Council feared this kind of archaic man—rapacious, single-minded, iconoclastic. It sent a Cadre One to interrogate the only one of the "shadow council" ever apprehended. Object: to unearth the identities of the shadow council and their methods of operation. He was the Cadre's best "milker," a humorless, passionless robot of a man, who delivered reports of uncanny accuracy after interrogation. Those who studied his reports were often mystified by the lack of corroborating evidence in the transcripts. They were the usual sort of thing—cautious or evasive responses, declarations of innocence, outright denials. But this milker's reports were invariably precise, factual assertions that were always borne out later. They could not trace the process from transcript to report. In spite of their confusion and their pleas to query the milker about his methods, he was never asked to divulge them.

Sparta was a loyal member of the Regnum, and it was angered by the revelations about Blis. The first attorney, its highest justice official, met Pol Tyrees at the Cadre's FSO, where the prisoner was being held. It was the prelude to the first interrogation session. The first attorney was an aggressive, no-nonsense man who tackled issues head-on. The two sat in the C.O.'s office, with Pol behind the desk.

"I thank you for getting this under way so quickly, Officer Tyrees. We Spartans find this affair distasteful—no, that's understated—we find it *intolerable*."

"So does the Cadre, First Attorney. I'm sure we can depend on your cooperation."

"Absolutely, yes. Anything we can do will be done. However . . ." The first attorney raised hands, palms forward, as if to soften his next words. "I must be frank. We would have preferred to deal with this ourselves. Our justice is swift and efficient. Vaas Blis is a blasphemy, and he would have been tried, convicted, and executed by now, under Spartan law. The evidence is damning."

"There is no question of the Regnum's jurisdiction in this case, sir."

The first attorney did not take offense at the blunt manner

of the Cadre One, for it matched his own. As he considered his next move, he fastidiously adjusted the sleeves of the austere gray tunic worn by all Spartan justice officials. Pol recognized the gesture as an unconscious ritual before the undertaking of a matter of importance.

"I don't contest the right of jurisdiction, Officer Tyrees. I urge you only to consider some practical points for your report. I know your recommendations carry weight. it may be possible to make . . . some compromises for the sake of justice."

The first attorney leaned far forward in his chair, his body a set of rigid lines. In contrast, Pol slumped in a pose of negligent ease, one that belied the uniform and the rank reflected in the dull black gleam of his collar piping. Cold, blue eyes; a thin smile.

"The Cadre doesn't indulge in backroom deals, First Attorney."

"Please! Just hear me out." With each of his points, he threw a stiff forefinger at the ceiling. "Fact: Blis controls incredible wealth and power, more than we suspected until the Cadre ripped him open. Fact: He can use those resources to delay and confuse Regnum legal machinery. Include the help of the shadow council, for all we know. These are possible if, *if*, he has the time. Fact: A swift and righteous justice here and now serves as an example to other vipers like him. I beg you— just recommend it—turn him over to Sparta and I will guarantee that justice. The Cadre cannot do that, because he's out of your hands after the interrogation. Who knows what will happen when he goes to the courts?"

"It is not my function to guarantee justice. I am here to interrogate the man and report my findings. That is my intention—with or without your compliance."

"But there is no question of our cooperation, sir! I have already committed that. All I ask is a recommendation supporting our jurisdiction in this case. The interests of the Regnum—and of the Cadre—will be better served by it." Now the first attorney was leaning forward, like a cat over a fish pond.

"You are ignoring the scope of this investigation. We need the *information* that Blis possesses even more than a conviction. He and a few others control the black market in this sector, and perhaps his influence goes beyond that."

"But you only lend weight to my proposition! You are limited to verbal interrogation until after a conviction. Sparta does not allow criminals such privileges. We can get that information for you!"

The first attorney settled back in his chair, certain he had scored a telling point, to watch the youngish man with the ancient mannerisms of authority consider his reply. He did not expect it to come in such a soft, uncompromising voice.

"That is one thing you can*not* guarantee, sir. Drugs and artificial detectors are often effective, but not dependable. Men react to them unpredictably. I will pass the proposal on, but I will not recommend it."

The first attorney sighed audibly. He wondered how the Cadre turned out these men. He had never dealt with a One before, and this man was carved from stone.

"Very well. I defer because I must, but I also say this: I was fooled by Blis, but I know him now. You will get nothing from interrogation. He made clowns of us all, exploited us for a whole generation, and we never questioned his integrity. He and his nest of rats will find ways to manipulate the Regnum courts. Be warned."

"The prisoner and his legal representative are in the interrogation room. I assume that you are Sparta's official observer?"

"I am."

"Then your presence is allowed, under the interrogation procedures. Shall we go?" Only that silver grain in his hair suggests the flint underneath, thought the first attorney as he shambled behind.

The interrogation room was bare, containing only a table with a pair of chairs on each of its sides. The walls were starkly white; table and chairs black. A high ceiling dropped a grid of glaring light on the table. Because the room was windowless and dampened sound, it provoked a sense of removal, of isolation and portent.

The sliding door hissed closed behind them, seals fighting air pressure. Two men sitting on one side of the table interrupted their low conversation. Both were middle-aged and richly dressed, but Pol had no difficulty in distinguishing Blis from his legal representative: the prisoner's tension level did not increase at the sight of the arrivals, whereas the lawyer was suddenly charged by their presence—a Cadre One and the first attorney. Blis was accustomed to men of power. He ignored

the first attorney and studied the man in black with interest.
He was a lean hawk of a man, with eyes set deeply, and bright
with intelligence. Everything about him suggested calculation,
studied deliberation. In contrast, his lawyer showed signs of
strain, looking quickly from one man to the other, as if anticipating a signal that might easily be missed. The first attorney
made introductions in a flat voice. Almost before he was finished, the lawyer spouted forth.

"Ahem. Yes. Well. On behalf of my client, I must be assured
that the ground rules are, uh, clear, and that everything is in
order before we begin. So . . ."

Pol halted the flow of words by simply shifting his glance
from Blis to the lawyer, who let his last sentence trail off.

"The ground rules are clear. Each daily interrogation will
last no more than four hours and will be recorded. All questions
must be answered by the prisoner. Observers must remain silent. The interrogation must last no longer than forty days, at
which time the prisoner may demand release or trial on the
specified charges."

"And there may be no physical or psychological coercion,"
piped the lawyer.

"That is a legality we may take for granted."

"And I need not remain silent if I detect any such coercion!"

"In this room, you do," said Pol in a monotone. "I will not
tolerate efforts to inhibit this interrogation by specious claims
of intimidation. You *do* have the right to terminate it temporarily by lodging a protest with the judiciary, but I have never
been removed from an interrogation yet. Several legal repre-
sentatives *have*, however, after their claims were found to be
tactical only." The first attorney nodded and smiled.

"But I may search this room? For . . . uh, any devices that
may be used surreptitiously on my client?"

"You may not. This room is free of any 'devices' save the
recorder—my statement to that effect is now part of the record."

The lawyer was about to speak again, but Pol turned from
him to the prisoner. Blis had not taken his eyes from the Cadre
One.

"You are the man under charge, sir?"

"I am."

"Identify yourself, please."

"Vaas Blis, second trader, citizen of Sparta." There was a disgusted snort from the first attorney. Pol's look brought a muttered apology.

"The indictment cites these charges: conspiracy to purchase and sell proscribed goods; illegal transport; bribery of customs officials; falsification of shipping manifests. There are thirty-two specifics. Do you wish them read?"

"Read" was not a literal term, because Pol was citing from memory. He had removed from his cape a small storage computer but had not activated it. It sat, a black, fist-sized cube, an accusation before the prisoner.

"That won't be necessary. I'm aware of them."

Blis's words were subdued. Pol had an impression of a man of infinite caution, of guardedness honed into habit.

"Should this interrogation result in a recommendation that you be put to trial, the charges may differ from those cited by the indictment. You are aware of that?"

"Yes."

"Do you wish to enter anything on the record before we begin?"

"Nothing, except that the charges are false. This is a deliberate conspiracy to use the law against me."

"Do you wish to elaborate?"

"No, I will do so when I'm in a proper court of law."

"Very well. Do you own the trading vessel *Forager?*"

"Yes, that is public knowledge."

Pol launched the interrogation with a series of rapid-fire questions, mostly innocuous and factual. The storage computer still lay inert between them. During the flow of question and answer, Pol watched Blis like a technic studying an insect plastered between glass slides. The questions were answered slowly, carefully. The words came from Pol like splashes of cold water; from Blis, like gobs of a viscous liquid dropping from a narrow-necked bottle. Through this uneven rhythm of conflict, Pol searched for patterns of motion and voice inflection that he could match with known facts. But Blis was difficult to read. He said as little as possible, and his body was a slab of marble. It was an intuitive defensive posture born of a lifetime of deception. The assumption of a cloaking outer layer had become as natural as the donning of a real garment—and he was aware that he never had more need of its protection.

Nevertheless, Pol was slowly building a telltale model, a template that he mentally placed over the image of the prisoner to make fine adjustments. When Blis was denying knowledge or hedging the truth, there was a minute change in the size of his pupils. The dilation was an automatic reaction to sensed danger and an increased effort to concentrate.

Another of the details Pol etched onto his invisible template was the medallion that hung from a long platinum chain around Blis's neck. It rested just above the folded hands, in his lap. Blis gently fondled the medallion with his fingers. This was the only action that an ordinary man might notice, if he were told to look for one. He would be unlikely to attach any significance to the unobtrusive motion, because it seemed only an idle caress. But Pol saw a pattern in the unconscious touches: a stroking of the medallion's edge when Blis was unsure and hesitating over an answer; a light fingertip tapping when he felt on safe ground; a clasp by thumb and forefinger when he felt threatened.

Pol concentrated on the microcosmic drama of the fingers and eyes—waiting patiently for Blis to tell an outright lie, waiting to make the match between it and the telltale flaws in the prisoner's façade. He had it a half hour into the interrogation.

"You were on Gamma for three days during their trade festival last year?"

"Yes, I represented Sparta."

Blis stopped tapping the medallion and held it tightly. Pol could see an image of a falcon embossed on the shiny surface. For the first time, he did not immediately throw another question across the table. The man's eyes narrowed as the pause lengthened. Slowly, Pol reached for the storage unit and activated it. The festival *had* lasted for three days, but Blis had been under surveillance by then, and he had remained on Gamma for *four* days. The number Two could only determine that Blis attended meetings with others from off-planet. Pol did not have to consult the computer to verify this, but he frowned at the tiny luminous screen before speaking again.

"You're certain it was three days?"

"Yes." The answer came quickly. Fingertip pressure on the falcon's talons increased. Eye pupils diminished. Pol's template was finished. He would test it a few more times, but he was certain now that he could detect a lie *without* backup information. He decided not to press his man until the issue was important. The next question was innocuous; he watched the finger tapping begin again and the eyes return to normal.

The first attorney was no longer pleased with the proceedings. A frown was deepening, and tightly folded arms contained his silence. Blis's lawyer was watching his client with approval. The rhythm of question and answer resumed until Pol knew that the prisoner was again feeling secure: then he went on the attack.

"You know of the epidemic on Bastion eight months ago?" Once again, the medallion was captured.

"Yes, I'm sure everyone in the sector knows of it."

"One hundred thousand dead. More than that with permanent brain damage. Do you know what caused it?"

Blis's eyes seared into Pol's. "Yes, a virus. It attacked cells of the nervous system."

"That's what caused the *disease*. What caused all those deaths?"

"I don't understand what . . . the disease . . ."

"The disease has a simple cure. An injection eradicates it. Enough vaccine to inoculate the whole population was en route when it was intercepted by pirates. Do you know anything about that?" All Pol knew was that the Cadre suspected an involvement in the ugly affair.

The prisoner's eyes were now orbs of glass encasing hard black pellets. "No."

"After the hijacking, vaccine was sold at exorbitant prices to wealthy Bastionites while the planet was under quarantine. Do you know anything about that?"

"No, I do not." The template gave its verdict.

"You are lying," said Pol in an even voice.

"The accusation is absurd—and insulting."

"I have not yet made an accusation. I will now. You are directly responsible for the deaths of one—hundred—thousand—human—beings." The two observers looked at one another in shocked surprise.

"My *only* connection with it was as a—horrified neighbor. Horrified."

"You are lying."

Inside Blis's head, white walls and black table began to spin. How did this man know? How could he be so *certain?* Blis's mask remained intact, but his resolve was shaken. He was familiar, even comfortable, with the unlit place of hiding inside himself, but now, as he crouched there in the darkness, a claw reached out to touch him. He held the medallion in a tight fist, not speaking. Finally his lawyer sensed a crisis and leaned forward.

"I must speak, sir! You are attempting to intimidate my client with baseless accusations. He is answering every question candidly, and you—"

"Keep your silence. A single word more and you will be removed from the interrogation room."

Pol's eyes returned to the prisoner, who felt them hit, penetrate, scour like a wash of acid. It was insidious, violating. Only the black table kept them apart. Something irresistible gradually took form out of the shapes and shades, the lights and wetnesses of Blis's eyes—terror—a terror born not of guilt, but of a sense of being raped. The ravager waited until his victim's recognition of it was full before he resumed.

"We are close to the time limit." The same mechanical, implacable voice. "Vaas Blis, you are not just a greedy mercenary guilty of breaking trade regulations. You are guilty of moral crimes on an inhuman scale. Some would call you evil. I can promise you that I will lay you bare. I can promise you that the day will come when ordinary people will think of your name when they speak of offal. But I will allow you one option—it may be the last you will ever exercise. It is within my authority to declare a closed trial. The result will be identical, but the public will not learn of the nature of your crimes. The price for that concession will be the full disclosure of everything you know. It is just within the realm of possibility that others have as much to answer for. Think about it until tomorrow."

Pol picked up the storage unit, dropped it into an inside pocket, and rose. His cape fell forward from his shoulders to close around him. The prisoner looked and knew what it was to see a man of powerful office when he was more the office than the man. The black cape and the high collar were more than a uniform—he was augmented by it, diminishing other men. He stood, long and still, smooth visage and cold blue eyes, a dark statue.

SY 3043

CADRE EYES ONLY

Field Agent's Report—**Pol Tyrees, Cadre One, Political Security**

Assignment Directive
- Interrogate prisoner Vaas Blis, second trader, Sparta (charges, investigation report, background data through local FSO)
- attempt to ascertain identities, operations of black market "shadow council"

Preliminary Report
- Interrogation terminated, plea of guilty as charged
- Prisoner agrees to divulge full knowledge of "shadow council" activities
- Details following

Transmission re . . .

PT—CI

SY 3049

Pol sat alone at one end of the spaceport's VIP lounge. A bevy of wealthy tourists chatted at the other end, while waiting for a final customs clearance. They were happy to be home, even after an indulgent holiday. To Pol, their home planet was just another ball spinning in the Void. It housed his current HQ. This was his first assignment out of Sector IX.

He stared down the long rectangle of the lounge at the babbling group. They were watching him, too, but only with sidelong glances or with sweeps of eyes carefully casual, arcs that crossed over but never rested on him. To them, the dark figure was a beast in an open zoo—pacified, even friendly, but foreign, perhaps dangerous. He could be ignored, but not forgotten.

A middle-aged woman, festooned with silk and sable, was opening an elaborate cage that had just been delivered to the lounge.

"Oohhh, poor Bitty-Loo. Poor Bitty. You're home now, darling. Come give Mommy a hug. Ohh, my poor little girl." She coaxed an armful of fur with pointed ears out of the cage. It snuggled to her bosom as naturally as a baby. A handlike paw popped out of the fur to caress her nose. Chuckles and chuckings and "isn't she cutes" came from the others. She stroked it lovingly and held it toward a smiling man beside her.

"You see, Georg? How could they keep a cuddle-bun like my Bitty locked up with the baggage all that time? Say hello to Georg, Bitty." Her companion reached out a hand, like a dutiful uncle about to chuck the chin of a newborn. Suddenly, savage eyes and hacksaw teeth exploded from the soft bundle. Then eyes and teeth and hand all disappeared into the fur for a half second before the man screamed, jerking back convulsively. He gaped in semishock at fingers spouting blood from several deep wounds.

Pol turned his head disdainfully away from the ensuing pandemonium. He forced his thoughts back to his own situation and his latest assignment directive. Once again, he was being kept out of the Trade Wars struggle. Once again, it was a "dry" assignment, posing no threat of physical danger. He had long ago decided that it was deliberate—as was his constant reshuffling from sector to sector. He even suspected that he was being watched, but he couldn't fathom why. He was a Cadre One, with all its power and prerogatives, but he felt like a small boy being patronized. His "milker" assignments had begun to gall. A pot-scourer, scraping at crusted lies, caked guilt. Looking on as they squirmed like fallen women hiding their nakedness. Looking on as their disgusting undersides were exposed. Others did the *real* work—finding and pushing over the stones under which these creatures crawled. He was forced only to dissect them, his probing fingers mucking through their ooze. The nature of his assignments rankled him to the core— almost as much as the fact that his efforts to change them were totally ignored.

But this one was different—a beam of sunlight. It was still a rocking chair assignment, but it would allow him to renew an old innocence, to once again breathe the clean air of an old enthusiasm. The Holtz Effect.

In all the years since his grandfather, nothing had been discovered that either supported or disclaimed the Alien Contact Theory. Ultimately, perhaps it was unsolvable. Perhaps it should be cast aside when the Regnum itself was rupturing from its core. But he was still tied, umbilically, to his grandfather's dream. He responded to the comfortable tug of almost forgotten harness. It *could* be the breakthrough. Tercet. He ran the encyclopedia entry across the backs of his eyes.

Encyclopedia Galactica
Computer Entry: SEC 9-EXP-TER 02
"Tercet" (new entry—updates monthly)

The planet Tercet presents an unusual occurrence in colonial history. it was officially "discovered" only a few years ago in SY 3024, but was actually inhabited about 2000. Tercet is only nominally part of the galaxy, because it is twenty light-years from the fringe of Sector IX, itself an outlying corner of the Regnum.

The rediscovery of the planet was accidental. A research vessel, *Boundless,* was commissioned in 3020 to investigate the black hole BH 189, 12.5 light-years from Sector IX's edge and on the same plane. In the process of circumnavigating the hole, *Boundless* found a tristar system whose presence had been masked from the galaxy. The rarity of a three-star system in synchronous orbit prompted *Boundless* to risk a dangerous incursion into intergalactic space. The system contained one small planet—Tercet—on which flourished a few hundred thousand descendants of a Sector II colony ship of a thousand years ago.

Technologically, the Tercians are quite primitive. Preliminary reports, however, reveal a rich culture bound to a mythology dominated by its three suns and the black hole nearby.

OPEN FILE, UPDATES MONTHLY ... OPEN FILE, UPDATES MONTHLY ...

Fascinating. Pol then dug his little storage unit from his cape and keyed for the Cadre's first and only report on Tercet. A digger had been sent, ostensibly to check out the HE readings, but Pol suspected that the Trade Wars part of the directive was of greater importance to those above. His own directive was very similar, and it was good security simply to have a Cadre man on Tercet. Because of its isolation and the shielding provided by the black hole, it would make an ideal hideaway for the Trade Wars barons. But why a number One *now?* The thought disturbed him. It tugged to the surface the old bitterness that had begun to grow back on Raven—perhaps even further back with Crazy Max—and had long since been nourished by the conviction that he was being used. But didn't the Cadre *use* all its personnel? Maybe this would be different. He shrugged mentally and began to read the digger's report again.

SY 3049

CADRE EYES ONLY

Field Assignment—Breeme Valtac, Cadre Three, Alien Security

Assignment Directive
  - Confirm Holtz Effect reading on planet Tercet (computer key S 09-ter-he for background material)
  - Gather data on Tercian culture seeking anomalies that may shed light on nature of HE
  - Remain alert to possibility of Trade Wars incursions

Report Procedure
  - Monthly progress reports
  - Emergency reports, field agent's discretion: re Trade Wars contingencies

It is not surprising that much of Tercian culture can be traced to the unique nature of their solar system (see Appendix F) and the strange story of their arrival on Tercet. Their way of life has evolved through one thousand years in total isolation. No other inhabited world (except Man's birthplace) can claim that distinction, and it is a matter of record that only ancient Tera has Holtz Effect readings comparable to Tercet's. However, I found no correlations between the two worlds that seem significant.

An important point must be stressed: It is extremely difficult to gather cohesive data on the niceties of Tercian culture. They make little distinction between subject disciplines or even between the five senses. A study of Tercian history demands also a study of their music; to understand their music, one is forced to look at their mathematical symbology, and so on. Each discipline is interwoven, often inexplicably, with every other. An example would be a reference to a color in terms of its "smell" or its "hotness." So much of their way of life is confusing to a non-Tercian; I suspect that only long immersion would provide the perspective necessary for even basic understanding. Their puzzling mode of logic (which seems to be an attempt to coalesce individual experiences into one total experience) seems to have little debilitating effect on their daily lives—it surfaces most often in their philosophical works. However, I am sure that it accounts for their lack of progress in the sciences.

Appendix A is a reproduction of *The Teraac,* their facsimile of a holy book. It is a gathering of homilies, philosophical tracts, and religious speculation. Tercians regard it as a compendium of their collective wisdom, a "guide to the single light." *The Teraac* is open-ended because it is added to irregularly by their "Seers." The attitude of the populace toward these writings is curious. It is that of a man working passionately on a work of art, not yet certain how it will turn out but dedicated to the task and confident of the final result.

Paradoxically, the Tercian "Seers" are blind from birth or have been voluntarily blinded in youth. I do not understand this brutal custom in a society that manifests little violence otherwise. Only men are Seers. They offer no explanation for this, though Seers do practice celibacy—as an exercise in self-discipline rather than morality, I think; Tercians probably couldn't afford such a "luxury" among their women when the population was so thin in the early days of the colony.

With some rather unorthodox programming, I subjected *The Teraac* to an etymological computer analysis. It produced two data of consequence: a rather obvious metaphorical derivative, the tristar system, and one that I could have predicted. Certain phraseology and syntax from the earlier writings (rather, writings inspired by an oral tradition) led to the probability that a space vessel's log was one of *The Teraac*'s sources. (Of course, Tercet was colonized accidentally by a Sector II ship in the 1990s. We have this from the Tercians themselves.) The lead helped me to ask the right questions, and I was able to track down the damaged captain's log crystal from *Forger,* the colony ship. It was kept—"enshrined" would be a better word than "kept"—in our equivalent of a museum. I had difficulty getting them to lend it to me, even though they've had no way of playing it for hundreds of years. However, they are aware of their origins and are very curious about us, their "cousins from the other side of darkness." In my opinion, the Tercian interest in Regnum membership is inspired by that curiosity, rather than any political or materialistic motive. Any talk of political intrigue confuses them. Our technology doesn't impress them any more than wealth. They take their pride in manual workmanship, like the building of a stone fence. The "darkness" that separates the Tercians from our galaxy is BH 189, a black hole that, until recently, escaped close investigation because it lay beyond the limits of safe astrogation where the graviton flow thins out. Tercian mythology symbolizes the hole as a negative force—as evil, dangerous, repressive, or blinding.

I was able to restore most of *Forger*'s log crystal. The captain seems to have undergone a profound experience that I can only describe as religious. I have selected several excerpts.

• • •

It is now certain. God help us. The malfunction which locked us into this course cannot be reversed. *Forger* is headed out of the galaxy. I have informed the colonists. I . . . Seeing their faces filled with fear and the death of their faith in me, I find myself praying that it's all over *soon.*

• • •

It's a black hole. We have detected a black hole. We are closer to it now than any vessel has ever been to one. Fate has chosen for us a more unique way to die than I anticipated—less lingering, at least. So be it. Depression is the real captain here. It is a deep, pervasive anticipation of the negative, a waiting for terror to stride in. You know it is coming; you do not know its exact nature or timing. So you wait, and suffer quietly. So you die slowly inside without hope. It is a tension that stretches lines from your throat to your groin and sets them thrumming painfully to the song of your solitude.

• • •

I am *caught up* and I am going to die. But so are all men. It is a *fact* that any individual, no matter how strong, is also caught up in a maelstrom of events like the Great Diaspora. The blast of mankind through the stars propels him, not like a leaf in the wind, but like a nail under the blow of a hammer. Or like a puny ship speared into a black hole.

The steam pressure of a population kept under containment for so long has been released. The explosion produces outward movement on a galactic scale; the ability of the individual to oppose this force is negligible. Time was when, on ancient Earth, a single man might have had the wherewithal to dictate the course of history; but when man's habitat grew beyond a solar system, he exposed himself to a plethora of new and mysterious forces beyond his control. Perhaps even in the past man's sense of free will was an illusion. If so, interstellar culture has shattered it.

In galactic space, distance is a concept that denies the senses. Our minds reject the paradoxical absurdity of the speed of light in the context of its crawling, laborious journey through the vast darknesses. Who can accept the reality that the heatless light from a faraway star began millions of lifetimes ago and outlives its own source? Oh, we can absorb such ridiculous facts by filtering them through instruments which cull them of their insulting— no, their *sinister* implications. The innocuous accumulation of zeros, the small superscripted digits representing overwhelming immensities, the little spike on the graph that takes passing note of a star dying—these things we can accept, after our devices have laundered out their threat.

*Inter*galactic space compounds these absurdities. There are one hundred billion galaxies in the cosmos, with as

many stars and as many planets in each. Even with our
machines busy, scraping the residue of terror from these
dark facts and presenting only blithe symbols, sooner or
later, one by one, we cry out, "No! This is too much!
Our lives cannot fit into it! It has no meaning. . . . How
can we have meaning? How can *I* have meaning?"

Yes, man's presumptuous journey into the stars has diminished his significance—perhaps denied it entirely.
He gazes upon an intimation of infinity, a dark shadow
dotted by the pitiful, cold light of a billion galaxies. He
is incredulous. He stands on the edge of this terrible idea
. . . and is afraid. I, too, am afraid.

• • •

We are going to miss it! The black hole is bending our
flight path. We are like a bird in a tornado, but we'll
enter a segmented orbit only, so this black force only
flirted with us, after all. We have reacted strangely. We
have known for some time that we would die and that
knowledge has rocked our sanity. But have we not *always*
known? Nevertheless, we feel some triumph now because we have looked upon its face: robber of light, void
maker, essence of nonbeing. Powerful—yes; fearful—
yes; but its power is a passive one, a dark maw that pulls
one toward it, but cannot reach out. Somehow, now that
we have "seen" it, we have the strength to cry, "No!"
We can resist. We can hope.

• • •

Back home, they would be interested in our readings. I
find it fascinating to come under the influence of such
a . . . a negativity. I know of its presence because I see
nothing there. Like trying to look down inside yourself,
something I intend to do more. Watery stars at its periphery, becoming fewer as we approach.

• • •

We plunged into the darkness and were afraid again. But
we did not succumb, and now the light—and what a
glorious and unique light it is!—now the light is brighter
and more beautiful than ever before. The *Forger* of the

incomprehensible black forged also our possible salvation. I tremble at the thought of it.

Screened from the galaxy by the black hole is a most magnificent, most unusual star system. Three stars—a red giant, a blue dwarf, and a yellow class G—dance in a complex synchronous orbit that is utterly spectacular. The hole swung us into a vector passing the system's only planet. It, from our preliminary readings, seems capable of sustaining life. We accept this miracle. Imagine! With its size alone, the cosmos only fails to humble the ignorant. Yet it provided *us*—less significant in the scheme of things than an amoeba to a star—with a chance for life. Men who have been given so much must justify their existence by keeping their spark of life aglow.

Forger must be abandoned. We will take to the shuttles. It will be a hard journey, but we will survive. We will survive!

I have uncovered no hard data of the landing period. However, there is a great deal of apocrypha melded into Tercian mythology (see Appendix D).

Most of *Forger*'s crew died in the struggle to gain and tame Tercet. The planet is hot and arid; it grants life grudgingly, but in the process forges a tough, resilient strain of our species. I've never seen a people more uniformly different from their fellows. They are pure gristle—an extra calorie is like an extra nose on them. Their skin is dried leather. Tercians generally ignore physical discomfort because their beginnings made them value self-discipline salted with stoicism. The evidence indicates a time of semiprimitivism after the shuttle landings. Because of a scarcity of food and water, the first real Tercians were nomadic desert tribes. Songs and stories celebrate feats of endurance and self-denial in the face of deprivation. Their victories are those of survival against the forces of darkness which they came to fear less, knowing them so well. The words and spirit of their brave captain is alive in them still. They fear death less than we; perhaps they revere life more. Certainly, mysticism permeates their culture.

I must emphasize that my views are the result of observation and extrapolation from their writings rather than firsthand. Aside from a natural reticence, their manner of speech is confusing. It is highly metaphorical, a synesthesia: that is, a mingling or interchanging of sense references. My Linguacomp was efficient in teaching me literal vocabulary and basic syntax (there are still many similarities to Standard), but I can communicate with the Tercians only on a superficial level. Here is a part of a conversation I recorded with one of their "Seers":

Valtac: What does a Seer do?
Seer: I see, of course.
Valtac: Since you are blind, you must mean that metaphorically.
Seer: I mean that literally.
Valtac: Then what do you see?
Seer: I see what is there to see.
Valtac: Do you mean in a mystical sense? Do you see a higher truth?
Seer: That smells interesting. I like to feel that is what I see. Perhaps. But "higher" than *what* truth?
Valtac: Well, let's leave that for now. Do you meditate? Do you leave this place or this time with your mind?
Seer: I do not taste meaning. How can I leave here and now?
Valtac: Well, there are those who claim they do that with their minds. They say it gives them a knowledge of those things timeless or absolute.
Seer: Ahh! Now I taste it. Yes. When I see the blue of Sentos, I leave now and here and hear the pure blue of all times and places.
Valtac: But you are blind! How can you see Sentos?
Seer: I am blind; hence, I see better, perhaps. You have eyes. Tell me of Sentos. It may be that I will learn from you.
Valtac: Well, it is blue, uhh, round, not particularly bright, compared to Eros and Logos.
Seer: I see all that.
Valtac: Right now? Here, indoors?
Seer: Yes, now. I smell it plainly.

That interview continued in a similar fashion for several hours. In the end, my patience was outlasted by his—and I learned nothing of consequence. I am a Cadre Three officer, trained in the gathering of data, and I am proud of my skills. But I remain confused about the full nature or function of the

Tercian Seer. Conversations with "ordinary" Tercians are even less productive. When the topic wasn't of mundane matters, I was always referred to their Seers. "We follow the sound of their footsteps. You must ask them."

There is a striking social anomaly on Tercet—their marriage custom. Excepting the Seers, they live together in triads—one male or female and two of the other sex. They say this is because each functions best sharing a three-part unity, like their tristar. Three lights become one. *The Teraac* (which is filled with obscure poetic images and philosophical musings) often alludes to the necessity for man to struggle for a balance of conflicting elements in his nature, like the senses, the passions, and the intellect. The marriage custom may be a manifestation of the concept. Nevertheless, its origin probably springs from the practical realities of the postlanding period—depleted populations, gene pool shallowness, an uneven mix of the sexes.

But none of my data seems to have a bearing on the Holtz Effect reading. It may be triggered by something chemical or radioactive in the atmosphere. It is a fact that Tercians are subject to an unusual mix of radiation from the tristar system. I brought back specimens of Tercian cell tissue for testing. However, even if we find mutational differences, links to the Holtz Effect would still have to be proven.

I will add a curious observation for which I have no corroborating data. During two local years on Tercet, I saw virtually no illness or disease. I saw death through old age and accident, and I saw *some* sickness, but only among the young. There are no medical facilities on Tercet, nor is there sign of even folklore curatives or herbal medicine. A hardy stock and a climate inimical to bacteria is insufficient explanation.

In conclusion, I was unable to uncover data with a demonstrable relation to the Holtz Effect. I do strongly recommend further research—perhaps by civilians with more sophisticated medical and anthropological expertise.

BV—C3

By the time he finished reading, a Cadre Four transportation officer—half again Pol's age—was waiting respectfully near the exit. He didn't speak until Pol looked up.

"They're finally ready, sir. Complicated programming. Tercet, nonstop."

SY 3050

A few months later on Tercet, a different Pol Tyrees stood, hands clasped behind him, neck bowed, glaring at an oral script machine as if it were denying him something vital. He was paler, thinner, his skin stretched into the translucence of an ascetic. His face was drawn into bleak lines, not of anxiety, but of deep concern. The silence around him was less perfect than his intensity.

The small room encapsulated him, bespoke solitude. It was rough-hewn, solid. Its walls were stone-studded and thick, breached only by a single high-set window and a heavy wooden door. The window was the only light source, but from it, brilliance exploded into the room as from the mouth of a furnace, leaving disconcertingly stark shadows in unexpected places. Heat hummed from the walls, ticked from the floor.

After a long time, the bowed statue came alive. Slowly, a hand reached out to touch a switch and the machine's drum began to roll. Softly, the statue began to speak.

COUNCIL EYES ONLY

Field Agent's Report (Entry 1)—Pol Tyrees, Cadre One, Alien Security

Assignment Directive
  · Take/recommend action re Holtz Effect, planet Tercet

Progress Report
  Where do I begin? How *can* I begin?
  Perhaps it doesn't make much difference. It may be that in the human framework, there *are* no beginnings or endings—even in terms of our births and deaths—though we would like to think so. Our thoughts and actions (and bodies, too) simply melt into something else. We trot out special days and special rites to celebrate beginnings and endings in order to sustain the illusion that they do exist. We need to convince ourselves that our actions do indeed have an effect on the universe—that our fingertips do indeed leave marks on the glass. So. I will do my part to paint the illusion.
  I have many things to say—but not in the official jargon of the field agent's report. That applies to form as well as content; Cadre standards are inappropriate now. Some Council members may think my words nonsense, the flotsam of a dis-

integrating mind, perhaps. But the Chairman will know better; so, of course, will you, Mister Cadre Proctor, *sir*. Forgive the sarcasm. I think little lately that it is not tinged with cynicism. Nevertheless, after half a lifetime sipping the heady broth of Cadre "honor" I still feel guilty. That will pass. Tercet is a fine and painful forge for such purging. I have plucked up the Cadre's skirts and looked at the underside. Like me, it is all too human. Its mystery, its glory, leak out like a bad nose cold.

What you read now is not the first beginning of my report, because I have rejected several conventional ones—ones with knee jerk lists of facts. Instead, I will tell the full truth. I will speak to you, Chairman, and to you, Proctor, who are in most need of its purity. The thought of addressing you directly fires my resolve as I speak to you from this bare room. I have not moved beyond its walls for four local months. Listen to me. Listen well.

You knew (you must have known everything) how naïvely happy I was when this assignment came down, in spite of the fact that the action was elsewhere. With the Trade Wars spreading virulently from the Hub, even Sector I was feeling its effects; but out on our thin spiral arm, the chaos and suffering remained an exciting challenge, something to tax the Cadre's skills. Then you transferred me to Alien Security—the "ghost-chasing squad." You sent me here to Tercet, on the other side of the other side of the galaxy. (You will come to realize that Tercet is beyond the pale in more than location). You wanted to keep me out of things, and you knew that the Holtz Effect was a grail quest for me. I came gladly. You assumed I was again mothballed for safekeeping; in reality, I was precisely placed for some startling revelations.

During the Great Diaspora, humanity spread in a radial wave through the Hub and beyond. With the Trade Wars, the whorl is turning back upon itself and the Pax Regnum is in jeopardy. Now, gentlemen, comes another spinning force hard upon the last. It may wrack the galaxy more than the other two, but I honestly don't know if it is an end or a beginning. I do know that whatever your wishes, nothing will ever be the same again.

But I get ahead of myself. I still have my oral script, though it falters when I order corrections or dictate too long. Perhaps it senses my struggle. I prefer it to a recording crystal because seeing the words helps me to think. My record commends me for dispassionate precision. I have a *real* need of it now. This

report is motivated more by my need to understand than by
my duty. Besides, I want to shove it down your throats. It's
petty of me, I know. But, you see, I'm not without the human
meanness that rat-scratches for revenge. Such is our history
and our shame—a mindless round of power and paranoia that
pastes us against the spinning wall of our sins. I'll quote you
a passage from *The Teraac*. It won't do you any good, but read
it, anyway. Then I'll resst forr a-a-a whileee.

> Behold Eros: vast and consuming, a blood-gorged pas-
> sion.
> Behold Sentos: delicate and moving, an azure caress.
> Behold Logos: piercing and bright, a searing gold.
> With these lights you can fuel, feel, see.
> Then behold the single light, the trilight.
> Use it to *know*.
>
> First, you must be asked: does Sentos rule Logos, or
> Logos Eros? Can you then allow the slicing blade of
> reason to let flow passion's biood, or the heat of passion
> to devour the gentle senses?
>
> Each is a gift of knowing, but each alone reveals only
> a pale shadow of truth. To see by a single light is to be
> drawn into the Hole of Darkness from which there is
> nooo returninggggg.

SY 3050

COUNCIL EYES ONLY

Field Agent's Report (Entry 2)—Pol Tyrees, Cadre One, Alien Security

Assignment Directive
· Take/recommend action re Holtz Effect, planet Tercet

Progress Report

I said in my first entry that this report is motivated by my need to understand; but I'm afraid it will be tainted somewhat by the impulse to berate the two of you. Bear with me. For the time being, I will concentrate on my story.

When I landed on Tercet six months ago, I was greeted by Valtac. He's a typical strait-laced Cadre officer and a good digger. However, it is *because* he is typical that he waded through the most revolutionary human phenomenon in history without noticing that his feet were wet.

I remember when I walked down the ramp to step on Tercian soil for the first time. Imagine looking down and seeing, faintly but distinctly, three shadows of yourself sprouting from your feet at unequal angles. With my cape, caught at just that moment by the three whirling suns obliquely above, my shadow looked like a black and sinister bird of prey. It startled me. I had a premonition then of a beast heaving under me, something ominous, like the dark shape in the red sand. The feeling left when I looked up into that glorious sky with its three gamboling suns. It's something purely aesthetic. You can never look up without seeing a different configuration, including some in which the red giant plays at swallowing up the yellow-and-blue youngsters but can't quite keep them both down at once. And the light! It varies in intensity; the sky is usually golden, cut with a thousand soft tints. Clouds are multicolored, always shifting pastels.

Although I wasn't fully aware of it at the time, that, gentlemen, was one of the many lessons taught to me by Tercet that is not in the Cadre repertoire. It is important, especially to me: to appreciate unabashedly something beautiful, to *give in* to it, to *feel* it without reservation. As you know, the reflex in me is to suppress such things. There was a girl once . . . But never mind. If you think that you now read the ramblings of a softening mind, you are not wholly correct. The three shining suns that shepherd Tercet through the Void are at the bottom of everything here.

Valtac found me like that—gazing upward, shielding my eyes against the glare.

"Quite a sight, isn't it, sir?" he said. He threw a rigid salute at me and introduced himself. He was easy to read: nervous, eager to please and, for a Three, unusually daunted by the black on my collar. He was about my age, but his manner made him seem younger.

"I read your progress reports en route, Valtac. Tercet sounds like a fascinating place."

"Oh, it's interesting, all right, sir. But I can't say I'll be unhappy to leave. The people are strange." He made a mild grimace.

"Isn't that to be expected, Valtac? Tercet has been cut off from the galaxy for a thousand years."

"Well, yes, sir. I guess they're just *too* different for me. Besides, I've found nothing solid on the HE."

The rest of our first conversation centered on the Holtz Effect. Valtac was at a loss as to why a number One was sent at all. In spite of the high HE readings, there was nothing to work on. As for myself, an opportunity to have another go at it was all I cared about, though even then I knew the Cadre was most concerned about Tercet's political leanings.

Valtac's mild aversion to the Tercians, I think, would have been the reaction of most Cadre men. On the surface, Tercians appear too "primitive" and "superstitious" to encourage an effort to understand. This, coupled with our "assignment directive" tunnel vision, kept him ignorant. He left with alacrity two days after I arrived. I think he found *me* a bit strange for his taste, as well. Most people do; but then, most people I know wear black uniforms. Don't misunderstand; I don't mean to condemn the Cadre wholly—that would be unfair. It would also be unwise, because a great part of me *is* the Cadre. Its ideals are worthy; its failing is its narrowness and its growing aversion to the common humanity it was intended to serve. This has come about because people like yourselves have compromised its ideals for nearsighted political reasons, and because, in doing so, you have made good men into an elite corps of blind minions who attack effects instead of causes. It angers me now that the Cadre is famous as an institution invulnerable to corruption. It is not. And you made it into a guardian of sheepy masses whose thoughts you mold.

My preaching will mean nothing to you. I preach to myself. I remember too well a man I loved—as well as I was capable of loving. The Cadre destroyed his spirit because it chose results over people; I destroyed what remained because I chose the Cadre over . . . over real brotherhood. It has been eleven years since I watched blood soak into that red hair. I . . . I have carried that memory locked in a hard place deep inside my soul. . . . His hands were ugly in death, like talons. You helped me to kill him, and then you rewarded me for it. All he wanted was the love of a good woman . . . Well, I'm glad I can speak of it now. But no more, to such as you. . . .

My life has two beginnings. The first was when I stood, as a boy, at the entrance of the training complex, and marveled at my good fortune. A beginning full of false promises. The second came six months ago, when I stood at another entrance (only this was metaphorical) and I was a man of forty-three looking at his shadow on the earth of the most unique planet in the galaxy.

I daresay that you are irritated with the plodding pace of this "report." Be patient. It will take time, because we *all* have a lot to learn. And learning can be a painful pro-pro-process.

I see-ee that my machine is acting up again. It functions smoothly only for limited timeee periods. I have already told you that I've been locked into this room for four months with-outt seeing or speaking to another human being. In the last feww days, I have begun to en-en-enjoy itt.

Back again, my black guardians. I'll clear up one of the questions you've been asking yourselves. My "imprisonment" here is not entirely against my will, though I didn't actually have a hand in it. My Seer and mentor, Meta-sol, lost patience with my faltering attempts at understanding. He said that if I wished to travel the road of truth with efficacy, I must place myself in his hands. Since I have come to trust him completely, I did. As a result, I have been locked in this room ever since. There was a point a few weeks ago when I called out and demanded release. When I got no response, I applied all the standard Cadre tricks to extricate myself. Obviously, all failed. Now I no longer try because I begin to *see*.

But I get ahead of myself. I must return to my first days on Tercet and my talks with Meta-sol. Just before Valtac left, he brought the Seer to me. Valtac and I had been cloistered in "The Tower" going over his findings. By the way, The Tower is misnamed by our standards because it's a wood-and-stone building, only two stories tall. One stands in every village, housing what records they keep and acting as a meeting place. Valtac had been given rooms there, close to the digs of the Regnum emissary, who had not yet returned form another village.

No more than a few dozen visitors have come to Tercet since it was rediscovered. It is a part of the agreement during negotiations toward Regnum membership that a Tercian Seer meet with *every* newcomer. (At first, this struck me as peculiar. I found out later that the Seers were looking for something that the Regnum has in rather short supply.) So this was my official visit.

There is little pomp on Tercet. Valtac simply opened the cracked wooden door and said, "Meta-sol, sir. Seer of Luta. Officer Pol Tyrees, Security Cadre One." To you, he would appear singularly unprepossessing. A little, wizened old man with a crooked cane and wraparound shawl. To a Tercian, he is the object of their reverence and holder of their destiny: priest, ruler, philosopher, and scribe.

He said nothing. He looked at me until I could *feel* it. Yes, he was blind and he looked at me with bright black eyes and saw things I could not see in myself. He listened to me breathe and heard the crash of blood striking the walls of my heart. He felt the heat of my skin and the wetness of my palms. He smelled my tension and tasted the touch of fear that was welling in my bowels. I know now that he saw the pell-mell electric skelter of my thoughts. Do not try to imagine it. You cannot. You do not believe me now, but you will.

On that edge of a moment, I felt only confusion and that touch of fear. Do you remember the first filter trial of orientation, Proctor? The one that's supposed to test behavior under data deprivation conditions? That trial was easy for me because of my "advantages." Well, those little extras helped me to advance in the Cadre and they have also cut me off from people I might have called friends. You are aware, however, that they were more refined by the time I reached Tercct: I read men's bodies as easily as you read these words. But I failed in _this_ filter trial. I looked at the Seer and saw _nothing!_ Valtac was standing formally at attention, waiting to be dismissed; yet, to me, he swayed as a slender tree in the wind. But the Seer was as still as a rock. All my senses, the abilities that set me apart from both civilians and Cadre officers, could read no data, make no inferences, concerning this man. I've seen such stillness in a human body only once—and he was dead by my hand. I felt a crackle in the dry air and could not escape the conviction that I was being charted as intimately as a technic traces channels on a chip under a microscope. Finally, as if a switch had been thrown, the crackle was gone. The statue of the old man came alive and turned to Valtac, who was by then beginning to fidget.

"We may be alone?"

"Of course," said Valtac. "But let me . . ." He had been about to guide the blind Seer to chair, but with an easy grace that denied his age, he moved unerringly to the chair, around it, and sat. I know that Valtac had seen such things before, and his response was the same on this occasion: he filed it under "unexplained trivia" and forgot about it. As for myself, I was dumbfounded. The Tercian and I sat there and listened to Valtac's fading footsteps, but he could hear them longer than I. Then he raised those sightless eyes to me.

"We had almost despaired," he said in a soft whisper that was as clear and pure as pouring water.

"I—I don't understand." Those inspiring words were my

first to a Seer. I was to repeat them often.

"I am sorry. Am I not using your mode of speech accurately? It is difficult and very limiting. I mean no insult, but many of your words and manner of using them cannot carry our meaning sufficiently. We—we had lost some—some hope and joy because you did not come before now." He seemed satisfied with this effort and fingered his cane, as he waited for my response.

"No, you speak accurately, I think. What I don't understand is *why* you said it. You were expecting someone like me?" I waited impatiently for his response. I think I had been waiting for this answer since childhood.

"You of the hidden stars are our fathers. The black hole has robbed us of your—taste for the span of many lifetimes. We have asked why your Regnum has not sent one of their Seers to us. Your . . . emissary said he was a Seer. He is not. You are a Seer. But you are . . . different, and so young. We must teach each other."

"The emissary probably misunderstood what you meant by 'Seer.' As for me, I think I would have little to teach you—sir."

"That is an untruth. I am called Meta-sol. What are you?" He took his cane and pointed diffidently upward. I came to realize that the piece of wood was used only rarely, as a guiding device—usually to trace the shape of an object rather than find it. More often, it was used to enhance a gesture. As well, it was a badge of office and all Seers had one. The Cadre has its cape, but somehow, the simple, gnarled piece of wood carried more significance.

I knew instinctively that this man would be important to me. I felt a compelling interest in something for my sake alone. I forgot the Cadre, its strictures, regulations, and need for information. Before Tercet, I would have answered the question, "What are you?" with conviction, saying "I am a Cadre officer." Now, knowing myself, I would say, "I am Pol Tyrees," and that would suffice. (The irony of defining oneself by what one does rather than what one *is* will probably be lost on you.) The time needed to read what I have said since the Seer's last words is less than the span before my response. Silence is a thing a Seer never finds uncomfortable. I chose my words carefully.

"Meta-sol, I *am* different from most of my kind. I have some acuities they do not. But their significance is small. I would be honored to tell you anything you wish to know. Perhaps . . . technology, the practical sciences—machines." For the first time, I was able to detect a hint of emotion in his voice when he responded. A touch of irritability.

"We will, because we are what we are, learn from each other what there is to learn. Seers can do no less."

"Please, Meta-sol. I mean no disrespect, but what exactly *is* a Seer?" There was another silence then, and I felt more of the dry crackle that had unnerved me before. A small, sad smile grew on the thin lips.

"I, too, mean no disrespect. But I see that you do not know fully what you are. And you are some things I am not. That is what I wish to learn—what I am not—so that I may . . . grow. When you learn what *you* are, you will know what a Seer is. I will help you, so that you may help me."

"Of course. I will do anything I can."

As I was speaking, he rose in a fluid motion to walk to the door. Then he turned and waited patiently for my question.

"But—what am I to do? How am I to start?"

"Read *The Teraac*. Then we will start together."

PT—Cl

SY 3050

COUNCIL EYES ONLY

(Excerpt from) *Field Agent's Report* **(Entry 3)—Pol Tyrees, Cadre One, Alien Security**

Assignment Directive
· Take/recommend action re Holtz Effect, planet Tercet

Meta-sol. His magic enchanted me from the beginning. He told me to read *The Teraac* and then disappeared for a time. An old man with a gnarled cane stood quietly for a few moments and, with blind eyes, looked into my . . . soul. Yes, I chose that word carefully, gentlemen. He knew I would push aside my duties and do as he asked. I wonder if he also knew that he had led me to the edge of a cliff.

Like you, most of my reading has been limited to Cadre reports. the difference between those and *The Teraac* is like that between a shipping manifest and poetry. Valtac's translation program helped, but there was more involved than picking up a local dialect. Nevertheless, I was able to understand better than Valtac because of a stronger motivation, and the synesthetic quality of the language was probably less foreign to my nature. And later on I had Meta-sol.

Actually, the descriptor is inaccurate because synesthesia means the *substitution* of one sense for another when the use of the Tercian language (especially by a Seer) *mixes* them, *blends* them. We have no appropriate word for the thing. Remember, language both forms and limits a way of thinking, so Tercian is difficult because it seems to contradict our cozy thought patterns. In fact, the brain's decoding process for sensual input is reflected more purely in Tercian. Take the smell of burning wood; it will trigger a "grooved' sequence of neuron synapses. Since that smell has been stored in the memory, it also fires a "reminder" sequence of past smelling experience. Any experience sends a clerk, as it were, into the memory banks of the brain to search for similarities. Let's say we sent a particularly bright and ambitious clerk after we smell coffee. Suppose he decides to look for *related* sequences as well— just to impress the boss. He finds one in the files under the general heading "taste," subheading "bitter." He runs the stuff back to his boss, who should be delighted because there is more data, his perception about the nature of coffee more accurate. He now knows its fragrance/taste as a *combination,* not as a single sensory perception. Reality is thereby experienced in an enriched fashion.

All of us have some sense of this phenomenon, if only unconsciously. I suspect that it has been a part of mystical experience since man evolved a complex brain. By mystical, I mean a "way of knowing" that seems to deny familiar laws of reason. It happens that the vast majority of us have no training in using this kind of perception, and we reject it as aberrant—the boss chucks the *taste* file into the disposal and scolds his clerk. We put people in institutions who have clerks bringing only the *wrong* file, so they might taste when they should smell. We call it insanity.

This is my theory. Something like that happens in the Tercian mind—at least, the Seer mind. The Seers also have acutely developed senses, an attribute I share in some measure. Amazing, isn't it? Look around and you will see primitive adobe huts squatting in neat triangles on the red-scabbed earth. You will see paths worn in the dirt by bare feet, and the char of open communal fires. You will see hardship and hardiness, marks of knife and axe and adze, of plow and shovel and hand-pulled cart. You will see the thatch of roofs curling in the heat of the tristar and the salt bleach on the bellows lever in the forge. You will see no machines as you conceive of machines, no progress as you conceive of progress. Yes, it is amazing, because in a thousand years they have made more real progress than we in a thousand generations.

The nature of that process is difficult to assess—or describe. I will tell you what I can, though I have no confidence in your ability to stretch toward a new awareness. It is possible that once, on ancient Terra, we were headed in the same direction, but there were more obvious frontiers to conquer, so we "progressed" in a linear path instead of the cyclical one chosen by the Tercians. Anthropology is not my strong point but I think that when we finally broke free—gained the life span that made survival something less than all-consuming—we chose to develop faculties that enhanced control of our *outside* environment. We made better tools, better machines. When the Tercians reached that point, they turned back *inward* to develop and control a more immediate environment—their own minds and bodies. (I think they are nearing an *outward* turning now.)

Why did they evolve so differently from the rest of their species? I think I know.

First of all, there's nothing magic about the human brain. On the one hand, it is inferior to a computer in speed and volume capacity for a "run"; on the other, it is capable of processing different *kinds* of data simultaneously, of moving in new directions to make its discoveries. It sometimes provides data for which we didn't know it was "programmed." Programming for the human brain is simply the mix, the input of experience there—*all* experience, including the senses, feelings, and thoughts. We do not know fully how the brain blends this experience, especially in those cases where it makes that famous "intuitive leap" to grasp a concept like the Gravity Field Theory. Somehow, it shuffles its data into new combinations to produce a totally new idea.

The Seers are working toward an understanding of the process of knowing, gentlemen, and they carry their laboratories in their heads.

It is time to enlighten you about Tercian history: Valtac did not see it in terms of their search for meaning. My sources are *The Teraac*, Meta-sol, and my own surmise.

As harsh a mistress as this planet is, Tercians regard her with reverence, simply because she was *there* when their ancestors had resigned themselves to the Void. Consider: anticipating a horribly designed death by implosion into a black hole; praying through one mind-searing escape with only the more lingering death of the intergalactic darkness to contemplate; seeing then the beautiful light of the tristar with its offer of salvation; committing themselves to suffer the harrowing shuttle journey; finally, after generations of death and deprivation, eking out an arduous but dignified existence. That is a pattern, that is a heritage, gentlemen, uniquely designed to forge self-discipline, to force men to look inward seeking some significance, some reason to continue the struggle against the awesome indifference of the Void. it takes a tough will to choose life over death when the pain of the first is so great and the peace of the second so alluring. A Tercian confronts the imminence of his own death more intimately than others of our race because his heritage displays it more dramatically. Think of it: if those struggling colonists had all died, there would have been *nothing* left—no children, no great works, just a distant place no longer visible, no longer accessible. The black hole would have *erased* them, rubbed them into an utter nullity on the dark slate of the universe. What meaning their struggles then?

So they looked *inside* seeking the answers, and they struggled harder. The original, terrifying voyage of discovery and the small Tercian cosmos became concrete metaphors for the inward journey. Our ancients had heaven and hell; the Tercians have the black hole and the shining tristar; but to reach that three-powered light of wisdom, it is necessary to travel *through* the darkness, to confront and defeat the black hole. It was so for the outward journey of their forefathers; it is so for that inward. One must smell one's own rotting flesh, feel the horror of one's own death, before the clarity of a bright inner vision is possible. Once this is achieved, the body-mind will no longer war against itself; as the three suns are one light, so are the self's many ways of knowing. The final stage of the journey is the struggle of those like Meta-sol: to form a unity of self and other-than-self, a state of being, in which body and mind merges with the flux of things outside, and one is an extension of the other.

I know it is difficult for you to accept these as the words of a Cadre foundling, gentlemen. Remember, though, that change is the essence of the universe. *The Teraac* says, "You have a choice: resist the flow of the tides and be drowned; or become a flex of their flux and master them." I cannot describe adequately this inner quest of the Seers, because the words are not there, and because I can only see it in tempting flashes. I know *I* am not yet ready. This turning drum helps me to trace my steps so that I can know better what brought me here and, perhaps, where I am going. I must go carefully. You are privileged to be close behind.

Like Meta-sol, I am aware now of what a flimsy tool is a word when it is asked to write to carry meaning beyond its capacity. I know why poets write and why they find it so painful: they realize that the best they can hope for is a pale simulacrum of the shining architecture in their heads. But the Tercian way of speaking is much better for the chore, and I am learning.

Not all Tercians are Seers, because their history is a story of raw survival, so their band of contemplatives is small. But their numbers grow slowly, and they take on likely youngsters for training that makes the Cadre trials look like my old nursery school. The population remains scattered because of Tercet's stinginess in doling out her meager resources. I can still say with conviction that the villages sprinkled around this thirsty planet have a sense of global community that is unmatched by any member of the Regnum. This is so because Tercians have two common goals that have remained constant for a thousand years: to stay alive and to gain self-knowledge. As the first gradually becomes easier, the second takes on momentum. Tercians depend upon the village Seers to show the way. When they aren't beating the stubborn soil into submission, they follow, slowly, faithfully, along the Seers' blazed trail. I have been struggling along that trail, too, but I don't know how far I can go.

The Teraac, if you haven't come to the obvious conclusion, is the record of the Seers' progress. It also confirms a suspicion I have harbored since my first meeting with Meta-sol: the Tercians are undergoing, *fostering*, a kind of evolutionary process—and they are succeeding. Gentlemen, you have aliens in your midst.

PT—Cl

SY 3050

Pol Tyrees spent a great deal of time with his mentor before entering his "prison." They walked often, talking as they went, through the red-baked lanes of Luta. Each step, each word added to the new structures of awareness in Pol. The foundations—laid by Meta-sol with infinite care—had to be strong, for each strand also added to his burden of pain.

Luta was laid out in rough triangles which enclosed small courts. These quaint, three-cornered enclosures provided gathering places in the cooler evenings away from the blowing sand. On one of these walks Meta-sol waved his cane at a rutted road leading out of the village.

"Luta's water source is a short walk that way," he said. Pol squinted into the sunlight, but the road disappeared into rounded knolls and short scrub.

"You must have to irrigate extensively."

"Irrigate?"

"Oh— a system of ditches to bring the water to your crops?"

"Ahh, yes. All villages must. All Tercians work on them. They are our survival. You will remember that *The Teraac*—likens them—to a man's bloodstream."

The village was virtually empty, attesting to the fact that work was more than a living—or a duty—here. Meta-sol turned off the road into a lane between stone huts, and Pol was again moved by the strangeness of strolling casually about with a man who could see—in the usual sense of the word—nothing. Meta-sol very rarely hesitated, almost never faltered.

"Meta-sol, try to tell me. How do you move without . . . bumping into things?" Meta-sol fingered the white wisps flowing from his chin.

"That is—difficult, Pol of the hidden stars. Can you explain to me how *you* see?"

"Well . . ."

"I must say only that I *sense* objects."

"Heat differential? Sound waves?" Meta-sol appeared to be thinking carefully about these suggestions. Finally, he shrugged, as if the question were of little significance.

"Perhaps. Perhaps. I must admit that dark, silent, flat places . . . disturb me, confuse me. It is sometimes even as bad as— what you would call vertigo, I think. At times I must seek these places out."

"You seek them *out?* Why?"

"We must all seek out the dark, silent places," he said with a mildly self-mocking chuckle. "We must learn to face them. To deal with them. they are our—weaknesses."

"Why do you choose to be blind at all?"

"It is in *The Teraac*. All our senses are—hungry, but sight is the most voracious."

"You mean it dominates? Distracts?"

"Yes. It slows the growth of the inner senses. Like Tercian soil, these must be carefully nurtured." He smiled. "Some things grow best in the dark."

There were a few people—usually very young or very old— who remained during daylight in the village itself. Those they came upon as they walked followed an invariable formula: Meta-sol was greeted with sincere, almost reverent deference; Pol with shyness, but no fear. When taking their leave they said, "Toil for us, Seer," and touched Meta-sol's cane. Pol was impressed by their common air of serenity. He sensed a peace in them that their simplicity alone could not account for.

"Your people seem so pacific, Meta-sol." The old Tercian frowned his lack of understanding, and Pol assumed it was the word he used. "*Content*, I mean. No anxieties?"

"Ah. A compliment. I have never thought of my people in that way. Perhaps we Seers carry their . . . anxieties, my young friend. Certainly no Tercian is anxious about the value of his work here. We need each and every one."

"You say 'one,' but Seers are the only real individuals on Tercet, as I understand it. Is that because—like sight—the bond of the triad would be distracting?"

Meta-sol nodded sadly. "A price paid higher than sight. Seers are alone."

"Why triads? You must know that outside Tercet, marriage is the norm—still is—a man and a woman."

"We have found that with three people, each is rendered more . . . functional. One person is not sufficient to dampen the excesses, fill in the lackings, of a single other. A three-part unity is best."

The two came to one of the triangular courtyards and sat on a stone bench. Their talk continued in its now familiar pattern: Pol's questions and Meta-sol's patient attempts to answer. Sometimes, in a fashion that reminded Pol of his grandfather (except that this man's strength was water, not stone), Meta-sol suggested exercises for him to try.

"Do you see that leaf? The lowest?" Again, Pol was startled by the Tercian's "sight." He was pointing with his cane to a single broad leaf on a dwarfish bush—one of the largest specimens of natural growth on Tercet.

"Yes, I see it."

"Look at it carefully. Smell it, if you can. *Feel* it. Take as much time as you wish."

Pol lifted his eyebrows but complied. He moved closer to the bush, sitting cross-legged on the ground, and concentrated on the red-tinted leaf as it stirred gently in the soft breeze. After several minutes he gave up, turning to Meta-sol with an expression on his face like that of a small boy too short to be seen and waiting under a counter for attention.

"All I can discern is its movement," he said peevishly. "What is it that I *can't* see?" Meta-sol waggled the tip of his cane aimlessly in the sand for a long time before answering.

"Its mortality, Pol of the hidden stars. Something you will taste in yourself one day when you make the inward journey. The leaf is . . . slipping, losing its hold on life. It will fall in a moment."

Pol sat dumbfounded. A few seconds later the leaf let go and wafted to the ground. From the Seer, a sigh.

"Man's time is also short. There is so little time for growth."

Pol picked up the leaf and smoothed it in his lap.

"How old are you, Meta-sol?" The old Tercian snorted and looked up at the tristar. He didn't blink or squint.

"Since I have been struggling with the sacred curse of life, Tercet has passed around Sentos, Logos, and Eros ninety-one times."

"But that's . . . over one thirty SY!"

"Many Seers are older," said Meta-sol mildly. Pol saw the gauntness, the filmy white hair, the crevassed face; but he also saw the skin glowing with vitality and the corded muscle where the weight of the thin shawl rested. A sand flea picked that moment to land on his neck. The skin crinkled like that of an animal, and the flea was gone.

Pol stood, heady with the sense of possibility. There, in the tiny, sand-blown court, unknowingly, he ceased to be Pol Tyrees, Cadre One.

"Teach me," he said.

Meta-sol did not stir except to say softly, "You have seen our enemy—our only enemy."

"What?"

"Death."

Pol turned away then, obscurely frightened. He blinked at the tristar and tears welled.

"Was I thinking of that?"

"And your guilt. Your Cadre. The Regnum."

"Yes."

"You have the power, Pol of the hidden stars. It is strong—stronger than mine. But it is . . . different. It must be tapped. Put to a use of your making. As yet you do not have the way of it. You dance on the surface. You are . . . a flat stone skipping across water. The depths unseen frighten you."

Pol dropped the leaf to the red sand and stared at it. He was bewildered.

"I want to believe you, Meta-sol, because . . . well, because I really don't feel useful as I am. A long time ago I thought the Cadre . . . But I have to give *everything* again, don't I? What if I *can't* grow?"

Meta-sol rose from the bench, let his cane fall, and lifted both hands to place his fingertips on Pol's temples. Pol felt a tremor course through him. Then the hands fell away.

"All is there but the will."

"You know that what you ask of me is . . . treason."

"Treason?"

"You said it earlier. The Cadre. It must be one or the other."
A nod. Pol kicked at the dead leaf.

"All right. What must I do?" Meta-sol smiled broadly, showing pale, almost translucent teeth.

"I think we must . . . arrange events. Stimulate growth."

"I hate to say it again, but I don't understand."

"You know that necessity . . . pushes us. Inspires us to heights
we think impossible otherwise. If a great stone rolled onto one
of your triad—forgive me—one of your family, you might lift
it then, when you could not before."

"Oh, I see. You're telling me I must expose myself to some
sort of danger to force it to the surface?" Pol's voice was thick;
he was thinking of Meta-sol being blinded. But the old Tercian
smiled the sad smile he had come to love. It was the smile of
a father.

"No. Nothing so . . . dramatic, my Pol. Do not be afraid.
This is a thing that requires time and . . . concentration. A sudden danger would not call it forth. I will consider the problem.
Since you have decided that you must follow the path of self-
knowledge, and you know that I would not harm you, you will
accept without fear."

"But I have made no such commitment! Are you reading
my mind?"

The smile again.

"Do you predict the future, Meta-sol?"

For the first time he heard Meta-sol break into a full, rolling
chuckle. He closed his black, sightless eyes and shook to its
rhythm. It was a *pure* sound of genuine delight, a natural
response, untainted by rancor, to something perceived as ridiculous. When he finished he put a bony hand on Pol's shoulder. By this time Pol was laughing himself.

"Are you reading a mind when you see a man's breath
quicken in the presence of his woman, and say he is in love?"

"Well, no."

"Are you predicting the future when you find him at his
table and smell meat over the fire and say that he is about to
eat?"

"No, not really."

"Then I cannot read minds or predict the future." Meta-sol
reached out to take Pol's arm in his, gently urging him back
to sit on the bench.

"How long have you been blind, Meta-sol?"

"Since just before my body reached its full height."

"Uh, how was it done? Were you . . . was it painful?"

Meta-sol's fingers lifted to touch oddly whitened eyelids. He nodded. "Yes. But the pain is . . . cleansing. In time I could see more clearly than before the Purging."

"The Purging?"

"The Purging removed the temptress of eyes that see only the surfaces of things." He reached down between his knees and pulled together a handful of the dry, red earth. "Can your eyes tell me if this soil will nourish growth? My people have need of such skills."

"No, not without a lab test. But I can arrange to have the emissary staff do one for you."

"I am my own . . . lab. This is my test." Cupping the soil in one hand, he probed it with moistened fingers. Then he raised the earth to lips and nose and nuzzled it.

"This soil has lost many of its . . . juices. No food-bearing plant will grow here."

Pol gripped his knees and stared hard at his mentor. It was not to be the last time he doubted.

"You still haven't told me about the Purging. Are you avoiding the question?" Meta-sol sighed. The brilliant sunlight glared up from the ground all around him except where his three shadows lay; they reformed as he shifted.

"You must read *The Teraac* with more care, Pol."

"It's there?"

"It is there. But I will show you the reality. You will be . . . disturbed; however, its taste may add to your growth. Come."

Meta-sol led him to the road he had pointed down earlier, and they walked out of the village toward the grainfields. The three suns were at their zenith, searing. Pol could feel the heat of the road through his boots. He looked up at the beautiful sky and marveled at its overlay of colors, thinking at the same time of the struggle that must be demanded to grow crops in such a climate.

They came to the village's man-made reservoir—about the size of a large pond—kept full for irrigation by the constant drawing of water from a nearby well.

The first hint of the Purging was the muted sobs.

A young boy, no more than fifteen, sat shoulder deep in the water. Little breeze-fed waves lapped at the back of his neck.

Pol couldn't see his face until he moved farther along the water's edge. Then his stomach convulsed.

The face was a horror: mottled and raw, blistered and grimacing, vise-pinched into a wad of pain. Shreds of skin hung from nose, brow, and ears. The nose was bulbous with fluid. It was difficult to distinguish blood from flesh. Tears brimmed from eyes sunk into black holes, gushed into deep channels that finally dropped them off the chin into the water. The boy's head was tilted so that his eyes—his eyes!—could take in the full, burning blast from the suns above. The Purging.

Pol watched the boy blink incessantly, struggling to keep his eyes exposed to the tristar's triple rays; when the lad could stand the pain no longer, he plunged his head into the water. That release lasted as long as he could hold his breath. Pol heard the sobs again, aware now that they did not come from the boy, but from a small knot of people at the water's edge—two adolescent girls and three adults of middle years who could only be the parent triad.

On the other side of the reservoir several men went about the business of extracting well water. They dipped the bucket end of a long, fulcrumed pole down the well and heaved it up for emptying. Down and up, down and up. Splash. Splash. Splash.

One of the parents—a woman—pushed herself to her feet and waded into the water to her son. Pol guessed that she was the birth mother because her face resembled his. Hers, too, was contorted with pain. She leaned forward to apply something with a shaky hand to the blasted flesh above the water line. Her son ignored her, blinking valiantly over her shoulder at the tristar. She returned to the bank and resumed her sobbing. Pol felt his anger burgeon from somewhere beneath where unconscious memories of his own purging boyhood rested in disquiet.

"Meta-sol. Meta-sol, this is not right."

"Not right?"

"If I had come upon this alone, I would have stopped it." Now there was a thin wash of anger on Meta-sol's face.

"To what purpose? This boy would never forgive you—nor would his parents. In time, he will be a Seer. He will help to guide his people."

"But this is a travesty! It can't possibly be necessary."

"Yes, there is terror in it. But those who have life and see no terror in it are truly blind. You must understand."

"I don't. This is a sacrilege—primitive and senseless. Look at his family." Pol waved in their direction. "A cruel spectacle for them."

"They are full of sorrow for his pain, yes. They are also full of pride for what he does—is able to do—and what he is to become. It is his choice. He has only to rise from the water to escape his suffering."

Pol shook his head. Another test the old exact from the young, he was thinking. His bitterness embarrassed Meta-sol, so there was silence for a time as both listened to the small sobs and the splash, splash, splash. Pol felt his eyes drawn once more to the boy in the water and thought of his grandfather and the Cadre filter trials. The comparison unnerved him even more. Finally, Meta-sol turned to him, lifted a hand slowly, and reached toward Pol's own eyes. He pulled back abruptly, and the gentle hand fell away.

"You will come to know," said the Seer, "that there is more to be purged than sight."

Pol snorted and, wheeling, fled toward the village. Meta-sol followed more slowly, his blank eyes cast to the ground. As the first huts came into view, Pol whirled on him and shouted:

"The boy is already blind, you know! He couldn't even see his mother in front of him!"

Meta-sol said sternly, "No." He pointed upward with his cane. "He can still perceive light. This is only the second day. Tomorrow, full darkness will come."

Pol looked at the old man standing there, three shadows thrown from his feet by the lowering suns, and saw only proud compassion in the shawled figure.

"The . . . the terrible effects of the sunlight on the boy's skin. Were they not extreme, even for Tercet?"

"Yes. There is an . . . ointment which the mother applies. It intensifies the burning. Sight *and* pain are purged. But remember, Pol of the hidden stars, life itself is a purging."

That night Pol found the reference to the Purging in *The Teraac*. As with much of what he had read from it, he had been lulled by the poetry into the assumption that metaphor had no direct connection with reality.

Dare you gaze upon the terrible beauty of the tristar? Such beauty burns white-hot through the windows of the mind to purge the darkness beneath. Pain comes. The lighted windows grow dark and close forever. But it is a joyful loss, a holy purging, for such pain is knowledge dearly won, truly learned.

Senses are given to embrace the reality without; so they are given to embrace that within. But alas, sight is the great tempter; it turns outward, away from the rich and terrible darkness in the deepest caverns of the mind.

Such is the covenant of the Seer: to be blind that he may see.

SY 3050

COUNCIL EYES ONLY

(Excerpt from) *Field Agent's Report* **(Entry 4)—Pol Tyrees, Cadre One, Alien Security**

Assignment Directive
   · Take/recommend action re Holtz Effect, planet Tercet

   I suppose it is time. Your curiosity must have a slash of fear through it—or *should have*.
   I will state it plainly: I know that the Cadre Proctor and the Chairman of the Regnum have been immorally (and illegally) conspiring to make me the object of a thirty-year experiment— that is the personal crime. I know that the Holtz Effect is a deliberate hoax perpetrated upon billions of Regnum citizens by their own Council—that is the political crime. I also know that you, Proctor, are my grandfather. . . .
   The guilt I felt at allowing my personal quest on Tercet to supersede my duty as a Cadre officer has been replaced by *rage*. I was *used* as Salaan and Ses were used. The rage is for all of us. I am fortunate that the objects of my anger are far removed, because I must, I will, defeat it, or I will never be released to my own destiny. I have denied myself the pleasure of seeing your vilification roll by on this drum. Given a choice

... But then, there has never been real choice in my life. That will be redressed.

How did I make my little discoveries while I was deposited for safekeeping on a backwater planet, hidden behind a hole in the fabric of the universe? I will tell you. I made them on a long, sometimes frightening voyage. No, gentlemen, not through outer space, through *inner* space, a limitless and alien ether that is impenetrable to most. Did I conjure up a vision of you pillars of the Regnum wringing hands in maniacal glee as you plotted the course of history? Did I scatter some dry bones on the hot sand, like a burning-eyed shaman and read the message of your megalomania? You may wish it so, when my story is finished.

It is alllmm . . . Itt . . . Welll. There itt goes againnn. La-teerrr.

You know, my oral script malfunction serves a purpose. It stops me periodically and I am forced to go carefully, to think things through as I search for understanding. It sees fit, at times, to warn me of misdirections, to caution me to keep to the highest path. Back to my story.

It is almost five months now, and I am still a prisoner; but I'm also my own jailer. I began this report a few weeks ago, when my rage first hit. It is less distracting now, and I have made some progress. After my escape attempts, I was forced to scrape away the rust of pride and came to some simple conclusions. I still trusted Meta-sol. He put me here for a reason—to learn about myself. Nothing had changed except my attitude and the passage of time. Obviously, Meta-sol believed that time and isolation were things I needed. I became ashamed of my escape attempts and decided to remain for as long as it took, either to convince the Seer of my inadequacies or to find out if he was right about me.

I put myself into the low metabolic state I often used when tired or tense and found it difficult to rest. As you know, my cage-keepers, I used it many years ago in the first filter trial. I was better at it by the time I came to Tercet because I had more conscious control over it. But I had never made *myself* the sole object of concentration while in this state; as a matter of fact, I never tried to think about anything in particular. I did so then, "emerging" every few days to eat the milk-soaked grain and bread someone, perhaps Meta-sol himself, placed in the wall locker from outside. (One of my escape strategies was to prop my end of the locker open, hoping to trap, or at least talk to, the hands that slid the tray in. I never saw the hands, because no food ever appeared when my side was open.)

Once I was committed, my first breakthrough came quickly. I was concentrating on monitoring certain functions of my body to see if I could improve control. I listened to my heartbeat, traced the rush of my blood, tried to adjust its flow through my lungs. But something went wrong. I stayed under too long, and slowly, so imperceptibly that I had no awareness of it, I lost conscious control. I was adrift and I didn't care. I was the explorer of a new and fascinating world, a primitive place of wind and river. I floated like an entranced scientist, charting courses, noting volumes and flows, cataloging curious details of chemistry. No drug could have produced such a sense of wonder, such an apathetic desire to be carried deeper and deeper into the dark nexus of self. Near the end, I recorded with detached surprise that the ever-merging rivers were a uniform violet, when earlier they had been richly red. Of course, I didn't know I was dying. My conscious control had ebbed away until I was nothing more than an enthralled observer, drifting with the currents.

I am sure Meta-sol saved my life—probably by the simple expedient of making a loud noise. Suddenly, my river-fed world was inundated by a quake, and I was buffeted by churning waters and tipped into a blurry chasm. I fell with the plummeting river and came to my senses on the floor, legs still tangled in the chair I had sat in a week earlier. And I was afraid. Fear has a sour taste, gentlemen. It begins ignominiously in the bowels and gouts up to fill the well at the bottom of the tongue. Its color is mauve, almost black.

That experience taught me caution, and the fact that inner space is as infinite as outer. The lessons had come at some cost: I was desiccated and had lost weight; my muscles were flaccid; my nervous system ajangle; I felt curiously disoriented. The inner world still seemed more real than the outer, but it was suddenly gone and I could find no reference point to put it in perspective. The closest I can come to an analogy is a numbing hangover after a wild but dimly remembered night.

I ate, slept, and went "in" again a few days later. This time, I kept a rigid grip on my level of conscious awareness. Soon,

I began to see and do things I hadn't known were within my capacity. I think the first plunge, dangerous as it was, acted as a breakthrough, and now the barriers were down. Before, I searched a cluttered house for an unfamiliar object which I suspected might be there: now, I *knew* it was there, and that made the difference. Like a boy carefully tinkering with a new toy, I discovered that I could increase my lung capacity by enlarging peripheral air sacs. I could stimulate the production of adrenaline. I could control my heartbeat within certain parameters before; now I could actually *stop* it.

The passage between the inner and the outer worlds became easier until it was just a matter of opening a door; finally, I was able to let the door *stand open*. With a little concentration, I could exist in both worlds simultaneously. I won't bore you with more detail, but I continued to progress. I can "see" my lungs, gentlemen, and other organs as well. I can see them as they function, and I can modify those functions. I can see them as clearly, more clearly, than you can see the backs of your hands.

I also saw something that, to say the least, blighted my joy of discovery—no, not evidence of your machinations yet; this was even worse, something that ripped through my very sense of being. I saw my own mortality. My body, my physical machine, is a very good one. I doubt there are many better at any age. But I can see every cog in it struggling against decline, forever postponing breakdown, forever postdating the inevitable. If your belly was slashed with a knife and you saw rotting, steaming worms spill out, you would not be as shaken as I was. I felt a new fear—a deep, pervading gnaw, an anxious horror that haunts, threatens to the last until its object, death, provides release. Did you know, gentlemen, that most people do not believe they are going to die? Intellectually, they know, but emotionally they deny it. They see it as an accident, like falling down an elevator shaft; it won't happen to *them*. But *I* believe it now. I can see the black hole waiting for me— yawning, hungry, dark.

It took me quite a while to get over that. No, not get over it—accept it—beyond that, I'll never get. it made me afraid to "look" further, because life seemed only a cruel joke, with death the punchline. But I had the encouragement of *The Teraac*.

If you flee the shadow of fear and
escape from thy self, you flee the
richest source of light in the universe.
It awaits thy reckoning. Seek it. Find
it. Plumb it.
You will be free.

My next disillusionment was more immediate. I refer to
your sins, gentlemen.

First you, Grandfather. For a long time after you were erased
from my life, I clung to the possibility that you were "officially"
dead for some security reason. It was more a hope than a
conviction, because it allowed you to live and still accounted
for your absence. I lost that hope, with time. Understand me.
I have not acquired new information; I have new faculties with
which to view the old. I see things that were always there
before but carried no meaning. Perhaps you can understand if
you think of a good holofilm mystery. Something happens and
you are surprised; but on thinking back, you realize that the
outcomes were inevitable. Things unnoticed the first time take
on significance. That is akin to what I can do now: I can look
into my memory and see definitions so sharp that I must fight
off the feeling that my senses have just put them there. Before
Tercet, an altered breathing rate or a change in vocal tone might
tell me an attitude or underlying state of mind—as they do for
you on a grosser level. Now I see in my memory minutiae that
reveal thoughts and emotions as clearly as the gestures of actors
in a child's drama. I'm looking at you now, Grandfather, as
you act out the scene of our last meeting, when I was fourteen.
You knew it was the last. I can see your mask of plaster imi-
tating the look of casual interest that was normal when we were
together; I hear the subtly altered tone of your words, the small
differences in syntax and diction that tell me as plainly as a
scream in the night of a man about to leave something behind
forever. I can quote the dialogue verbatim. You didn't like it,
but you did it. I don't blame you for that; with the values I
possessed a few short months ago, and the lure of the most
glamorous and (forgive me, Chairman) powerful office in the
Regnum, I would have made the same choice.

Condemning me to a rat-in-the-maze existence for all these
years is a different matter. When I realized that you were indeed

still alive, Grandfather, I knew one day of sheer joy. But you see, there were fourteen years of intimate images stamped on the mind of a young boy who worshiped his grandfather. Even after all this time, there is no one who knows you better. Perhaps a Seer could lie to me now, but you couldn't again. I can recognize those behavior patterns even in official documents from the desk of the Cadre Proctor; I can look back and see superiors (on orders) lying to me without knowing why: I am shamed when memory shows me images of "friends" (I had even fewer than I supposed) who were really surveillance officers watching the guinea pig. I can see your designs in the nature and pattern of my assignment directives; I . . . enough! The evidence is so overwhelming that I should have seen it earlier. You abandoned me and made me your puppet, and I was devastated. They say that you cannot unlove a person. They are wrong.

So one thing led inexorably to another. Why did you become the Cadre Proctor after only a few years as a VP? Your passion was the Holtz Effect. Once I thought that a connection was possible, everything fell into place. Hans's writings predicted the present turmoil in the Regnum and bewailed the lack of a unifying sentiment among its members. Although its findings were made secret, it was public knowledge that Hans chaired the special commission on galactic stability. And his closest friend became the Cadre Proctor. I put these things together with the scenes in my memory of our talks about the Holtz Effect, Grandfather—scenes in which your attitude changes to one of anxiety before avoiding the subject altogether—and I came to the only possible conclusion: xenophobia was an official scam to shore up Regnum unity. The "sentiments" chosen to do it were hatred and fear. The object of these all-too-human emotions was the fictitious alien. You wanted to lather up the natural (but inglorious) tendency in us to fear the unknown. The Holtz Effect was a part of that conspiracy. The masses would huddle together as a defensive reaction to the bogeyman, and they would *need you*. More treason: if such cynical manipulation is necessary to hold the Regnum together, then there is nothing worth holding together.

Here, too, the evidence is overwhelming: cutbacks in the ghost-chaser section; sensationalism in the media; the lack of hard evidence of alien contact in spite of the research. Part of my rage is the thought of all those dedicated men who were, quite literally, chasing ghosts, thanks to your godlike assumption of the right to rule their thoughts.

It is easy to see now that as the Trade Wars escalated, so did your efforts to spread the lie. I remember a line from one of Hans's books: "I hope they not only exist, but also confront man on his little island Galaxy." I know he was sincere when he said that, but if our species can remain viable only through confrontation, then we should at least confront *real* enemies.

Chairman, Cadre Proctor, you have been brought, more or less, up to my present. I don't know how long I will be in this room, but there are still many thing I must "look" into. I was a sculpted figure, never feeling the cut of the chisel's edgeeee. Now I musst do some of my own cutinggg. I will continue this report, but I have not yet decided whether or not it will be senttttt. Grandfff—Ggrraaa—Never mind.

SY 3050

The guilt still gnawed.

As he walked to the courtyard for his daily meeting with Meta-sol, Pol felt it like a soldier feels old shrapnel near a bone. It was almost two months since he had decided to take up his commitment with the Seer, and that had not diminished; nevertheless, in spite of the resentment that memories of Ses and his own exploitive, rocking chair assignments always produced, the guilt of the runaway son still nagged. He had done nothing in connection with his assignment, and he knew instinctively that the time was approaching when he could no longer attempt to embrace both the Cadre and *The Teraac*.

He had just come from the Regnum emissary, who was growing impatient over the slowness of Tercian membership negotiations and his shunting from village to village to prod a favorable consensus from the Seers. Meta-sol had told him that the time was near, and that he must be "isolated" for the "journey." To cover himself he informed the emissary that his work required an extended field trip of indefinite duration. Perhaps, he told himself, whatever Meta-sol had in store for him would simply demonstrate his inadequacy, and that would be the end of it.

He entered the courtyard in the midday heat. Meta-sol sat

on the stone bench leaning with both hands on his cane in a pose so still and so much a part of his surroundings, with the haze of heat dulling detail, that he seemed stone himself. Pol had come upon him silently and obliquely from behind, but he knew better than to assume his presence was not known. He watched the bent figure for a long time as the red dust stirred in the courtyard. Finally, he heard a whisper.

"Come closer. Look in the air. In front of me."

Pol stepped closer and looked. "What am I supposed to see, Meta-sol?"

"Look carefully," came the whisper.

Frowning, Pol studied the space in front of the old Tercian—and saw them. Glinting capriciously in the sunlight were dozens of tiny spangles suspended in the air. They were barely distinguishable, mere flittering glitters sparking a touch brighter than the sunlight. Eyes other than Pol's would not have seen them at all.

"Yes! I see them! What . . . what are you doing?"

The whisper said, "They are just small . . . motes of dust. Watch with care."

Pol concentrated on the flecks of light, mesmerized. He felt like the cradled child who looks for the first time at the miracle of his father's hands held above him. Slowly, so slowly that he thought it his imagination, the motes began to move. When he refocused his eyes, he saw that they were locked in the universal dynamic, orbiting in stately symmetry around each other and a revolving cluster at the center. Because single motes appeared and reappeared, reflecting the light, he knew that each tiny world spun on its axis as well.

Pol was so fascinated by this new manifestation of the Seer's power, that he forgot about its source—until he heard the stressed breathing. Meta-sol's brow had become speckled with perspiration; his face was suddenly ancient, drained and flax white, and covered with violet splotches like the victim of some deathly plague. His breathing became a choking rasp, and Pol, now alarmed, cried out.

"Meta-sol!"

The Seer's chin fell to his chest. The motes lost their light and fell also.

"Are you all right, Meta-sol?"

The Seer lifted a heavy head. Some of the light had also been lost from those strange black eyes. "Yes," he whispered.

"This exercise is . . . demanding." His voice gradually grew in volume. "I have been able to do it for only a short time. Already it begins to require too much effort. I grow old."

He turned away, but Pol had heard the despondency in the words and could see it rimming the set of his body. It was some time before he returned from that dark place, once more the vigorous old man with the sad smile.

"My . . . resentment shames me," he said. "You and I, we watched a mindless leaf fall with more . . . peace than I keep with *my* falling."

Meta-sol's thin crack of weakness—if such it was—fissured into Pol's heart. Meta-sol was less fallible than any man he had ever met. But he was still a man.

They sat through that day talking as the three suns teased each other to the horizon. In the last light, Meta-sol rose and signaled the end of Pol Tyrees, Cadre One. This time, he knew it.

"Pol of the hidden stars. I envy you the time you have to learn. But I must use what remains to me to learn also. We need each other to grow, so we must be about our business. Your place has been . . . prepared. Remember the dance of the dust motes."

The next day Pol entered his "prison." With all that preoccupied him there—the beginnings of his inner journey, the revelations out of the past, the long report he was writing—he had actually forgotten those specks of light until he came to a point when he wondered, Is it not time? Have I not truly *seen?* Why doesn't Meta-sol release me? He came to the obvious answer: He *still* had things to learn, things his mentor had seen in him. It was then that he remembered.

He looked up at the single window, small and high up on the wall. It was glazed with the thick, rough glass common on Tercet (he had been unable to break it a few weeks earlier when he had grown desperate), but a strong beam of sunlight was still able to penetrate. He positioned his chair so the beam fell in his lap.

The bits of dust floating a handsbreadth from his eyes seemed an abyss away. His breath alone could stir them; but otherwise, they moved in lazy arcs downward, reluctantly obeying the laws of physics.

He had spent too much time in the universe of his own body over the past few weeks; now, the outside seemed alien and inviolable—totally independent of him. But he was determined. He sat there for hours, in the end concentrating on single motes only, and failed. His mind-set refused to budge from the simple conviction that the few centimeters of space were an impossible span to bridge. When the sun moved from his lap for the third time, he kneaded tired eyes with the heels of his hands and just thought about it. If a man could progress from a conscious control over his limbs to that of his autonomic functions, even his chemistry, why not of his immediate environment? *The Teraac* hinted of such things. Had he not Meta-sol and his own eyes for witness? Why should a man not be able to affect electrical and perhaps magnetic forces outside his body by altering those inside? After all, what was so magical about a simple magnet?

When he hitched his chair closer once again and lifted one hand into the beam, the answer was there. This time, he went simultaneously "inside" and "outside." He followed the course of his arterial blood into the tiny capillaries in the topmost surface of skin on the back of his hand; with his physical sight he concentrated on a few dust motes above it. He pumped more blood into the capillaries, watching the slow fall of a single speck as it neared his skin. For a moment time was suspended altogether, and the image of a falling leaf—Meta-sol's leaf—came into his mind. Then, with a surge of awareness the two foci of his attention became one. Inside-outside became "one-side." Surface of skin with its tendrils of electricity merged with the charged air. As the mote fell, the hair on the back of his hand rose up to meet it—and it stopped!

It was for only a fraction of a second that the mote hesitated in its slow plunge, but he knew *he* had done it! His initial excitement had broken the delicate spell, but as soon as he could calm himself, he began again.

In an hour or so he was standing—with a silly grin on his face—haloed by the beam of sunlight, playing at being god. A whole galaxy of glittering motes whirled to his tune. He created intricate orbital patterns in the bright air. He choreographed a ballet of dust and light. With childlike glee, he made clusters of tiny stars collide and fall in coruscations. He giggled the joy of the infant who discovers that he is, indeed, master of the universe. He whirled in his own ballet.

"Meta-sol!" he cried. "Meta-sol! I've done it!"

No answer. In spite of the fact that Pol had no reason to

expect the Tercian to hear, he was instantly sobered. Surely no more was expected. He wanted release again. His recent efforts and the quick passage from triumph to despondency had drained him. With a sigh he thumped the heavy door softly with a fist, then leaned on it heavily, forehead pressed to the grainy wood.

He thought, What do I do now? I'm locked in this . . . The *lock*. A concept that hadn't undergone much evolution on Tercet, and as he leaned against the door he remembered his own. It was a long, rounded wooden bar placed across the outside face of the door and resting in wooden hooks that were attached to the sides of the door itself. When he had tried it earlier, he'd found he could pull the door a millimeter or two inward before the bar hit the outside jam. Crude, but more than adequate.

Then he *really* remembered. Memory storage is a virtually indelible electrochemical function. He could find his memories now—*any* memory—and he saw again Meta-sol bringing him into his prison. He smelled again the fragrance of unfamiliar, newly worked wood. He watched Meta-sol solemnly lift the bar from the room's single table, carry it with him, and gently close the door. He heard him place it across the hooks on the outside of the door. But . . . but the hooks were strange. They were not parallel. Resting on them, the bar would have to form an angle of about thirty degrees off the horizontal!

In a frenzy Pol seized the handle and tried to shake the door hard enough to vibrate the bar into a slide. The fit was too tight.

"Meta-sol!"

When he calmed, some questions posed themselves. Thirty degrees was too much not to be deliberate. Why were hooks and bar *round* instead of square to better serve their function? His original impression of rough utility did not fit the facts; on the contrary, care had been taken to make his "lock" *less* efficient. Bar and hooks had been sanded to a glossy smoothness.

Now he knew.

Meta-sol had been careful to let him see the exact nature of the device, but he had not offered information at that lowly stage of his apprenticeship. If he had, thought Pol, I would have found the notion ridiculous. Even now, recognizing it as a final test, a filter trial designed uniquely for him, it was too much. He was to slide that bar off its hooks—with his only resources those inside his head! He banged the door with his fist again, this time in anger. A stupid game. Another filter

trial. Another grandfather. And another memory to deal with:
the scene of Meta-sol racked by the strain of making his
motes dance. Pol knew the Seer could do no more, and he had
already gone beyond him.

Very well, he thought. In return for what he's done for me,
I owe him the attempt at least. He began immediately, before
the smirk of reality deepened.

With the sensation that he was about to attempt breathing
underwater, he pressed his upper body into the heavy wooden
door that stood between him and the bar, between him and his
self. Through one cheek and his palms he could feel the rough
texture of the wood's veins. He closed his eyes. Its patterns
became more and more distinct, until its ridges and valleys
seemed a part of him. But it was a surface thing only. He
couldn't think himself *in*. It was like that for a long time, as
he tried to extend some kind of awareness through his skin and
into the wood, through the resisting surfaces to the invisible
bar beyond. The "feel" he had reveled in when he'd played
with the motes was no good anymore. This filter trial dismayed
him more than any before, because he knew that what had to
be filtered out was a way of thinking, a part of himself. Something had to be left behind.

But the will was there now. As he clung to the door, forehead
beading with sweat which soaked into the wood, a fragment
from *The Teraac* flitted through his head.

The will is there
But what if a tree
Should will to walk?

See it, then:

A mighty, green-shagged head
Is thrown back
To borrow voice from the wind
And bellows, *Let me walk!*

Strength thrums through its rooted girth,
Strength that could power
A hundred fires,
Strains, quivers, cracks
With potent desire . . .

But its roots obey
Their law of stasis.

Make thine own law.
Take that woody will.
Couple it with thine own legs.

Then the earth will upheave
And give way.

But Pol was still nailed to the door, arms outspread, willing his roots to heave the earth. He was drenched in sweat, trembling, and near collapse when he sensed the change. His moisture was penetrating the wood, drawing awareness with it. He was suddenly seeing/feeling the delicate whorls within the coarser grain. His perspiration was acting as a transition medium; molecules of water were reacting chemically with the dry wood; electrical activity from his nervous system formed images in the shapes of its texture. He tore off his shirt and plastered himself back to the door, boosting the electrical charges and his rate of perspiration. He pushed between the heavy whorls deeper . . . deeper . . . until he felt absurdly attenuated, and a diminishing part of him remembered the awful danger of the world of red rivers that had almost claimed him. He ignored it because—once again—he just didn't care. He was as much wood as flesh now.

As he penetrated ever deeper, he became very conscious of an intoxicating aroma—an effect of the wood's resins, he thought—but he didn't know if he were seeing it or smelling it. The "softer," less dense pathways had a sharper redolence and he was lured by it, dizzy with it. Down the luscious, curving channels, he pursued the siren fragrance.

Finally, he could feel/see/smell the difference in texture where alien pegs secured the wooden hooks to the door. Dimly, only dimly, he knew that a thousand parsecs away, his body was shuddering violently, epileptically, but he was too close to stop. Courage had nothing to do with it, because he was nearing a boundary of another dimension, and no man has ever been able to stop at such a place.

He could smell/feel/taste/see now the thin membrane of slippery interface between bar and hooks. With a mental heave he gushed the last of his energy down the tenuous line of his passage to the two points of delicate joining and built a negative charge to oppose the positive that shimmered on the surface of the bar. . . .

It was enough. He felt a soft implosion—and he felt the smooth bar sliding down through the hooks as sensually as an oily pipe is felt sliding through a fist. He heard the clatter from the other side of the door as the bar hit the floor. With that sound his awareness snapped back and resonated, releasing him.

Only then did he have the presence of mind to be horrified by the low ebb of life that remained. With the convulsive movements of a man deep in shock, he pulled the door open on Meta-sol's proudest smile.

It blurred and faded with everything else as he passed out.

SY 3050

COUNCIL EYES ONLY

(Excerpt from) *Field Agent's Report* **(Entry 5)—Pol Tyrees, Cadre One, Alien Security**

Gentlemen . . . leaders of the Regnum: This is probably the last time I will address you. I now know who I am; where I am going remains a wonderful mystery. From you, I ask only the right to find my way without interference. It may be that we on Tercet will someday add to the mix of humankind an element of worth that history will remember with pride. For that, we need time and—I hesitate to use the jaded holy word—freedom. In return, I offer you this report and the last of my bitterness. If your honesty matches mine, you will agree that I have no moral obligation to the Cadre or the Regnum. My last assignment directive will have been fulfilled. I have traced the cause of the Holtz Effect.

I have just returned from the Gathering of the Seers. An attempt to describe the nature of a Gathering is probably absurd, but I will try. It is a form of communal meditation, and it filled me with pride and humility. My life has been a cold march through time, that missed, even avoided, most of the simple human warmth that gives the least of us a sense of value, and the best much more. That sense, with the mingling of the minds

of the Gathering, impacted on me with such power that I felt—
empty. There was an absence in my past. I felt it like a wounded
soldier feels pain from a missing leg. The Gathering changed
me irrevocably.

There is a place in the hills a few days' trek from Luta
where the Seers gather every three years or when something
of pressing importance demands the consideration of Tercet's
best minds. High places are sacred here, perhaps because there
are so few of them. Imagine a deep, natural bowl formed by
the slopes of three rounded hills high over a desert plain. Imagine a twilight scene—shot with dark violet because on this
day, Sentos was the last to set—of old, sightless men, shawled
and carrying canes, moving gracefully over the gentle curves
of earth to meet one another with easy touches. They could
not see, but they knew their old friends' names before their
fingers felt a forearm or cheek. Regnum politicians talk of
unity; this was . . . I think this was love, in a fashion strange
to us. They share a goal so earnestly that motives are never in
question; each knows that he has a part to play, a step to take
on the long journey. Often I saw a solitary figure pause to
"look" up at the deepening night sky. Overhead was a sight
you will never see: a rough ring of stars, a round band that
becomes more solid at its edges, as if reinforcements are always
arriving. And the ring shackles a vast smear of pitch . . . nothing, nothing but an awful blackness. The hole.

Meta-sol presented me to the Seers like a doting father.
"This is Pol of the hidden stars," he said. "He is the one we
have been waiting for, and he has much to teach us. The Maker
of the Void caused it to be that we must dwell in fear under
the round eye of the black hole. It hides us from the sight of
our fathers who flourish among the hidden stars. The Maker
willed it that we might seek worth in ourselves, that we, the
sons, might kindle a light out of our aloneness. This light, we
have come to believe, might be seen by our fathers, though
they are blind and far away. If we touch ourselves truly, the
fire will be kindled and our fathers will rejoice with us."

This was part of the formal opening of the Gathering, though
Meta-sol's words seemed only metaphorical, until later. He
also spoke of the "learning" that could be gained from those
of the hidden stars, the Regnum. I felt—embarrassed, because
I could not but compare such as you with such as they.

There is a cactuslike plant, the "life-without-water-root" (a literal translation) that grows everywhere on Tercet. It's a stubby, leathery, misshapen thing with stringy roots that reach deep into the sandy soil for moisture. The desert rodents gnaw on them for food, but their only practical function here is as fuel. After dusk on the second day of the Gathering, several of the Seers ended a period of silent meditation by suddenly rising in unison and moving into the little valleys between the hills where the plants grow in abundance. With pious gestures and intricate deliberation, they began to uproot them. The other Seers had surfaced from their still journeys and watched, as a family watches the preparation of a ceremonial meal; in fact, that is what I thought it was, at first. Nothing had been eaten since we had arrived at the high place at dawn of the day before.

A high mound of the life-without-water-root was formed at the bowl's center, between the three hills. Stretching out from the mound, and placed so as to join it to the foot of each of the hills, were three long, triangular offshoots fashioned with care by the Gatherers. When they were finished, they had formed a three-armed star that stamped some order and symmetry into the darkening terrain beneath that horrendous black circle in the night sky.

The other Seers rose when they were finished and moved down the slopes into the spaces walled by the arms of the star. They sat in silence, but I could sense an anticipation—hope, perhaps. I touched Meta-sol's arm.

"Meta-sol," I whispered, "what's going on? Is this a ceremony?" He seemed surprised that I should ask but smiled and leaned toward me indulgently.

"No, Pol of the hidden stars. It is not . . . a ceremony. It is a . . . test of power, an effort of . . . communion."

"But what is to be done?"

"We must try to give light to this star." He gestured with his cane at the nearest arms of the formation. "We must touch it with fire." He was very matter-of-fact, very casual, like a father who had just explained away a simple mystery to his son.

"You mean, ignite it? Set it ablaze?"

"Yes. You must help us."

Yes, gentlemen, I sat there in the semidarkness with a hundred or so old men in strange garb, on a strange planet, and in strange confidence went about the chore of setting fire to a pile of dry rubble in the shape of a star—through an act of will. It didn't seem unusual to them, I thought. Why should it to me?

I sat there, cross-legged like the rest, and tried to wipe everything from my mind, make it into a clean, blank slate ready to accept what I wished to put there, rather than what comes unbidden. Remember when I spoke of the frustration of poets who must find that their words are only a pale simulacrum of the shining architecture in their heads? That invisible structure is as real, as true, as any ever built physically— but we think in our ignorance that it cannot be fashioned outside of the mind.

I gazed upon that empty slate awaiting my touch—and I saw something already beginning to form there! It had its own life! It was energy/warmth/being seeking shape, and I knew immediately it was the communal mind of the Seers. You will not understand how I perceived it, because you cannot see a taste or smell a color. But never mind. I suppose I'm really only trying to explain it to myself.

I "saw" in the black hole of my mind the energy awaiting expression, demanding function, and I joined with it, adding my own energy, my own will. Together, the Seers and I forged a flaming ball and augmented it—I swear this is true— I could feel waves of heat on my face. My physical eyes saw exactly what *you* would see: a fiery ball, suspended above the central mound of the rough-hewn star, pulsing light off upturned faces. Slowly, we allowed it to settle, and the star burst into flame.

Believe it, if you can.

The Seers ignored the heat from the roaring fire, the nearest absentmindedly brushing at sparks carried by the wind into their hair. Their reaction was strange: they smiled and chuckled and murmured with delight, but their sightless eyes were wide with wonder and they—all of them—"looked" at me.

I leapt up and stumbled closer to let the heat wash over me. Their hands lifted, like those of children trailing a father in a crowd, to touch my cape as I moved. I spread my arms to the fire and felt joy, and awe, and . . . well, I can't explain how I felt.

The blaze fed ravenously on the dry roots, gouting higher and higher. The light bounced off the hills and the small sea of shining old faces and pierced the darkness above until the black hole was no longer discernible. I ran back and pulled Meta-sol from the ground.

"Meta-sol!" I cried. "This is wonderful! Wonderful! Why didn't you tell me? I never dreamed such things were possible, even with all the Seers together!"

In my excitement I hugged him, and he hugged me back. He was proud, but, I think, a little afraid.

"Yes, I believed such things were possible," he said softly, "but this is the *first*. It was *you*, Pol of the hidden stars. It was your power, your guidance."

"What?"

"It was you." Tears glistened on his cheeks.

"Meta-sol . . ."

"You—are—first—among—us."

Three days were spent, in small groups and large, each teaching each, all gently prodding, wanting to be sure of steps taken in a new direction. I was the main subject of their questing. I was told that they could not assess the full potential of my powers of "knowing" with accuracy; they were amazed, they said, but also afraid. They took care in testing my sense of responsibility as a possessor of such gifts.

With their help, I continue to learn. I am no longer Pol Tyrees, Cadre One; I am Pol-Nesol-Rast, *Seer*. Truly now, I am called what I am. Incidentally, my name, roughly translated, means "Pol, son of Meta-sol, out of the darkness." That says it all.

I have been purged of all but a lingering regret that so much of my life has been wasted by moving in a grooved pattern channeled into the cold granite of what you call reason. I became afraid to feel, because I knew only deep loneliness. My body and mind were armored against feelings because they hinted at chaos, a loss of control that threatened a return of emotions I had never learned to accept as a natural part of living. Passion—any kind of passion—was anathema to me. I didn't realize it at the time, but the fear and loneliness forced upon me in my Tercian "prison" were a resurfacing of what I felt as a young child. You taught me how to repress them, Grandfather, with your example and your careful training.

So I never got drunk. I never loved a woman—not really— and I could not laugh or cry or share fully with others . . . and

I never understood the pain that my only real friend suffered. He called out in his suffering to one he trusted . . . and he died for it. So the atonement must be mine.

The Cadre was a steel cocoon, keeping me from the knowledge of being fully human. I know what it means to live inside that shell; your store of compassion thins with each atrocity, and the shell thickens. I stagnated in the arms of an institution and forfeited my *self* to my duty. But now I begin to *see,* so I also know the thrill of balling up the flimsy of a life gone sour and flinging it away.

Enough. I will finish my report and fulfill the last of my Cadre duties.

I recommended to the Gathering that it withdraw any consideration of membership in the Regnum. The Seers agreed that inasmuch as its function was to provide a universal law, it was good; inasmuch as it forced an artificial unity and encouraged only economic and technical growth, it was not good.

The Tercians wish to remain friendly and invite individuals to share in their learning; they wish to travel among the "hidden stars" and share yours.

My recommendation to the Council, not as a Cadre officer, butt ass a mman, isss thaaat you acceeeed.

Farewelll.

Pol-Nesol-Rast, Seer

SY 3050

(Excerpt from) *The Personal Diary of Petr Tyrees*

Pol's report is . . . devastating. That burst of flame in the wooden star is also a burst in human evolution. I read it as soon as it came out of graviton transmission. I am afraid. I cannot prevent the Chairman from seeing it. If I were religious, I would pray for God's help . . . but prayers are wishes cast to the winds.

I can only hope for time, hope that the Chairman is preoccupied with other matters. I must think of a way to protect my grandson. I have lost his—I suppose I can say the word—love. I lost his father in much the same way. I thought I at least had the Cadre, but I was wrong—the Cadre has me. I have nothing. I am a strong, intelligent man—and I am a fool—a fool!

I have lost him, but I will not lose his life as well; it is even more unique than I suspected, and he has much to give.

There are some who can help. I will speak to Hans. He must share some of my guilt, and some of the risk too. After all these years, I am still a worm in the apple. I take little solace from the thought that there were more poisonous worms there before me.

SY 3050

COUNCIL EYES ONLY

(Excerpt from) *Recording Transcript*—**Chairman's Automatic Surveillance System**

Recordees: Chairman, Council of the Regnum; Proctor of Security Cadre
Time: 49 45 3050
Place: Chairman's private offices
Occasion: Automatic surveillance

(RECORDING BEGINS—TRANSCRIPT BEGINS)

Chairman: Sit down, Proctor. We have a serious matter to deal with.
Proctor: (sighs) Obviously, you've read Pol's report.
Chairman: I certainly have. It's the most amazing thing I've ever come across. Do you believe what he says?
Proctor: I'm afraid I do, sir.
Chairman: He can't be missing a gyro or two?
Proctor: They aren't the words of a madman, Chairman.
Chairman: No. You realize, of course, the implications of his report. Both for the Tercians *and* for him.

Proctor: Implications?

Chairman: Your grandson has—*on the record*—disavowed
              both the Cadre and the Regnum. The Tercians—

Proctor: Come now, Chairman! His circumstances are un-
              usual in the extreme! Allowances must be made—

Chairman: Come now yourself, Proctor! He calls *himself* a
              traitor!

     (Recording crystal verified—legitimate eighteen seconds
                              silence)

Proctor: I'm sorry I raised my voice, Chairman. I apolo-
              gize. I'm sure you must . . . be angered by Pol's
              personal remarks, but they were really meant for
              me. I found them painful, perhaps because they
              were true. I made decisions befitting a command-
              ing officer instead of a grandfather. I put Pol in
              an untenable position; if you seek justice, then
              punish *me*.

Chairman: You *are* his commanding officer, Proctor, remem-
              ber that. I am not seeking justice; I am trying to
              eliminate a problem. Justice would punish *me* for
              allowing you to let Pol go his own way. I can only
              use the Trade Wars as an excuse; I haven't even
              bothered to check the surveillance on him lately.
              You never volunteered information, did you? Just
              how much had he "changed" *before* Tercet?

Proctor: If you'll permit me, sir, we've both made mistakes,
              but there's another side to this. Look at what he's
              achieved! What he has become represents the most
              important evolutionary breakthrough in the history
              of mankind! He is now *more* than human. He's
              gone beyond the Tercian Seers themselves, in just
              months. And we were always concerned whether
              or not his abilities could be learned, were trainable.
              Pol's report suggests they are; the fact of the Seers
              suggests they are. They can teach us. I once said
              that Pol could be the Cadre's most valuable re-
              source. Now, I'm convinced of it! We must do
              everything in our power to—to bring him back
              into the fold, to explain our motives for treating
              him as we did. I—

Chairman: Stop right there! Your judgment is blurred, Proctor, contaminated by a sense of guilt. I see things quite differently. What your grandson has become is not a "breakthrough," it is a *threat*. That band of— of *Seers* is a threat. You are responsible for the security of the Regnum: have you not considered what would happen if that primitive tribe of mind-tinkerers were unleashed in the middle of a civil war? There would be no such thing as security! The Trade Wars barons would stop at nothing to gain their services or learn their insidious little tricks. Just before you walked through that door, I was informed that your grandson's life implant stopped sending—now, don't get excited! Obviously, the timing is too much of a coincidence. He's not dead, he's interfered with the implant *himself*. Pol Tyrees is not "more than human," Proctor, he is *alien*—and dangerous.

(Recording crystal verified—legitimate twenty-two seconds silence)

Proctor: Chairman. Those are the words of paranoia. If you are suggesting... The Council will never permit—

Chairman: The Council will do as I say! I've demonstrated that to you often enough in the past, Petr. Accept the inevitable: in less than two months, that festering little ball—Tercet—will be reduced to a cinder. Its location is ideal because no one will ever know.

Proctor: Chairman!

Chairman: And if you don't know where your duty lies... Remain seated!... Thank you. You should know better, Petr. One more second, and you would have been a dead man. There are elements of my security system even you don't know.

Proctor: Strange, you've never called me "Petr" before, have you? I wonder how far *I* have gone—from grandfather to Cadre officer..... Oh, Pol, forgive me.

Chairman: In spite of all that steel, you do have a maudlin streak, don't you, Petr? You're getting too old. How far have you gone? I'll answer that one. When you accepted this post, you took it as a bribe for your silence on the Holtz Effect. No—let me finish. Never mind the rationalizations about Regnum unity. You took the bribe. I offered it when there were other ways, more certain ways, to keep you quiet, but not because I have your latent soft spots. You've been a good Proctor, Petr, one of the best. Without you, the Trade Wars might have reduced Regnum to a farce by now. Listen, my friend. The office of Proctor of the Security Cadre was vacant, as I told you, because of the sudden death of its previous holder, right? Well, he died because his opposition to me at the Council table was becoming a nuisance. You see, Petr, the Proctor's personal safety isn't the only reason for keeping his identity a CEO classification: it's a very powerful office, and secrecy makes things so much simpler, if he should become expendable. You are becoming expendable, too. There is no bribe this time, Petr, just a choice. . . .

(RECORDING TERMINATED. CHAIRMAN'S
CODE WORD SPOKEN.)

SY 3051

The attack vessel moved silently through cold and empty space, shrugging off the tug of Black Hole 189 to move toward three points of growing light—red, yellow, blue. The long black shape was the most destructive artificial force in the galaxy. It was a sleek, dangerous animal in uncontested territory, so it stalked lazily, confident of its kill.

Two men stood on the bridge on a raised dais, to either side of the command chair. They looked morosely over the tensed backs of the flight control technics at an overhead screen. A theater buff would assume he was watching a staged drama: eerie, flickering light threw shallow shadows; soft hums and clicks flecked the silence, only to deepen it; dominating the upper background, a screen tilted downward, displaying dark swirls and three wavering, colored globes of light. The observer's impression of contrived drama would harden as he considered the two silent figures. They were posed, outside of real life. They were costumed in the ageless, symbolic colors of antagonists—one in black with a long cape, the other in sleek, sheeny white. Both wore expressions of serious intent; both stared at the three lights above, as if waiting for some terrible resolution. A bit overstated, the observer would think, but potent nevertheless.

"Why are we going so slowly, Captain?" asked the man in black. "Or is there some point in drawing this thing out?"

"Please remember, sir, that there is a full emissary staff on Tercet, with detection and communications equipment. They will know we're here quite soon, as it is, so I don't want to alert them by screaming in there. The orders say 'surprise attack.'" The captain's tone held a touch of patronage.

"Fast or slow, I don't see how it could be anything *but* a surprise, when they don't know our purpose."

"Undue speed might reveal our purpose."

"To what effect? What could they do about it? The quicker it's over with, the better. I'm sure you've noticed the signs of strain on your crew." The caped man's voice was low and hard, and it jerked the eyes of the captain away from the screen to him. He had not taken proper note of the increasing tension, but he was less acutely trained in such things than his guest, and he resented comments from *any* outsider about his crew.

"Would you rather have them know they were about to be atomized? I don't like this any more than you—sir. Obliterating a planet—whatever the reason—is not a distinction I relish." The captain's sarcasm was not directed at the Cadre One, but at the circumstances; nor was the pause before "sir" meant as an insult. He was simply not accustomed to having a superior aboard, and certainly not one from another service who knew little about military tactics.

Before the Cadre officer could speak again, a soft "ping" froze the bridge. The captain whirled to face the jittery technic at the communications console.

"Uh! Signal, sir. Request for transmission reception!"

"On our frequency?"

"Yessir."

The captain hesitated. "They know about us," he said in a grim mutter to the Cadre One. "I'm sure they know all about us."

"How could they?"

"I don't know how, but that's the battle frequency. The emissary would know it, but he wouldn't *use* it unless he knew why we were here—and this is at maximum range, so he was expecting us. Damn!"

"So he knows. Put him on."

"What! Sir, I can't do that. My orders—"

"Your orders say nothing about receiving a transmission,

Captain. Obviously, there's going to be no surprise attack."

"With all due respect, sir, the whole flavor of this mission is contrary to any communication with the—the enemy."

The Cadre officer's cape swished softly. His next words came in low-voiced slashes.

"You are in command of this vessel, Captain. I am in command of this "mission," as you call it. The orders are clear on that. You will put the Tercian emissary on transmission acceptance, please." The captain stared at the square, implacable face for a moment before turning again to the technic.

"Accept the transmission, Vinil."

"Yes, sir. Receiving signal—now."

Suddenly, the three wavering lights on the screen were replaced by a grainy image of the emissary, the man charged with coaxing Tercet into the Regnum. His features were pinched with strain, his voice distorted by distance and emotion—determination, fear, hope, anger. His eyes bored into the bridge crew, whose intention was to turn his temporary home into a fireball. Beyond name and title, there were no amenities.

"I am Neet Pristor, emissary to Tercet. As a vessel of the Regnum battlefleet, you have my voiceprint in storage." He paused, to allow time for a check on his identity, but he was also mustering his will. The crew waited.

"I know that I am addressing a war vessel, and I know its purpose. Whoever is in command *must pay heed to my words*.

"It is probable that you do not know the *reason* for your orders. It is this: Tercet has, unknown to me, harbored a few dozen mutants whom the Council considers a threat to the Regnum; one of these mutants was—is—a Cadre officer, a Cadre One." The captain looked sidelong at his companion on the dais. "All of these men are now off-planet. I repeat: All are now off-planet."

There was another pause. The emissary was breathing heavily, and his glare from the screen intensified, as if he were determined to exorcise the invisible watchers with his eyes.

"A few days ago, a research vessel made landfall here, bringing Councilman Leeth, minister of information and research, and Dr. Hans Bolla, who identified himself as a Regnum commissioner. They informed Officer Tyrees of your mission. I was told of the Council's orders as well, but only after my offices were occupied by armed Tercians. Since emissary staffs have no weaponry, resistance was impossible. Tyrees and the Seers have fled in the only two space vessels. We have not been harmed, and are no longer prisoners. You must not *waste our lives*.

"I have a recording crystal here"—he held up, in slightly unsteady fingers, a sealed packet—"from Tyrees for the Chairman.

"You *must* believe my words. The destruction of Tercet is now absolutely senseless. Please acknowledge."

The screen went blank before it was again filled with the ever-growing image of the tristar. The two men on the dais faced each other.

"Aren't you going to acknowledge?" said the man in black.

The captain was confused and bewildered by the emissary's message. With the eyes of the bridge crew on him, however, his face was hard with decision. "No, nothing has happened to affect my orders. I will—"

"Nothing has happened! Don't you believe the emissary?"

"It doesn't matter *what* I believe—or what *you* believe, either. The black hole cuts off communication with the galaxy. We would have to break off for a week for new orders, which might destroy the effectiveness of the mission. We still do not know for certain why it was launched. Pilot!"

No!" The Cadre One held up a hand in the pilot's direction and slowly lowered it. This time, he didn't attempt to lower his voice; he no longer cared whether or not the crew heard.

"Captain, I know the military is accustomed to following orders without question. Perhaps that is as it should be. But I cannot operate that way because my work demands flexibility. You must rely on my experience and accept my judgment, Captain. Discretionary powers must be assumed here."

The captain was now red with outrage, and he was quick to fight back.

"I don't need lectures on 'discretionary powers' or Cadre individualism. I know my duty and I know my orders."

"Your orders place me in command!"

"Not of my ship. And no specific order can supersede that of the mission itself. Pilot!"

"Captain!" The Cadre One's voice lost all inflection. "You will acknowledge the emissary's transmission, and you will tell him we are touching down to investigate. If you do not, I will kill you—now."

A long moment passed as the man in black and the man in white confronted each other silently, on levels private to themselves. The man in black, a heavily built block of a man, had not produced a weapon or even changed his body position; but the captain knew that if the caped man wished it, he would be dead in seconds.

After the ship touched down, three men—the two Regnum officers and the emissary—stood in animated conversation in her shadow. One of the Tercian suns, the red Eros, tarried above the horizon. Finally, they trudged across the beaten sand toward Luta. The man in black held a sealed packet in his hand.

At the edge of the landing area, they neared a dark shape crumpled lifelessly in the red sand. The Cadre One broke off from the others to pick it up. It was a long black cape. The others did not see his hands trembling under it. They trembled because he was thinking of a sterling time in young manhood when bonds that took were layered under the skin where later time and events could not penetrate to alter them. He was thinking of Pol and Ses. He was thinking that no one ever called him Ttig anymore.

SY 3051

CHAIRMAN'S EYES ONLY

Recording Transcript: **(Recorded message delivered to the Chairman, Council of the Regnum, through Neet Pristor, emissary of Tercet)**

Recordee: Pol Tyrees, Cadre One, Alien Security

(RECORDING BEGINS—TRANSCRIPT BEGINS)

Chairman. I am Pol-Nesol-Rast, Seer and spokesman of the Gathering.

Nine days ago, one of your Councilmen, Amos Leeth, and Dr. Hans Bolla came to Tercet to tell us of your crimes. The murder of a man who devoted—I cannot—I cannot even speak what you can do. You . . . No. This is not to be a message of my loathing, because a man like you would find it amusing. I will not curse you from a distance. I will say this: Whatever else my Grandfather was, his motives were formed by what he saw as the good of the Cadre and the Regnum—concepts larger than himself. I can say the same about men like Bolla and Leeth, except that they will not place ideas above men. *You* are made of a more grisly fiber. Leaders like you make our choices ridiculous. Unknowingly, we pick from alternatives that you paint on the innocent walls of our minds. When we find that they are only your hideous graffiti, we become frustrated and destructive. I was a rat in a maze for many years; you are a rat in a maze of your own making and will ultimately provide your own vilification. History will record it closely, Chairman; it will spell your name in blood and curse your being. And I will guide its hand. That is my prophecy.

To more immediate business—conspiracy to commit planetary genocide. You will have to devote your talents to less ambitious crimes against humanity, because before your war vessel reaches Tercet, we will have left in the two ships now under our control. Information of your crimes—the murder of a Cadre Proctor, the intent to massacre a defenseless planet, and others—will be stored and code-locked into the Regnum communications net. Leeth, your ex–minister of information, assures me this *can* and *will* be done. Should any harm befall Tercet, the information will be unlocked and automatically disseminated throughout the galaxy.

I and my Seers will take to intergalactic space.

A warning: Do not assume that our escape is a flight of despair, that we run in fear, choosing the Void over your wrath. We have plans to make and forces to marshal . . . and they will be formidable. Know that the combined strength of my Seers is a power you cannot even comprehend. Know also that they are guided by a former Cadre One, who shivers with anger when he hears your name and who now possesses the ability to *read and follow the intergalactic graviton pathways. . . .*

Yes, Chairman, we can ring and stalk your puny galaxy with the impunity of a hawk at a beached and bellowed whale. We will strike where and when we wish, with new weapons. . . . Their exact nature I leave to your imagination. You will not escape our purging. Know and be afraid. You are about to be invaded by aliens.

(TRANSCRIPT ENDS—RECORDING ENDS)

STEVE PERRY
THE MAN WHO NEVER MISSED

Khadaji was ruled by the brutal forces of
the Galactic Confederation—until one day he had
a revelation...and walked away from the battlefield.
He was a new man, unknown, with a secret plan that
he shared with no other. Not his mentor.
Not even with the beautiful exotic whom he loved.
Now, no one can understand how the Shamba Freedom
Forces are bringing Confed to its knees.
No one sees them. No one knows who they are...until
Khadaji is ready for them to know.

_____ The Man Who Never Missed
by Steve Perry/0-441-51916-4/$2.95
